WHERE LOVE IS FOUND

24 TALES OF CONNECTION

Edited by Susan Burmeister-Brown and
Linda B. Swanson-Davies of
Glimmer Train Stories

WASHINGTON SQUARE PRESS
New York   London   Toronto   Sydney

Washington Square Press
1230 Avenue of the Americas
New York, NY 10020

Library of Congress Cataloging-in-Publication Data
Where love is found : 24 tales of connection / edited by Susan Burmeister-Brown and
Linda B. Swanson-Davies.—1st Washington Square Press trade pbk. ed.
p. cm.
ISBN-13: 978-0-7434-8879-2
ISBN-10:   0-7434-8879-2
1. Love stories, American. I. Burmeister-Brown, Susan.
II. Swanson-Davies, Linda B., 1952–
PS648.L6W46 2006
813'.08508—dc22
2005048024

First Washington Square Press trade paperback edition January 2006

10 9 8 7 6 5 4 3 2 1

Manufactured in the United States of America

Pages v-vi constitute an extension of this copyright page.

Dedication

There are at least three notable times in our father's life when he's chosen to put his own needs completely aside: In WWII, when he, as an American officer, entered a wire enclosure meant for five thousand enemy POWs that was, at war's end, packed with twenty-five thousand. He felt compelled to push through the exhausted men, tell them not to panic, that the situation was not intended and would soon be resolved. He was afraid they would, in desperation, attempt to break out, creating a killing crush and then a shooting by the equally exhausted Allied soldiers standing guard. He could not stand for another ghastly and unnecessary loss of life after an already horrid period of hate, pain, fear, and loss. In 1970, after our mom died of a brain tumor, we two sisters broke through the lock on our father's door with a bobby pin to find him sitting with a loaded gun. He wanted desperately to join his wife. When we explained that he had to stay—*had* to—because he was all we had left, he said he would do his best, he would try. And he did that for us. Just a few years ago, he wanted, again, to leave, because he felt his body and his mind failing; depression was taking hold. Again, for love of his family, of his dear Carmel, wife of over twenty-seven years, he decided to stay, and, this time, to at last trust enough to leave his fate in the hands of God, of those he loves. Finally, still alive at eighty-eight and unsure of who, exactly, everyone is, he has not forgotten he is a man committed to and by love. We dedicate this collection to him.

Acknowledgments

We are indebted, as in all things *Glimmer Train,* to Paul Morris and Scott Allie, without whom we two sisters would be lost. Our hearty thanks go to our wonderful editor, Sarah Branham, and to our agent, Bob Mecoy, who have brought this collection to life.

We are in awe of the wonderful people whose writing created *Where Love Is Found*. In these times, we are especially grateful for fiction that reminds us of our inescapably shared humanity.

Our husbands and our children fill our hearts daily, making it possible for us to move through the world with joy and curiosity.

Lastly, we must thank our readers, the people who keep meaningful literary fiction alive in this world.

Contents

Foreword

Where is love found? Everywhere. In the determination of a woman tracking down the recipient of her lover's donated heart. Under a tree, where a dog holds vigil for the spirit children held there. Between devoted old friends at a pivotal moment, at the end of their lives. In a man's faith that the Virgin Mother can save him. In the call of a goose made by a man in love with a woman who loves a different man. In a foreign country, where a desperately lost Westerner is embraced by kindly Muslim cabbies.

It is certainly found in these twenty-four stories, where, in spite of losses of life, voice, faith, and trust, there is the powerful—and hopeful—urge to connect, to find and offer love and comfort, to somehow stretch the threads of our lives between what is possible and what we cannot live without.

—SUSAN BURMEISTER-BROWN AND LINDA B. SWANSON-DAVIES

WHERE LOVE
IS FOUND

Christopher Bundy

❧

MORNING PRAYERS

*Somewhere in the middle with the haze
and the sky like a bruise*

Prayers in Arabic floated to the domed ceiling as a small crowd of men knelt on simple rugs and straw mats in front of a young white man. In blue jeans and a T-shirt stained with Val's blood, and his own, the same black cherry, the young man had wandered into the remote mosque after police had taken his unconscious wife away in a taxi. Clumsy old ambulances like fat cartoon vans overflowed with wailing Chinese, traumatized Malay, and a family of Indians that spoke only in terrified gazes. The police had not allowed the young man to go with them no matter how he pleaded and shouted, no matter how well he cursed them. Men in ill-fitting blue uniforms stuffed the young man's wife into the backseat of a dirty yellow taxi, folding her legs, still bleeding from the glass that cut them, into the tired Fiat as if she were a tattered mannequin on her way to the scrap yard. The crushed bus below appeared to the young man as if through frosted glass, a gauzy gray spot below him. Women cried and men yelled hasty instructions as headlights broke through the morning fog and cars began to arrive at the scene of the accident. The ceaseless squeal of police sirens

1

pushed the young man to bang his fists furiously on the hood of another taxi—this one a dented and dusty red, unmarked and anonymous—bringing automatic frowns from two men left standing by the car, watching and wondering at the white man with blood on his shirt and a bandage around his head. With the departure of the ambulances and police, the scene was quiet and the young man was left alone. He pounded again on the hood, his fists hurling into the air and back down again, a windmill of fury and frustration. The taxi driver, a young Malay in dirty brown trousers and a dress shirt opened to his navel, rubber thongs, and a baseball cap, grabbed the young man by the arms, using his feet as leverage against the bigger man.

"*Let me go! Where's Val?*" The white man struggled against the small Malay.

"Sorry, sir. Please come."

The taxi driver pointed to the inside of his taxi. In the hysteria of the crash scene, and with so many others injured, dying, and dead, they had forgotten the young man, a hasty bandage placed over his forehead, his wounds minor in comparison with the others. As the sun began to rise behind the haze and the sky lightened into purples and yellows like the bruises that would soon rise on his arms and legs and neck, the young man surrendered and slid into the backseat of the old taxi. As they drove east toward the brightening sky, his head hurt, like a rope tightening around his skull by degrees, and he heard the echo of song, a rhyme and rhythm that he did not understand, growing louder, over and over, the same stanza chanted through loudspeakers across the Malay morning. Morning prayers had begun and their melody rang over the flat land around him.

The Caretaker greeted the young man without surprise, directing him to sit down on one of the prayer rugs inside the remote mosque. Everywhere men bent in prayer. The taxi driver and his friend guardedly watched the tall stranger, bandage around his head, dried blood on his face and T-shirt. He clutched a dirty day bag with the strength of panic in trembling hands. Birds perched in the open windows and a blend of prayer and birdsong reverberated through the breezy mosque. In a matter of seconds the young man had gathered himself up onto a frayed and faded rug in a fetal ball, tired, his head foggy, a knot of fear and bewilderment in his throat. He felt a hand on his shoulder and a fever swept over him with the rhythm of morning prayers.

Itinerary

Berdy never liked the bus rides: the highways so lightless and somber, the grind of old bus transmission gears and snoring passengers, the cramped spaces, and the chill of winter nights, or the relentless heat of summer. On the bus he could only think of arriving, and when, if ever, that relief from cramps, too much cigarette smoke, roadside food, and sleeplessness would come. The Malay bus ride was no different than any of the others that he and Val had taken. Val slept, her legs across his, a blanket pulled tightly over her shoulders, but Berdy could never find a hole to crawl into and rest. The buses were kept either too cold or without air-conditioning altogether. Some stopped at lightless street corners in anonymous towns so that passengers could find roadside meals, have a smoke and a piss. Others plowed ahead without concern for what was in between, rocking along horrible roads at dangerous speeds, simply start and finish on the bus driver's mind. Berdy typically spent the sleepless hours clutching his money belt and pushing earplugs deeper into his ears, struggling with a need for a cigarette, too nauseous and miserable to actually enjoy one. Yet despite his desire to escape the sluggish isolation of an overnight bus ride, there was something peaceful and reliable about the dark journey over empty highways, the sounds and smells of two dozen of the sleeping and the sleepless, the drum and rattle of an old diesel or the clean, cool churn of a newer one. Berdy recognized the precious moments, to be awake when others were not, his thoughts keeping a steady rhythm with the roll of big bus tires, wondering where he and Val, newly married, were going and what they had left behind.

Not that he and Val had left much behind. They were simply ready to be in someplace different yet again, the getting there just as important a part of their plan as being there. A bus, a ferry, a train ride to the very next place, and *always* another place. It was important that they get there successfully—the connections of bus and ferry and train sketched out in their guidebooks, Val's tidy handwriting in the margins: prices, times, and intricate maps that exemplified precision planning; cross-referencing; constant updating; and suggestions from other travelers. They were interested in the kind of travel that demanded the best of what could be assembled from guidebooks, word of mouth, and their own road savvy. They shared an affinity as travelers, their trustworthy travel books and backpacks and well-worn, comfortable clothes; wet and dry gear and travel blankets assembled somewhere en route; boots as reliable allies; knives; flashlights and sunglasses; hats for sun, rain, and cold winds; novels, essays, and dictionaries that rotated in and out of their portable library; and a small stack of journals adorned with the tatters and tears that were wistful memos of time and places done. That was the plan: always another place and always the journey that came of practiced study—a deliberation of a treasured itinerary. So bus rides—where Val slept deeply and easily and Berdy stayed up, shifting his butt from side to side, furling and unfurling his aching legs, suffering for a cigarette—were a part of it, the pleasure and pain of late-night fitfulness and getting there.

Berdy and Val had still not spoken since leaving Hong Kong except for mundane utterances on directions, the price of a room, or a place to eat. In Singapore for one night, Val ate in the room while Berdy searched the harborside for a cheap beer. He feared their long silences in Hong Kong had put something between them he could not name, something that would keep them remote from each other—mute travelers guided by a common itinerary. Berdy assumed they had both wanted to leave that silence behind in Singapore, the curiously quiet time a necessity for a couple so closely joined by geography and agenda. But the act of solitude had turned tedious and absurd. He imagined their scheduled connection in bright and shiny Singapore would give them an excuse to leave the creepy hollow that had opened between them in the rush of Hong Kong. But they had not spoken since, and the silence between them grew.

The night clerk in their guest house—an old Chinese man sweating in a worn T-shirt and smelling of garlic, onion, and soy, as if he had spent the day inside a bowl of noodles—told the young Americans that they must catch the 6:00 AM bus to Kota Bharu near the Thai border. Up early, Berdy and Val stood ready. But there was no morning bus to Kota Bharu. There *had* been, but it no longer ran that route, guidebook and concierge both wrong. So Berdy and Val waited in the heat and smog of Malaysia for the 10:30 PM bus to take them to Kota Bharu, eating a breakfast of cheap, sour noodles and rice, their backpacks underfoot as diesel exhaust and dust settled over everything. They read novels, journal entries, a limited English newspaper, and more of the faithful guidebook. Val scratched a thick black star in the margins by the erroneous bus information, so hard that she tore through to the other side of the page. When the sun began to set and the shade of the station awning began to actually comfort, they opened cold bottles of beer and the guidebook to read passages as if from a book of prayer. Berdy and Val recited to each other in the cool tones that they had adopted for temporary exchanges of the words that formed their expectations and plans, their gospel. It was the first time in two weeks that they had spoken to each other beyond necessity. Their faith in the faulty edition had only slightly diminished, but their confidence in the method remained.

The guidebook outlined the east coast of Malaysia and the islands and towns they calculated would be their stops. Color photos of empty beaches and Spartan bungalows rekindled their desire to head north along the coast, a contingency plan already developing around a new schedule. The sun set behind the thick haze that hovered above, and they pulled bandanas tighter around their faces to keep the smog out while the fires of Sumatra burned strong and unbridled in the aggravating summer of 1997, the currents of the Indian Ocean driving cloud after cloud of dense, unbearable smoke over the whole of Malaysia, trapping heat and dust and exhaust inside the crowded, watchful cities.

A season of forest fires

Sleep came so quickly to the young man that he had no awareness of actually falling asleep. He dreamt wild burning dreams that left him feeling as if he had not slept at all. He dreamt of forest fires so bright, so high above him that the sky was consumed by flames and he felt the hair on his arms and head singe from the heat. He tried to get closer to the fire, to walk through to the other side, to see what was there, if anything, beyond the wall of burning forests and foothills. To his left and right he saw an infinite length of flames that reached beyond the sky as if straight into space and on and on, eating up the moon, the planets, and all the stars that he could remember from the unforgettable cloudless skies over the Gulf of Thailand. But that was before the fires; now he was hot with them, the flames burning closer and stronger, louder in his ears. His throat was scorched dry and he could neither swallow nor breathe. With an irresistible lightness, he let himself rise with the heat and the flames toward the sky. He raised his arms from his sides and relinquished himself to heat and sky, following the channel of fire higher and higher toward a purple yonder.

The peculiar stillness of Hong Kong

The bus north finally departed at 11:25 PM, chugging up the east coast of Malaysia through the states of Johor, Pahang, and Terengganu, escaping some of the dense haze of the Indonesian blaze. Val slept while Berdy tucked his arms inside his shirt to keep warm, the powerful air-conditioning chilling him shivery and sleepless until he felt sick.

In Hong Kong, Berdy and Val had gone in different directions, two weeks of hardly seeing the same patch of ground on the same day, out on their own, solo and away from each other. Eventually they would visit all of the same sites—Macau, Discovery Bay, ferry rides and a laser show, dim sum and giant malls, boutique upon boutique of the same European fashions—but on different days and at different times. In the evenings they lay silently on sagging hotel beds with the same smells of cigarettes, rain, and oily Chinese food issuing from their undress. Val and Berdy liked the same things— waiting out afternoon rainstorms in open-air food stalls and drink- ing beer until sleepy; following step for step the museum guides, headphones and pamphlets on and open as they soaked up history and culture; haggling for fruit, for the incense that they always car- ried, for rooms, for anything familiar—but, for the time being, they didn't like each other. At night, they met in a tiny room with twin beds, an odd coincidence of availability that matched their moods. Berdy and Val saw each other only in the hotel room, the noise of Nathan Road down below their sixth-story room, the lights and sounds of a stirring, restless city filling the void of silence. Berdy smoked cigarettes and escaped the business and bustle of Asia through Wallace Stegner and the American West. Val wrote con- stantly in her journal, a bottle of duty-free bourbon on the win- dowsill, smoking and carefully studying herself in a small mirror over a worn-out wooden dresser. They did not talk about their day or compare notes on what they had seen. They did not share anec- dotes or impressions or frustrations over the candid, enterprising Hong Kongese. Instead, they read and wrote, drank, smoked, and slept without a word to each other. Two cameras were placed each night side by side on the dresser, filled with images of other people and none of themselves. Except one: Berdy had asked a Chinese woman in Macau to snap his photo in front of the ruins of St. Paul's Cathedral, alone on the steps, wondering why he was alone after all, eyes cut to the sky as if he were mocking the photographer or the place.

Their period of silence and withdrawal began over a cigarette. Berdy had come back to the hotel their first afternoon in Hong

Kong to find an acrid odor in the room. Val slept in her underwear on her stomach with the covers kicked off to reveal her naked back, shoulders pink from a day outdoors, a light layer of sweat in the cleft of her spine, and a hole in the sheet. Her cigarette had dropped from the ashtray beside the bed and slid down against her hip where her weight caused the sorry bed to sag. The charred butt lay embedded in the cheap foam mattress, an ugly black opening where the sheet had burned. Berdy stared at the hole and the butt of the cigarette so close to Val's skin, so close to burning her up in a seedy bed in a big busy hotel in Hong Kong. He choked at the thought of Val ablaze in her bed—her hair, her pink blistering skin—and knelt down next to her. Picking the cigarette butt from the mattress, the foam stretching gooey from the filter, he held it before him. The jagged hole in the sheet was the size of his fist and his finger fit neatly into the hole in the mattress. Berdy wondered what had kept it from burning further, from burning Val and room and hotel to the road six stories below. He watched his wife's face on the pillow, sweat over her lips, a ring around her hairline, a slow run of it along her neck. He replaced a strand of hair that had stuck to her cheek and leaned in to kiss her when she opened her eyes. Looking into her husband's face, there was no hint of expression or recognition.

"Huh?"

"You just about cremated yourself, that's what," Berdy scolded.

"What?" She rubbed sleep from her eyes.

"Here." He pushed his finger into the hole again.

"Is that right?" She followed his finger, did the same with her own, and rolled over. "I was sleeping."

"So you were. Well, don't you remember what the sign says, *No smoking aloud?*"

The malapropism had made them laugh when they arrived a day earlier, and they pranced around the room, trying to smoke *loudly*, huffing and puffing, making sucking noises and *tap tap taps* against the ashtray, laughing at each other until they fell into the new, tem-porary space, and eventual silence.

"I thought I *was* smoking *quietly*." She played along with her head turned away.

"Guess not. Next time, though, it might not be so pretty." Berdy got up quickly from the bedside; his teeth ground irrepressibly together, and with his hand open, he reached out and spanked Val hard, really hard, a sharp slap against her bare thigh that was meant to sting. As soon as he had hit her leg, his hand recoiled as if Val were indeed on fire and too hot to touch.

"Owww, goddammit! Why'd you *do* that?" She rubbed the growing red mark on her thigh, jumped up from the bed, landed on the floor like a cat, and punched Berdy in the arm with her fist, a swinging, furious jab, and then again harder and again, the fight in her already ebbing. Her eyes watered and she wiped her hand under her nose. "That *really* hurt, you shit. What the hell?"

"You should be more careful, could've burned the whole fucking place down."

"You know, you suck. Leave me *alone*."

Berdy spent the next hour in the dirty bathtub, mad at Val for being so careless, so vulnerable there on the bed when he had first come into the room. Her bare back, long legs, and white underwear, and the hole a big black stain next to her sunburned skin, such a blot, such an ugly portent of what could have happened to her while he was gone. In the tub, he smoked cigarettes until they got wet, lighting another and another, a pile of soggy butts on the floor by the tub. Val leaned out of the bedroom window tapping ashes over Nathan Road and hundreds of oblivious passersby.

Accident

Then Val lay somewhere along Malaysia's east coast between Berdy, a bus, and the bottom of a steep hill. Berdy could not find her in the dark, the screams of the other passengers stirring the panic and pain that bounced around inside his head, quelling his other senses. His vision had gone blurry because of the blood that dripped into his eyes from a gash above them, and he felt a sticky patch just above his hairline. Rubbing his finger along the wound, Berdy felt again the tumble of the bus as it rolled, throwing them from top to bottom and back again and again, each roll another punishing throb.

Berdy had been in a light dream of watermelon and trees when they were sent tumbling off the road and down a steep hill, the bus groaning as its frame twisted and split, the horrible sounds of separating metal mixing with the screams of men, women, and children. Berdy regained consciousness back in his seat, but the bus was on its side, its front end pushed into the cabin, the engine hissing steam. Val was not where she should have been. Lying across his seat, Berdy stretched his hands out to feel for his wife, but found only pieces of broken glass and fruit from someone's basket. He heard cries and whimpers, calls in Malay and Chinese, so many puzzling sounds, whispered prayers and glass crunching under bodies. The cassette player continued to rattle out a Hindi song through torn and frayed speakers, the volume up so loud that it, above everything else, made his ears and head hurt. When he crawled away from the bus through the broken window, bent into an odd polygonal shape, he found others already huddled outside. The bus rested against the tree that had finally stopped its long, sick tumble. His body ached and his head throbbed even stronger as he moved about. In the early-morning darkness, Berdy realized the shape of a bearded man in a torn sweater cradling a young girl. As his eyes adjusted, he saw that the young girl's eyes were closed, her mouth open, and her pale dress pushed up around her thighs. A dark stain spread across her chest and the man's hand appeared to be swallowed up in the bloody darkness. The young girl lay so still, so quiet in the man's arms as he recited prayers over her, that Berdy wondered if she was simply sleeping, silent in the comfort of the old man's arms. But the dark stain broadened to her belly and blood dripped from her thin dress onto the man's pale pants. The man looked up at Berdy, unintelligible prayers still coming from his mouth, his eyes focused not on the young American but somewhere beyond, his face calm, almost serene. The taste of diesel fuel mixed with the warm blood that ran from Berdy's nose. Behind him rubber and oil fueled a smoldering wreck. Feeling his way over the rough terrain, the hillside too steep to walk along upright, Berdy grabbed at bushes and bent trees that clung stubbornly to the barren slope. He tried to call out Val's name, but his throat was burnt and bruised, a pungent taste lingering in his mouth; he could only squeeze out a hoarse gurgle that barely rose above the cries of women, the tick-ticking of the wounded bus engine, and the squawking Hindi music.

At the top of the hill, the same darkness left everything an oily black, neither moon nor streetlamps to light his way to Val. Terror rose again in Berdy's belly, working its way up into his throat, the hoarse gurgle trying to come cleaner and louder, to find her. He tried again to scream her name, but still could get no sound to rise from his mouth—a desperate dream scream so silent and awfully futile. Berdy clung to a small tree, trying to find balance so that he could descend the hill and find a bottom, but his head spun, his stomach rolled, and he plopped back down to the ground, the pain in his head so sharp and dizzying that he could hardly breathe. Just as quickly, Berdy got to his feet again and began to slide down the rocky dirt slope. And twenty, thirty, forty feet down there she appeared—Val—rolled over like a discarded sleeping bag, her face buried in her arm, her legs twisted in a way that brought dread fast into his mouth, so that all he could muster was a series of choked *oh*s and compressed whimpers. When he reached Val, he found her name in a whisper and put his arm on her shoulder, a faltering gesture. Fear swelled inside him like a bubble of emptiness, a cold, hard heart attack upon his chest that sank horribly into his gut, so quick and so terrifyingly true that he nearly fell onto her in panic. But Val moaned and Berdy knew that she was alive, giving him such a flash of hope that he raised his head to the sky and smiled.

Learning to pray

The Malay Caretaker examined the young man's head as it rested against the prayer rug. He considered the dried blood over his face, the bandage on his head, the bruises on his arms and neck, and the sweat that covered his body. He has a fever, the Caretaker thought, but as Allah will watch over him he is safe here from bus accidents and the misery that they bring. The Caretaker had heard of the bus accident that killed four people and wounded others with cuts and bruises and broken bones. Inside the mosque, dramatic retellings already swirled of the crushed bus and its bleeding passengers, a morning full of so many horrible things. He let the young man rest and left to prepare breakfast. In the narrow room where the Caretaker slept and ate and read from the Koran to ponder his place in the everyday of God's world, he poured hot water over tea leaves in a sieve into a short glass, then stirred in condensed milk, letting the tea sit until a thin, pale layer had formed on the surface. He pulled two warm rotis from a clay bowl and removed a small iron pot from the portable gas stove on the table that served him as cooking counter and writing desk. From the iron pot he spooned a light lentil soup into a bowl, placing it with the tea and the plate of rotis on a serving tray. With a patience that he had exercised for more than thirty-five years, the Caretaker walked back to the young man. The two brown men from the taxi in identical mustaches and dense black beards stood by the young man, pointing to the bandage around his head and the blood on his face, scratching their beards and running their hands over their prayer caps. The Caretaker knelt, placing his hands on the young man's shoulders.

"He's resting and I think he has a fever. He's probably very tired and confused from the bus accident. There was a white woman who was taken into town. His wife, perhaps."

"What shall we do?" one of the men asked.

"Give him peace. Let him talk to God, maybe. To find answers for the pain he must feel. Mostly just quiet, I think."

"Is he a Muslim?" another man asked.

"I don't think so. But I think he still needs to talk with God and here, here he will most likely find him." The Caretaker pulled gently on the young man's shoulder, speaking to him in English. "You would like to eat, my friend?"

The young man's eyes popped open and he grunted in surprise. The two Malay men jerked backward, startled by the sudden movement and the noise from the sleeping white man. The young man looked up at them and they back down at him. One of the men smiled in return.

The young man jerked his body upward, "Where's Val?" He gestured with his hands, pointing to the ring on his finger. "My wife, *wife,* where is she?" Trying to stand too quickly, he fell back to the floor.

The Caretaker studied the young man's face, recognizing the fear and confusion.

"I have tea and rotis for you. You eat something."

"What? No. *No.* I gotta find Val." He tried again to stand, but could not pull himself all the way up. "Oh Christ, my head is killing me."

The young man studied the men around him: their apprehension and curiosity; the Caretaker with his plain brown face, receptive eyes, and shaven head. He looked down at the prayer rug and out a window that faced east where the sun rose, plump and promising. He tried to stand again but sat down clumsily—*oh hell*—dizzy and weak. The two men immediately reached to lift him to his feet. The young man turned his head left, then right, to stare blankly back. He let them carry him to the Caretaker's room, the Caretaker himself shuffling along in front of them, the tail of his long white kurta floating out easily behind him. The young man ate the roti and lentils while the three men in black beards sat around him in silence. He did not speak again, and ate slowly, sipping occasionally from his glass of hot tea. The fiery panic that the Caretaker had seen in the white man's eyes had paled and was replaced with the warmth of hot tea and weariness. When he had finished his meal, the young man wiped his hand across his mouth and whispered, "Thank you." The three men leaned forward, each of them smiling. The Caretaker answered, "You are most welcome, but God you should thank. Thank God." The young man touched his forehead with his hand and looked at the blood on his fingertips. His head hurt, and a wave of nausea rolled over him again; he struggled against the discomfort and uncertainty, faced the Caretaker, looking hard into his dark face, his black eyes, and placed his hand on the old Malay's shoulder.

"What's happening?"

The ache of her survival

Berdy was told to wait. So he sat on the prayer rug, his knees bent stiffly under him, though they ached terribly, and throbbed with the shock of the accident. He felt that he needed the sum of all his pain to keep Val alive in whatever sort of place they had taken her. The greater the pain, the greater the chance that Val might be alive; so he folded his hands together in prayer and whispered words to God—a god he knew nothing of—and he let the pain in his knees and back and head roll like the tides through his body, crest and trough over and over. The pain in his head thumped just above his eyes and he could not see clearly or focus on the front of the mosque. Berdy whispered his wife's name and engaged the pain, so strong in his back by then that it made his eyes water, and he felt as if his spine might simply crumble, leaving him limp and crippled on the dusty rug. He felt the eyes of the two men as they watched him from behind, stirring restlessly, uncertain of his presence there inside their holy place. The Caretaker who had fed Berdy, and showed him how to wash himself before praying to God, roamed the temple greeting others and sweeping dust from the floor, leaving the foreigner to his pleadings. A gentle morning breeze blew through the temple and Berdy felt the sweat from fever, cool and dangerous on his forehead. He smelled smoke from a cooking fire, a suggestion of spices in the air that he could not name. He murmured his wife's name again, the only word that formed in his throat. Berdy tucked his knees in tighter and twisted his back to ensure that the pain would roam his body without favor to him or any part of him. An eye for an eye, he made his deal. Behind him, the two men watched in silence. Berdy heard them shuffle from foot to foot. He turned to see them rubbing their mustaches, one after another, nervous and unsure of what to say, scratching their heads at the foreigner where he sat bent from the pain of his wounds and his pitiable petitions to God.

Passage

The Caretaker volunteered the same two men to take Berdy further on into town. When Berdy got into the taxi, the Caretaker pressed his hand into his shoulder and said, "Yes, do not be afraid, it is only morning. We have prayers for each part of the day." Berdy thanked him for the food and the kindnesses and shut the door, his words hollow, echoes of the sounds that his voice made. As they drove away from the mosque, the Caretaker calmly waved good-bye, standing white in his pajamas against the orange sky that blossomed over the wide, flat earth behind him.

Berdy rode in the back, the taxi driver and his friend up front. Sleep came with the wind of open windows and the sound of the taxi's wheels ripping across pavement, and then, so quickly, without warning, the sound of the bus turning over, wrenching in pain as its metal twisted and tore, glass and human bones shattered, and people crying out in fear and shock. Berdy closed his eyes and let the wind blow across his face, trying to keep out the image of the big man and the broken child so limp in his arms, peaceful against his broad chest, blood dripping from her dress. He tried to quiet the sound of Val groaning with the pain of her shattered legs. He tried to erase the look of panic that spread across her face when she saw him kneeling over her.

A voice rose amid the crackle of the radio up front. It sounded years away, lost in static and swell. The driver picked up the transmitter, responded in Malay, turned to his friend with his eyebrows raised, and returned his gaze to the radio in wait of an answer. His friend turned to Berdy and smiled weakly, uncertain, it seemed, of what he wanted his face to tell the young man. In another second, a reply came over the radio, more a remote voice on a wave of sizzling air. The driver and his friend did not look at Berdy again and they rode on in silence.

The silence made Berdy nervous and he dug through his backpack in search of their guidebook. It was turned up at its edges, swollen and stained with moisture. Flecks of tobacco were stuck between its pages along with Val's notes and scribbles of the previous day, when their greatest threat was a missed connection. From the map and the description in the guidebook, it seemed that they were just south of a popular fishing village. Huts had begun to appear along the water to the right and fishing boats rocked in the surf, verifying Berdy's guess. Val was somewhere near that fishing village, he told himself, perhaps in a tidy, modern hospital, or dropped into a provisional clinic, surrounded by gifted midwives, a rural but capable young doctor, sick children, and nervous parents, a funny travel story already simmering in her head. With the silence of the two men, Berdy's sense of urgency and panic rose again, and he traced his finger under the names of each hospital trying to rub the answer to Val's whereabouts from the page. The panic subsided briefly as he deduced that his wife must be in Marang, some forty-five minutes north. He placed his hand on the taxi driver's shoulder and held the book up next to his face, tapping the name of the hospital with his finger.

"Marang. That's where we're going, isn't it?" Berdy spoke up against the whine of the wind and the taxi.

The driver looked at the guidebook and nodded his head. His friend in the passenger seat pushed a cigarette toward Berdy, who accepted the charity, nodding his head thanks. Berdy checked for road signs, but saw nothing on the lonely, two-lane road. He leaned back in the seat and inhaled deeply from the cigarette, certain that he had gleaned the correct answer from the reliable guidebook, the words written on the page, the presence of those very words, the map and the compass, and the scale at the bottom of the page bolstering his mood. The man in the passenger seat curled his lips inward, a look of empathy in his mouth and eyes. He guaranteed nothing in his drawn lips and discerning eyes except an affirmation of the fear and the panic that edged around Berdy's chest, and upward into his throat again. Then the taxi slowed and pulled up to a narrow beach. The man that had offered Berdy his understanding turned again, pursing his lips with thought, nodding to the ocean that smelled brackish and brown and rumbled softly fifty meters away.

"We stop, okay?" the taxi driver said, his smile appearing in the rearview mirror.

"Stop? Why?" Berdy asked him.

"We stop, okay," he repeated, this time more a statement than a question.

"No. No, not *okay*. Not okay. Keep going. We gotta find Val. In Marang, right here." He tapped the page in the guidebook again.

"We stop, now, okay."

Berdy clenched his fist at the repetition. "Okay? Okay? Fuck this!" He banged his fists against the backseat and kicked at it with his feet. "Start this fucking car and move it. Marang, goddammit! Marang, Marang, Marang!"

"I'm sorry, but we stop now."

"Don't you fucking get it, don't you realize that my wife is hurt, probably in some goddamned country hospital?"

"Yes." The driver looked back with such earnestness that Berdy felt the air leave his chest, his fists unclenching. He did not have the strength to fight him anymore, or any idea of how to make him understand what he wanted, but he did not want to leave the security of the car, the only thing bringing him closer to his wife. The driver and his friend stretched their legs and arms, lit one another's cigarettes, and wandered off toward the ocean water, glancing back at the angry foreigner as they wondered what he might do next.

But Berdy only sat in the taxi listening to the sounds of waves crashing one over another. He felt no sense of urgency, and the panic in his throat had descended into his belly, where it floated, an irritating swirl of emptiness and a stranger's empathy. He wondered at the two men and their reasons for stopping along the seaside. He could see them from the taxi, their rubber thongs off and pants rolled up to their knees, smoking cigarettes and walking through the surf. Every few minutes one of the men turned toward the car to see what the young man was doing. His cigarette finished, Berdy felt the desire for another, and considered getting out and walking himself to the water, an imaginary crutch lifting his body across the sand and dropping him into the cool ocean. But his body was limp and comfortable in the backseat, the morning air cool, an ocean breeze through the small cab, and he felt an apathy that he could not explain. He stared ahead as if he had been napping on an autumn afternoon, an electric fan humming at his feet, circulating balmy air, the sounds of monotonous inactivity, just cool enough to pull the light blanket over the top of his body, no need to get up, no appointments to make, no itinerary to pursue, no place to be, no haste or hurry to pull him from his catnap and drowsy daydreams. Berdy and Val had plunged from their plan right into a crack in the road that had no regard for their schedules, notes, and journals, their meticulously managed alliance of system and process, every step procedure and purpose. And yet the bus—itself shackled to schedules, routes, service procedures, lists, and inventories— betrayed them their journey, depriving them of their getting there and away.

The taxi driver stood in the ocean engaged in a sort of dance, body moving back and forth in water just below his knees, smoke drifting up from his side, the haze of Indonesian forest fires behind him. The driver smiled broadly and waved for Berdy to join them on the beach. Berdy pushed himself up from the backseat of the taxi and placed his feet on the ground, where he felt stronger, and pulled at the door to get himself up and out of the car. On the beach with his feet in the water, Berdy smoked another cigarette, another offering of empathy and occupation from his new friends.

He wondered at the idleness that had overcome them all while his wife Val lay in a Malaysian hospital somewhere. He looked at his watch—12:25. He and Val should have been in Kota Bharu already, on their way to catch a small boat to the Perhentian Islands and a small bungalow next to the jungle where, the guidebook told them, the owners fed you fish from the day's catch and an Indian man named Pijar told you wild stories as you shared his secret stash of homemade whiskey that tasted curiously of vanilla and Coca-Cola. He and Val would have unpacked and been for a cleansing swim, perhaps ready for the day's first nap. They would have congratulated themselves on a job well done, getting there without missing a bus or paying too much for a taxi, their tiny, spare bungalow exactly as they had imagined it from the picture in the guidebook. He would have rocked Val in her hammock while she blew smoke into the air and laughed at their silly stubbornness in Hong Kong. Berdy would have apologized for smacking her and kissed her on the forehead. Together they would have anticipated a walk under a budding new moon, holding hands as they talked to each other again.

The size of God's hands

The sun moved through its zenith over the ocean as the taxi driver and his friend closed their eyes and repeated a few words of praise for Allah. They willingly placed their fates in his hands, knowing that any minute he might choose to pluck them up out of the ocean and take them to heaven. The taxi driver wondered at the size of God's hands. How many could he hold? How many lives? Beside him, the young white man who had been dropped into their lives from a crushed bus began to move his feet back and forth through the water. The taxi driver still heard the scratchy reverb in the policeman's voice over the radio as he told them of the white girl's fate. He felt tears burn in his eyes as he realized that he did not know the words to tell the young man what had happened to his wife.

The young man raised his head up to the sky, smelled the air, and put his hands together. "She's okay, I think." He looked to the taxi driver. "You think, okay?"

The taxi driver looked to his friend, unable to return the white man's gaze, and pointed to the sky. "Allah . . ."

"Yes, of course . . ." As seagulls circled overhead and the sun shone over the sea, the young man closed his eyes and whispered *thank you*.

Karen E. Outen

BENEATH THE EARTH OF HER

Stokely

She says, "I just don't think about it like you do. Babies have never been at the top of my list."

Her face is closed when she says this, lips tight, their pouty fullness disappearing against her teeth. I'm leaning toward her in my chair, as open as she is closed, my arms and legs wide for her.

She knows my point. I see myself as a father. I see that child on my lap, pulling through my pockets looking for my candy and coins, listening to the same damn story five times in a row. I smell the licorice on his breath, the hair grease in her braids—a little coconut scent like she's a tropical baby, full of sun and sand and ripeness. Wait, now, do I want a girl? I've always seen my son, but I'm seeing now a sweet little girl to wrap her arms around my neck at night, *ahhh* . . . I see her head tucked against my chest, those little-girl barrettes shaped like roses with long, flat petals just under my chin. I tickle her, she giggles. Her laugh is that high squealing thing girls do in octaves off the charts. And her smile is lovely, animated, with those thick, wavy lips from her mother.

Who still isn't smiling at me. "Freida," I say, "it would be a positive thing."

"Uh-huh," she nods, her voice neutral, and walks away from me. I let it drop. Except I hear it, that little-girl squealing followed by the strike of her laugh echoing and falling like a bell. I rub my hands slow over my knees, ringing out the last bits of sound, and I gotta laugh. Here I am, a brother with a biological clock.

I'm looking out the kitchen window in the morning, watching little kids fill the corner in front of our townhouse—I mean, tiny tiny folks, with backpacks half as big as they are. I could practically balance one kid in each hand. These little folks wait for the school bus. A bunch of mothers stand behind them. No fathers—where the hell are all the brothers? There is one who comes sometimes, stands at the back of the group so I can't tell who his kid is. He doesn't seem particular—see, I don't understand that. Go claim your kid! I say this to myself and Freida hears me. She plunks the cast-iron skillet down on the stove. I look at her.

"Stop staring out there," she says. "Those people will think you're a pedophile."

Her hair is natural, softly nappy, brushed wavy and neat back into a thick braid that trails below her shoulders. I go tug on it, to loosen her.

"I just think they look cute," I say. "Little folk with all that purpose. With their backpacks on, waving good-bye and going off in the world and whatnot."

She nods, unimpressed. I move closer and lean down, press my face to the back of her head, my lips near her ear, calling for her. She leans into me.

"So, that's what you want, Stokely? Somebody to send off into the world?"

"You know what I want."

"Yes. To propagate the race. To be fruitful and multiply."

That's my point, all right. But she's got the wrong tone with my message.

She looks at me and her face softens. She smiles slow, a smile that leaks sadness at its edges. "You just wanna be a father. That's all."

I look back out the window. A little naked. A little sad. The school bus pulls up and blocks my view. When it rolls off, the kids are gone.

That night we go to a reading at the bookstore on the corner. Best bookstore in the city, and not just because they carry my chapbooks and my brother Eldridge's paintings—that's right, my mom named us after Stokely Carmichael and Eldridge Cleaver. No, the bookstore's good because it handles books respectfully; that is to say, they don't segregate all the books by black folks on one shelf in a corner, architecture next to literature next to fashion how-to. Also, they hold readings by young brothers and sisters, poetry slams. I come here and listen to what poetry sounds like now, hip-hop some of it, and long on rhetoric, but I love it, the necessity of it. Sometimes you'll hear something *live,* some traditional craft with contemporary rhyme, full of imagery and language that's particular to us, something that speaks to a way of preserving the past. That's what I'm talking about, having a link to the past and some stake in the future. I see my son as my connection to ascendance, descendance.

Tonight we come hear one of my former students. He's one of only three young brothers to graduate in his class (fifteen other brothers failed), so I gotta support him. Freida says, "I can always tell your students. They come having rediscovered dashikis and big afros." She laughs.

The room's full, mostly sistas and some interracial couples. Used to be you could count on some young hardhead-looking dudes to show up, but not anymore. Not even a handful of brothers are here, so I stand out, one of an endangered species. I get glances from everybody. Sexual glances, curious glances, puzzled glances. When the reading starts, I sit forward in my chair, riveted. I glance over at Freida beside me. She's preoccupied. Next to her there's a white woman with a brown baby, round-faced, straight-haired. The baby looks Central American, some Asian ancestry to her, but definitely some African influence turning up the melanin in her. (Don't you love how you cannot hide us in ancestry; we show ourselves some kinda way.) "A world child," Freida would say, "a bit of everything." The baby's fussing even though her mother tries to bounce her or occupy her with toy keys and some rattling thing. The baby keeps hitting her mother in the chest. Freida's squirming in her seat, disapproving. I watch her face shift like fast-moving clouds: light, dark, clear, stormy. She'll be the stern parent, I'll be the peacemaker. Finally, the mother sighs and shifts the baby under her left arm, unsnaps her shirt, pulls at a bra, one-two-three, and there's her breast with a long pink nipple. She pops it in the baby's mouth.

I get flustered, man, sit back, look away. How the hell does a woman do that in public? Something so nakedly . . . essential. Whew! The image of that baby grabbing on to the breast plays large for me. As much as I try to erase it, it stays until I just surrender. I turn and watch the baby with her feet in the air. She's happy just playing with her toes and getting fed. As I'm watching this woman, who's too wrapped up in her baby's pleasure to notice me, I'm seeing Freida opening her blouse with that much easy power—yeah, it's a silk blouse that floats on the air—and she exposes the brown globe of her breast for our child. Look at Freida now: she stares straight ahead and concentrates on the reading. Her face is blank. She crosses her arms tight against her chest. Then slowly, so slow maybe she doesn't know it, her hands move up over her breasts, over her nipples like shields. Her face shows nothing. All she does is cover her breasts, dam up her sweetness. I gotta wonder, what's she hiding?

Later at home I follow her through the kitchen while she gets her chamomile tea, into the living room where she sorts the mail. She says over her shoulder, "You're like a puppy on my heels." We go upstairs, and at the bathroom door she turns to me and says, "Stay," then closes the door.

She's right, of course, I'm following her like a seductive aroma wafts through the air behind her; you know, like in a cartoon, that ribbon of scent rising from a fresh-baked pie.

Only when she comes out of the bathroom and sits at her vanity—brushing the tight silk of her hair, swathing her arms, legs, and feet with lotion—I know what it is: not scent but vision riding that ribbon from her to me. It's Freida, hands clamped over her nipples, damming up from me—that's what's irresistible.

I sit on the bed with my feet up, arms clasped around my open knees. She comes to sit beside me and looks at me long and steady. We hook up like this once a day. It's a steady draw on the pilot light, a few minutes of hearing a calibration set between us while we offer ourselves, waiting for the leap of our flame. Doesn't take me long, never does. The familiar broadness of her temple, the wide reach and flare of her nostrils, the delicate rise of her cheekbones, and the slight point of her chin call to me. Her skin is even brown, a red undertone like fine clay giving rise to the glow of her. This is so familiar, but still I know she keeps secrets, even after nearly two years together. So when I pull her to me she's total mystery. Seems I'm always looking for some passageway to Freida. Ah, all the openings of a woman . . . I pull down the thin straps of her gown, kiss her collarbone, make my way to her breasts. Her nipples get hard. I latch on. Like I'm suckling her, like I'm getting her used to the idea. I see them—what are they? I'm reaching for knowledge from biology class, some name that sounds feminine . . . areolae? Yes? The ducts that make milk? I don't know, but I see this like a map: her breast filled with little sacs that burst with milk and find a path to her nipple, this closed hard knob I pull on now. Strange to think it could open, even as Freida opens to me, her long legs around me, her big thighs warm and shaking as she lifts them and pulls me between her hips. I'm thinking of all the points where I could enter her, eyes, mouth, lips, her sex, but I'm fixated on her breasts. I suck with desire so deep, it must've come before me, must go on afterward. She moans, then strokes my cheek. I draw steady on her. I want more of her, so much more. I imagine all her riches pouring from her, feeding me.

Freida

Since puberty I have often envisioned my ovaries, their full seedi-
ness and their small bloody eruptions each month. Like most
women, I feel the sharp twinge as the egg bursts, spewing bits of
blood and membrane. The egg sails fast and high in a graceful arc
toward the fallopian tubes, which wave their fibril arms like anxious fans of the game, longing to catch the pitch.

I see the lushness of my ovaries. They overflow with luminescent, pearly caviar. As a teenager, when menstruation and ovulation
were first explained to me, I took as a sacred task the business of
nurturing and releasing my eggs. That these functions were performed without my overt prodding, and regardless that I may never
use their capabilities, made the process all the more amazing. I was
that strange breed of woman who enjoyed menstruation from the
start, and I suspect I will until the last. I love the magical femaleness
of my body. Even if at the moment I recognize the occasional
imperfection of that magic.

A nurse enters my room, walks purposefully to my bed, and
pulls down my damp, tangled sheets and bandages. She examines
the sutures above my shaved pubic hair. Every few hours, a new
stranger comes to take such liberties. As my reward, they straighten
my sheets and place towels under the damp parts of my body.

I stare across the hall. The door to the hospital room opposite
mine is open also. A cast of blue light pools to the left of the doorway, reflected from the pale blue curtains and the muted television.
I watch the woman in bed there, a perfect patient, with arms at her
sides, her sheets pulled straight and carefully folded, a portrait of
blissful maternity. We occupy the surgical-gynecology ward, a jumble of cesareans, hysterectomies, and laparotomies, all of us somehow entered and altered, relieved of babies or wombs, or simply
cysts and fibroids.

In the dark, my mind plays tricks on me. First I hear Stokely's
voice, his laughter rising from someplace in me, from my incision
perhaps. It is the best part of him, that deep genuine laugh, unre-

strained, the kind of force that knocks him a bit sideways. I know he has seeped into me; I feel it in all ways. First, in the copious sweat of his body when we make love. The soaking rain of him spills into my mouth, my ears, even into my eyes, where it washes my corneas and clears my irises. Stokely's laughter is not all I hear at night. A cry, high-pitched and insistent, as I fall asleep, as I awaken, as I turn or pull myself to stand; the sound, even in its faintness and distance, is salty and stinging. A baby's cry. I dream that it is Stokely's cry.

In my second day here, I have found a certain peace. After all, I am not ill and my life is relatively unaltered by my surgery. I lie here, drifting on painkillers and watching the passing parade of women. They are mostly new mothers taken by wheelchair to the nursery and their waiting babes. I enjoy the quiet of the ward and the stealth of the night nurses as they enter my room to check my IV. It is so different from my life with Stokely. He allows me no space, my slightest sigh anticipated. I grow weary just remembering how it is, like a constant hand pressing on my shoulder. Without him here at the hospital, without that metaphorical hand, I first felt some guilty relief: *Thank God, that pressure is gone,* the rush of coolness and blood feeding the space so long held. But I do miss him, his expansive dreaminess. I desire things now that I did not before Stokely. For instance, I do not have a specific desire for a child (I never have), only an earnest wish to desire one for him. At night I have often crawled into Stokely's arms to inhale his scent and breath; with one hand over his heart, I have hoped to evoke and assimilate this particular yearning.

Today, I attempt to stand, although I cannot move easily. I elevate the head of my bed, descend the foot of it, and grab the high arm rail so that I can roll myself to the side, and push until I am sitting upright. Then, gingerly, I slide my feet down and stand. A nurse holds my arm and I go to the bathroom for the first time, the trip across the room unsteady and long. Only the woman across the hall, perfect and still in her bed, makes the arduous journey worth-

while. Are her eyes open or closed? The man at her bed—the husband, I decide—gazes attentively, awaiting recognition or simply
consciousness. His face is expressionless. In fact, there is something
indistinguishable about him in general. I cannot tell his ethnicity:
he is slightly brown—but by nature or the sun? His hair is shaved
so close that it loses texture and assumes a general buzzed nap. She,
however, reminds me of myself: medium-brown skin with high
cheekbones and full lips, an understated sheen to her skin. Her television remains on but muted around the clock—another reason I
wonder about her state of consciousness. As I walk, a nurse wheels
an isolette into her room. Inside lies a tiny form: spongy, spindly,
splayed out like a frog awaiting dissection. As I near the bathroom, I
get a closer view of them. The Husband covers his face a moment. A
slight shudder crosses his shoulders, then he removes his hands
and reveals a slow smile, an unconvincing pantomime, and says to
her, "It'll all work out in the end."

In the bathroom, my body resists the memory of peeing, still
traumatized by the recently removed catheter. The nurse hands me
a small wand that sprays warm soapy water on my genitals, and
soon I pee haltingly. I concoct stories about Her: She is comatose
from improperly administered anesthesia. She delivered the first of
twins—quintuplets?—and now must remain completely still to
prevent miscarrying the rest. Of the stories, I like this best: How
does she conserve energy for the babies she carries, but nurture her
fledgling now in the world? What to give, what to withhold? What
an odd statement the Husband made, not one of real hope and opti-
mism, but a weary resignation.

When the nurse leaves I ask her to keep my door open. The hallway is hushed, its lights dimmed. A deep stillness rises from its core.
A baby's cry colors the distance. I watch Her. Light flashes and fades
across her face from the muted television. She is a human incubator,
a gestational woman—Ges, I'll call her; that is all I know of her.

On some level, I am indistinguishable on this ward; we are all black
women (from what I have seen) connected by uterus, ovary, blood,

and sutures. But I stand apart in this ward primarily composed of mothers; I am a woman who does not yearn for a baby. And a black woman, too. As a rule, we are seen to be fruitful.

Perhaps that illusion fooled Stokely. We met as volunteers at a community center. Even before we met, the women there asked me the same question loudly or in a hushed whisper, depending on their level of discretion and their age and whether they asked me on a dare while a small clump of their peers waited breathlessly, hands at their giggling mouths: "Don't you want kids? Ain't you getting a little old?" These inquisitors were often pregnant teens. I thought of their youth, of the easy way their bodies had given over to conception. "I am not too old," I told them with pride, "my body still works"—I pictured my ovaries, lobbing their skillful pitches—"but just because I can, doesn't mean I must."

This is how Stokely first saw me, surrounded by disapproving young girls, and those of their mothers who found me suspect as a deliberate nonmother, and therefore kept an eye on me. All of them seemed to question my claim on womanhood. While I did not question that particular thing, I sometimes wondered where I fit in among them. Perhaps Stokely sought to rescue me. But two years after meeting Stokely, these women still question me.

"You and Stokely should have kids, set an example for these young folks, show 'em how a family oughtta be, mother *and* father *then* kids," says another volunteer, a woman slightly older than I am. She wears her hair in a tight bun and draws on her sweeping eyebrows with a dark gray pencil.

"I do set an example," I say. "I'm here every week helping them with homework, teaching them job skills, trying to guide them to the future. This is my contribution."

"Yeah. Well, I guess you gotta do what you can do. He's just so good with kids," she adds, as Stokely leads the small children in spirited song and imaginative play. "It's just a shame," she says, and looks at me with an insulting pity.

We did not discuss babies concretely before we married. Often Stokely would jokingly point out a child, dissecting her Nubian features—a full mouth like mine, round dark eyes like his. "I see how we could make her," he'd say. The notion of our child seemed part of Stokely's seduction of me, an idea that conjured sex and a particular partnership between us. (Or, did I simply wish it not to be a literal desire?)

Lately, an insistent tone has colored his exclamations: he calls out to me across the community center. "Freida! This could be us, next generation," and points to a small boy, handsome but unremarkable. In bed that night I hold him, my arms around his broad chest, my hands straining to meet and close our small circle. "We don't have to have a baby," I say. "I'll be your home, I'll be your family."

He turns so that my arms fall away. He touches my face. "I know you will. But don't you want more?"

"No," I say, my life full to brimming with Stokely. "This is enough."

"Not for me," he says gently, but it penetrates me, a deep and unrelenting truth.

A week later on a crowded day at the Boardwalk, Stokely and I stroll. A passel of kids darts in between and around us, their circuit thin and silky, their shrieking laughter circling overhead like birds. They play exasperatingly close to us. As they run between us, dart in front, double back, in some out-of-control tag game, Stokely reaches for my hand. A few minutes later, he barely breaks stride but bends down, retrieves a lost doll, her glasses crooked, hair flying, dress askew, but smiling nonetheless. He walks ahead two steps quickly, pulling me along. Stokely taps a young girl on the shoulder. She seems maybe seven or eight and carries a bulging backpack full of dolls, a protrusion of arms and shapely calves, unruly mushroom clouds of hair. When she sees her doll in Stokely's hand, the girl's face becomes wide-open shock. She dropped it a few steps back, Stokely explains. Her thank-you is so genuine, a lifesaving sigh, a flash of her clear brown eyes and the sly dimple of her left cheek. Stokely's face turns aglow. They hold that doll between them, each grasping an arm, for a few beats too many. When he releases the doll, the girl moves ahead, folding seamlessly into the crowd. He looks at me, his face gentle, pleased, then longing and slightly veiled. I feel it then, my desire to want this for him, a feeling that swells full and meaty at its edges, but is ultimately hollow. I raise our two entwined hands to my lips—it takes a while; Stokely drifts from me—and I kiss his hand.

I never saw the doll. I would have trampled it like everyone else. I am always looking somewhere else when the ball rolls away from the child, or when the toy is just out of reach. But inevitably Stokely is there. I often turn to discover him in a private encounter with a grateful child. I have a feeling not unlike walking into the middle of a movie, not unpleasant but curious, wondering how much I've missed, whether I'll catch up.

Stokely

I'm inside her and not. I mean, I definitely feel the heat of her, the curve of her body beneath me, the way we sweat, and it's a glue that bonds us. I still hold on to her breasts; she's with me. But not. Like she's vapor in my arms. Hold her tighter, reaching deeper for her. I'm close: it's a cave, a deep cavern that closes in on me, and there it is up ahead, some kinda glow, some golden thing that I take for her soul—can I reach it? A lava that bubbles sticky-hot from her— there, there, the truth of Freida, I'm almost there . . .

"Stop, Stokely, wait," she says, breathing hard like sobs. "Something hurts."

She pushes my hips up, pulling away from me. Turns on her side. I'm still over her, pushed up on extended arms and wide legs. Jolted. She draws up in a ball, holding her belly. Both of us breathing like it's our last breath. My body feels hit, tumbling between motion and stillness like walking into a door, *bam!* and the aftershocks tremble through you.

She turns to look at me. "What is it you're searching for, going so deep?"

"What—did—you—say?" I exhale, fast and startled.

"I said, something hurts, like you hit against something."

I sink down behind her. My body gets a chill. "I'm sorry." I kiss her shoulder, then wrap my arms around her. She faces away from me and feels tense, like any minute she'll spring out of my arms, so I try to hold her loose; but it's hard, hard not to enfold her, her skin sweet and tangy with my sweat. "I'm sorry." I kiss her shoulder again.

"You go too deep sometimes."

"I know. I don't mean to hurt you." I brush my lips along her shoulder. It feels soft as dew. She hunches forward like she's gonna leave. I relax my arms and pull back. Hold still a minute. The coolness on my chest, between our bodies, stings. I close my eyes—how far away will she pull? If I wait here, give it some space, maybe—damn. Damn. Wait another beat.

She eases back against me, the touch of her giving me a warm flush. I wrap my arms around her like blankets, encircle her, small and still panting in my arms. I close my eyes. So what now, I have to play around the edges of her? Make love to her tentative, like we're strangers? Like it's nothing? Damn, all the ways of keeping me out! I look down at her breasts, which seem soft and limp, a little useless.

"Don't get upset, please," she says, and places her hand on my arm.

"I'm not. I'm not. I'm just. Sorry." This time when I pull her close I hold back a little and she turns her face into my neck and sighs.

It's not that I sleep, just calm into unconsciousness, and then this thought jolts me up. "Freida, Freida." I wake her, shaking her shoulders.

"What, what, Stokely, what?" Her arms flail around her face like she's falling. I take her hands.

"Maybe it's a baby."

"What?"

"Remember your sister said she felt this knot inside her when she got pregnant? Remember?"

"What? Stokely, no, I don't recall this."

"Yeah, yeah, I heard her telling you and your mom."

"What? I don't think so. I use a diaphragm, remember?"

"They fail sometimes, Freida." I stroke her brow, trace her lips with my fingers. "This could be it." She finally opens her eyes wider than a squint and focuses on me. When I kiss her, she parts her lips slow, like she always does. Building my anticipation. Until she offers her lips, the firm palate of the roof of her mouth, that slippery slope of tongue, all for my excavation.

This time inside her I'm easy, gentle. I'm thinking about mystery, the alchemy of cells, the heated fusion of conception in Freida transforming her, transforming us. Our cells dividing and growing, mutating. In liquid and darkness, the journey to her womb: some route I don't know, but a survival-of-the-fittest voyage, some middle passage that requires faith, but, as I said, is all about mystery. So I am gentle, slowly caressing her. After all, this is what she responds to best. I know if I had more patience all the time, more . . . subtlety, yes, I could win her better. I used to have it, used to just calm myself to her rhythms. I try to be easy with her. But even now, this hunger comes over me, and man, I close my eyes against it, I push it away. Even as she pushes me away again, tearful: "I'm sorry, something's wrong." She cries, soft shudders, and hides her face from me. I sink down, my face on her stomach, mouth at her belly button, calling into that place in her where hope grows, tender and sore. I call, "Hang on, hang on." I cup her hips, hold on to her heat until it fades.

From the get-go, there were certain things I knew about Freida. She was a whole lot more Miss Uptown than me. Yeah, we both have good educations, jobs, et cetera, but she's more closed. She gives off this self-contained thing—I think it's in the tilt of her head—almost a "don't mess with me" vibe. So I didn't, just watched her at the community center with the teen mothers, doing her tough-love routine. Then at the center's block party I saw this different Freida, looking out of place in the crowd. Don't know what it was. Maybe there was just too much going on, all that whooping and hollering, the bands playing, just a real good time. But, as I say, Freida seemed lost. So I went to her. I took her inside where it was dark and cool, sat her down, waited for her to recover. She looked kinda tussled, her dress slipping off her shoulders, the sweat beading on her upper lip. Maybe she was overcome with heat, but it wasn't that hot, just loud and rowdy. She seemed . . . tender is the only word for it, like if I touched her, something in her would yield, her skin glistening and soft with sweat. There in that place, just me and her, she was suddenly mine. I let her take her time coming to herself. I figured I would just wait a while, take her back out there; maybe I thought I could shield her some. After a couple minutes, this quiet spread over her and disarmed me, and then it was me, a little off balance. Who was this woman? I think I lost myself a little then, in the stillness of her. I took it as need.

She won't let me go see the doctor with her. "I am not pregnant, Stokely, I can tell," she says.

"Yeah, where'd you get your medical degree? How d'you know? Have you had a period?"

"Back off," she returns, then slowly says, "No."

My heart leaps a little.

I'm watching her from the sofa. She sits at the desk that butts up against it reading something about flying planes, another new interest of hers. She's doing all kinds of new things. She's trying to learn the flute. (Good God! That's some painful listening.) Yeah, I said we should keep trying new things, you know, expand ourselves in a sense, but I meant something else. Like having babies. I lean until my arms rest at the edge of her desk. She's trying to act too het up in what she's reading to talk to me. She won't even look up. So I study her. The crazy way she stashes pens between her breasts so she won't lose them. Tonight her breasts will be covered with ink, long blue milky streaks.

"I take it you don't want to talk," I say, and she nods.

Something about the wrinkle that fades in and out across her brow, the set of her shoulders, makes me want to compile a list of everything I know about her, see what it amounts to. I guess I'm leaning forward, because she looks up and sighs, "Stokely, you're blocking the light here. Could you lean back, please?"

I can't say there's a reason it takes me so long to do what she's asking. It's a reasonable enough thing, right? I can see I'm in the shadow of the small lamp beside us. Still, my first thought is: *Don't give up no ground.* Ain't that something? She looks at me and her eyes are clear, her tone is easy. And I'm holding on at the edge of her desk like a dog with a bone. I see, rationally, that I'm pushing up against the desk blotter, the dictionary, her opened books. Making them slide toward her chest. But I don't move. Confusion creeps up over her face, rises over the wide ridge of her cheekbones, and darkens her eyes like a low cloud. She's getting pissed off and trying to hold it in. And still I'm not moving. I'm telling myself, *Leave this woman be!* But thinking, *I'm already on the edge of her, what's the big damn deal? What am I asking, sitting here holding her in a gaze, what is so fucking much for her?!*

"Stokely," she says flat and slow. I snap to attention, see that the blotter pushes against her breasts. I relax and pull the blotter back in place, turn away from her on the couch.

Funny, it's supposed to be me, the distant one. That's the acculturation. Like in the movies, you know, I'd be some tight-lipped black man, hardworking, somebody who always has some "b'ness" to attend to; a cold, distant man, hard-fucking some woman to a Hollywood screaming pitch. And the woman, well, she'd be a walking pool of emotion, laying herself open, talking about: "Baby, just let me in!"

Maybe I've been that. I can think of a couple weeping women in college, showing up at my door all hours, laying themselves open to pour me into their veins. As unattractive as that was, I've got some sympathy for them now.

"Look," I say, and Freida's shoulders tighten up with my voice. "This isn't right."

"What."

"I ought to be with you at the doctor."

"That's not necessary, it's just a checkup."

"Or maybe not, how do you know?"

"Okay, okay. If I say yes, can we drop this?"

I can't tell if she's about to cry. Sometimes I swear her voice, her face, seem fragile to me. I mean, she's usually sorta placid, but sometimes I know there are these hairline cracks, a kind of fault line beneath the earth of her. Sometimes I think: *Go ahead, Freida, let go, I'll catch you*—doesn't she know that? Is she on that edge right now—maybe this will be my time to step up to the plate: *C'mon, baby, I'll catch you*. You know, there are these thrill seekers who chase earthquakes, the folks who talk about "the big one" hitting and go around staking out their territory, waiting for the earth to peel back, to tremble and crack at their feet. I know what they want: that glimpse inside. Is there solid rock or liquid at the heart of earth, gold or ash, bones and ruins, or just air and the purest water? What's at that unseen core? "Yes," I whisper.

She sighs. "Fine, then."

When I watch women with kids, I'm looking for those small moves. The way a woman squats down and spits on a tissue, then wipes it all over some poor kid's face. Or a woman biting the nails of a sleeping baby so he won't scratch himself. Or chewing up some food a little before giving it to him. Lifting him up to sniff the diaper. Bizarre behavior. Unless you're somebody's mother. Or father, now, I can see me doing that. No qualms. But do I see Freida doing these things? Freida, who's shy about holding hands in public. Freida, who keeps her lips a little too closed in the first minutes of a kiss. Do I see her doing all that? Well. Let me just say this: I *want* to see her this way, in that unguarded moment.

Freida

He crowds me. I am reading a book, writing an article for a trade journal, and Stokely bears down on me. He leans in so that my books and papers slide across the desk toward my chest. I should be accustomed to this, it happens so often in the kitchen when he leans over me at the stove, in the bathroom when he peers in to view our joined reflections in the mirror, in bed when he latches onto me with a desperate heat.

I try to hold myself out to him. But he barrels toward me so that I cannot fully brace myself, his face too close, his body too insistent, his presence flooding me. What rises in me then is a knot in my chest that fans out through my body. Sometimes I feel near tears, other times I could scream. I breathe in slow and deep, but I seem only to draw in his exhaled breath. He has radar for these things and closes in tighter until I must draw away.

He presses in on me as the crowd did the day we met: At a block party given by the community center, it seemed the noise, the people, the heat of the day converged around me. The street was abuzz with demonstration booths, double-dutch contests, stilt walkers, and a boisterous drill team. Frying chicken and fish, grilled burgers, cotton candy, and the sweat of concrete in the sun formed a staggering haze. I experienced a kind of sensory overload; as if my pupils were dilated, I could barely focus even a few feet ahead. I recall the feeling of seeing so much so quickly that it became useless information. Stokely came to me. He led me inside to the cool, quiet hall of the center. He sat near the window and described the sights to me frame by frame, and I thought: *He sees what I need.*

Later, when we rejoined the celebration, my focus expanded, taking in color and movement easily. I left the building cautiously, preparing myself for the rising noise, the assault of color, the press of the crowd. I made a studied reentry. Stokely, however, burst onto the street, taking on the crowd in one easy breath. He seemed brave and bold and kind and passionate, but also able to offer quiet sanctuary.

"Stokely," I call now, in as measured a tone as I can muster. He is startled, but seems to see how he has me penned, the desk blotter pushed against my breasts, my back against the chair. He retreats but watches me closely as I work. I once felt that if my life were a room, there would be empty corners and landings. Stokely seemed to fill them so well. I laugh a bit to myself, thinking wistfully of the pleasure of dustballs collecting in corners of minimalist rooms.

"What?" he says. "What're you thinking about?"

I shake my head. He gazes at me insistently. "Nothing, Stokely." But, naturally, he remains unsatisfied, this man of mine who harbors no unexpressed thought or impulse. "I was thinking of music," I say. I arise and find my flute case. I retrieve the instrument from its case with care. I position the music stand in front of me. When I lift the flute to my mouth, it casts an aura around me, a gauzy filter for the world. I fade into the notes of the scale, the studied progression of sound. My focus shifts so that I see nothing but the music before me.

"I'm going for a walk," Stokely says, and leaves the room. When the front door closes, I stop playing. I hold the flute in my palms and stand still, listening to the silence crackle and settle around me.

After my doctor's visit, we are dinner guests of Shelley and Jason, a childhood friend of Stokely's. They live within walking distance. Jason seems to me the sort of friend who would land you regularly in after-school detention: a schemer. He smells of old cigarettes and a newly acquired taste for cigars, and a vat of Polo cologne worn as unsuccessful disguise. But he is funny and gracious and Stokely's best friend.

Their two-year-old, Miles, seems attached to Shelley's leg; Shelley walks as if carrying a weighted ball. Miles bounces along, riding her foot. Stokely smiles at this and mumbles something about the mother-child bond. I find myself staring at Shelley—she refuses my help with the final stages of dinner preparation. I met her at her baby shower two weeks before Miles's birth and he has been attached to her breast or hip or leg ever since. I have a chilling thought: *What if a child does not appease Stokely, but becomes just an added weight for me?*

After dinner Shelley turns to me conspiratorially: "So I hear you and Stokely are gonna start trying."

"Trying?"

"To get pregnant."

I glare at him across the table. "Well," I begin slowly. "There are some complications. My doctor's doing tests. It seems I have a cyst on my ovary."

"Oh," she says slowly, and places a hand on my knee. "My sister has them all the time. Are you worried?"

"No, I'm really not. My blood tests were fine. I have faith in my body."

"I'm sorry to just be all out there in your business. Stokely made it sound like this was a done deal."

I stare at her a moment too long, uncertain what to say.

"Oh," she says, "uh-huh," and lifts her wineglass to her lips. She swallows. "So. He's in denial about this?"

"We're. We're just considering kids."

I follow Shelley upstairs as she puts Miles to bed. He is a sweet boy, his head perfectly round as a marble, his eyelashes beguilingly long, his baby teeth straight and white and perfect. He offers me a hearty hug and a kiss on my cheek. His lips feel wet and wispy. Shelley and I kneel beside his bed with him for prayers. I study the little-boy perfection of his room: a colorful kite in one corner, a wallpaper border of trains and boats and a matching round throw rug beside his bed. Miles thoughtfully includes Stokely and me in his prayers. It is sweet and charming; it does not fill me with desire.

Shelley and I retreat to the den across the hall. "Mommy will be right over here, sweetie. Go to sleep," she calls to Miles. She studies me for a moment. "You know, not everybody feels a burning desire for it. But having a kid is nice. It's the deepest bond you'll ever have."

I nod.

"Oh. Heard that one, huh?" she laughs.

"I guess I wish for it. For Stokely," I say, and feel an uncharacteristic wave of confession overtaking me. "I try to . . . I mean, it's just not . . ." *what I want,* I think, and the thought causes a surge of dread that has been rising slowly in me. Ever since Stokely hit against it when we made love, the truth has threatened us, solid and unmovable. "I mean, so many other things keep occurring to me.

Lately I've had a recurring dream of trekking outside Katmandu, spending time at the monastery there. It's so peaceful."

"Katmandu, huh? Why can't I picture Stokely in the Himalayas? Or at a monastery in meditation, for that matter," she laughs.

"Stokely?" I say, and realize I had not pictured him there either.

She looks a bit unnerved. "I wasn't sure either, Freida, about babies," she says quietly. "I guess it just happened while I was making up my mind."

She shrugs and we stare out the window. We watch a skittish squirrel climb a tree, pause and look over its shoulder, climb, pause, then drop its nut and run away.

"What if you're pregnant right now? How 'bout that?" We are in bed and Stokely sidles up to me. He reaches to rub my belly.

"I'm not."

"But what if? Right this second, baby, it could be happening." He looks at me: *Play along, Freida.* But we seem so far beyond games. He waits for me to join in; when I do not, he sighs and sits on the edge of the bed. He turns to me, his face so distressed I expect an anguished cry. I feel the start of a headache and a familiar knot in my chest. He gestures inarticulately, and at this moment I am painfully aware of how very much we cost each other.

I reach for his hand and grasp it in both of mine.

"I guess I don't know what it means to you. Having a child. Just . . . one word. One thing it means to you. Tell me."

"One word?" I stumble. I think of nothing, my head pounding. I want to give him what he needs. Nothing comes. My chest tightens.

He stares across the room, a melancholy veil covering him. "Salvation," he says dreamily.

"From what, Stokely?" He shakes his head slightly, a faint shrug of his shoulders. He is trance-like. His need is unfathomable, a thing that would swallow me and still hunger. Salvation, he says— could it be as simple as a child? Could anything really be enough for Stokely? Frightened, I lurch for him, hugging him around his shoulders, but he does not fully return to me.

* * *

An older woman, perhaps sixty-five, watches my movements in the cement-blocked office of the community center. "You sure look purposeful," she says. I look up at her and smile. "Look like a woman with a lot to do in life. I see you carrying around that instrument case, what's that?" She walks toward me, pointing to the flute case beneath my chair, but scanning the piles of paper on the desk, my opened purse, my outfit, my hair and nails.

"I'm learning to play the flute," I answer. She raises her eyebrows, which are slowly turning gray, and shakes her head. I see myself reflected in her gaze; I am foreign to her.

"Guess you got time to fill." I am not just filling time, I want to say, but when I turn toward the main room, there is Stokely, joyful, with one child on each knee. Greedily he beckons others to climb on. I recall one of the young girls quizzing me: "Miss Freida, don't you wanna keep your man? Then why you not having his baby?"

Stokely

She gives in on the doctor's visit, so I get to go along. Me and one other guy sit in the waiting area. He looks miserable, restless, shifting back and forth in his chair. He wrings his hands, then puts them in his pockets. I laugh in sympathy because I'm doing my own restless dance.

All the women here, half of them big and pregnant, and this guy and me are the only brothers in the room. If you didn't know better, you'd think we were responsible for all this. Where are all the brothers?

I don't get to actually be in the room during the exam, which is okay. Except part of me is curious: What's the big deal women always make about getting in stirrups? I guess it's a wild concept: you prop your legs up in the air and pay somebody to peer inside you, someplace you can't even see yourself. I wonder what that doctor will see. If I peered over her shoulder, would there be something new to see about Freida? That's one thing about her being pregnant, I'd have a spy. First thing I'd ask the baby: What'd you learn about her?

"I need to have an ultrasound," she says as we walk to our car. "The doctor doesn't seem to think it's such a big deal. And they did a pregnancy test, just to see. Since I'm late." She glances at me. "Stokely, thousands of things happen to a woman's body other than pregnancy."

"Uh-huh. But it's all *about* that, right? About it happening or not? Am I right?"

A cloud covers her face, and there I go again, going too deep, hitting up against something.

"You mean, we're judged by that? Yes. It does seem that way."

She turns in, quiet. Nothing I can read about her. She doesn't have much to say for the rest of the afternoon, a grunt maybe, or yes or no. I just watch her like she's a house on the block, someplace vacant. Maybe where my best friend lives. I'm watching the stillness, the windows shut, the doors locked. Waiting for that porch light to come on.

We go to my buddy Jason's house for dinner. Me and Jason have been tight since junior high. Freida seems to like his wife, Shelley.

Jason pours us all some wine after dinner. Shelley and Freida sit across the table from Jason and me, talking, friendly. Freida shoots me a quick angry look. What the fuck did I do now?

Jason talks trash about old friends, long-gone brothers, a lengthy, sad list. While we talk, his son, Miles, climbs down from his high chair and runs to Jason. He tugs on him until he manages to climb up onto his dad, settle into his lap, curl in. Miles plops a thumb in his mouth. Jason wraps his arms around Miles, real casual, from memory—this is your place, little man—and keeps talking. Miles pulls at a loose thread on Jason's sweatshirt, bunching up the fabric, turning it.

"You got lust in you, man," Jason says.

I meet his eyes and we both look down at Miles. He's got this half-smile behind the thumb in his mouth, like yeah, I'm happy, I'm with my dad. "I'm jealous," I say. "You got the future right there."

Jason nods slightly toward Freida and says, quiet, "She getting with the program yet? Y'all working your thing out?"

I give a lazy shrug.

"I tell you what, man, if you don't have it together before this here"—he play-swats Miles's bottom—"you gonna be miserable as shit. There won't be time later."

"I'm not sure I got time now," I blurt out.

Jason gets that slow, deep grin, and I know this brother's about to start some shit. "No, see the problem is," he starts, loud as hell, "it's that we've relegated the future to sixteen-year-old girls. We're lettin' them have all the babies. I'm saying, all educated, gainfully employed sistas—I'm talking *grown* women—oughtta have a child. Like, that oughtta be in the handbook."

"The 'handbook,' " Shelley groans. "Here we go."

"Yeah, you know, the black folks' handbook. All the unwritten rules, like don't root for the Celtics, don't talk about somebody's mama if you can't fight, if you have Kool-Aid it's gotta be red."

Shelley says, "Umph," and shakes her head. Freida doesn't move, just looks to see what I'll say. Nothing at all.

"You see my point, Freida, right?"

"Hmm," she says, and smiles, but her back hunches up. "Sure. Babies as a political marker: 'How down are you with the cause?' "

Shelley laughs. "Exactly. Politics. Still tryin' to keep us barefoot and pregnant." She gets up. "C'mon, Miles, let's clean you up." She scoops him up from Jason (why do my arms want to reach for him?) and leaves the room calling Freida to follow.

"I tried," Jason says.

"Yeah. To get me killed."

We're walking home and I get brave. "I think Jason's got a point."

"I know you do."

We walk a few steps in sync.

She says, "I know we have all kinds of things to offer: love, a sense of heritage, we can afford to expose a child to all sorts of experiences. But it's just convenient, isn't it? Jason's point doesn't get to the individual heart of it, of what goes on between two people. Stokely, sometimes we are so disconnected. How does a baby fix that?"

"It's just the strain of this baby thing. I know, I know, I'm pushing."

"What is it you really want?"

"A child, Freida. Just that."

"Really? See, I think we haven't talked about this the right way yet. It's as if we don't have the language."

We walk, silent. I'm not sure what to say, how to sell my point, and I hope that doesn't make her think she's right.

"It's so complex," she says.

"Yeah, you are."

She looks up sharp, then laughs. "Yeah, well, you should have married that little pep-squad girl you and Jason drooled over all night in your memory. Pulling out the yearbook and staring at her. I'll bet she was 'easy.' "

"Oh! That's low," I laugh. "Nah, I knew you were a trip when I met you. Difficult. My brother says there's nothing like a woman to make you suffer a little."

"No," she says seriously. "Oh, Stokely. Why should you suffer for me? Please, don't."

Moonlight washes across her face, touches it just like I would: faint across her brow, a shadowy sweep on her cheek, full concentration on her wavy, thick lips. Why, she asks, her lips moist with that doubt, the quiver under her bottom lip taking all breath, losing itself to moonlight.

I hear the shouting—"You little son of a bitch"—and turn on instinct, ready for whatever's coming. We turn the corner and there are two cops wrestling a kid maybe thirteen, fourteen, some young brother out late and wrong on a Saturday night. I walk toward him. He looks familiar, like a kid in my class or from the community center. Probably needs somebody to call his mom. They're rushing him toward the paddy wagon, same beat-up looking rolling jailhouse they had back in my day, the thing my mother and father warned me against when I disobeyed: "You gonna end up in that paddy wagon."

I walk toward it, about to call out to the young brother. The cops swing open the doors and I stumble back. All the faces, bodies, young black men, handcuffed and herded into that wagon. Yelling, begging, spitting at the cops. Some of them break a sweat, some of the youngest ones tear up but hold in a cry. The cops push the new brother into the wagon and turn to me: for a minute, I see my fate. I'm ready to resist capture.

"You know him?" one cop asks me. I look at the young boy, at the defiant fear in his face. Freida comes to me and takes my hand.

"Ma'am, is this your son?" the officer asks her.

"Yes!" I spit out.

"No," Freida says quietly.

I'm looking face to face to face, memorizing them. "Treat 'em like they're all my sons," I shout.

The cops close the doors. The wagon drives away.

"Stokely, Stokely," she's calling me. I'm breathing hard. I don't answer her.

When I wake in a cold sweat that night, I'm alone in the room. Freida's side of the bed empty. Can't move. No light. No sound. Nothing. I am the last black man on earth.

Freida

The healthy babies are crying in the distance. My nurse approaches me. "Today we're going to take a real walk," she says. With no use of my abdominal muscles, I brace for the task. She pulls me upright and binds my stomach with towels. We shuffle slowly to the door. The nurse holds my hand as if I am a debutante being presented at court. I clutch my IV pole and study the exasperatingly slow movements of my feet. At the door, I notice a steady clatter. Two women with IV poles in hand are already in the hall. They proceed unassisted, gripping their whining and clanking poles. Three other women wait at their doors with nurses, awaiting a clear path to enter the hall. We are to fall in line and promenade down the right side of the hall, circle around and up on the left. I consider each woman, how she has come to be on this ward, and I contemplate where I should enter. A woman smiles at me as she passes. She wears the outfit we all do: blue checkered hospital attire, one as a gown, one as an open-front robe. She is entirely gray, perhaps in her mid-fifties. Hysterectomy, most likely. My nurse presses me to enter the hallway, and I do. The woman who follows me moves with great effort, grimacing and biting her lip. She appears to be in her mid-twenties and wears a short, tapered afro, diamond studs in each earlobe. Her breasts look swollen and her gown features two growing wet spots around her nipples. Cesarean section. How strange to walk between them. I have no lost womb to mourn, no healthy baby to rejoice. I am another variation of woman.

There are six of us altogether, evenly spaced in our orbital walk. We smell of milk and blood and the slightly twangy stickiness of our most private parts. They regard me with kindness. Several of them smile or nod, a simple tenderness. Thankfully—finally—I feel welcomed without judgment. I pass Ges's room. She is as still as ever. Where would she fit in our circle?

Our blue paper slippers slide along the ivory marble of the floor, its surface speckled and shaded with blue veiny streaks. Clouds beneath our feet, clouds and sky: Womanhood is the solid inhabitable earth beneath us and we spin through her atmosphere, the specter of motherhood hanging a low moon, eclipsing some, simply shading others; for some of us it is so distant as to fall out of phase.

In our mothers' wombs, we each carried between six and seven million eggs. By birth, that number had decreased by half. At puberty, we each had less than half a million eggs. Now, I estimate that over, say, thirty-five years of fertility, with ovulation occurring an average of ten times per year, a woman will have produced approximately 350 conception-ready eggs in her lifetime. The millions of eggs between us—where have they gone? Fertilized and born, aborted, unused, they link us here. Their magic is ours. Through my light-headed fatigue, I see clearly where we meet, and where I fit here, our bodies at the vortex of what is known and what is possible. In our dizzying orbit, our praise song to our bodies, we tell a particular story: of those who make babies, those who do not, those who have not chosen, those who begin to claim their choice even now.

"Had enough?" my nurse asks, then wipes my brow. "Okay," she says, and our group splinters, each of us to our rooms.

Dr. Xavier angles her chair so that she sits squarely between Stokely and me.

"First of all, you're healthy. Okay. Now, your husband mentioned to me that you were ready to start a family."

"He did?"

"Yes, when we talked after surgery. So, I want to be sure you understand. This was not an aborted fetus or an ectopic pregnancy. It was not viable. It was a growth attached to the left ovary."

Stokely shifts in his seat. "A growth that had hair and teeth, some skin, but you say it wasn't really human?"

"Yes, that's correct. It was what we call a dermoid cyst. You see, the cells in the egg are capable of differentiation into various tissue, including teeth and hair. But not in a normal, coherent manner. It's more a jumble of cells." She has long, caramel-brown fingers, which she rubs together back and forth as she talks.

"So it could've been a baby, it just—misfired or something?" Stokely leans toward her in his insistent in-your-face manner. "Can this happen again?"

"No, no," she says quickly. She leans back from him and reclaims her space. "This was not a fertilized egg. Just an egg with a mind of its own." She opens the medical file in her lap and pulls out two Polaroids of my ovary. Stokely snatches the photos and stares greedily from one to the other. "As you'll see, it's just a cyst on an ovary. With some special features."

Stokely cups one photo in each hand. He studies them and then gives me a searing look. I glance over at the photos. Not at all the radiant sac I had imagined, my ovary is dull gray and deeply pitted. I ask if that is normal.

"Ah, yes," Dr. Xavier says, "for a woman your age. Those scars just mark where ovulation has occurred previously. They become more scarred as you move closer to the end of your fertility. Not that you are there yet, just that you are closer. It's normal. It means your ovaries are doing their job."

"So," I inhale sharply, "what happens to the eggs I don't ovulate?"

"Well, good question," the doctor responds. "Millions of your eggs just break apart. They get reabsorbed into the bloodstream. Eventually all your eggs are ovulated and, potentially, become a child, or are destroyed and incorporated into the body. Not every egg is meant to be fertilized."

I see my eggs as iridescent and beautiful as pearls. They rise and burst as bubbles, their wispy fragments raining down on me, setting my limbs ashimmer. They remain my small miracles. I glance at Stokely—has he heard the real truth of me? A truth I have known instinctively since puberty, but only fully embrace now. That my eggs do not necessarily await his sperm. That while my body ovulates, it holds out another possibility for me, surreptitiously destroying my eggs. They innately offer a choice. Either way they are transformed, reborn within or outside of me. Does he see that truth? That I may never give him what he desires?

Stokely catches me with that long, probing look of his, holds my ovary in the palm of his hand, a dull gray extraordinary thing that fails him. As do I.

"What did we do wrong?" Stokely asks, his eyes fixed on me, but closing, closing, the pupils pulsing smaller and narrowing. He turns his head.

"Nothing at all. This doesn't mean you won't have healthy pregnancies." She stands to leave and retrieves the photos from Stokely.

I think of Ges, still unconscious across the hall, diligent in her maternity. And I embrace the truth: No matter how much I have loved Stokely, I will never desire a child.

Stokely looks bereft. Perhaps we know the same things. I see in his eyes that like me, he is not certain there was no conception.

After all, it makes perfect sense that this fantastical conglomeration of desire and retreat, this tangled jumble of cells that collected but did not take root, might be our truest child.

I take Stokely's hand in mine, stroking the veins that rise there. I wonder about the faded scar across his palm—why have I never known its origin?—and a small mole in the well of his pinky finger—had I noticed this before? I stroke his hand and think of all the ways we have not seen one another.

Stokely

Before I go into Freida's room, I stop to look in across the hall. She's still there, still in limbo. She's a nice-looking woman, about Freida's complexion, rich brown, smooth skin. I overheard some nurses talking about her. They said she had a bad reaction to anesthesia and a small stroke. They think she can hear, they think she'll come out of it at some point. I know they brought in her sick baby hoping the sound of his crying would jolt her back. Until yesterday, when that poor baby died. Every time I come the door's half open like this. I see somebody's by her bed, a man, I figure, judging from the trousers. I've never seen him, just, like I said, his knees in those trousers, but I feel for him. Living in a kinda hell. You don't ever think something so, so straightforward and positive as creating a child could make you lose everything. So I stop by this door every day and say a little prayer. Or maybe it's really an incantation, warding off that kinda luck.

I sit here looking at Freida, at this doctor telling me what they removed from Freida's body wasn't partly mine. But it had teeth and hair, maybe skin? Doesn't sound right to me.

"Look," the doctor says, and gives me these photos of Freida's ovary. I gotta say first, I'm freaked. But then it hits me. While Freida was lying there sliced clean open—and don't they use retractors, some kinda metal clamps to peel back the skin?—there was somebody standing over her with a camera recording everything. It pisses me off. Look at how surprised she looks now, seeing these pictures. She didn't expect this. I sure as hell didn't. Because I would've wanted to be there. If anybody's earned the right to see what she's made of, it sure as hell is me.

Gray, pitted, a little shriveled, lumpy, sort of like a walnut. The doctor says this is what an ovary oughtta look like. Fine, what do I know? I'm studying it hard. There is nothing written here that I can read. I gotta laugh at myself. I must have expected hieroglyphics, maybe, something ancient but decipherable. Well, then, there it is, in the pitted craters of her ovary, the language of some miracle. Trying to read it like it's a crystal ball, trying to see my future. But it's her own private language and I'm a fool. Naive and a fool. To think I could know all about her this way. Certain that if I searched far enough, I could find something of myself there. I look up at Freida. I don't know any more about her now than ever. Except that we are different people, Freida and me. I look back at the photos one last time, look at how this ovary hangs in the dark cave of her body like a secret.

Freida takes my hand. Her eyes, her mouth, these are things I wanted to duplicate in the world. Across the hall the door stands wide open. The man hunches over his comatose woman—wait now. He looks . . . what is he? I check out the paleness of his skin, then the undertones of it, looking around the ears, the temples for his color. Yeah, I see it. The palest trace of melanin, I mean, fading out from the edges of him. Like he's being erased, all his dreams, his fears, whatever else he brings to hunch over that woman he's lost.

He leans back in his chair out of the light of the hallway. Slowly leaning back, his face and shoulders gone to shadow, now his arms and even his legs invisible. Erased. God. I'm running out of time.

Nomi Eve

Esther and Yochanan

My father has researched our family history all the way back to the seventeenth century. What I am doing is juxtaposing his written family history with my own fiction. Everything my father has written is true. Everything I write is what I imagine.

My father writes:

    Rabbi Yochanan Schine, a student of the famous Chatam Sofer, was engaged to Esther Sophie Goldner Hersch, the granddaughter of the Chief Rabbi of the British Empire. Esther and Yochanan were my great-great grandparents. They migrated to Israel and married in 1838 in Jerusalem.

I write:

    Esther was pious but in a peripheral way. She knew the mitzvot, she knew to make the Sabbath holy, but she felt that there was no real harm in putting her own creative interpretation on the old rules because certainly creativity was an essential and blessed quality of Man and it would be a sin not to use it.

    At first she did not like Jerusalem; she was from a long line of people who lacked sense of direction. The stony city, with all of its obscurant walls, twists, and turns, seemed to her a nasty place without any recognizable plan.

    Four months and two days after the young couple arrived, she ventured out alone for the first time. Quickly lost, but not frightened, Esther decided she would just wander. She knew that if she wanted to, she could ask someone to show her the way back to their house, which was a half-grand, half-decrepit habitation on Rev Pinchas Street. It was located across from the American colony house in the center of town.

And then Esther smelled the bread. She walked forward, turned a corner, continued forward a few more steps. Soon she was standing outside an arched open door watching a baker slide a tray of dough into a furnace. Esther stood and stared. The steam and sweat and dough and bare baker skin created in the room an atmosphere magnetic, carnally alluring. The baker was a young man, no more than twenty. Esther, married less than four months, was nineteen.

Although she was not ordinarily a believer in astrology, and had absolutely no idea how sailors used the night sky to tell them where to go, she felt certain that crucial stars had descended into that tiny bakery room to make for her a perfect navigational tool. In short, she was inspired, and knew for once in her life exactly in which direction she was supposed to go.

The baker stood before her—a destination slim and brown. He was lithe and beautiful in a coltish, boyish way. Small. Only a bit taller than she. Esther immediately took in his huge almondy eyes, and his hair—thick dark brown hair gathered in a low braid at the back. He seemed to her like something carved out of precious wood; miniature, masculine, and muscular, and all at once.

The bakery was only two rooms: one with a low wooden baking table rutted and eternally floury from years of use, and the other with a brick furnace that had been hewn, by the baker's grandfather, out of the limestone wall. It was behind what would later be the Russian Compound but was then a rubbly clump of lower-class homes bordering the more prosperous center of town. When the baker saw the young woman with the full skirt, cinched at the waist, when he saw the big brown eyes of the woman, when he saw her white skin, full lips, and attractive face, he invited her in. He gave her a fresh roll and asked her, in nervous, clumsy Yiddish (which like a mule kicked and brayed itself off of his tongue; he was embarrassed at his language's lack of manners) if she would like some sweet mint tea. This was the start of her nine-year love affair with the baker and lifelong passionate entanglement with Jerusalem, the city whose twists, turns, bakers, and twin arcane whispers of piety and perversity ultimately spoke straight to her heart.

Esther would make love with her husband at night "through her front door," and then, in the daytime, she carried out an affair with the baker, a third-generation Palestinian Jew who had a voice that made her think, for no good reason, of clouds. Their sexual game was ruled by the fact that the baker would only enter into her "rear door." Both euphemism (which in the entire nine years they never breached) and position (which in the entire nine years they never varied except slightly in angle) suited each of them, titillating not only the tenderest parts of their anatomies, but also the deeply humorous sense of sex that they found they shared.

She came once a week, on Tuesdays, in the late afternoon when her husband would be busy participating in his civic meetings, and the rest of the town, in classic Mediterranean style, would be indoors either scheming, studying, or sleeping. The baker, whose hands Esther always thought were strangely thin-fingered, uncallused, for a baker, would lock the door to the back of the shop. And as he walked over to her, she would be laying a clean cloth down on the baking table. She loved lifting a finger to his lips, putting her fingers in his mouth, and then with her wet fingers she would trace the graceful outline of his face, from mouth to nose, eyes, and into ears.

Always, when they were both ready, she would turn away from him and lean her body over the table. He pulled up her skirts, down her undergarments, and down his own pants. Then he licked the fingers on his right hand and slowly, passionately opened her up. Soon he slid right into her. She loved the feel of his body angling its way upward. She loved the feel of her heavy breasts hard pressing into the wooden table. He gripped her buttocks and thrust himself deep.

They kissed and panted and hungered at and for each other's skin, more, not less fervently as the years went by. Theirs, they agreed, was an ancient elemental passion that must have existed, like sand, earth, and sky, long before either of them had been born. And despite the intense physicality of their togethering, both Esther and the baker always felt insubstantial, flimsy, oh so light in the presence of this passion. But this was not a bad feeling. When they made love it was as if they were wrapping their bodies not only around each other but also, and more essentially, around something else that had before been naked. It was, they agreed, as if the passion were the real creature and they, though temporarily deprived of the normal trappings of personhood, were lucky to have been chosen as its favorite clothes. They dressed the passion in carnal finery, and the passion wore them with secret frequency.

My great-great-great-grandmother, Esther Sophie Goldner Schine, granddaughter of the Chief Rabbi of the British Empire, thought her husband's coming in through her front door and her lover's coming in through her rear door was the perfect arrangement for a Jewish woman. Something about the notion of separate facilities fit nicely into the ready framework of kashrut. Milk here, meat there, and as long as there was proper distance between things, everything stayed quietly kosher.

My father writes:

Yochanan came from a part of East Prussia called Sheinlanka, which means "pretty terraces." Today it is part of Poland, not far from the town of Posnan. He came to Israel under the following circumstances:

In 1836, the Chief Rabbi of the British Empire wrote to a famous Prussian Rabbi by the name of the Chatam Sofer, and asked for a shidach for his granddaughter Esther, under the condition that the young couple move to Israel. A shidach is the Yiddish term for a marriage match. This was before the existence of Zionism. Most Jews still believed that Israel should not and could not be established until the Messiah came.

The Chief Rabbi disagreed with prevailing thought. He was among a group of radical, European, liberal Orthodox Jews who believed that moving to Israel was not in opposition to the messianic idea. The Chief Rabbi wrote to the Chatam Sofer because he knew that this Rabbi was also of this thinking.

The Chatam Sofer sent his favorite student, Yochanan, whose father was himself a great scholar.

I write:

On the second Tuesday in Iyar, four months after they arrived in Jerusalem, Yochanan finished early with his civic meeting and decided to make for home. He was just about to walk past the American Colony when he saw Esther step out of the front door of their house and turn to walk the other way. It was late fall, and chilly. She was wearing her long maroon coat and the wide-brimmed black hat that tipped down over her right eye and made her vision, she always explained, "a bit drunk feeling, you know, only half there and wobbly, but not too bad, I find my way after all." Yochanan loved his wife's way of speaking. Her sentences were curvy and full of original character.

Yochanan called out to Esther but he was too far for her to hear and so he walked on and meant to call again, but then he found himself walking quietly, stealthily, after his wife around a corner, and again, another corner, and then down the street and into an alley. He stopped at the mouth of the alley and watched his wife walk through the bakery back door. Her maroon cloak wafted behind her for several seconds and then, too, disappeared into the warm realm of dough and yeast.

Pulling back and into a doorway on which was graffitied the word *sky* in sloppy Aramaic, he looked up at the real sky, which was darkening with the foredream of a storm. He watched as the baker poked his head out and then shut the front door of his shop. Hidden, but only ten feet away, Yochanan didn't say a word. Then he walked to the closed bakery door and put his ear to the old wood of it. Soon he could hear his wife groaning. He stepped away from the door and looked up and down the street. No one was in the alley, nor walking toward it. He walked back and listened some

more. He became aroused almost immediately, and soon was pic-
turing the baker holding Esther's naked breasts, petting them gently
and then lifting up the nipples to his mouth. First one and then the
other. And the baker's hand, Yochanan imagined the baker's left
hand reaching in between Esther's legs, which she pressed together
tightly. Soon, in his mind, they were pressing their naked bodies
together and moving, back and forth, toward and away, with the
tempestuous ease of a storm just brewing. The storm outside began
to blow. Yochanan huddled into his coat, raised his collar, and
ducked deeper into the doorway. Shutting his eyes, he leaned into
the images as if they were the real door, open and welcoming, while
the wooden one, closed and cold against his body, kept him out of
all this. Now he heard the baker groaning. Esther let out a small
passionate yelp. And as the two lovers inside reached satiety, the
one outside reached down and touched himself, pressed there,
pressed and pulled himself to solitary, intense pleasure. Only then
did he leave.

Yochanan put his hands over his hat and ran through the rain.
His feet swish-swished into puddles already forming in the narrow,
stony streets. As he ran, an angry litany, like an opposite prayer,
wrote itself on his brain:

The baker has a face of moldy clay.
The baker has hands of heavy, stinking wood.
The baker is a deformed gentile in disguise.
The baker is an eater of clams.
A descendant of Amalake.
The devil of devils.
The baker is . . . the baker is . . . the baker is shtupping my wife!

The rain hit him harder now. Pelting from every angle and also
straight up from the ground. He felt slowed by it, slowed and
assaulted, as if each raindrop were a separate obstacle. Reaching
home, he went inside, took off his greatcoat and hat, and set them
upon the fine wooden rack that they had brought with them from

London. Shaking out his beard and hair, he ran his fingers through them. Then he held his hands up to his mouth and breathed into his open palms. The warm air hovered there, but only for a second, and soon his skin was cold again. He breathed again, felt warm for several seconds and then cold again, warm and then cold. Cold. He dropped his hands down to his sides, thrust them into his pockets, and sighed a silty, grainy sigh. One that seemed to come from the bottom of his soul's ocean. But then everything changed. His mood rocked and swayed, and Yochanan felt a smile flutter to his lips.

Laughing out loud, he turned and looked at his image in the gilt hall mirror. My, how shaggy! Wet! How disheveled! But happy! Happy! He found himself possessed of an excited and yet cautious confusion.

He had taken great pleasure outside the baker's door and yet there were so many sins and so much shame growing on the fields where this kind of pleasure bloomed. Where was his anger? He could not feel it now. Where was his litany, his sour prayer, his anger? Putting his hands over his face he pulled back on his own scalp, up from his forehead, feeling the prick and pull of each hair being stretched back and some even breaking. Yochanan loved his wife, and trusted her, too. Strangely, he still trusted her. The image of Esther in the baker's arms was an excruciatingly beautiful flower. Vicarious, criminal, devastating, and yet thrillful. He ached with every petal, leaf, and fresh-cut stem of it.

Once again, he imagined the baker's dark hands thrusting upward into Esther's body, her mouth half open, lips wet. Yochanan imagined and imagined, and grew once again aroused while standing alone in the antechamber, still dripping from the rain. But he didn't touch himself this time. He was in his own house and the walls were lined with holy books. Yochanan could not bring such odd, illicit flowers home with him. Here they wouldn't be fragrant, but sacrilegious, most foul.

Rubbing his hands together, he put them once more through his beard and hair. As if he could comb out the confusion. A servant walked into the antechamber.

"Oh sir, I didn't hear you—come in, sit by the fire, take off your wet clothes, and eat some fresh rolls, just come from the baker. Esther, the Lady, your wife, she has just brought them, in through the kitchen courtyard door."

My father writes:

In 1837 there was a horrible earthquake in the northern mystical city of Sefat . . . Over five thousand people were killed, and those that escaped left the city and wandered throughout Palestine. Many half-mad old Kabbalists made their way to Jerusalem. The streets were full of their ragged and deranged numbers. Yochanan and Esther, working with the British Consul, set up a charitable foundation to aid their cause. Amongst other projects, they raised money for an orphanage. Once the money was raised, Esther became its de facto director.

I write:

While her husband had come in wet, Esther arrived home soaking. She had gotten caught in the brunt of the squall. And although both her color and her spirits were still lifted from her doughy tryst, everything else about her dragged. Her hair had come loose under her hat and was lying in sopping tendrils all about her face. And her long maroon cloak, drenched on the bottom, dragged around her feet.

In the kitchen she threw off her floppy hat and stepped out of the cloak, gratefully peeling its wetness off of her body. The only dry thing about her were the rolls which were curled into a cloth that she had stuffed under her cloak and which she had held tight into her chest as she made her way home. Suddenly laughing, she thrust the rolls away from her body and into the hands of the servant, who laughed along with her for no reason at all. They continued laughing, Esther and the servant girl, as Esther unconsciously ran her hands up and down her bodice. Her nipples were cold and hard. And they stung a bit, too. Esther dropped her hands and walked upstairs to change into dry clothes for dinner.

When she saw Yochanan standing in the front vestibule she

stopped, gave him a smile. His look was neither vacant of affection nor full of any familiar warmth. He was in between something, and she knew not what, but did have a frightful idea. She knew not how to respond. Again, she tried to smile. And this time was successful. But the smile brought another shiver. As if there were a bit of cold contained in the subtle upturn of her own lips, which, with her smile, spilled out over her whole body. She hugged her arms about her. And she needed to speak. It was odd to stand there not speaking.

"One of the Sefat men begged to be let into our house, out of . . . ," she began.

"And so you let him; it's raining, of course you let him."

"I led him to our door but at the last second he—"

"Ran away. Yes, they always run away."

"My husband. You look tired."

"My wife. You are very wet. Go dry yourself. And then we will eat. I smell the bread. It smells good."

Esther walked toward her husband and continued to speak. "But just as I opened the door, the man ran from me." She stopped in front of her husband and held out her hand to touch his. Yochanan felt how cold she was. Esther spoke again. "The baker put in an extra roll. He is a good baker."

"My wife. Esther. You are very wet. Go upstairs, dry your—"

"My husband, I am going."

Yochanan watched after her as she climbed the stairs and rounded the landing. And as Esther disappeared from his view he felt that he could hear his own heart and smell his own blood and even feel his skin encasing his face and fingers, his legs and feet, his toes, too. He felt taut and uncomfortable inside of himself. As if he were more a creaky machine than man, more a sum of mismatched parts than any sort of ethereal spirit. Whereas usually he felt the opposite. So comfortable with the feel of his own soul. And so familiar with it.

But now was not a time for soul. Actually, he couldn't feel his soul at all. Only his bones, and his body and all the blood running through it. Looking up the stairs again, he saw only emptiness. Then the green spot at the top of the hall snared his eyes; it was the picture, a landscape that his father had sent them, a present from Sheinlanka. Sent with the messenger whose eyes rolled this way and that, and in whom Esther had recognized a distant cousin's husband's younger brother or at least the form of someone remote and inconsequential whom she had once known.

"Well maybe not you," she had said when the messenger protested, "but definitely someone like you or at least like your face." Then all three—Yochanan, Esther, and the messenger— laughed at her rather silly if not poetic persistence.

"At least like your face." Now Yochanan mouthed his wife's words to himself, "At least like your face." The words didn't mean anything, but he felt an odd and pressing need to repeat them. As if this one fragment of nonsense could save him from having to live in a kind of wholeness that made too much sense. He knew that he would not mention what he had seen to his wife but that she knew that he knew and that this was to be their secret. And he also knew that the secret would become, over time, a mistress to both of them, or rather, his mistress and her mister, a hermaphroditic silence that they would share and bed and ultimately believe in. For what is a secret, he painfully mused, but a kind of religion that leads the silent to constantly pray.

Focusing on the picture at the top of the stairs, he ran his fingers through his hair again, pulling each follicle upward from his scalp. And then he lowered his hand to his teeth and gently bit the knuckles. The skin gathered up like soft leather in his mouth. He pulled and then sucked, unconscious of the action but fully immersed in it. Meanwhile, watching quietly from the kitchen, the servant thought her master most strange.

My father writes:

Yochanan's father, the chief assistant of the Chatam Sofer, was the blind Rabbi Mordechai Schine. A legend has been passed down that his students never knew he was blind. According to the legend, Rabbi

Mordechai Schine tricked his students into thinking that he could see by listening for the turning of pages as they studied the Talmud and following the text in his head. He must have known the entire Talmud by heart.

I write:

Esther changed quickly out of her wet clothes and came down for dinner. They ate in relative silence, whereas usually both chatted comfortably about their days. Then right after they had finished eating, the couple went up to their room and got into bed. It was much earlier than usual, but neither knew what else to do.

Esther was pious in her own way. She knew how to keep the Sabbath holy but in private she often broke the rules. Yochanan was pious but in a serious way. He knew the mitzvot and he always kept the Sabbath holy. To him, creativity could come only as a consequence of prayer and piety, not as a shaper of it. Esther and Yochanan lay in their beds, side by side, barely any space between them. As it was not her time of the month, the beds were pushed together. On the days when she was bleeding they would be pulled far apart. Esther fidgeted and couldn't lie still. She sat halfway up and flipped her pillow over, fluffed it up, and then rested her face into the cool linen. She watched Yochanan's back. He was turned away from her, facing the window on the east wall, which looked out over the Mary Church and farther in the distance also faced the garden the Christians call Gethsemane, after the olive trees that grow there, crooked and squat.

Esther sat up again and turned the pillow another time. But the linen on the underside wasn't cool yet and this made her fidget some more. She did not know what or how or how much he knew, but she knew that Yochanan knew something. And Esther wondered how this something fit into his prayers, let alone into his pants. He was a most prayerful man, her husband, from a long line of Rabbis reaching all the way back to Rashi, the great eleventh-century commentator.

Shutting her eyes, Esther tried to sleep but she could not. She kept seeing images and having odd thoughts and memories. She felt

filled with them. Her whole body dreaming, remembering, thinking. One image would not leave her alone. It was of Yochanan's
father. She could not stop thinking about Yochanan's father, a man
whom she had never met, but whose story fascinated her. Esther
had a picture in her head of an old man sitting at a table in the
House of Study. He was surrounded by many students and many
books.

The image dissipated, leaving her alone with Yochanan in the
almost-dark. Esther closed her eyes and listened to her husband
breathing. Heavy and deep were his inhalations, and every couple
of breaths a restless comma of a cough inserted itself into his
repose. Sighing, Esther feared that he had caught cold in the rain.
She rubbed her eyes and took a finger up to her right nipple, which
was still tender. The baker had taken her nipples into his mouth
and sucked them until she felt like screaming in pleasure, but she
hadn't screamed; instead she turned the yell inward as she had
taught herself to do, inviting it into an inner cavern where voices
were always echoing and the trick was never to try to contain them
but just to let them joyously be. She moved her hand off of her
breast and traveled it down in between her legs, but only for a second. Not for pleasure, but for the comfortable and warm, close feeling of touching herself. And then she curled over on her side and
shut her eyes.

She pretended that every time Yochanan inhaled was the turning of a page and every time he exhaled was the ending of a chapter. In this way, she read the Talmud of their togetherness. It was a
big book. A book that contained all that had already passed
between them as well as all that would ever pass between them.
Past and present and future all were written there. She read for a
long time, so many shared stories, some intimate, some silly, others
dark and uncomfortable, some so beloved that she almost cried
from them.

The night passed heavily. No, thought Esther, Jerusalem is not
a place for regular sleep. Only for a kind of restless snuggling
inward that leaves a soul dreamily awake all day long. Yochanan

slept deeply; his breath was a parchment of air that she read from for a long time. And then, as the sky lightened, Esther moved toward her husband and roused him gently. Yochanan wrapped his arms around her and nuzzled his lips into her hair. She pressed her body into his, and together they slept, adding another page there.

Paul Rawlins

OURS

> . . . I imagined
> for a long time that the baby, since
> it would have liked to smell our clothes to know
> what a mother and a father would have been,
> hovered sometimes in our closet . . .
> —Robert Hass, "On Squaw Peak"

The ghosts of children haunt our house. They gather at corners, huddle in the closet just above the mound of heavy winter clothes piled on the upper shelf. There's a coolness you sense when you draw on a sweater, the edge of a scent that scurries up and past you, a column of clean, bright air instead of musty wool. I take this to mean that whatever, whoever they really are, they want to be close—but so far as I know, they can't be touched.

In the backyard this spring, they've taken to hanging from the dripping limbs of the peach tree. Teddy, our dog, knows they're there. He'll whine to be let out the back door, then trot over to the tree, where he sits on his haunches and stares up into the branches. I followed him out once to check for nests or maybe stray leaves—frozen, black ones that had clung through the winter and might be making a shadow or a sound—but there was nothing. Teddy looked back at me over his dog shoulder to make sure I saw whatever it was, too, or to check that he was doing okay—he had that look of wanting to know he was doing this thing right. I nodded, and he went back to watching the tree while I stayed there looking past the branches to the marly sky until the water coming up from the grass had soaked through my shoes and I could feel the chill in my feet.

"Come on, Teddy," I said. He followed me to the patio, but when I slid the door open and stepped inside, he turned and jogged back to the tree. He came in later, scratching at the glass door after dark. Lystra, my wife, stared from the kitchen table while he hustled past her to the porch, where we heard him lapping from his dish. Lystra stacked my plate on top of hers without saying anything, then carried them to the sink.

She knows they're out there, too, and when Teddy came back through the kitchen, she crouched down to take his pointed face in her hands.

"You're a good dog, Teddy," she said, then let him go.

Lystra goes on with her housework, her gardening, the grocery business she runs over the phone, taking a bath, all of it with them around her. She surprised me the first time I went to tell her I'd felt as though there were someone perched on the arm of the couch. I thought maybe I'd seen something, too—a smudge, or a tear in what should have been seamless air—and the hair rose on the back of my neck. I found Lystra in our bedroom, folding towels and sheets. She stopped long enough to look up when I came in the room, then went back to pinching a pale green towel in the middle between her fingers, folding it in half again lengthwise, quickly, as though she were clapping her hands.

"I know," she said when I told her.

"You know what?" I asked. I scooted the laundry basket over and sat on the edge of the bed until she scowled at me. We'd just bought a new, fancy mattress, a thick one with white-on-white striped ticking that was stuffed with layers of horsehair and spun-cotton batting. We were supposed to turn and rotate it head to foot every first of the month, and we weren't supposed to sit on the edge—no jumping, either, of course.

I pulled a chair over.

"You know what?" I asked her again. It was only a weird feeling I had come to tell her about, really.

"They come and go," she said while she bussed a stack of folded towels to the hall linen closet.

"Who?"

"Those children," she told me from the doorway, where she stood with her arms folded across her stomach. She had just cut her hair short, the way women do sometimes in their thirties, and it had left her face looking more open, fuller. "They're children," she said again. Then she came for her wicker laundry basket on the bed and left for the washroom downstairs.

I know that Lystra's tried ignoring them. I have, too, but you can't always or forever. She's tried to guess what they might want, but there's nothing she can think of to do for them. She can't feed them and doesn't believe they could be cold, only lonesome, perhaps. I have heard her sing songs while she works around the house, silly ones that children want, with nonsense rhymes like "hey diddly, diddly, dye-die-die" and such. She sings under her breath, almost to herself, in that unconscious way you do when you're thinking about something that makes you sing, rather than the song itself.

She never used to sing. It used to be the radio when we first married, eleven years ago, and she couldn't stand the quiet of the house when I was working swing shift and she was home for hours alone before me. I came home one day, and she had bought a little black Sony with luminous green numbers that from then on she left playing on the kitchen counter.

She got used to being home alone when she started her grocery business. The radio stayed on, but it stayed turned down to where it was forgotten, and we sometimes heard it from our bed at night. That led to a game we used to play after one of us got up to go turn it off, where the one left behind might or might not hide in the dark house along the way back to the bedroom. It was terrifying to walk back, and then, if you survived, to find the bedclothes rumpled and empty. You had to look for the other one if they were gone—that was the rule—and no lights. When it was me, searching for Lystra, I used to close my eyes sometimes, squatting on my haunches and swirling my hands out in front of me. Somehow this seemed to put us on more even footing. Sometimes I would feel her heat as she moved past my reach, a fold in the air at my side, luring me down the hall. Once she even hurdled over my shoulder, brushing me like a bat might, or an owl swooping past in the doorway of a barn when your eyes hadn't yet adjusted to the dark.

That game is an old one. Lystra stays up now on her own, while I go to bed myself. I'll wake up after an hour or two most nights to see if she's there. Sometimes she'll answer from the bathroom or the patio; a light will switch off, and then she'll lift the covers and slide into bed. Other times I find her in the kitchen with her glasses on, reading at the table. Or in the spare bedroom, sitting with her feet up on the daybed, the curtains opened to let in light from outdoors that turns her nightgown pale and silver.

"Usually they're pretty quiet," is what she told me when I asked if something in the house was keeping her up. "They go to bed at night, I guess, like everybody else."

I can't think of spirits needing sleep—spirits, clouds, reflections, dust, whatever I've thought them to be once.

"They're only children," my wife reminds me. "They've got to have their rest."

They're our children, of course. By my wife's count, there could be at least five of them. There have been five she knows of. Two more she suspects. Others rejected by her body early—maybe in the first moments, maybe hours later, as if my seed is poison to her, or the eggs she bears are hollow, like the ones we've blown for Easter, thin and practically translucent, with no more strength than tissue.

We talked nonstop after we lost the first, trying to be sensitive to one another, to reassure ourselves. It was so common—how many friends did we have who had gone through it?—that it seemed it could have been our due, but now the odds were with us. Our love-making became fraught with determination to make a child so beautiful, so perfect and strong, as though our raucous force could assure it—as though we could pound nails a little deeper and set the seams and joints too tight to leak or split. As though strong love alone could produce strong life—which, perhaps, it has. But no bodies that could live in light and air.

The second was followed closely by a third. And then hiatus. Rest. An autumn season, and a winter, as things go, with the silences that grow up between you when a part of life is scarred beyond the point of your being able to keep looking at it.

The next time we were cautious. I curled around Lystra afterward, and she seemed to make herself small to fit, as though I were a shell or a case closing snug around a jewel. She finally stopped shaking and she went to sleep, while I kept watch for most of the night and made my bargains there with God or whoever might be listening.

The next time was by accident. Since then, we've grown more careful.

Lystra started the grocery business she runs out of our home because this was where she planned to stay and raise her babies. She quit her job the week after she found out she was pregnant the first time, because she wanted to make her recruits and get her system pat long before the baby came. The business was going to save us money while it made us money, too, which it has. Lystra has seven women under her now in her downline, plus her best customers, whom she's on the phone with once a week taking orders. The commodities are bought in bulk, and Lystra arranges for drops and distribution from our garage. My wife and two out of the seven women under her have done well with this system, providing toothpaste and toilet paper, cold cereals, diapers, canned goods, even an off-brand motor oil and tires for their neighbors.

She keeps the business up, she says, because she likes it. I worried that it would remind her of why she started it in the first place, of all the plans we'd hatched while she lay there patient as I thumped her naked belly, claiming that I was testing it for ripeness, pretending I knew anything at all about what was going on inside of her.

The grocery business doesn't have anything to do with that anymore, she tells me, and the women she sells goods to are her friends. Her business now isn't supposed to be any different than the home we live in, which has three bedrooms with room for more and sits in a neighborhood where herds of elementary-aged children walk past to school in the mornings and scream through the streets in the summers. Downstairs there is still masking tape on the floors from two more bedrooms we had planned, and a long family room we argued over whenever it came up—over how big it needed to be, colors, a fireplace, carpet, lights. We marked the rooms off with the tape, sticking it down, then measuring and pulling it up again, over and over, to move the imaginary walls. It's all just gray space down there now, and junk, aside from a laundry room.

Lystra said once that these children don't go down there, and it's true, I've never noticed them to. They stay upstairs, where we are mostly, and I've seen Lystra haul the ironing board up to the living room or kitchen for no other reason I know. Even so, they never do come around directly—and they don't stay if you move toward them.

I was arguing once with Lystra about it, not sure what was going on. I wanted to know, if these things were really there, what they were hiding all the time for, whether they were teasing us or if they were afraid.

"I don't know," Lystra said. "They might just be upset about what's going on."

"So you think whatever they are, they're mad at us?"

"They could be angry, but not necessarily at us. You see what I mean?" Lystra said. "Angry that this happened, but not because it's our fault."

"It's not our fault," I said.

"I know it," Lystra said.

It's something I've told and retold her, and sometimes she's told me, around the table, in our bed, digging in the flowers out in the backyard. You take turns at being the one who knows, like you take turns at being most everything after you've been together for a while—the strong one, the grouch, coach, prophet, martyr.

Flowers are something new to Lystra and me, a hobby she took up on her own a few years back. There's no history of it in her family or mine, but I've gotten to where I like joining her to work on the egg-shaped hills we've mounded up in the front yard and in back. There's a familiarity to it now I enjoy, the triangular holes cut by the little hand shovels, the transplants from the nursery with their cubes of soft new roots cupped in my palm, Lystra's yellow watering can with a grinning frog on the side.

This year, Lystra wanted the sweet alyssum she planted in the backyard last season taken out. Out back she wanted tulips now, and in front, roses. It was cool out, overcast and damp, but we were working anyway, wearing windbreakers and kneeling on burlap sacks to keep dry and out of the mud. Off as the day was, it was still the warmest yet all year. While we were digging, there might have been something on the step. They stayed, mostly, at the edge of things, and you saw more when you weren't trying.

This year, Lystra wanted a scarecrow for the garden, too. She had an old coat and a pair of denim coveralls wadded up in a box in the garage, and I'd noticed she'd been adding other items—a hat, which seemed obvious, and a bandanna, a pair of threadbare gardening gloves to make hands, a pillowcase she'd embroidered with a face. I'd seen last week that we were going to have a smiling scarecrow, friendly and benign—one who would probably go ahead and husk the corn for the birds. It would be a scarecrow these children would like, like one of the old men at church who passed candy from his pockets to the kids when they shook hands.

When something moved around the corner of the house, I stabbed my shovel into the soil and sat back on my sack, looking at the peach tree with Teddy under it, wagging. I had thrown a rock at that tree just last fall, sent it cracking up through the branches so that it startled Teddy and landed somewhere in the neighbor's yard. I made Teddy come inside, and he spent the afternoon whining at the door until I shut him in the garage. I don't know if it was Teddy or the rock I was feeling guilty for, but I'd gone back out later that night while Lystra was in the shower and stood there in front of the tree feeling foolish.

"We've tried," is what I finally said. "We wanted you. If you're really here, you know that." A neighbor had a sprinkler running, a rain bird, and there were crickets chirruping, but nobody answered. I checked behind me to see that the bathroom light was still on in the house before I went on. "You should just go." I had my hands out, like I was holding a bowl, explaining, trying to win my case.

Now I sat with my hands wrapped around my knees while I stared across the yard. Behind me I heard Lystra stop jabbing at the earth while she rearranged her sack. The clouds were settling down the face of the mountains across the valley, gray and full of awful silence, driving everything indoors.

"What?" I said when I realized Lystra had been talking.

"Are you finished?"

"No," I said.

She waited, but I left my spade where it was and sat looking out over the yard until she said why didn't I go get a rake and start over at the corner.

In the garage I left the rake and drug out Lystra's scarecrow box and some old, dusty sacking with a coarse weave that burned my hands when I stuffed it down the pant legs I'd tied off at the ankles with twine. I used a coat hanger to help form shoulders and crammed the shirtsleeves with newspaper I knew was only going to deteriorate from the wet. For the torso, I pulled two pillows off the bed. I shoved one halfway down into the tops of the pants, then folded the shirt around the other and tucked it behind the bib of the overalls. For the head, I used a dirty foam basketball. I snugged Lystra's pillow slip around it, tied it off at the neck, then stared at the grinning face before I turned it around backward. I practiced faces on the floor of the garage with a piece of charcoal. I drew a smile and then a frown. Then I worked on a scowl, something that looked like a scream, then a snarl with jagged saw teeth. Finally, I settled on a howl—three elongated Os, two for the eyes and a long, distended mouth.

I found a hammer, and I hauled the straw man outside, flapping limp under my arm.

Lystra was back on her haunches, watching as I came out of the garage.

"Where are you going to put it?" she said. She got up to help, brushing off her knees, but I turned up the back steps instead of heading for the garden.

"What are you doing?" Lystra said.

I let the scarecrow slump on the porch so I could drive a nail an inch deep into the back door, then I hung him there, looking out at the tree where Teddy stood with his nose turned up toward the empty branches. Lystra moved back to the edge of the patio to look. She stood with her hands on her hips, then motioned me out of the way. I went down the steps and stood halfway between her and the door until she started to laugh.

"Was it supposed to be scary?" she said.

"I guess so."

She nodded; then she turned sober.

"He looks more like somebody kicked him in the balls."

I turned back and saw the face, eyes and mouth wide in shock and innocence, with less menace than there was fear. I squatted, banging at the grass with the hammer.

"Are you going to leave him there?" Lystra said.

"Are they still waiting, is that it?" I said. "Is there still supposed to be a chance?"

Lystra shook her head.

"This isn't limbo or purgatory or whatever. Why should they have to stay here?"

"I don't know," Lystra said. She tossed her silver garden claw toward the flower bed and squeezed her hands between her knees. "Unless they're just ours."

I felt a raindrop splash on the back of my hand.

"How can they be ours? How can they be anything?" I said.

"That's just what they are," Lystra said.

"That's crazy."

"If that's what you want to be." Lystra sounded stern.

I stood and looked out over the yard. "Teddy," I yelled. "Get over here." While he jogged over I turned back to Lystra. "What would you do if I cut that tree down right now? It's old, and the fruit's never any good. I think it's got peach bore."

"Do what you want," Lystra said. She was trying to keep her eyes on me and away from the spot where Teddy had been standing.

"You don't think I could. You watch."

"You could," Lystra said. She bent down for her gloves where she'd dropped them. "I know you could. What good's it going to do?"

When she got to the top of the steps, she lifted the straw man off his nail. She twisted his head around, turned the smiling face out and looked at it for a minute; then she pushed him over the porch rail into the flowers and went inside.

The exhaustion that came with living in our house surfaced sometimes and burst over everything in an enervating flood, and I found Lystra on the bed, asleep, when I went in. It was after I'd thrown the hammer out in the yard and sworn at Teddy, then locked him in his pen when he wouldn't stay away from the tree. I'd gathered up the garden tools, stacked the sacks of bulbs and peat moss in the garage. The scarecrow I sat up in a plastic chair under the eaves, safe from the rain, his grinning face turned out to the world in welcome.

To watch Lystra while she slept, you wouldn't know she wasn't perfect. But there was something inside of us that couldn't come out and wouldn't be kept in. Something inside of us that made shades instead of children. We weren't supposed to try anymore. There were reasons, one on top of the other, all things the doctors understood. And there had been doctors, one after another, for Lystra and for me. Doctors with no shame, for whom your most private moments, your starkest nakedness meant nothing. We'd had arguments as well as silence, fights vicious enough to leave bruises inside that you couldn't see a way to keep from rising to your skin. And at different times we practiced hope, or we tried for understanding.

"You're going to adopt," my mother told Lystra after the last time, after we had considered this and everything else. She had said it before. "You're going to raise a wonderful family, and they'll be yours, one hundred percent yours." It was what we probably would do, we'd decided. We just didn't know when. We were always thinking it would be soon. I didn't know, though, and Lystra didn't know if we could ever crowd these others out. They might be jealous or cause trouble—or, then, they might just leave. You couldn't say.

I rested my chin on Lystra's shoulder while I lay beside her, wanting to tell her that, to tell her anything just to hear us talk. The mattress we'd bought raised the bed four inches, and from the dripping window I could see Teddy out back. I'd let him out of his run, and when the storm had started, he'd come in from the yard to lie in the doorway of his doghouse. That's where he was now, with his long face cradled between his paws, looking out to where the tree stood beading up with rain, keeping watch over everything that love had made.

Robert Olen Butler

Hiram the Desperado

Mr. O. E. Malsberry
Instrument man P. R. R.
Gorgona, C. Z. Panama

Dear Owen—This is the school where Cousin Hiram reigns supreme & curries the town ruffians. All's well. Chas.

Postmarked Charleston, Wash.,
Apr. 24, 1908

Say, don't you think they need somebody to tell them what to do? These kids all around me? Another kid to tell them, I mean. Me. Not like the things they hear plenty of already. Elbows off the table and quiet down and be in this room on that tick of the clock and add up these meaningless numbers and eat your greens. But things that have something to do with something. So for instance I tell the six- and seven-year-olds to steal cigarettes for me from their dads, just one every other day and only from a near-full pack, nothing the old man'll even realize is gone, and for this I'll keep the big kids off their backs; and then I tell the thirteen- and fourteen-year-olds not to rough up the six- and seven-year-olds, and I keep them in cigarettes for going along with it. I perform a service for everybody, and it has to do with what they really need, in this case protection and smokes. And sure, along the way in this one particular part of the doings, I keep a few extra cigarettes to smoke for myself and I get a few extra favors from the biggest of the older kids. That's only fair.

Say, we're just trying to get out of childhood in one piece, all of us. It's a new century, so they keep reminding us. There's some swell

75

stuff going on. But I'm sitting around in a kid's body and I'm wait-ing for influenza and diphtheria and dengue fever and the black cholera and infantile paralysis, and if you go out to play, one of those swell automobiles will run you down or an aeroplane will crash on your barn with you in the hayloft or a sixteen-foot cedar-cut will roll off a logging sled and right over you or your dad will drink the whole pailful of beer in about one hour flat, not to men-tion half a bottle of whiskey, and he'll beat you near to death for breathing too heavy or you can get knuckled to death by anybody who happens to have been born a few years before you—they say kids have died having their brains scrambled up by a good knuck-ling to the temple while in a headlock—and there's always being bored to death sitting in a schoolroom all day with George Washington staring down from over the blackboard looking like he's as bored as you, not to mention a Sunday afternoon when it rains all get-out and you are doing so bad you still have your churchgoing collar on and no strength to even take it off, this Puget Sound rain is coming down so hard. Kids have been known to seize up and keel over dead sitting in a window seat or on a porch swing with the rain coming down on a Sunday afternoon.

The boy who moved in next door—he was twelve, same as me, though I never got a chance to play with him—had himself a growth on his neck. He was a Catholic and went to parochial and so he wasn't on display at our school, where we hadn't had a good goi-ter for several years, and I made better than a dollar selling a nickel view of him from our attic window, which could see down into his fenced backyard and him sitting there in the sun. Then last week he was gone and they put up the black wreath and I guess it was some-thing worse than a goiter, and that kid didn't need anybody telling him to divide thirteen into a hundred and four or to sit up straight. I don't know what his dad was like.

So ain't I already saying how I can be fidgeting to death in a front desk of a classroom on a spring day that's working up to rain as soon as the bell rings? I'm not in that front desk out of choice or even the alphabet. I'm put there to be in knuckle-striking range and where I can't whisper worth a hoot or pass a note, and it's like that from the first day of class anymore, me being a known desperado. It's the price I pay. I saved others, but myself I couldn't save, which is one true thing, at least, that I learned while being brought to the brink of death-by-boredom at my weepy mother's side in church.

Anyways, I'm sitting there in school one day this spring and I can't find a place in that chair where my tailbone is happy about anything and there's a terrible itch in my left heel and digging at it with the toe of my right shoe isn't helping. Mrs. Pickernose is droning on about something—that isn't her real name, but I saw her with her finger up her nose once after school when she thought nobody was looking, and I'm still waiting to give out that information in some useful way sometime. But I'm sitting there when I see out the classroom door and Miss Spencer walks past.

Say, I can be in love, can't I? I don't have to explain any of that. If most of the hundred-something other boys in this school would ride me down the hill to Port Orchard Bay on a saw blade and dump me in if they figured I was mashed on a girl—not to mention a full-grown woman, not to mention a teacher—then that's just why I'm the guy who runs things and not them, because they're all a little backward, is how I see it, and I don't have to fess up to nothing, much less explain myself. Not that I ever got any advice about this sort of thing. Pa don't talk about nothing. The few boys who some girls think of as their beaus, they haven't got the first idea about it. It's something I just know to do. She's past that door in one second flat, but she's as clear as can be in my head. She's got her hair all twisted up in the back like that princess who Cupid was stuck on that's in our reader. Miss Spencer has never been my teacher, and I guess it's better that way, her not having a direct chance to think of me as rotten, though if she had to crack my knuckles with a ruler I'd be pretty happy just to have her thinking that strong about me at all.

This has been going on for a few months already. On this particular day, after the bell, I go out and she's walking away fast, her purse and her books tucked hard against her chest, and I follow her for about a quarter of a mile past the logger cutoff and she's still walking fast like she's got serious business downtown, but I've got things to do and I let her go.

I've only ever spoken a little bit to Miss Spencer. Once, she came upon me out back of school collecting dues from a mollycoddle who didn't understand the workings of the Grand Fraternal Lodge and Benevolent Association of Cedar Weevils.

"But when do we meet?" he says to me.

"We don't meet," I say.

"So why do I pay dues?" he says.

"Say," I say, "don't you have even a little sense? There's privileges."

"What sort?" he says.

I'm not quite ready to knuckle his brains. He's two years younger and kind of on the small side, and that's always a final argument, but I've found there are fewer problems if you use reasoning. "The secret handshake," I say, wiggling my fingers at him. "The code of honor. And ain't I letting you skip the terrors of initiation? Do you think a privilege like that ain't worth ten cents? What would your fellow Weevils think, them having paid up and also bearing the scars of the rites of initiation? You need to take into account how subject you could be to this and that."

Which is when Miss Spencer walks up, right as I'm doing a serious forefinger tap into the center of the kid's chest and he's finally getting that look in his eye like logic is going to prevail.

"Hiram," she says, and I didn't even realize that she knew my name.

I stuff my hands into my pockets and turn to her. Her face is swell, is all I can say.

"Are you playing rough with this little boy?" she says.

I smile slow. She knows my name but not his. "Not at all," I say. "We was just discussing."

"We *were* just discussing," she says, stressing the word I already knew I got wrong. I'm not stupid. I pick up more than they realize. "And what might that be?" she says.

I say, "Oh, *this and that,*" which the Weevil-to-be understands right off.

"This and that," he repeats, and I look at him and give him a very friendly nod. He gives me a nod back, like we understand each other. Miss Spencer made the mistake of calling him a "little boy," and that reminded him of who he really depends on. I even turn to him and grab his hand like I'm shaking it, but I sort of jiggle it around a few times right and left, and he's beaming now with his first Weevil secret, he thinks, the handshake.

"That's all right then," Miss Spencer says.

I turn back to her, wanting the conversation to go on. I say, "Nice weather we're having, Miss Spencer, isn't it?"

She looks at me with just a little pinch in her forehead, like she's not sure she wants to talk about the weather to a kid. Then she says, "If you like rain."

"You're not used to rain?" I say, and I'm thinking what I've heard about her, which she now tells me.

"Last year I taught in California," she says. "It's very wet up here by contrast."

"That's what puts the *wash* in Washington," I say. I'm pitching like Christy Mathewson here, but she has to go.

"All right, boys," she says. "Be good."

"Sure," I say. And that's the longest conversation I've ever had with the woman I love.

So it's a couple hours later on the day when I follow her from school. It's working up to time for Pa to come home and I go into the kitchen and get the beer pail. It's sitting next to the door so I can just step in and take it without any talk. Ma is rolling out some dough and usually she's all over me about something I've done, but she acts like I'm not even there, which is how it goes at pail time.

I head on down the hill toward the bay and I can see the smoke-stacks of the USS *Iowa* in dry dock at the navy yard, which is pretty swell, and I dream a little about somehow having control of this view, and I'm selling admission and toting up dollar after dollar. I dream a little, too, about the Great White Fleet that our president has sent off to circle the world and show them all who's boss, six-teen battleships and six torpedo boats, and I feel bad for the *Iowa* that got left behind, it being a big hero in Cuba and all. Even battle-ships can get a raw deal. This all is what's going through my head, with Pa's beer pail swinging in my hand, when I get down to Front Street and see Miss Spencer.

I've made the turn up toward the docks, heading for the saloon, and the trade's a little rough along here, and there she is, the last person I'd expect to be walking along. She's on the other side of the street heading the opposite direction from me, and at first all I see is her—there's nothing else on the street, or in the whole state of Washington for that matter—her in her white shirtwaist and black skirt. Her face is lowered a little, like she's concentrating on where she's walking, which is a pretty good idea around these parts, actu-ally. Then I realize there's a guy at her side, a navy guy in his blues. I don't know he's with her till I see them go a few steps and keep alongside each other. But she's not looking at him and he's not look-ing at her and they're not saying nothing. She'd have me put that different, I know. I'd always talk perfect around Miss Spencer, because I can if I want to, and it'd make her happy.

I think they're heading for the nickel motion-picture show up the street. But I don't like how her face is down and how they're acting. Something's wrong here. I cross the street and follow them. He's a little guy, not even quite as tall as Miss Spencer, which makes me real edgy inside, like this could be me beside her as likely as him. They pass the motion-picture show right by, and the brick-yard, and they cut in at a footpath through the waterfront park. They circle the bandstand and nothing's changed about how they're walking. There's a little space between them like they're trying not even to accidentally bump into each other, and there's no talking as far as I can tell, and she's still got her head down. Yet it's not like they've just met or something. There's a real familiar feel going on between them, too. Like you pick up from somebody's parents, my own Ma and Pa even, when she gets him to go off to church once in a while and I'm walking behind them. Finally Miss Spencer and her bluejacket slow and stop and they start to turn around to sit on a bench and I duck off the path and into some shrubs and crouch down and wait for them to get settled. A Port Orchard steamer out on the bay toots its whistle. Another couple walks by and the guy shoots me a look, and I'd give him a *Bugs* or a *Dry up* except I don't want to draw attention to myself. But even this dope has his girl's arm through his. Then I peek out at Miss Spencer and this guy she's spending time with who's maybe a problem for her.

They're sitting side by side all right, pretty close now, and he's talking and then she's talking, but they're not looking each other in the eye, and then they just sit for a while. I settle down where I am. I've got a Piedmont in my pocket and a dry match, and I light up and puff away. I don't look at the pail. I know it's there and time's passing and I'm going to catch something bad for doing this, but I'm not ready to leave Miss Spencer out here with this guy. Though I'm not looking at them, either. I'm just sitting in the middle and smoking a cigarette.

When I look at them again, they're just starting to stand up. One thing I notice. She puts her hand just below her stomach, but very light, like it hurts. I know right off what's been going on, like I knew the first time I saw them on the street. Pa's smart. He don't like me showing his handiwork, usually. Ma cares about that. She's got to tote me off to church and she don't want folks knowing how bad a boy I really am. When it's not a strap or a lath or a shake across the back of me from my collar to my shoes, it's a fist right where she's touching.

They're coming this way and I duck down and hunker into the bush. They could see me if they turn, but they don't. They drift past like a dark cloud and I wait a bit and I'm pretty angry and trying to think what to do to this guy. For now I follow them. And there's two more things I notice. On the footpath, with nobody around and Front Street coming up, he tries to take hold of Miss Spencer's hand and she jerks it away. That just shows me I'm right. And if he wants to get tough with her right here for taking her hand away, I'm ready to run up on him and do what damage I can with this pail across the side of his head and my fingers in his eyes and my teeth taking chunks out of his ears. But he doesn't do a thing. He keeps walking. Which figures. It's a public place. Guys like this know how to keep it all private.

Then the other thing I notice comes a few minutes later, along Front Street. He tries to take her hand once more and she lets him. She holds his hand for a moment like it's still okay between them, and then they let go, but they move a little closer to each other as they walk.

Say, don't I know how that happens? Don't I realize I have to stop and let these two go on to wherever they're going, and don't I double back to my Pa's favorite saloon and go around to the back door? Some woman with a tired face is there ahead of me and she's just starting to move off with a pail of beer, and I guess she loves her man, and I'd rather do this myself than have Ma come down to Front Street every day. Fat Ed in his apron takes my pail, and he's okay, Fat Ed. He gives me a couple of cigarettes and a handful of radishes from the free eats and I pop the radishes on the way home and they're real good. They taste sharp, a little bitter, just what I need.

The next day the father of our country is watching me squirm to find a way to sit in my desk that don't hurt too bad, and he's not changing that little smirk on his face. Being father of the country, he had his hands full with all the backs to whip, I guess, about a million. So I keep my mind on what to do with this bluejacket who normally I'd think is pretty swell, him fighting for his country and having a swell uniform to show for it. But say, there's only so much you can allow somebody for being whatever else they are. The main thing is he's hurting Miss Spencer.

So I go to my two best hard-boiled eggs, a couple of fourteen-year-olds who I find smoking out over the knoll behind the school and who I've done some things for way beyond the Piedmonts they're sucking on right now. Joe's dad is a logger, and Joe's taller by a hand than the guy I'm after. Billy's only a little over my size, but he would bite an ear clear off if he needed to. I see their plumes of smoke and I come up over the knoll and they jump up fast from where they were crouching.

"Yay, Hiram," Joe says. "I thought you was a teacher."

"Yay, Joe," I say. "Yay, Billy."

"Yay, Hiram," Billy says.

"I may need another note from my mom soon," Joe says.

"You know where to come," I say. My handwriting is a lot better than any of the teachers realize. I say, "I need a favor from you, too. Both of you."

Joe lifts a clenched fist before his face. "You just point me," he says.

"Bet your knickerbockers," Billy says, lifting his own fist.

"Good men," I say. "Good men. And you're right about needing this." I lift my fist with theirs. "The three of us."

"We need to recruit some more Weevils?" Joe says.

"There's a sailor in town we've got to teach a lesson," I say.

The fists fall and the eyes widen. It's true this is nothing like what I've asked of them before. Or of myself, either.

"A *sailor*?" Joe says.

"An *adult*?" Billy says.

I don't need to listen to any more. I suddenly understand I'm standing here with children. I turn and head up over the knoll. "The note for my mom . . . ," Joe calls after me.

Sailors drink. This is something I know. They get drunk and then they stagger around Front Street late at night. I'm a kid. I still look like one. Nobody notices a kid or thinks a kid can do certain things. I don't need some damn army of children crusaders with me to do what I have to for Miss Spencer. So my Pa has some old logging tools in the stable out back and I fetch his beer and tonight he passes out before he can get angry, which happens four nights out of five, to be honest, and Ma is passed out too, mostly from tiredness. I go to the stable and find me a billhook, which is just right, pretty short and easy to swing, but with a nasty curved blade. It still has a good gouging point to it and it's even rusty so I can give him lockjaw on top of whatever else. I wrap it in burlap and put it under my arm, and I go into the night and down the hill, and there are electric lights shining all around at the navy yard. You can even see the *Iowa* sitting there half lit up against the dark, and I guess maybe Miss Spencer's bluejacket is from the battleship, though he's too young to have been at Cuba. That was ten years ago, when I was still pretty much a baby, and this guy was probably knuckling little kids at his public school. Not for me, he wouldn't have. Not this guy. He's bad seed, as Pa likes to say.

There are three saloons on Front Street at the navy end. I spend the next couple of hours drifting from one to the other and poking my head in now and then to check out the faces of the sailors, and then hanging around where I can, outside in the shadows, ducking the police when they come by, 'cause they'd take me as a boy-gone-bad. They'd nab me for loitering and street-roaming and for whatever they'd make of my weapon, though I'm ready to say my logger father needs it for work and I'm just trying to find him, the poor harmless drunk who's going off to the woods at dawn without his billhook. But I keep out of the way and nobody pays me any attention, and though the sailor I'm looking for isn't around yet, I'm ready to wait till he appears, and then till he's drunk and he can be taught a thing or two.

Finally, as I watch the sailors who got an early start at the saloon drifting out and back to their quarters, I realize they all have to go down Front and past the park. So I find a thicket of bushes at the street edge of the place and kind of burrow in where I can't be easily seen, but I can watch everyone going by. I wait and wait. And then I wake up with a start. I grab fast at my billhook and it's still there beside me. I look around. The street is quiet. It's very late. I come out of hiding and go down Front, and I look in at the three saloons and they're almost deserted. The guy I'm looking for isn't there, and I head on home. Ma and Pa are both still sleeping so deep that for a second I think maybe a crook snuck in while I was gone and killed them.

The next day I'm a perfect model of a schoolboy. I definitely don't want to be kept in, even for twenty minutes, 'cause when the final bell rings I go down the road and find the billhook all wrapped up by the tree where I left it, and I slide around out of sight and wait for Miss Spencer to go by. When she does, I step out and follow her. Today I'm going to stick right behind her all the time. I'll take my beating for missing dinner and the damn beer pail and bedtime and breakfast, even. Not to mention I'll take my hanging, if it comes to that. If this bluejacket starts beating on Miss Spencer, even if he's cold sober, I'll go at him right then and maybe that'd be just as well, with the cause real clear to everybody.

She's moving kind of slow. She doesn't really want to go to him. I don't blame her. If only I was somebody, I'd just go on up to her right now and say, Come with me instead, and we could do that, we'd just walk off together. But she leads me down toward town and I can see the bay out in front of us looking real blue and peaceful, and then Miss Spencer does something I don't expect. She takes a path off the road and heads up into the hills, up toward the old growth on the edge of town that the loggers haven't got to. The bluejacket and her are meeting somewhere secret this time. He thinks he won't have to worry about people seeing him if he gets upset with her and he can do what he wants. It's good I'm along. We're on barely a walking path now, through a shaggy meadow coming up on a big wall of trees as tall as a Seattle skyscraper. I don't want her to know I'm around, so I hang back quite a ways and she never looks behind her.

We go on into the dark of the woods and I have to stay closer to Miss Spencer with all the turns in the path. But there's more places to duck behind, as well, and I tread real light, like a redskin, staying on the mossy parts when I can. We play up here sometimes in the summer. We sneak around with rifles carved out of wood and we hunt the Suquamish and the Chimakum and the Muckleshoot, some of us being the Indians. When I'm Chief Seattle no one can ever find me till I plug them in the back, and I never have to give away nothing to the white man. There are real Indians out here, too, real off-the-reservation Indians, hop pickers mostly, farming and fishing between seasons. So we never know when we're going to run right into someone real, face to face.

I think about giving the bluejacket a few extra blows for making Miss Spencer come all this way alone. She's just turned out of sight ahead, beyond a tangle of dead trunks, and there's a strong smell of decaying wood in the air. I make the same turn she did around the dead trees, and ahead of me the path falls down a little slope to a clearing where there's a couple of shacks close by each other made of waste slabs from the sawmill, and Miss Spencer is heading straight for them. Then a couple of Indians step out to meet her and I jump off to the side so they can't see me, but I flatten out on the ground and crawl under a thicket at the edge of the clearing and peek down on them.

The Indians are an old couple. The man, in raggedy overalls, is moving over to the second shack, which has cattails drying on the porch and woven hop baskets bunched up beside it. He goes in. The woman is wrapped in a blanket and her braids are hanging on her shoulders, and she's real old. Miss Spencer has turned this way and the two women are talking. Miss Spencer lays her hand on that place below her stomach where he hits her with his fist. She's crying. I can see that from this far away. Then the Indian woman puts her arm around Miss Spencer and takes Miss Spencer's hand in hers and they move off to the other shack, the old woman talking low and gentle all the time.

It's now I realize he's not coming. This has to do with how he's hurt her. I don't like the doctor in town either. He comes with his black bag and never says a word, and he looks over his glasses at me like it's my fault, even if I've got a broken rib. Maybe this Indian woman has some medicine that'll help Miss Spencer. And maybe her coming here alone means she's quits with him. I reach into the burlap and squeeze the handle of the billhook, and I think about catching this guy on Front Street tonight. I wonder if maybe I'll find out what my Pa is thinking when he does what he does to me. Of course, Pa's never actually gone and killed me. Or even hacked at me with a blade. But it's got to be pretty much the same. I'll lift my hand to the guy from behind and I'll strike at him over and over, and he'll crouch down, bleeding heavy already from the first strikes, and being too weak and drunk to put up a fight. He'll cry for mercy for a while and then he'll see it's no good and just shut up and take it. That's him. But what about me?

I sit and wait, trying to imagine. What if I was Pa. And then it seems real simple. I hate your guts, is all it is. I just hate your guts. I'm starting to cry. And then there's crying from inside the shack. A sharp shout and then some crying like Miss Spencer knows I'm here and she can feel what a kid feels and she knows. I'm ashamed of my own tears but they keep on coming. Say, don't I want to go help her, if she's hurting? But don't I realize that Indian woman is doing all she can, and she knows things I haven't even dreamed of? And say, aren't I crying myself like the child that I am? So I get up and drop that old billhook at my feet, and I go on along the path through the trees, and to hell with my Pa if he wants his old billhook ever again. To hell with him.

Ron Carlson

GARY GARRISON'S WEDDING VOWS

ary Garrison gave Radcliffe a second try, but when she came home to New York having completed her sophomore year, she announced her academic career was over. "It isn't a good idea for me to be up there cutting classes to sit around my room having feelings," she told her mother. The classes were excellent, if large, but all they inspired in her were feelings. She took differential calculus and got feelings. She took philosophy and got feelings. She took Advanced French and The American Renaissance and they gave her feelings. She walked the campus and through the town at odd hours, driven by emotions she could not control, an urgent sense of the size and magnitude of all knowledge, and she sat in her room and felt her emotions surge in her like an uproarious tide anxious on a steep shifting shore. She made the actual decision to let go of college in a tree on the quad. She entered the thick umbrella of an ancient pine and then climbed the puzzling and ready ladder of limbs around its trunk until she was two hundred feet from the ground and could see the lights of Boston. She was twenty years old.

"I am destined to go through life as an exposed nerve," she said. "That's what I learned at college. I hope you don't feel I wasted your fifty thousand dollars. The food was good."

"You're going to be fine, Margaret," her mother told her. "You're the kind of girl who will look out the window while you talk to people. You are high-strung, but you won't explode. It will make you a good listener. Your life is going to be lovely if you can find the right company."

Gary was looking out the window now and she turned to her mother, defiant and understood. She sat with the fingertips of her left hand touching the fingertips of her right hand, a posture of power and fragility at once. "I'm going to get a job," she said. "And try to grow some insulation." She didn't know what to do about being the kind of person who was driven by emotion, who climbed trees, whose eyes watered three or four times a day from a feeling she could only take as happiness. She saw meaning everywhere, but couldn't interpret it, and this made her alert constantly for signals from the world. Some people viewed her therefore as superstitious and others as overly sensitive, but everyone thought she was charming, for she represented a stage they'd all known but could not sustain, a dear wakefulness that had in them subsided.

For this reason no one was surprised a year later to hear of the shape of the nuptials she had fashioned, the conditions, how the whole wedding would work. She was a lifetime away, in Utah, and was marrying, if all things came to pass, a successful lawyer who chaired the board of the bird sanctuary where she'd taken work. The ceremony was being held in a little church north of the village of Brigham City, a building that looked like a child's drawing of a church, and it stood among cornfields there. The wedding would commence at the moment of sunset, December tenth, and the only light would be the twelve candles, one on each windowsill of the plain building, and there would be no spoken *I do*s. In her time west, Gary Garrison had learned to love geese, and had had moments when she felt she understood what they were saying, was sure of it, though not as something she could translate, but as something she could feel. The large wild birds affected her. The wedding vows would be read in the candlelit church, and then

Gary Garrison and her husband-to-be, William Brookes, would stand with the minister until they heard the call of geese. The call of the geese would seal the deal. The invitation said it this way: "When the wild geese call, we will be married heart and soul, and only *if* they call."

Her mother smiled to read the invitation, imagining Gary's new life in the larger world, seeing a hundred wedding guests in the dark room listening for the winging birds.

After leaving college, Gary Garrison went west to wear out her feelings, shuck them, use them up, but it didn't happen that way. She traveled by car and now all the new places gave her feelings, fresh electricity every morning, noon, and night. Times, many times, she pulled off the interstate onto some back road and stood arms-folded against her car, breathing deeply and trying not to cry. Traveling this way, fits and starts, she arrived in Utah and took the job a friend of her father's had arranged at the Brigham Bird Refuge.

"She wants out of doors," he had said. "We'll arrange it."

There her story begins, for she fell under the spell of the sky and a man. It was September, which offers up a crazy fragile blue, a season of crumbling summer and its crushing light, light about to fall off a polished table like a crystal vase, light that filled Margaret Garrison like fire in a bowl, and in her September days, she walked upon her toes to get her head up into the air as far as possible.

Where she walked upon her toes was along the causeways that formed a large grid through the wetlands well north on the giant Great Salt Lake. These were little more than gravel dikes grown with reeds and marked by the single trail where the manager of the refuge and his minions marched. On such a narrow path with water on both sides in great blue-sky sheets, she felt herself drift away more than once. What she had in her hand was a notebook with a green canvas cover, and inside the cover on the lined pages of the thing were two types of entry. One was the bird count at each station along with the time and the date, and one-line descriptions of any birds she did not recognize, exotic ducks or the like. The other entry in Margaret's official book was her poetry. The back of her book began to thicken with blue pages of her free verse, written, like so many things she did, because she could not not do it. If she did not write the poetry when she sat alone in the barrel blinds and on the platforms watching ducks settle and feed, she would not have burst or had a breakdown, but some small gasket in her would have surely cracked.

It was as if she were born for the task of learning birds, for their names came to her immediately, and she could distinguish them by their profiles in the sky at some distance and by the way they sat on the water or landed, and she knew the various geese and ducks by their calls of succor and distress, and her notebook thickened with her fall census.

The manager of this private wetland was a trained wildlife ranger named Mark Faberhand, who was thirty-one years old and had become at that age a flinty expert in the western flyways and in all birds, even exotics. He was tall and permanently tanned and taciturn, and he struck people on first meeting as being furry, for he shaved once a week on Sunday and blond hair grew everywhere on him. His role had evolved on the thousand acres of the refuge to that of policeman, really, and he had grown into that part reluctantly, but now it was what he did. He'd pull up to the pickups full of scouting hunters or young lovers or older lovers who were off from their lawful spouses, and he'd step to their vehicles in his green refuge uniform with his flashlight and he'd ask them to move on. The hunters would kid with him, pleading, Come on, you've got so many Canadian honkers, share a few, scare some over this way.

The skies were busy all September, and that doubled in October, the steady migration of waterfowl loading the morning and evening with sublime traffic. No day or part of a day was lost to Gary Garrison. She was out early, 5 AM, walking the reedy pathways in the chilly dark to count the incoming ducks and outgoing ducks, and she learned to tell by the way some took off that they were actually going off to feed and would stay another day. The first thing she heard every day in the sky was the whistling wings of the low-flying, fast-flying ducks, and the last thing she heard at the sharp edge of the short fall twilight was the honking of the Canadian geese as they settled.

The geese became her favorite, and their cries felt personal to her, and at the same time part of some larger fate, tied to the vastness of the sheeted waterlands and the mountains as they flared and faded. The geese in their afternoon squadrons arriving or departing or crossing high overhead seemed part of a force that she longed for, and that is why they figured later in her wedding plans. When the time came, they would perform the ceremony.

The other intern in the wetland sanctuary that fall was Juanita Dubois, a young woman who had recently graduated from Utah State University in wildlife management. Juanita already had been hired by the state of Utah, and she would be working the Central Wildlife District starting in the spring. The two women roomed together in a new trailer across the gravel yard from the one permanent structure on the grounds, the administration cabin. Three days a week the women went together in the refuge truck to six ponds in rotation, and their census involved a check sheet of time of day, water temperature, bird count, et cetera. Every Friday they met with Mark Faberhand in the little cabin, entered data, and planned the coming week. It was a regulated pattern that fall, but in her heart as always Gary Garrison felt as if she had a secret and it was ineffable, unspeakable, and it filled her and emptied her like a bellows. Mornings when the first wings would whistle overhead in the starry black, she'd gasp and sit down and feel the water burn to the surface of her eyes.

She wrote to her mother: "I will not climb a tree and quit this place! There are no trees, and simply this has claimed me, incurably. Not curable. Incurably incurable! There's no cure for this love, if that is what it is. I love the sun, the mud, the traveling birds too much!"

Juanita Dubois was a level-headed, steady friend for Gary. She was smart and energetic and plainspoken. She was annoyed to have done so well in her classes at Utah State that she'd scared away possible boyfriends, and in the evenings while Gary lay in her bunk and listened to every living thing moving in the sky, Juanita listed each man she'd almost dated. Her admiration for Mark Faberhand was immediate and complete, and over the weeks of the fall, it crossed over to affection, which she also reported to Gary Garrison in their night quarters.

With Mark, on their forays in the field and at their weekly meetings, Gary kept quiet. She also admired many things about him, but she didn't think about them, because she saw they would never end. The list would start with his speaking voice and move from the hair on his wrists to his walk in his heavy brown lace-up boots and to his general ethic, and she didn't know how to control such a list or the feelings it engendered. He was a good man, and she hadn't known any. Being around him vexed her because it was like interference; she could feel him there more clearly than the pulsing world. The only time she was surprised by incoming flights or ducks in the reeds exploding into flight was when she was out with him. She also understood her feelings because she could never face him full on, turn to him openly, even to stand and talk. She kept to one side, nodded his way, and spoke looking past his shoulder the way she'd seen baseball coaches talk to pitchers on the mound.

When she was out alone that fall, she thought she might die of the beauty or whatever it was about this wild world. And then she thought that double because each day was shorter than the one before, and each day there were fewer birds, as the thousands of wildfowl rested and went on toward Mexico.

Some days the three of them came across trespassers and had to intervene. Mark would stand out of the truck with Juanita behind him while whoever had camped on the property packed up their gear and drove off. A couple of times Mark had Juanita walk up to a pickup on one of the dirt access roads and say, "Listen, boys, you're going to have to move on. The property line is a half mile back."

"You the bird woman?"

"I am Officer Dubois, the citation person." And she'd reach into her back pocket for her ticket book. "And who are you?" She lifted her pen. "Or were you leaving?"

At such moments, Gary would watch Mark smile at the proceedings, and she could feel static across the top of her heart. He was slow to smile and a smile made his face a wonder.

Juanita would stride back to their truck and say, "In the line of duty, from time to time, there is no better posture for a conservation officer than to be a hard-ass." She'd salute Mark and move past him to get in the vehicle.

"Where does he live?" Juanita asked that night. "Is he married?" But she didn't wait for answers; she was building a solid theory on the evidence. "His lunches, in my opinion, are not made by a woman. I haven't seen anything in those thick sandwiches except packaged cheese and salami. And he's using that same brown paper bag four, five days in a row. I haven't seen a napkin or a treat large or small."

Gary agreed with all of this and could have taken it a step further because she'd had half of one of Mark's homemade sandwiches a day or so before, and it had sandwich spread inside too, something made of Thousand Island dressing and pickles that she had never tasted before in her life. Since he had handed her the sandwich, she had not been able to think to the end of a sentence. His fingerprints were in the bread and when she put her teeth into the thing, she was changed and she knew it.

"I figure his heart got broken when he was up in Missoula at school, and he's been out here for six years, living in a basement apartment in Brigham, oiling his boots and ironing his own shirts. He's pretty good at it. He doesn't go out much. He's afraid of love. Hasn't met the right woman." Juanita was silent a moment. "Until now."

"You go on the count tomorrow," Gary said to her friend. "I'll lay in. I could use the sleep."

"Are you okay? Do you feel sick?"

"Juanita," she said. "I'll sleep in tomorrow. Say hello to all my babies. And be nice to Mark." But in the morning as soon as Juanita left, Gary dressed and sat in the chilly morning on a folding chair in the trailer yard and watched the light come. Her thoughts changed channels for hours.

When she'd been out with Mark alone, they didn't talk. He wasn't a talker and she said nothing, afraid that if she ever started, she could not restrain any of the words, the feelings that rose in her. So they sat in one of the large barrels that served as blinds and watched the geese. They were so close that every breath, every small movement, shift, seemed like code. At one point she saw him tilt his head to look closer at something and his mouth opened, and when his lips parted, she heard the sound they made, they were that close. A group of a dozen Canadian geese came from the north and went behind them when suddenly Mark put his hand on Gary's shoulder and nodded before making a sharp barking noise, two loud syllables she recognized as the honking of geese. His hand on her shoulder emptied her head and she focused, such a relief. He called again, honking, and then three more in succession. He nodded his head again, and she saw the flock turning toward them, calling back. They circled past and then came in a splashing assault on the pond where Mark and Gary hid in their barrel. A moment ago they had been at eight hundred feet and now they swam and settled in the dusk, twenty feet away. When Mark lifted his hand from her, Gary thought she would float away.

The big deal of the fall was the Trustee Tour and Dinner. The annual event was key to fund-raising for the year, and it was held the week before Halloween when the foothills of the Wasatch were crosshatched with gold and maroon, every orchard gone orange and rust, and the giant yellow cottonwoods dotting the hillsides. The desperate world was magnified and Gary Garrison couldn't take a step without feeling the blue and the straw, the ivory and green burning in tiers up the graduated and massive slopes. The first snow had already cut triangles in the tops of the steely peaks. One noon two catering trucks came out into the refuge's dooryard and set up tables and lamps and portable heaters and a bar for cocktails.

It was in this circus of color at the high center of the last season of the year that she met William Brookes, the head of the trustees, a young attorney from Laramie, and their meeting, by torchlight in the open air of Utah, led to all the rest.

He saw her right away when the assemblage disembarked from the four blue vans that had delivered them from Salt Lake City. Within a minute he had taken in her carriage, the elevation of her face, her easy confidence, and he was a goner. He was thirty-two and had never felt anything like his awe and yearning for the young woman. Mark Faberhand led them out the primary embankment just as the sun set, and the fifty important personages, casting shadows that were a quarter mile across the shallow ponds, watched the birds cross and recross the sky, settling, seeking shelter, and calling. Mark answered questions as did Juanita and Gary, all dressed in their refuge uniforms, pressed and perfect. Back at the open-air dinner, William Brookes, lit by a fire he didn't even understand, delivered remarks about the importance of the mission of the refuge, which made disciples of everyone at the long table; it was the best speech of his career.

Mr. Brookes was back the following afternoon in a plaid shirt and Levis. Gary Garrison had never been courted before. There had been some boyfriends, but boys. Everyone assumed a person of her beauty and idiosyncratic demeanor had a complete life, chapter and verse, and she was let alone. When she had received flowers, they were from her mother. William Brookes drove her to the Old Mill, the fanciest restaurant in the county, where the waiters wore lederhosen and green felt hats and stepped heavily around the wooden-floored room. William Brookes called her Margaret, which she didn't correct, because with all this new noise she felt like someone else.

After dinner he drove above one of the apple orchards, the trees all bright wrecks in the moonlight, and he pointed out the deer moving through the scrub oak. Deer that should have undermined her ability to breathe, sit still, but she watched the small herd move through from a new distance. Her mind on Mark, and now William in her face, the smell of this big new car, a night plucked and stolen from the continuity of her electric life. He talked, a man's voice this close, about how much he loved the West, his life, the air, the dark, the mountains, et cetera, an unending inventory that she heard and after half an hour began to trust. His sincerity walled her in. He leaned to her and tried to kiss her and kissed her and still tried. A man's lips on her own crushed the circuits, and she kissed him back. He professed his love for her, apologized for saying it, and said it again. He drove her back to the refuge, stopping every fourth mile to kiss her and apologize.

In the trailer, Juanita waited until Gary sat on the bunk to say, "Mark came by to ask where you had gone to."

Gary was in hard flux and looked across the dark space to Juanita on an elbow on her cot. "And I told him, since he was so interested and has never asked you where I go when I drive to town to do the laundry and see a movie alone, that you were on a date with the king of this place."

"Don't be upset, Juanita."

"I'm not. Or maybe I am, but it's okay Mark asks about you while you're out with William. It's strange for me. Envy rises from some deep pit. Oh well, I say, you get all the men, I get southern Utah this spring. It's a tough call."

When Gary saw Mark a few days later, he had already closed himself up like a resort town in winter.

William Brookes did not return to Laramie and his practice; he stayed on in Brigham City and pressed his suit with Gary. The days shortened, the sun like a weak flare rising, and then the brief afternoons like an invitation to the brittle wind. The reeds along the ponds stiffened and there was lacy ice every morning. Walking back to the trailer in the broken light at day's end, Gary was as confused as she'd ever been. William's Land Cruiser idled in the yard.

They ate at the Old Mill three more times, saw two movies, ate at his hotel, necked in his room until every time he sat up and stopped them, placing his forehead against hers. He was in. He wanted something larger than sex in November in northern Utah. He said it to her that way and then asked her to marry him, come to Laramie. She told him she'd have to think. She needed a week.

It was late in the year now and the census told the story; every day fewer birds, and a magnificent golden loneliness fell upon Gary Garrison as she walked the embankments of the sanctuary. And every evening the day dropped away sharper and birds still called.

One afternoon at four o'clock she sat on a levee with her notebook, her mind splintered. She wanted to sleep with William now, and she wanted to talk to Mark, who had shown her the power of this place, and she wanted no men at all, just a year of these creatures flying and calling. The sun rolled from east to west and the birds flew from north to south. It felt like the sky was being asked too much; it seemed that she was being asked too much.

It was then she heard the geese, a string of seven, calling in approach. She sat down in the dry reeds, and she put her head in her hands and sat still. She listened as their calling came louder and louder, her feet nearly in the icy water, and she wept without moving. When she peeked between her fingers again, the seven geese were settling at her feet. She could see the grain of the fine feathers on their necks and the glistening black center of each eye.

The large birds looked at her without remark, and she knew what she was going to do, and that she would schedule the wedding at four o'clock, and like everything she had done so far, there would be an *if* in it. *If* the geese called, *so be it until death do us part.*

Gary's mother flew out a week early and in the hotel said, "I'm not surprised. I cannot be your mother and pretend to be surprised.

It is sudden and strange, but he is a fine young man, and marriage might redirect the voltage in you. I'm an optimist."

Eighty-five people attended the little wedding north of Brigham City: two dozen of Gary's friends from New York and a few from college, her parents and her aunts, and a handful of her parents' friends. William Brookes's family, friends, and many of his associates from the greater west came to Utah for the event, happy for him, and curious about what they'd read on the invitation. They almost filled the wooden pews in the old church as they sat in the dusk, many watching the candles struggle in the leaky window boxes.

William Brookes looked like every young man looks when he gets married: serious and pretty, and those who knew him could see him breathing.

Margaret Garrison came up the aisle on her father's arm while one of her friends played Segovia on a big Gibson guitar, and the minister, a former state senator of Wyoming and a close family friend of the Brookeses, read the sheets that Gary and William had created. It was noted that this was an unusual ceremony, but that marriage sometimes required the unusual, and that there were forces beyond this room, beyond this moment, forces that understood the world perhaps better than we do. Geese mate for life and travel together, and that was the intention in this bonding. "And so we agree and know that if we hear now the call of the wild geese, then Margaret and William will be man and wife." Then it grew quiet in the darkening church, and it stayed quiet as the candles worked against the larger night.

Juanita Dubois had done what she was to do at the appointed hour. That is, drive the refuge truck out to the stubble field on the high end of the wetland—but when she arrived there meaning to stir up the two dozen Canadian honkers that had been loitering for weeks, and who came and went with a casualness that made it seem they might try to stay all winter, they were gone. They were all gone. There were none, not a single goose.

Juanita checked her watch. It was nine minutes after four. She had her red satin dress hitched up to her knees and she was wearing her workboots unlaced. Her pumps were in the truck. She went to the far ditch and shined her mighty flashlight through the field. There was a last ribbon of green light in the west.

She found Mark Faberhand at the Clock Cafe on Main Street at 4:20 PM. He had just ordered the hot roast-beef sandwich and was folding the menu up when she came in. To her credit, she did not run in and grab him by the collar. "Juanita," he said. "What is it?"

The cafe light was bracing and full of hope, and she took a breath. "It's Gary. Do you think you could help us out?"

A quarter mile from the little church north of Brigham City, Utah, is a park that gives onto an open field that is sometimes winter wheat, sometimes alfalfa, many years simply volunteer growth of any kind, and Juanita parked the truck there as Mark had instructed her. The wind was at their back, blowing toward the building. They could see the candles in the windows.

"They've got candles in the windows," he said.

"They do," Juanita said.

Mark had a bottle of George Dickel in the truck, and he leaned against the grill of the vehicle for the engine warmth, took a slug of the whisky, and offered the bottle to Juanita.

"I'll have some," she said, and she tipped the bottle back. She kept having to finger the hair away from her face.

"You don't have to do this," Juanita said. "If you want me to just take you back, I'll do it."

"No," he said. "Season's over. We'll take in the dock and lower the water this week. It's been a fall."

"You want me to put my arm around you?" she asked him.

"I do," he said. "I appreciate it." They stood side by side in the dark. "How long they been waiting?"

Juanita looked at her watch. "Thirty minutes."

"That's a long time to stand there. This is going to be the last singleton of the season, coming in late from somewhere." Then he stood and cupped the side of his mouth with one hand and made the call, the two-part song of the Canadian goose, in a rhythm he'd learned from geese: one, four, then two, repeating one, four, and two. Then he did two, and took a sharp sip from the bottle. "They're married now," he said. "That's got to serve."

All Gary Garrison heard was the first call, because by the second everyone was applauding and gasping and crying out and like that, but it was all she needed to hear. She knew all about it, and she raised her finger for the ring.

Andre Dubus III

❦

THE BARTENDER

Robert Doucette met his wife-to-be while tending bar at a dance club on Hampton Beach. It was Labor Day weekend, the season almost done, his sunburned customers already beginning to wear sweatshirts and light sweaters. He had spent the summer living in a one-room rental above the bar and he had three thousand saved, enough to get him through until late winter, when he was thinking of hopping a bus to the east coast of Florida to work a topless bar called Skinny's. But late this morning while lying in bed listening to the beach traffic out on the boulevard, a phrase occurred to him and he thought he might start a poem with it. The words that came were of a woman "with eyes of black hope." He wasn't sure he liked this line; he suspected it sounded mawkish and falsely heroic, but its unexpected arrival left him feeling there might be something within him worth mining for after all.

Then she walked into the club. She wore a white sundress, her long, curly black hair held back in a loose ponytail, her bare shoulders and arms thick for a woman, but tanned and hard-looking. She was with two laughing blondes, both thin and inconsequential. They sat at his bar, one of the blondes ordering piña coladas for all three, and the dark one sat quietly watching him, her stillness a force that pulled him closer, though he did not approach her until setting the fresh rum drink on a napkin in front of her. She smiled and looked up at him, and there were the eyes he'd written about just that morning, eyes of black hope, and they seemed not to see him so much as all he might represent. The women only stayed for one drink. In the half hour it took them to finish it, Robert worked the service bar but kept feeling the dark woman's presence behind him like good news in a letter he wasn't opening. When they stood to leave Robert took a chance and wrote his name and phone number on a napkin and set it down in front of her. She glanced at it, then took out a pen of her own, crossed out his number, and wrote hers.

Her name was Althea, and throughout the fall they dated; they went to movies and restaurants in Portsmouth and sometimes Boston. She was a good eater, always finishing the entree and salad, then ordering a dessert, too. She was quiet, more of a listener than a talker, which at first unnerved Robert. He was used to being around waitresses and barmaids, women who seemed to talk about almost anything as if they were experts. Althea did not present herself as an expert on anything, which left Robert feeling he might not be either. But one night driving her home while she sat quietly beside him, he forced himself not to turn on the radio, or to tell her another tale from the bar business: of the fellow bartender who had skimmed ten thousand dollars from the register one winter to pay off back child support; of a cocktail waitress who was kidnapped by her boyfriend after her shift and found tied up in a motel room two weeks later—dehydrated and hysterical—her boyfriend having hung himself in front of her; or any of the dozens of bad jokes he knew, tools of the trade that felt, in Althea's presence, like dried mucus on a handkerchief. He'd already told her of his dreary childhood growing up on his family dairy farm inland, and of course he'd told her that he was a poet, that for ten years he'd been working on a book of poems he hoped to one day publish. She nodded knowingly at this piece of information, but even then, remained quiet. So he drove in the silence and fought the urge to ask her a question about herself, for he already knew the essentials: Althea was an upholsterer, working in the basement of a house she rented and shared with the two blondes, bank tellers Robert didn't like because they talked of interest rates and attractive men who owned property, and they wore makeup even when they stayed in at night. But Althea wore little makeup; her mother and father had immigrated from Greece, only to return there to care for ailing relatives now that their girl was a woman with a trade she'd learned on her own. She had a steady line of business from local antique dealers who trusted her to strip and redress their ancient chairs and settees in floral brocades, classical damasks, and gold and burgundy tapestries. She had no brothers or sisters, which perhaps explained her silence, Robert thought, her feeling there was no one in the room to whom she had to speak.

After two months of dating, she invited him to spend the night in her room, and as they made love, Robert moved carefully, as if he were trying on new clothes he didn't want to soil in case they had to be returned. Afterward, they lay quietly together in the dark, the faint sounds of a late-night television talk show coming from downstairs. When he had softened completely, he eased off his condom and was trying to lower it discreetly to the floor when she held out a white tissue for him to drop it in. He did, and she took his seed and placed it on her bedside table next to a copy of the New Testament, and two Willa Cather novels she'd withdrawn from the library. Outside, an October wind blew dead leaves against the house and across the yard. Her room was spare, no rug or carpet on the pine floor, nothing but a dresser, a cane chair, and at the foot of the bed an old trunk that had once belonged to her grandfather in Sparta. One wall held a framed poster of the Wyeth painting of the young woman sitting alone on the grassy hill staring up at a farmhouse, her hair lifting in the breeze. Robert could see just the shadow of it.

Althea kissed his shoulder. "Robert." It sounded like more of a statement than an inquiry, as if she were assuring herself of who he was.

"Yes?"

"I haven't done this with anyone I wouldn't want to have a baby with."

There was a slight itch in the hair at Robert's temple, but he didn't move to scratch it. He wondered what his heart sounded like beneath her ear.

"That's good."

She lifted her head and studied him in the dark. "For you? Or for me?"

"For both of us."

She was quiet now. Robert's cheeks grew warm, and he felt he'd just lied.

"You mean that?"

"Yes."

"Completely yes?"

"Yes, completely."

She kept her head up a while, looking at him in the dark. Then she rubbed her nose against his and kissed him deeply, opening his mouth with her tongue. They made love again, this time without a condom. The wind picked up outside; it sounded cold to Robert, though here with Althea it was warm, almost hot. A lone leaf scuttled across the window and was gone.

Two days later, a Monday, the weather was warm, the orange and red leaves on the branches and ground like flames giving off heat. Althea carried the frame of a wingback chair from the basement to work on in the sunlit grass of her rented yard, and Robert had no shift later so he sat close by drinking beer and trying to read from an anthology of twentieth-century poems. But he kept watching her instead, the way she sat on her calves with her back straight, a long curved needle between her lips as she pushed a spring into the seat then began to sew it down, her wild black hair tied back loosely with a purple scarf, and he had to look away because the word that came tumbling down against the back of his face was: bride. *My* bride. He said nothing to her, but in the days and weeks that followed, this knowledge began to transform her silence for him; sitting in the car or across the table at a restaurant, it now began to feel comfortable, like she had accepted him for who he was already, without him having to go on and on, the way a home should feel to a child, Robert thought, and he proposed to her the day after Christmas as they lay in her bed watching it snow out the window. "I think I should marry you."

She turned and looked at him, her eyes dark and moist.

"I know I should, actually."

Her eyes were filling up now, but she said nothing. Robert took her hand in his. "Will you?" In the shadows of the room Althea's eyes looked black, but she was smiling and she nodded and hugged him tightly, and they were married the first week of January in Portsmouth with their hands on the Bible of a justice of the peace.

They spent their honeymoon making love in an inn on the waterfront, the mussel-shell, freighter-oil scent of the Piscataqua River filling the room. They ate long dinners in restaurants, and though Althea wasn't a drinker, they both drank too much and Robert would lean forward and recite the poems he could remember from William Butler Yeats, John Donne, and his dead mentor, Robert Frost. In the candlelight, he saw the moisture in his bride's eyes at what Robert could only assume was her perceived good fortune at marrying a man of true romance and high calling. No one had ever looked at him like that, and it stirred in him a low, animal calling, a central pull to the dark depth of her quiet womanhood, a nest in which to sink and blossom his own muse.

Within the first month of their marriage she became pregnant, delivering the news to him one morning after an exhausting and lucrative shift whose end he had celebrated with too much bourbon and beer. Lying in bed, his face feeling like clay, the inside of his mouth so dry it had surely cracked, Althea came into the room, kissed him firmly on the mouth, then held up the small white tab of the home-test kit, the pregnant end pink. She smiled at him, her dark eyes full of hope, and he sat up and hugged and kissed her, though his head pulsed and he had to close his eyes. Walking to the bathroom, he felt every bit of the floorboards beneath his feet, and it was an effort to lift his head; it was as if the earth's gravity had just doubled.

In the shower he kept thinking of his father: his substantial shoulders stooped and rounded, his mouth always set in a grim line, even on Sunday afternoons when he would finally allow himself to rest *if* it was a day when no heifers or cows were giving birth, none were hurt, all the calves were fed and dry, if there was no equipment to repair or paperwork to catch up on. When all that had to be done was another three-hour milking at the end of the day, then Robert's father would lie on the sofa in the living room with an *Almanac* or *Yankee* magazine, the television tuned to an old movie, maybe a bottle of Miller on the lamp table beside him. When he was a boy, Robert and his mother and younger sister would be there, too. On Sundays his mother baked cookies or a cobbler and she'd let them eat a serving in front of the TV with a glass of milk. His father would have some then. He'd sit up on the couch to eat, quietly chewing and watching whatever was on the screen. Sometimes Robert would see him looking at him and his sister, studying them the way he did his Holsteins, looking for any defects that might cost him even more further down the line.

Althea's visit to her doctor confirmed the home test, and Robert willed himself to try and rise to the occasion. He ordered his wife a dozen roses, and she placed them in three separate vases throughout the bedroom of the house they now shared with the two bank tellers until Robert found something better. On one of his nights off, Robert insisted they sit down and come up with a name, starting with a boy's. If they were to have a son, Robert wanted to give him a strong name, the sort a boy couldn't help but live up to, the way a poem must earn its title. He wanted to name him Ajax, Greek for eagle, after the hero in the Trojan Wars. But Althea had balked and without a word, as was her way, simply showed him the scouring powder of the same name, then shook her head and pinched his cheek. But Robert was taken with the image of the eagle, his possible son a lone and majestic bird whose natural surroundings would be life's peaks and precipices.

So they settled on a variation of the Old German for eagle, Adler, a name Althea thought was softer, more gentle and reflective, the way she viewed Robert himself.

For a time.

During the months of her pregnancy, they moved to a place of their own, a one-room motel cabin on a salt marsh across the boulevard from Hampton Beach. It had a sleeping loft, a hot plate, sink, refrigerette, and a shower-stall bathroom with a toilet that flushed its contents into pipes whose smell did not seem to make it out of the reeds. Built on short creosote piers, there were five of these cabins alongside one another, each identical to the next. In front of them, across a crushed-shell parking lot, loomed the Whaler Restaurant, Bar & Hotel, a four-story, fifty-two-room attraction open only five months out of the year, when its manager rented the marsh cabins to its best waiters, waitresses, and bartenders. The hotel's clientele were mainly dentists', bankers', and architects' families from the Midwest and upstate New York, and Robert—with his literary charm and quick reflexes, his ability to light a cigarette for one while serving a drink to another, all while giving the punch line of a joke to a third—was head bartender and worked the restaurant's bar six nights a week. At the end of his shift, after storing the leftover garnish and mixes, after restocking the beer chest and rotating the older bottles to the front, after wiping down the speed rack and soaking all the pourers in a hot rinse, Robert served himself a cold draft and a jigger of Maker's Mark bourbon. He drank off a third of the draft, then dropped the full jigger into the mug, the bourbon spreading up and out into the beer like armed reinforcements.

Tonight, a Thursday in mid-August, the main restaurant's lights were off save for the ones over the bar. The kitchen staff was gone. The barback and busboys and waitstaff had all gone too, and the manager had left Robert and Jackie, the head waitress, to lock up. She sat a few stools down from the register inhaling deeply on an unlit cigarette she didn't want to light. She had thick red hair, gold in places from the late mornings and early afternoons when she would lie on a chaise lounge in front of her cabin in a bikini that barely covered her ample breasts, wide hips, and round buttocks. Sometimes, when Althea was reading or washing the dishes, her back turned, Robert would allow himself a peek out the window. Once, he looked just as Jackie was turning over onto her stomach, her breasts swaying, and he imagined his face nestled in the sweaty freckled crevice there. Now Jackie's breasts strained against her white Whaler blouse, the top three buttons undone, her skin a deep pink, and Robert felt a surge of guilt that he felt no real guilt about viewing Jackie in this way, his pregnant wife sleeping in the tiny loft of their cabin behind the hotel.

On days with no sea breeze, the cabin filled with the smell of sewage from the marsh and Althea would usually feel nauseated and they would leave for a walk down the boulevard, which was almost worse with its canned rock and roll blaring from the shops, the sidewalks crowded with sun-beaten tourists, the smells of fried dough and teriyaki steak from the Frialators and grills, the roar of a Harley-Davidson out on the street, a gang of seagulls shrieking above. Althea would squeeze his hand, holding her protruding belly with the other, and soon Robert and his wife would have to go into a restaurant for a bathroom where she might throw up, and Robert would sneak a quick tequila shot or two at the bar while he ordered two Cokes, one to hide the tequila—a fiery friend and confidant in his gut—the other for her. They would sit in a booth or at a small table in the shadows away from the bright street, and she would sip her Coke stoically, staring at the rug or sometimes just at Robert's hand or chest, which left him feeling she was a bit simple, taking her pain in an unquestioning and almost bovine way. He would think of the heifers on his father's dairy farm, the vague indifference in their eyes as his father loaded the breeding gun with thawed bull semen, his entire arm covered with a lubricated plastic sleeve. But other times, the surreptitious tequila shots spreading out in his belly like a purging grass fire, Robert would feel moved at her silent suffering and he would lean over and kiss her clammy hand, this woman he was so wise to choose as his wife, this pregnant woman he was beginning to bronze in a maternal cast only.

Because she was quiet, Robert knew some thought her aloof. Often on a Monday night, the slowest night at the Whaler, the waitresses would throw a party at one of the cabins. They'd prop their speakers in open windows and play loud rock while they barbecued hamburgers on one of the tiny front porches. Other off-duty waitstaff would join them with coolers of beer, wine coolers, and sometimes a blender, ice, and a bottle of rum. Robert and Althea joined them, too. As head bartender, Robert enjoyed his place of leadership, and he would mix up a batch of frozen piña coladas or daiquiris and drink three in twenty minutes while Jackie and two of her best waitresses cackled and howled about getting their revenge on bad customers, like the chronic butt-pinching doctor whose béarnaise sauce they spiked with a tablespoon of urine every time he came in. There were other stories to fall into, and while they did, Althea sat quiet and pregnant in a lawn chair in the parking lot apart from the smoke of the cigarettes and barbecue, and Robert would sometimes feel her presence the way some felt the ghosts of disapproving ancestors. Jackie or another woman would become a waitress for her, asking if she wanted another cup of ginger ale, or did she want to put her feet up on something. But Althea would shake her head no, no, thank you, and sometimes Robert would finish laughing at the tail end of another story or joke, then go sit next to her a while, watching his restaurant friends laugh and drink and smoke, flipping hamburgers and bobbing their heads to the music, and he would feel he was missing something sitting there with his expectant wife who was always quiet, a quality that, when they were alone, he had actually come to admire. It now seemed to him she was waiting for something only she knew about, something transcendent and holy that would be good for all of them. Alone with her, this woman who had chosen him and was carrying his child, Robert felt believed in, felt called once again to great and important things—namely his poetry, becoming a published poet.

But when the Doucettes were not alone, Robert was beginning

to feel Althea's abstinent quiet like the penetrating gaze of a chaperone, and he wanted to flee. Once, when he was in the Whaler's walk-in cooler, the door ajar, he heard Jackie and two of the younger waitresses at the coffee machine talking about his wife, using words and phrases like *conceited* and *holier than thou.* Robert did not agree: he had never heard Althea utter an ugly word about anyone; she was simply quiet. But as he left the walk-in cooler carrying his bucket of lemons, limes, and oranges, he said nothing in his wife's defense and instead smiled at them, hoping he looked friendly and handsome as he passed. He was immediately ashamed of himself for abandoning Althea like that, his shame soon turning to resentment, though—not at Jackie and the girls, but at his wife for putting him in the position where he would have to defend or fail her on so many subtle fronts, and again, he felt the urge to flee.

Now Jackie was switching from her melon ball to a Mount Gay on the rocks with a splash of Coke. Robert made himself another boilermaker, set it down in front of the stool next to Jackie, then joined her there with the register drawer and night deposit bag. She was copying the week's schedule onto a clean sheet of paper, still sucking on the unlit cigarette, and as he sat next to her she reached over and gave his knee a friendly squeeze, leaving her hand there a second or two as Robert sat up and began to count, log, and bag the night's receipts. Her fingers slipped away and he could smell the coconut lotion she used on her skin during the day. He took a long drink off his mug, the shot glass clinking inside like a badly kept secret.

"My grandfather drank those, Robert. That's an old man's drink."

"It does the job."

"A lot of things do that, honey." She was looking right at him, her bright green eyes mischievous and kind. Robert and Jackie had been locking the place up together all summer. There had always been an easy camaraderie between them, an oiled, lubricated quality that came from coming off the same shift together, from working in close proximity with one another. But the last few weeks it had been harder for Robert to look into her face directly, his eyes sure to betray the fact he simply wanted to kiss her, to feel her freckled breasts up against him. So now he shook his head, smiled, and looked down at his hands on the bar, hoping this gesture of genuine shyness would endear him to her. It was after two now, the restaurant and hotel so quiet he could hear the surf out on the beach across the boulevard. Sometimes, when Jackie finished her work before he did, she'd leave first, blowing him a kiss from the door before she closed it, and after she was gone Robert would turn off all the lights and sit in the dark with his drink and watch the ghostly phosphorescence of the waves breaking on the night sand, white breaking over and over again in the darkness.

Jackie got up and made herself another Mount Gay, then surprised Robert with one, too. "Nobody does shots and beers anymore, Robbie. Get with it."

Robert laughed; she was the only one who called him that. She sat back down and they drank and finished their night work; the bourbon and beer had already opened up the veins in his head, relaxing and widening the possibilities, and now the rum was a tight ball of fire rolling through without an obstacle to stop it. He wanted to see the night surf; he wanted Jackie to see it, too.

"Hey, Jackie, I want to show you something." He hopped off the stool to go hit the light switch behind the bar, but then he felt her at his back, her confusion about where he was going to take her to show her something, when all he'd wanted to do was turn off the lights. And when he turned to tell her wait right here, what I want to show you is out the window, his hand brushed both her breasts, their cotton-covered give and release, and she giggled, then smiled, her eyes pleasantly alert, and she lifted her chin and there was nothing to do but lean forward and kiss her. Just this, he thought. Only this. But she opened her mouth, her tongue warm and yielding, and soon they were on the gritty carpet that smelled of sand and ketchup and ashes, Jackie lifting her black Whaler skirt up around her waist while Robert fumbled with her mint green panties, leaving them around one of her ankles as he pushed himself inside her. She gripped his buttocks with both hands, her face hot against his, her hair smelling of coconut oil and kitchen smoke. Outside, the surf pounded, then was silent till another wave rolled in, then another, and now Jackie was moaning, and soon, too soon, he could no longer hear the surf, could only feel the next wave as it began to build and gather, then roll itself out of him and into Jackie.

Just before dawn, Robert stood in the dark bathroom and washed his hands and face three times. He considered a cat bath for his genitals, but lately Althea had been getting up several times a night to pee, and he feared her walking in to see him doing that, washing his penis at the sink. He should have done it in the restaurant, but had let the self-locking door close before it had occurred to him. And he couldn't take a shower because he never did that right before bed. He dried his face and hands, then climbed up to his place beside his wife. As soon as he stretched out she turned over and lay her leg over his, her arm across his chest, and he tried to breathe normally, wondering if she could feel his heart beating beneath her wrist in a way it shouldn't.

He may have slept; he wasn't sure, but later that morning, the air still, the slight smell of sewage and seaweed in his cabin, Robert's pregnant wife woke from her sleep and straddled him, and Robert tensed with the knowledge that Jackie's dried juices were still on him and now they were inside Althea. For the first time he thought of the virus, something deadly he could have caught and would now be passing on to his wife. His wife and baby. But Jackie was not the type to sleep around, he told himself, and Althea seemed to be enjoying it, moving up and down, her round stomach hard against his, and Robert felt sure she would begin to sense something different somehow, that a deep and womanly part of her would detect the evidence of another woman's depths. But, instead, Althea came softly and then he did too, and last night's indulgence felt for the moment harmless, forgivable, and behind them both.

But that night, as Jackie ordered drinks from him at the service bar, she looked particularly radiant, her eyes brighter and more mischievous than ever. When Robert put three Bombay tonics on

her tray, she squeezed a lime wedge directly onto his hand, the juice
running down between his knuckles, and five hours later, the bar
dark and quiet, they took their time and did it on the restaurant
floor, in the kitchen on the prep table, and, finally, in the manager's
office, Jackie's bare bottom on the desk blotter, her heels on his
shoulders. After she had left, blowing him a kiss from the darkness
of the shell parking lot, Robert went to the men's room and washed
his hands, face, neck, penis, and balls. It was very late, probably
close to sunrise. He poured himself a tall Maker's Mark on the
rocks, his third of the night, and sat at one of the tables at the front
window feeling what he viewed as a uniquely male mix of pride
and remorse; Jackie was unquestionably the most attractive woman
on the waitstaff, respected for her earned authority with the other
waitresses, known to be an easy date for nobody. And here she was
giving herself to him freely, which left Robert feeling an echo of
what he felt with his own wife—special, singled out—but it was a
bastard echo, one he knew could gratify though not fulfill. Over the
years he'd done this with many waitresses and barmaids, sometimes
in their apartments, but usually like this, somewhere in the dark of
the restaurant or bar or back office after hours, a few drinks in him
and them. One, a single woman with two small kids at home,
pulled her panties back on and said, "Will you write a poem about
me?" And besides their own nameless hunger and the liquor in
their veins, he knew that's what got to them, the fact he professed to
write poetry when so many other bartenders tanned themselves at
the beach and worked the numbers on big football and basketball
games. The fact they thought he was a poet.

Now Althea's dark faithful eyes came to him and he drained his
bourbon and poured himself another, splashing it with Coke to go
down faster. Tonight the surf was loud enough to hear clearly
through the glass, the white froth of the waves easier to see out on
the dark beach. Robert began to feel somewhat imperiled, his chest
a bit constricted at the real possibility that on a loose and drunken
Monday night, Jackie might tell one of her waitresses about the two
of them; and he had no doubts the news would then spread

through the Whaler and its cabins as thoroughly and predictably as the smell of their own sewage on windless days. He had no doubts about its effect on Althea either; she would leave him with barely a word. Her faith in him would simply vanish, and she would vanish as well, taking his child with her. For a bourbon-floating moment, Robert felt relieved at the prospect, a reprieve from husbandhood and fatherhood and all of their weight. He drank from his adulterated bourbon, his thoughts already tilted on their axis inside him, his relief gone as he feared this to be the true state in which he would find himself if he were ever to lose his wife: off-kilter, foggy-headed, and directionless. He imagined himself alone in his cabin, perhaps ironing his shirt and vest, preparing himself for a shift of high tips he would squirrel away so he could take time off to be alone and do what? Write poems? Really *write* some? Who was he shitting? For without Althea, without her unquestioning belief in him, he wasn't sure he'd really be able to make that leap onto the page, a leap he truthfully hadn't been making too well *before* Althea. For months and months he would not write one line, or even read a poem; he'd work his shifts, spend the day running errands or watching two rented movies on his VCR. Sometimes a line would come to him and he might write it down on the envelope of a bill he'd end up throwing away. Other bar and waitstaff would talk of the accounting course they were taking up, or the realtor's exam they were studying for; if they turned their attention to Robert he'd smile shyly and say he was working on a book of poems. Then Althea walked into his bar, the woman he'd conjured with words that very day, and he began to actually feel capable.

Some late mornings as he lay in the loft waking slowly, Robert would look down at Althea as she swept the floor or fixed him some eggs, or simply stood at the window with a cup of tea, her belly round and full and heavy, and he was certain he felt an ethereal measure of the same thing, his head and heart germinating what he hoped would one day uncoil and spring into a book with his name on it. After breakfast, if Althea had no upholstery work and wasn't driving to the basement shop she still rented from the

two blondes, she'd kiss him on the cheek, then climb back up into
the loft with a novel, and Robert would sit at the table with his
open notebook, put his pencil to it, and wait. He'd hear a single-
engine plane running an advertising flag out over the beach and he
would write: *plane*. He'd hear an off-duty waitress laugh in one of
the cabins and he'd write: *woman laughing*. He'd try and combine
these to see if some poetic alchemy might ensue, a Robert Frost–like
rhyming couplet, maybe. But when he did come up with a couplet
it sounded more like an old woman's effort at a cheerful greeting
card:

A plane flies by
a woman laughs high—
The man sits at his table
wondering if it is stable—

But nonetheless, he saw these as seeds, the sketch before the painting, and usually, after a half hour or more of recording them, he felt
he'd laid some important and necessary groundwork, and he'd
close the notebook, place it carefully on the shelf beneath the window, then open a beer and climb the short ladder to the loft, feeling
virtuous and almost triumphant.

Once Althea had asked to read one of his poems, but Robert had
told her the truth: "They're not good enough yet, honey. They're not
done." She smiled at him knowingly, a smile that seemed to respect
his honesty about his craft, but she knew better—they were already
wonderful—and Robert had felt once again the surging hope she
may be right and that he was destined for an exceptional road after
all.

But now there was the feeling he was laying booby traps in that
road. Robert finished his bourbon, washed out the aftertaste with a
quick draft, then placed the mug and glass carefully in the sink,
closing and locking the rear door to the Whaler. He could smell the
ocean. He turned and stumbled over something in the shell lot and
landed on one knee. It was an empty Bacardi bottle that had fallen

out of the full Dumpster, and he threw it back onto the heap. It was
nearly dawn. The air was cool, and the cabins were five black sil-
houettes against the dark marsh. He looked at his own, the farthest
shadow on the south side of the lot. Inside the front-porch window
was the dim glow of the table lamp Althea left on for him every
night. He imagined her standing in her full cotton nightgown, leaning forward to switch on the light before climbing with sure-footed
care up to the loft.

He looked at the other cabins; Jackie's was just two over from
his. He wondered if she was asleep yet. Did she share the loft with
her cabinmate, a dour veterinarian student and waitress named
Anna? Or did she sleep alone, and there was room for him to crawl
up there and sink into her one more time, because after tonight this
would be it? It would only be a matter of days before word got out
among the waitstaff, and then how long would it be before Althea
would hear a comment through an open window or from one of
their tiny front porches? And he knew then, standing in the slight
sway of a bourbon swoon, the five black cabins standing before him
like a line of executioners, he was going to have to leave the Whaler
before the season was up, just take Althea, load up the Subaru, and
rent a place inland. He'd tell her he didn't want to subject her and
the baby to any more raw sewage; he'd say he wanted to get more
work done on his poems. The Whaler always had a waiting list for
his job, and he'd tell the manager, Danny Sullivan, a round and
sober Irishman who never smiled sincerely, that his wife's pregnancy needed monitoring from her hometown doctor, something
like that, and then Robert Doucette would start anew.

He took a deep breath and struck out in the direction of his
cabin, but then veered slightly north and stepped softly onto
Jackie's porch. He cupped his face to the screen door and peered
in. The room was all shadows, the loft a pale strip hovering in the
darkness. But then there was another shape, lower, on the floor, a
cot or small bed, a woman's hair fanned out on the pillow. Robert
swayed a moment then caught himself. He could hear morning
birds in the trees beyond the marsh. He had ten, maybe twenty

minutes at the most before it was too light to slip back home. *Under cover of darkness*. The phrase rippled through his head. Shakespeare, he thought, and he fancied himself with billowing white sleeves, a long sword, poetry on his tongue. He reached for the door handle, turned it, and was not surprised when the door opened; most of the cabins' doors were swollen from the sea air and would not close all the way without slamming, and then you needed a pry bar to open them in the morning. He stepped inside the cabin, which could have been his own, but the air smelled strongly of pine air freshener and hand lotion, and one of the women, the one in the loft, was sleeping deeply, a slight rasp in her breathing. Robert concluded it had to be Anna, as Jackie would not be so deeply asleep yet. She was on her side in the cot, just a few feet in front of him. He recognized her thick hair on the pillow. He would slide in beside her, lift her top leg, and enter her from behind, his hands on her bountiful breasts.

Robert took off his bartender's vest and dropped it to the floor. He squatted and untied his shoes, stepping out of them and his pants and underwear, walking over the floor in his shirt and socks, his penis already half-hard. He glanced up at the loft and saw Anna's hand, her fingers curled in sleep. He leaned over and lifted the cot sheet, and was about to whisper Jackie's name when he saw Anna's profile instead, the low cheekbones and perfect nose that because of her cheekbones was not attractive, the same profile he saw every night as he placed drinks on her tray and she scanned her tables, eyes narrowed in worried concentration. Now her face was slack, her lips parted, a dime-sized drool spot on the pillow, and Robert lowered the sheet and stepped back.

The thought came of climbing the loft and placing his penis in Jackie's cupped hand, but outside already seemed less dark than moments before, the high grass of the marsh becoming defined in the soft blue light out the rear window. The morning birds were calling to one another louder now, more frequently, as if they were already into their second cup of coffee, and Robert began to feel the whiskey-dulled punch of remorse in his stomach. He crept back to his clothes and stepped into his underwear, but had to hop to get his second foot in, and when he finally stuck it through he was breathing hard and standing three feet past Anna's cot. She turned over onto her back and let out a long breath; Robert held his own, his heart pulsing high above his ears. But her eyes were closed, her lips still parted. He had neglected to cover her all the way, and her white tank shirt was twisted on her. Poking from the arm hole was half her breast, her dark nipple as solitary and inviting as a chocolate morsel. He glanced back longingly at Jackie's empty hand, then tiptoed to his pants and sat down on the floor before pulling them on, then his shoes too, leaving them untied as he backed out the screen door and slowly pulled it back into place.

It was dawn now, the shell parking lot salmon-colored. A lone white gull landed on the Dumpster and folded its wings in before jumping onto the heap. Robert began to tuck in his shirt, but something was missing, his vest, and he was just about to reach for the door handle one more time when he felt something a few yards to the south.

Althea.

She stood there looking directly at him, her long white sleeping gown bunched slightly on her belly, the hem raised in the front, showing her thick ankles and bare feet; most of the shells were broken and jagged and nobody walked on them barefoot. Robert let go of the door. His shirttail was hanging out in front and he wanted to tuck it in, but knew that motion would surely reveal everything, though *nothing* had really happened inside the cabin. And this is the truth that emboldened him to step off the porch onto the crunch of shells, speaking gently his wife's name: "Thea?"

She didn't say anything, just looked at him with dark, dry eyes.

"Honey?" The air itself seemed to be stretched tight as he walked through it.

When he got close she raised her chin: "Which one?"

"What?" Inside Robert an elevator cable seemed to snap.

"Jackie or Anna?"

The descent was terrible.

"Anna?"

"No, Thea, honey, what are you talking about? Let's go inside."

Robert touched her hip, was hoping to turn her toward home, but she gripped his wrist and looked directly into his eyes: "Jackie."

The elevator slammed into the pit. Robert shook his head, but Althea was nodding; she dropped his hand and walked quickly over the broken shells toward Jackie's cabin. There was a great silence and time seemed to slow down to nothing, as if he were in a car breaking into speeding pieces on the highway and all he could do was roll with the fragment he was strapped onto; he watched her go, her curly black hair and white sleeping gown and bare feet as she stepped up onto the porch. Now time moved again and he bolted after her, but his foot slid out behind him and he did a near split and had to catch himself with his hands, then his knees, and then he was up. But Althea was already inside, the screen door a slam Robert was late for, stepping into the room just as his wife grabbed Jackie's empty hand and jerked her completely out of the loft onto her back and buttocks, her bare feet slamming the floorboards and wall, Anna jumping to her knees in the cot, screaming. Jackie was screaming too, flailing behind her at what had her hair; then Althea screamed, and it was the only one Robert heard now, a sound that seemed not to come from all that was unfolding because of him, a long wail followed by a panting whimper. She held Jackie's hair with two hands, but no longer to do damage, it seemed; more, it was to hold herself steady. She was bent over, squeezing her knees together, and blood was coming in slow, sure rivulets, moving down her olive calves onto the floor, onto the floor and Robert's black bartender's vest.

It was Jackie who called the ambulance. Althea kept moaning, her face empty of color, and Anna had her lie on the floor and rest her bare feet up on the cot. Robert had just stood there a moment, saying nothing, doing nothing, but then Althea began to cry, covering her eyes with her arm. He knelt down and touched her hair, but she shook her head away from him so violently that he stood again, then ended up sitting on the cot, holding her bloody feet in his lap as Anna squatted and did something with a towel beneath his wife. Jackie stood off to the side in nothing but light blue panties and a New England Patriots T-shirt, her hair still ratty from Althea's grip, looking from Robert to his wife on the floor as if this were something she couldn't possibly have invited upon herself.

Robert had wanted to ride in the ambulance, but the EMT shook his head no and closed the doors, his partner already inside there wrapping a blood-pressure cuff around Althea's arm. Robert followed in the Subaru, the ambulance in front of him impossibly white, its siren off but its orange and red roof lights blinking and spinning as the van sped down the empty boulevard. And the sun was the same color, sitting on the water, the beach deserted. Robert had to push down on the accelerator to keep up with the ambulance, and he felt he was actually chasing it, that they were fleeing him, whisking his wife off to safety and high ground. He began to feel afraid. The towel Anna had wedged beneath Althea was dripping when the EMTs arrived. And when they lifted her onto the gurney her face was yellowish and she didn't look at him or anyone, just closed her eyes tightly against what must've been a terrible pain. *Two months early.* And what about the baby? Was the *baby* in pain?

The ambulance left the boulevard and barreled past the wide salt marsh. Robert kept the Subaru two car lengths behind, though they were moving close to fifty. He wondered what the EMT was doing to her behind those white doors. How could you stop the bleeding if it was coming from inside? Robert's face prickled with heat and he felt nauseated, his mouth nothing but a sticky shot glass, his head aching behind his eyes. Over the years he'd had a handful of girlfriends, mainly women he worked and drank with, and on shifts when they hadn't been around he would sometimes cheat on them; but he had never cheated on anyone as loving, trusting, and faithful as his wife. The wind was blowing in against his cheek, the smell of the ocean and the mudflats of the marsh, and for a moment he could feel his heart beating in his ears, and he heard nothing else as the wind pushed silently at his face like unrelenting bad news: *What if you lose her? What if you lose your child, too?* He got an image of himself alone in the fall, working at Skinny's in Florida, a youngish man with all his promise gone: squandered and lusted away. If he'd ever had any in the first place. No one at the University of New Hampshire thought so; the resident poet there, a Pulitzer Prize nominee, told him his work lacked a beating heart, that he should start looking at *other* people instead of expecting everyone to look at *him*. There was the week of drinking and skipping all his classes, then leaving school, and then his father standing in his bedroom doorway saying, "You're all talk, aren't you, son? Nothing but talk."

The ambulance hit its siren once as it pulled into the emergency bay. Robert parked his car nearby. He was shutting the door when they wheeled Althea through the doors, her profile small and anemic. He hurried inside, his head pulsing with no sleep and the leftover Maker's Mark. But there was only an emergency waiting area, a woman at a desk typing something into a computer, her glasses pushed to the tip of her nose. He approached her and was conscious of his bloody white shirt. He wanted to tuck it in, at least, but the thought felt ludicrous.

"Where did they take my wife? I think she's having the baby. Where would they take her?"

The woman glanced at his shirt, then up at his face as if she weren't sure she'd heard him correctly.

"Have you preregistered?"

"Excuse me?"

"For the delivery, sir. Are you in our computer?"

He told her no, they were going to do that later. His wife wasn't due to deliver for two more months. "She's bleeding. Where would they take her?"

The woman looked at him over the rim of her glasses.

"I need to see my wife." Robert's voice cracked and his eyes began to fill.

"Of course you do, dear. But first you need to sit down so I can enter her into the system."

Robert sat in the chair facing her desk. His legs felt momentarily useless and he was grateful someone had told him what to do. The woman pressed a few buttons to clear away old work, then sat forward and, looking only at the computer screen to her left, asked him questions about Althea: her full name, her date and place of birth, her next of kin—"Me, her husband." And as he spelled out his name, he began to feel the strength return to his legs and feet. He sat up straighter and perched himself on the edge of the chair. He answered they had no medical insurance, she could bill him directly. And he gave her the address of the Whaler Hotel—they would either be there or they wouldn't, but at the thought that he and Althea and their son or daughter might *not* be living in the Whaler cabins, Robert forced himself to imagine it was because they would move, and not because there would be only one returning there instead of three.

Soon enough she let him go, directing him to the maternity ward, where a man in a turquoise smock told him his wife was being prepped for surgery. *Why? What's wrong?* But the man just told him to have a seat, then disappeared behind a swinging door. The small waiting area was six cushioned chairs, a table spread out with magazines, and a water cooler and Coke machine. Robert sat down, but it was a comfortable seat so he stood. His mouth and throat were dry, and there was an evil taste in his mouth. In his right pocket was the cash from last night's tips. In his left were a few stray coins, enough for a Coke. As the can came clacketing down through the machine, two women in those same turquoise smocks walked quickly and quietly down the hall. Their shoes and hair were covered with blue-green netting. Their white breathing masks were hanging loosely beneath their chins. They pushed through the swinging door, and Robert did not know if they were going in to help with Althea, but their silent and urgent rushing left him feeling queasy and lost, like he was falling backward away from all this, his mouth dry, his stomach a terrible mistake, his knees liquid. He sat with his unopened Coke, rested his elbows on his thighs, and breathed deeply through his nose. He saw his shoes were still untied and left them that way. He remembered Jackie's heels on his shoulders; he remembered the sound Althea made as she wrenched Jackie off the bunk, a deep sustained cry that could only come from a well of quiet.

He sat there a long while. He felt he should call someone, but Althea's family was in Greece and, except for a couple of regular customers—Dennis, the lobsterman; and Geoffrey, a funny and obese trial lawyer from Lawrence—Robert had no male friends he could call. And even those two he had spent little time with, simply allowed to stay after closing for a few more on the house while he closed up. There had been one friend in college, before he quit over a decade ago: his roommate, a thin, sad-eyed existentialist with whom Robert would often go drinking.

Robert thought of him now and suspected that even if he knew his phone number, he wouldn't want him here; at a local bar or at a dorm party, the existentialist would get morose and sneer at the young men and women dancing or huddling together over a joint in their loose jeans. "We're all going over the falls, man. Drink up, Doucette! God drowned in the first boat!" And Robert would drink up, then leave his friend and join the others—women mainly, those with delicate throats and wispy hair that, when they danced too close, would catch on his face if he hadn't shaved—women who smiled at him because he was almost handsome, which meant cute; and when he told them over the music and through the smoke that he was an English major and wanted to be a poet, their interest would deepen, and some of them wanted to drink alone in a corner with him, talk about life and beauty. And so he adopted the sentences of his poetry teacher, and he'd tell them life was a song that had to be sung and *forget* iambic pentameter—too cold. "Life's a burning building; life's a ride through the rapids before we all go over the edge, and we only have so much time to get things down. Like your delicate throat," he'd say to one. "Like your eyes," he'd tell another. "The way they make me think of minks in Russia, a family of minks in the snow." He'd leave with one of them and later, after he'd ejaculated into her, after he'd slept in her room, the dawn's hopeful light piercing the windows, he'd *know* he was a poet; he just hadn't put it all on paper yet. He'd slip out of her warm bed, sometimes taking one last look at her naked buttocks while she slept, or at that sweet triangle of pubic hair between flaring hip bones, and he'd dress and leave the dorm that smelled of cigarettes and cold pizza boxes and beer soaked into the carpet. He was Rimbaud, Baudelaire, Wilde; he was all the rascal poets he'd been reading. And as Robert left the smells of the dormitory and stepped into the cold New Hampshire air, he was grateful he no longer smelled hay and silage, warm udders and oak-handled shovels and hoes, cow manure and diesel fuel, the smells of a life he thought he'd never escape: in the winter, the twice-daily mud-and-ice trek to the barn to lead six dozen Holsteins eight at a time to the milking room; to clean the valves and tubes after; to rake manure and haul corn silage from the silo to the feed bunk; to keep the calves dry and fed in their stalls; to inseminate heifers, then calve them months later, changing the hay they slept in, hauling bales as if he hadn't hauled enough in August, the baler shooting them out at him when he only had a few seconds to hook his fingers into the twine, heaving and tossing the bale into place onto the trailer behind him, the sweat in his eyes, his back a tight cord about to snap. And in the fall they'd have to pack the silo with load after wheelbarrow load of the corn they'd planted in the spring, and the vacuum chute was always getting clogged or breaking down, so when his father climbed the ladder with a tool apron, Robert would build a huge mound of corn cobs he'd have to load into the silo once it was fixed. There were always things breaking down: the tractor, the picker, the baler, the milkers. One summer the freezer went and hundreds of dollars of bull semen thawed and died. And if all the machinery was running smoothly, a storm would come in and there'd be a roof leak, soaking some of the stock who were too stupid to move, and then they'd get sick or just more dopey than usual, and one might trip on her way to feed and cut a foreleg, and

Robert would have to nurse that, clean it and wrap it with gauze. But sometimes an infection would come anyway and the cow would get a fever, and even if she could make it to the milking room the milk might be tainted, and Robert's father would have to sell her off for scrap beef: cat and dog food, hot-dog filler.

In college, Robert tried putting all of this and more into a poem. And when he finished he felt it was the most honest thing he could possibly have written, the most passionate. How could anyone read it and not know how life at Doucette Dairy was for him? How could they not know all of its tedium? He stayed up till almost dawn typing it and retyping it into the shape he wanted, the right stanza length, the right verse. After a few tries, he found the title, too: "Dairy." He slept in his clothes on his bed, but woke before his alarm went off, then went to poetry class, handing the Pulitzer Prize nominee his manuscript. His professor said he would read it that morning and to stop by before lunch.

"It has the authority of lived experience, Robert, but I don't believe there was no joy in any of that work. You've written in the voice of the suffering hero and I don't buy it. Try writing a poem without you in it. Show me the cow's fever without your bitching about having to change the bandage. The farm life's the subject, not your whining."

Robert had just stood there, his mouth a dry web. The Pulitzer Prize nominee sat down at his desk and began to read a hardcover book. "Write it again, if you like."

Robert had spent the day in his room lying in bed. He had an afternoon class but didn't go. He read the poem over and over, but kept hearing the poet's last three words, *if you like*. They were completely apathetic. Would he say those same words to someone he thought had talent? The following week he skipped all three poetry classes. At a dorm party he got drunk and the next morning at dawn he woke up at the base of a red maple tree planted by the class of 1945. He was hungover and cold and could see he'd covered himself with leaves the color of bright blood. There was a stone engraving on the ground: DEDICATED TO THE VALIANT YOUNG

MEN OF THIS UNIVERSITY WHO GAVE THEIR LIVES FOR FREEDOM—1945. And Robert wished there was a war *he* could go fight, but it wasn't fighting he craved, or danger even. More, it was something to be honored and known for—an ability, an act, anything. The night before, he'd told a girl that the poet had praised one of his poems, saying it had the authority of lived experience. She'd had a sweet milky face and thick red hair, and she'd looked at him askance, as if he were a real blowhard for repeating praise like that.

He didn't know her name and never saw her again, but in the last ten years her skeptical face would sometimes come back to him, the way it came to him now, along with the question to which she seemed to have the answer: *Was* he? Was he a blowhard?

"Mr. Doucette?"

Robert raised his head. It was the same man from before, his curly hair matted from the surgical cap he now held in his hand.

"It was a placental abruption, but we've stopped the bleeding and your wife will be in recovery soon. Your daughter appears to be healthy as well, though we'll have to monitor her pretty closely."

"Daughter?"

The doctor told Robert he could see his child in the neonatal unit, and his wife would be going to ICU after the recovery room. He said congratulations and offered his hand. Robert, still sitting, reached out to shake it, then stood quickly and squeezed; the man's hand was small and soft, and Robert was acutely aware that it had just performed two miracles: saved his wife, and delivered their baby. "Thank you, Doctor. Thank you." Robert did not want to let go, but the doctor stopped squeezing and glanced down at Robert's shirt. He said it would be a little while before his family was ready for a visit, and he should feel free to go home and change if he'd like. The doctor let his hand slide out of Robert's, offered his congratulations once more, then disappeared back behind the swinging door.

Robert did not want to leave. He wanted to find the neonatal unit and see his child. His daughter. Be with her. Let her hear his voice. Smell his skin. But what would she smell? Jackie's scent?

Coconut oil? Old bourbon and her mother's blood? And later, when he visited Althea, would he want to show up in the same clothes he wore when everything went wrong? No; he would drive home, shower, shave, change his clothes, and buy flowers on the way back.

Jackie was sitting on the porch step of her cabin when Robert drove over the shell lot and parked alongside the marsh. She was smoking a lighted cigarette this time, and she still wore the baggy Patriots T-shirt she'd slept in—that, and a pair of shorts, Robert noticed, her hair pulled back. She was barefoot, and when Robert turned off the engine she sat up straight, blew smoke, and waited; she was a beautiful woman, her thick red ponytail hanging straight down her brave back, her thighs and calves hard and supple-looking, covered with tanned freckles. Robert's cheeks became warm, his throat dry, and he took a long drink off his Coke before he got out of the Subaru and walked over to her.

She was looking up at him, her eyes empty of mischief. Instead, Robert saw fear in them, and something he could not begin to name. But he must have been smiling, because Jackie said, "Everything's okay? The baby? Everything?"

"A girl. We have a little girl." He was conscious of the word *we,* the exclusion of her in that, and, as if to make up for it, he sat on the step next to her, their hips touching.

"You're smoking."

Jackie nodded, took a final drag off the cigarette, and flicked it out into the broken shells of the lot. "How'd she find out?" She was looking at him, her eyes full of sorrow, as if *she* had been betrayed, and he knew then Jackie would never have told anyone.

He shrugged. "She saw me come out of your place. I snuck in to see you, but you were asleep, so I let myself back out again."

The screen door opened behind them and Anna said excuse me and didn't wait for Robert to finish scooting over before she stepped between them and off the porch. She was dressed for work, the early lunch crowd, her white blouse and black skirt freshly ironed, her bare legs lean, disciplined, and moral. She walked straight to the Whaler's service door and didn't turn around once.

"She hasn't talked to me all morning." Jackie looked halfway over at Robert, her eyes fixing on his shirt, his bloody shirt. "I feel really bad." Her voice broke and Robert put his arm around her. She seemed to be crying, her shoulders bobbing slightly, though he couldn't be sure because he didn't hear anything. He could smell her hair, the natural oil in it, the linen of her pillowcase. He began to get hard, and he pulled away. "I should get my vest."

She looked at him, her green eyes shiny and dull. She blinked twice, as if she were trying to focus on what he'd really just said. She sniffled, wiped under each eye with one finger, then stood and led him inside. His vest lay on a towel on her bunk, the top sheet balled in a heap at the foot of the bed.

"I rinsed it in cold water."

"Thank you."

"Why weren't you wearing it?"

Robert picked up the vest, dark and damp. "I was carrying it. Just forgot about it." He didn't like lying to Jackie; he should not lie to at least *somebody*. He could hear the beach traffic out on the boulevard, the clown horn of a motorcycle or truck. The air in the cabin was still and hot, and he smelled the sewage, all of theirs, his and Jackie's and Anna's, all the other barbacks and waiters and waitresses, the ones who waited. And Jackie seemed to be waiting too, her face sad but open to spontaneity, her nipples erect beneath her shirt.

"I'm sorry about what happened, Jackie."

"Me too."

Robert moved toward her to give her a hug, he told himself, that's all, but she stepped back and held up her hand. "Don't."

Disappointment and relief twisted inside him. He nodded, thanked her for the vest, then left the cabin and walked back to his own, where he showered and changed into khaki pants and an oxford shirt Althea had ironed and hung in their tiny closet beneath the loft. He was sweating a foul sweat: bourbon and desire and a profound weakness; he was almost certain he would have done it with Jackie one more time, a final time. All the windows were open, but there was no sea breeze at all, just the smell of sewage and salt water from the marsh, the faint scent of garbage from the Dumpster on the other side of the lot, rancid fried fish and clams, hot metal and dried soda, and he could not imagine bringing his wife and baby back to this. *If* she would come—there was the way she'd turned her head away from him as she bled on Jackie's floor, her placenta "abrupted."

A cool sweat came out on his forehead as he slipped on his loafers, combed his hair back, then crossed the shell lot. It seemed an entire night and day had passed since he'd closed up, but it was still early, the lunch staff pulling chairs off tables, running the vacuum over the sea-green carpet, setting each plate with silverware, cloth napkins, and a Whaler's place-mat menu. Anna was drinking coffee at the window table with three other waitresses who were taking a cigarette break, and Robert didn't have to guess at the topic of their conversation. Still, he waved to them on his way to the manager's office. One of them, a dark-haired, small-hipped woman who owned her own video store a few miles west, asked if his wife was doing all right. Robert nodded and smiled, though he felt as if he were lying again.

His manager, Danny Sullivan, was sitting at his cluttered desk with a clear glass of creamy coffee, smoking a cigarette and studying last night's receipts. He had a thick red mustache and a wide double chin. He wore reading glasses. A small paper-clip holder was turned over on the blotter at the edge of the desk and Robert remembered Jackie's hand bracing herself there. He'd forgotten this was the last place they'd done it, and now he felt like a house burglar walking by one of his victims in the grocery store. His own face was lost behind a sudden veneer, and Dan Sullivan glanced up at him, then back at the receipts, the smoke from the cigarette wafting in front of him.

"We're switching over to Sprite on the guns, Bobby. When you lock up tonight, have the barback put all the 7-Up canisters outside, all right?"

Sullivan flicked on his adding machine. Robert scanned the desk for any more evidence of last night, but there was none, just the general paper clutter of beer and liquor orders, the only hint a clear semicircle of space at the front edge of the desk where Jackie had rested her ass.

"We had our baby today, Danny."

Sullivan looked up, his eyes suddenly empty of numbers. "Already?"

"Eight weeks early. Everything's okay, though." Robert felt himself smile, and now, telling the news to a man, a father, though twice divorced, Robert felt genuinely happy. "We have a little girl. She'll be in the hospital for a while, I guess."

"Your wife?"

"She's good." Robert's forehead felt like plastic.

Dan Sullivan stood and offered his hand. "Good for you, kid. Sit down." He waved at a sawed-off bar stool, its upholstered seat sealed with duct tape. He left the office and was back before Robert had even sat. He was carrying a bottle of Bushmills Irish Whiskey and two highball glasses, still steaming from the machine. It was the last thing Robert wanted, his bourbon-dry gut already shrinking back at the news, but when Sullivan poured him three fingers and put the glass in his hand, Robert knew he would drink it. His manager raised his own glass, said something in Gaelic, then tapped Robert's, and Robert drank the Bushmills slowly, enough for his insides to acclimate themselves, and when they did things weren't so bad: it was a warm, amber day on the beach and his gut was lolling in the water. His manager must've seen something in Robert's face and poured them each one more, though this one was shorter.

Sullivan raised his glass again. "A girl's the way to go, Bobby." His manager drank down the Bushmills and Robert followed suit, the second glass feeling a bit shy in kick and weight, Robert remembering something about Danny's grown son tending bar here till his father had to fire him for stealing from the register. Sullivan sat back behind his desk and took a deep drag off his cigarette, the numbers back in his eyes again. "I'll get Davey to cover for you till you're all set. Give yourself a couple of days, all right?"

Robert thanked him and left the office. He'd meant to give his notice too, to tell him he was done for the season, but Sullivan's gesture of the Bushmills and toast had thrown him. The aftertaste of the Irish whiskey was a bit coarse in Robert's throat, and he walked to the bar and filled himself a glass of ginger ale from the soda gun. The waitresses were gone from the window table. It was set now with napkins and silver and a clean ashtray. Outside and across the boulevard, the beach was already full of people sunbathing, others throwing a frisbee or football back and forth, still others wading out into the green and white surf. He was exhausted, the glass in his hand heavier than it should've been, his legs stiff and unsure. And he felt the toast too, his face and head a wide, reckless expanse with no borders, and there was the feeling of being left behind, something important going on someplace else he really should not miss.

Then he was in his car backing over the broken shells, perhaps breaking more himself. Though the windows were rolled down, the inside of the car was hot and he began to sweat beneath his ironed shirt. A screen door slammed back on its jamb and there was Jackie standing on her porch in her sunbathing bikini, holding her folded lounge chair and a glass of something iced. She'd pulled her hair out of its ponytail and now it hung thickly just past her shoulders. He didn't wave or acknowledge her in any way, mainly because the car was moving forward, he told himself, but in the rearview mirror he watched her watch him go, her lovely face looking small and sad with resolve, her breasts as ample and inviting as two peaches on a limb on the other side of a steep gorge.

In Exeter, Robert stopped for coffee and flowers. He parked across from the small gazebo off the main square and stepped up under the awnings of the shops and restaurants that filled the old mill buildings all the way to the river. The air was warmer here than on the beach, no breeze, and his mouth was dry, his shirt sticking to the middle of his back. Down a side street was a florist. He went inside and ordered a dozen long-stem roses, but then changed his mind; red wasn't the appropriate color for the occasion and, under the circumstances, he didn't want Althea to think he was trying to romance her. He asked the lady behind the counter to make up a fifty-dollar mixed bouquet, then stepped outside to escape the earth-strangled odors of all those green stems in water. Across the road was a Mexican restaurant, its doors open. In the dark bar two men sat laughing. Robert considered a quick beer, but the Bushmills had worn off, leaving him sleepier than ever, his eyes burning slightly, the terrible all-nighter behind him like a faraway sound. The sight of the two men bruised him in a way he couldn't pinpoint, and when he walked into a newsstand at the corner for a cup of coffee, he saw the humidor of cigars and knew not only was he genuinely afraid of Althea leaving him now, but he was lonesome too, lonesome for at least one male friend to whom he could hand a cigar.

He immediately thought of calling his father. It was almost noon in August: he'd be putting up the hay, driving the baler while a couple of hired hands caught the bales, then stacked them onto the trailer. At this moment he was a grandfather and didn't know it, and as Robert paid for the wrapped flowers he told himself to make the call from the hospital, though he hadn't seen or talked to his mother and father in over four years. What would they have talked about? Robert's tips? The tuition money he still owed them? The poetry he wasn't writing? But now there was something to show, something worth his mother calling his father from the fields to the phone for. But the notion of his baby girl being identified as his father's grand-daughter left Robert feeling naked and weak, like the better man would get picked to step in and finish a job with which Robert, of course, could not be trusted. And he thought of Althea's anemic face and dark, dry eyes. Jackie in her bikini watching him go.

Robert drove slowly. The coffee was bitter and too hot and wasn't mixing well with the Bushmills. A band of sweat came out on his forehead and he wiped it off with the back of his arm, then dumped his coffee out the window, the plastic lid falling away. In the rearview mirror he watched it roll and flip over onto the yellow divider, then lie flat, seemingly accepting its fate as the tires of a pickup truck just missed it. But Robert didn't feel so lucky; the surge of joy he'd felt earlier when he'd told Sullivan of the birth had now backed up on him and turned into an almost suffocating awareness of his own worthlessness, and as he took the left turn for the hospital, his stomach queasy, it seemed inconceivable that in his short marriage to Althea she had, in her quiet way, left him feeling not only worthy but exceptional, a man capable of being not only a real poet but a husband and father, too.

The hospital sat on a rise surrounded by woods, its windows reflecting the glare of the sun. Robert squinted, his head aching. He parked in the shade of a sugar maple and got out with the flowers. When he swung the door shut it pinched off the heads of a daisy and a flower he didn't know. He opened the door to retrieve them, but they were both crushed. He reached inside the bouquet for the flowerless stems but couldn't find them, his fingers feeling thick and clumsy. He left them there, hoping Althea would not see them. Inside the hospital at the information desk, he asked an elderly woman for his wife's room number. It was on the second floor, she told him, room 214. Robert asked about the neonatal unit too, and the woman said it was on the third floor, though this time she smiled at him, an understanding and encouraging smile, one with which she obviously hoped to fortify him. Robert hadn't been looking for or expecting that; it frightened him. He walked quickly to the elevators, remembering the doctor's words earlier, that his daughter *appears* healthy, and Robert's face flushed with shame that this hadn't been the primary word on his mind since he'd first heard it.

In the elevator he pressed the button for the third floor, bypassing his wife's. The neonatal unit's door was locked. Robert had to press an intercom button beside it to announce who he was. He cleared his throat and leaned close to the speaker, his throat dry from the coffee, a bad taste in his mouth. He pressed the button.

"Your name, please." The voice was clear and free of static.

"Robert Doucette."

There was no answer. Robert saw he was holding the wrapped flowers tilted to the floor, their heads lolling on their stems, and he righted them.

"We have an infant girl Doucette."

"That's her—I mean that's me. I'm Robert. She's my daughter." And it occurred to Robert their child did not yet have a name. She had come too soon for a name. The door buzzed loudly and Robert entered the floor. There was a polished passageway, and in it was one chair next to a sink beneath a fire extinguisher. A dark-haired nurse greeted him and smiled, this one genuinely warm, but brief and businesslike. She handed him a yellow gown and said he would have to leave the flowers on the chair and wash his hands at the sink. Robert did as he was told. He dried his hands quickly, put the gown on over his shirt, and was tying its sash at his waist as he followed the nurse into the unit.

At its center was a brightly lit nurses' station with four or five women sitting behind a circular counter writing or reading something, or speaking quietly on a phone. One stood and pulled a clear bottle from a cabinet. The nurse led him past a large, dim room whose windows were covered with closed blinds, eight or nine tiny cribs scattered in the shadows, transparent bassinets on wheel stands, really. At each one was some sort of electronic monitor. Some were unplugged and dark, others lit up with green, red, and orange lights. Next to these were metal stands with intravenous bags hanging from their hooks. Two or three babies were crying, their voices high and strained and plasticine, as if their vocal chords were only thin distressed membranes. Robert tried to swallow, but his throat was too dry, his heart beating in his palms and fingers. He followed the nurse into another large room, this one a bit brighter, its window blinds pulled up halfway. There were four bassinets, and the nurse stopped at the first one on the right. There was an intravenous stand and an electronic monitor. All of its lights were lit up green and red, its screen an opaque orange showing the graphic rise and roll of a beating heart.

"Here she is."

Robert's eyes filled.

There were so many tubes and wires running into the bassinet Robert was at first not sure what he was seeing. Then he saw her bare chest in the folds of the linen; it was red and orange, really, a network of tiny blue capillaries beneath the skin. She was not much larger than his hand.

Her arms and legs were thin, crooked, and short, and her eyes were closed, her face the size of a small apricot. Her lips were tiny rims of purple, and they were parted, her dark round mouth smaller than a dime. She had no hair and hardly any eyebrows or lashes. On her bare chest and stomach were the monitor wires connected to what looked like small round Band-Aids. Just above the minuscule diaper was the stump of her severed umbilical cord, pink and blue, still bloody at the tip. Around her upper arm was a blood-pressure cuff no wider in circumference than a cigar band, and taped to her wrist was the IV tube, which dwarfed it.

Robert wiped at his eyes and nose. "Is she all right?"

"Yes. She just needs a little extra help right now. Would you like to hold her?"

He looked at the nurse: she was smiling, her eyes bright with a certain knowledge she seemed to know Robert did not yet have, one she was happy to give him now. For Robert it was like looking into an angel's loving face while sitting on the toilet, or masturbating, or stealing money, or standing there with a sleepless, hungover head and body and freshly washed genitals while your wife recovered from surgery she probably never would have had, this infant deprived of eight precious weeks in her mother's womb, this miniature infant girl, her belly rising and falling in short, almost desperate-looking breaths. How could he hold her?

How could he not? A cool sweat came out on his forehead and the back of his neck.

"Here." The nurse stepped closer, reached into the bassinet, and picked the baby up with cupped hands, her head fitting snugly between two of the woman's fingers, the wires and tube reaching only so far. Robert held out both palms. They trembled slightly, and as the nurse slid his child onto his hand he was terrified of dropping her. The infant turned her head to the right and left, then nudged her nose and cheek into the soft flesh at the base of his thumb, her feet barely reaching his other hand. The flowers he'd bought were five times heavier than this. She began to blur. He sniffled and held her close to his chest. Her ear was pinkish red and perfectly formed, but as small as if he were seeing it from a hundred feet in the air. The nurse covered her with a light blanket smaller than a man's handkerchief. His daughter blurred again. The nurse dragged a rocking chair over and set it beside him. Robert was afraid the tube and wires wouldn't reach. The nurse began to uncoil some slack from the IV stand, but Robert shook his head and told her that's okay, he'll stand. She looked at him briefly, as if she were making sure that was what he really wanted; there was something like satisfaction in her eyes. Warmth, too. Wisdom. She turned and took all that to another baby in another room.

Robert looked down at his daughter, this infinitesimal baby girl curled under a piece of cloth in his hands. He held her as close to his chest as he could. He stroked the top of her head with his thumb, her eyes closed, her mouth a dark oval. He wanted to feed her. Shouldn't they be feeding her something? There was the tube in her arm, but was that enough? He would ask the nurse about this on his way to see Althea. Althea, who had stood barefoot in the shell backlot of the Whaler, her cotton nightgown fitting tightly over her pregnant belly, her dark eyes afraid but strong and ready to act, when all fear ever did for him was scare him away: scare him away from the farm and his father's joyless toil, from the poet's class, from school, from the pitiful jottings in his largely empty notebooks, from his quiet wife who had loved him so faithfully and unquestioningly he had taken refuge in the dim chaos of the Whaler and the warmth between Jackie's thighs. And now this three-pound baby girl in his hands needed a refuge, a solid nest in which to grow, and Robert felt certain he had already failed in giving that to her; and he felt the need to place her back in her bassinet, leave the flowers on the chair in the hallway, and drive away from here. He would go to the bank and withdraw half their savings, almost four thousand dollars. No, he'd leave Althea and the baby all but a thousand. That would be enough to get him to Florida or the West Coast, where he'd soon find a job and a place, where he'd go back to just working his shifts, sleeping with an occasional waitress or barmaid, telling himself he was a poet gathering material the way he'd seen so many waitresses use the story that they were only doing this while they saved for night classes; it was just the lie restaurant workers told each other so they wouldn't have to admit the truth, that they'd rather watch life's swimmers go by from the deep warm sand of the beach. That's who he was. That's who Althea married. And she can do better, he thought. She will do better. This one, too.

Robert stepped closer to the bassinet, but when he began to lower her inside a loud beeping went off, and he stopped where he was, holding the baby in midair as the nurse came walking swiftly into the room, her face calm and smiling again, when Robert had expected a look of alarm, or at least chastisement.

"Her IV's sensitive." The nurse stepped in beside him, so close he could smell her hair, the lingering scent of shampoo and the deeper scent of her scalp, just skin, the skin of a woman working, and he felt strangely calmed. He let her take the baby and nestle her back into the folds of linen, patting the wires back into place, pressing gently on the intravenous tube in his daughter's thin arm. Robert took one step back. He breathed deeply through his nose and a sound came out that surprised him, and his eyes filled so much he had to wipe them away. Then there was a hand on his shoulder. "She's really fine, you know. We didn't even have to ventilate her. She's a little trouper." She squeezed his shoulder and let go. "Is this your first?"

Robert nodded but could not look at the nurse, not after what he'd just been planning to do. Instead, he looked down at the baby, at his daughter, the rise and fall of her first breaths, at the way her sleeping face was turned to the side, her lips parted, her clavicle almost visible beneath her skin.

"What are you going to name her?"

"We don't know yet."

And he meant it, not the not knowing, but the *we*; as far as he knew, he and Althea were still a *we*. "Has my wife seen her yet?"

"No, would you like to bring her to her room?"

"Yes." He took a breath. "Yes, I would."

"I'll call down and see if she's awake."

The nurse left and Robert kept his eyes on his daughter for a moment longer, then turned and walked to the window. The sun had disappeared and he could see a cloud bank to the east, the air not as bright or dangerous-looking as it had seemed earlier; it was probably raining at the beach, on the Whaler, the cabins, and the marsh. Jackie had probably jumped up and carried her chaise to the porch, maybe stood there in her wet bikini looking out at the rain. He imagined it coming down on the fields of his father's farm, maybe a downpour. That would stop the baling and send the men into the house, into the kitchen, where his mother would serve them coffee or iced tea, probably something sweet she'd baked. Robert had been one of those hands himself: sitting at the table with his shirt sticking to his back and arms, his pants damp and matted with hayseed, his work boots still on because his mother knew they were going right back outside after the rain had passed, the soles heavy with mud and bits of manure and silage, his father sitting in his chair at the table, chewing and staring straight ahead into the rest of the day's chores, barely tolerating this momentary interruption from the work that called him.

From the doorway the nurse said Althea was still asleep and they would ring when she was ready for the baby. Robert thanked her and looked back outside. Down below in the parking lot was a young family: a man in sandals, shorts, and a T-shirt, and a woman in a sundress holding a little boy with a blue cast on his arm. In his hand was the string to a large red helium balloon floating over their heads. The father opened the rear door for his wife and son, and while the mother lowered the boy into the backseat the father took hold of the balloon with both hands to keep it from popping or drifting away. He stood there a moment and looked past the parking lot to the stand of pines beyond, his face tanned, maybe from outdoor work, Robert thought, landscaping or carpentry or roofing—honest work. The man was smiling in the gray light, holding his young son's balloon. His wife straightened and her husband watched her walk around to the passenger door, his smile deepening. He leaned into the backseat with the balloon, handing it to his son, waiting for him to get hold of the string. Then he kissed him, straightened, and shut the door gently, clicking it shut with his hip.

Robert's heart was beating fast. He turned from the window, walked to his daughter's bassinet, and touched two fingers to her tiny forehead. She was warm and stirred slightly. He left the room, smiling politely at the nurses at the counter, though his wasn't there. In the passageway he hung up his gown, picked up Althea's flowers, and carried them close to his chest all the way to the elevators and down to her floor.

Room 214 was directly across from the nurses' station, and Althea's door was closed halfway. Robert slipped in shoulder-first; he was relieved to see her still asleep, but her face was puffy and still yellowish; her lips dry, almost chapped; her wild black hair matted and tamed-looking. Beneath the sheet and light blanket, her belly was flat.

Robert's face grew warm and he felt queasy again. He sat in the chair near her bed. It was deep and soft, welcoming his body as if it had been made for just him, and he knew he could easily sleep in it, would sleep in it if he weren't careful. He sat forward, looked at his wife's sleeping face, noticed how even her eyes seemed swollen. Her mouth was closed, and she was breathing steadily through her nose, her breasts rising and falling.

Robert's mouth was dry again, his fingers trembling. He was afraid of her waking, but more afraid of not being the first human being she saw when she did. Then he remembered the flowers still in his hand; some of them looked as if they were beginning to droop, and his heart began to pound an insistent echo through his throat. He stood to find a vase. But in the small room there was nothing but the chair in which he sat, Althea's bed, her table and movable tray, a TV built high into the wall, and the bathroom.

He went in there with the flowers. He thought there might be a water pitcher or a plastic urinal container or something, but there was just the sink, toilet, and mirror. He could put them in a sink full of water, but then she wouldn't be able to see them or know that he had brought them. He plugged the basin anyway and began to fill it with cool water, afraid now the sound would wake Althea; he pulled the door closed and when the sink was half full he shut off the tap, unwrapped the flowers, and lay them in stem-first. He took a long breath and let it out. He opened the door and saw his wife still asleep. He knew he would not be able to hand her the flowers now when she woke, to use them in the way he'd imagined, but that no longer seemed to matter.

He walked to her bedside and stood there, then sat on the edge of the chair. Althea's bare arm lay at her side on top of the blanket. He reached for it, but then stopped, not wanting to wake her, not wanting to see her eyes yet. He lowered his hand and looked at hers. It was small and he could see the sewing calluses at the tips of her fingers. His own hands looked softer, and he thought of their daughter's, pink and curled into tiny fists. He wanted her here now, but first he had to see how Althea would look at him in all of her silence. He would wait for that, truly wait. Soon enough she would open her eyes, and he could only pray that when she did they would be the ones she'd first shown him, the ones he'd received for a poem he never wrote and knew now he probably never would, eyes he did not deserve but hoped to earn—eyes of black hope.

Yunny Chen

FOOTSTEPS

The doctor tells me that my wife is sick.

My wife, Mei-ling, is changing in the examination room and cannot hear him.

"It doesn't look good," he says, and frowns at the X-rays in his hands. Then he takes out a piece of paper from his desk, and with his blue pen sketches a square with rounded corners. "This is the liver." Then he draws two round wedges, the shape and size of two lima beans, into the middle. "This is the abnormality."

I stare at the lima beans, wondering what an abnormality is, exactly.

"Come back next week and see Dr. Wu," he says, crumpling the paper in his hands.

There is a knock, the door opens, and a nurse comes in and holds the door for Mei-ling.

"Wife! The doctor and I just finished talking," I explain.

The doctor stands up behind the desk. "I was just telling your husband that—"

"He has another appointment. Right now, actually." I pick up my jacket. "We better get out of his hair!" I grab my wife's arm and march her down the corridor.

Driving out of the parking garage, I turn into the traffic slowly so that she will not nag me about my eyes again, but like always, the front right tire of the car runs over the curb and bounces onto the street. I steal a glance at her to see if she will say something, but her eyes are closed, her head hanging to the side. Her hands lie limply in the lap of her skirt. So weak.

"Wife," I say to her. "The doctor thinks everything is okay. No need to worry."

She doesn't respond, but I keep talking anyway. "He says the tests show nothing. No cancer. He says to go home, sleep, and everything will be okay."

I reach over and shake her. "Wife, you hear me?"

At home, we take off our shoes in the foyer. She sits on the steps and watches as I balance myself on one foot and then the other to untie my shoes.

"What did the doctor say?" she asks.

I wonder if she knows that I was lying in the car, or if she really was asleep. Instead of answering her, I return my shoes to the shelf and crouch down on the floor to tidy up the scattered newspaper. The Taipei City Little League is in the play-offs, and I have been collecting articles about the games.

She tugs on my shirt, her face full of concern. "I saw how tense you were when you came out of his office. It's no good, lying to me."

Sighing, I sit beside her and try to tell her what the doctor told me, but the words don't come. Instead, I take a piece of newspaper from the pile, and over a row of score boxes begin to draw what the doctor showed me, except that my liver looks like a television and the abnormality fills the box like the television screen.

My wife holds her breath.

"Maybe it's smaller." I cross out the picture and draw another one; this time, the abnormality is the shape of an apple, my shaky attempt at a circle.

She pats my knee. "Don't worry," she says. "I'll be fine. You'll see."

Then she goes inside, stopping by the dining table to hang her purse over the back of a chair before she walks into the study and closes the door behind her.

The study is her private room. There, she will take her old leather-bound Bible from the bookshelf. She will sit at the desk and read it, and when she is done, she will shut it and pray. In her prayer, she will confess all her troubles to God, and he will listen to her, and when she has told him her worries, he will give her peace.

She calls God by the name of *Father*. When we were first married, I didn't know why she had to pray to her father and if she wanted to pray, why she would not do it at the temple. We had many of those in my village where we were married. I said to her, "Your father lives on the other side of the bridge. Why don't we walk over and talk to him?" She laughed at me and told me that my idol worship had clouded my brains.

"Father is God. *Shang-di,*" she said. "He lives in heaven."

"With the Buddha? Do they know each other?"

She shook her finger at me and said that I was only trying to be difficult, that I really didn't want to understand, and that my heart had closed itself to the gospel.

That was forty years ago. We lived with my mother then, in the village where I was born, and I would shush my wife when she talked about such things, using words like *gospel, Savior,* or *Jesus.* Heaven help her if my mother should ever hear that talk again. Even in her old age, my mother still wields a quick tongue and a faster stick.

I knock lightly on the door of the study. My wife gives me no answer; she is probably already praying. As quietly as I can manage, I push the door open and peek inside. She is not praying. She has the book open before her, but her head is down on the table, her arms hanging limply by her sides.

I enter the room. "Wife, what is the matter?"

She raises her head when I trace the few strands of white hair at her temple. "I can't pray," she says. Then she lets out a brittle laugh. "I'm too tired, old man."

* * *

I have only seen my wife pray sitting at a table, usually at the church when I pick her up after service or sometimes later, when she stays for lunch and talks to her friends. The church is on Tian Mu Road, near the Takashimaya department store. It is the first floor of a five-story building and was once a convenience store. My wife calls the church women her sisters and the men brothers. They're always praying in there. Sitting together around a table, their heads propped on their folded hands.

Sometimes I go inside with her and sit in the back for the singing part of the service. Sometimes I even sing along. My voice is not half bad. It makes my wife happy when I stay. The longer I sit, the more she glows, until she can't sit still on the bench. Sometimes I let her put her offering on the offering plate without scolding her afterward. But before the pastor can begin his talk, I leave. That is why I sit in the back of the church, so that I can make a quiet exit.

My wife sometimes prays on her knees when she is alone, she once told me. She said that her father, a retired pastor, sometimes prayed that way for emergencies. I asked her what kind of emergencies, and she said an emergency meant that someone was dying or possessed.

"Possessed?" I asked her.

"Yes, possessed, when evil spirits take over your body."

I thought to tell my wife then about the priest at the temple in my village. People believed that he was possessed; that's why so many of them went to see him, because whatever possessed him made him powerful. Then I saw the expectant look on her face, and I pursed my lips together. When my wife says things like that, I keep my thoughts to myself.

She tries to stand up. I help her push the chair back and let her lean on me as we walk to the bedroom. "Maybe you can pray in bed," I tell her. "Surely he wouldn't mind."

She seems surprised and even considers it. "Maybe," she murmurs as she lies back on the bed. I take off my jacket and climb onto the bed beside her. She takes my hand and places it on her stomach.

As she sleeps, I concentrate on the warmth of her beneath my hand. We have been married for forty years, yet her womb has never known the presence of a child, and my hand has never felt the butterfly kicks of a small foot.

My wife being barren is one of the reasons why my mother despises her. My mother also hates the matchmaker who brought us together, for she told us that Mei-ling would bear her many grandchildren. I was twenty-two that year and Mei-ling was nineteen. The matchmaker brought her to a teahouse in my village for a meeting with me and my mother. That day, I wore black slacks and a white shirt with the sleeves rolled up to my elbows. It was an important occasion, but I didn't want the girl to think I was too eager. When Mei-ling came into the shop with the matchmaker, I was taken with her at once. It was the way she held her head, so high and proud, how she looked a person in the eyes, none of the coyness I found so annoying in the girls I knew. And when she smiled, it was like watching a water lily bloom at dawn. My head was filled with fantasies of our first night together.

The girl stayed quiet and the matchmaker did all the talking.

"What kind of work are her parents in?" my mother asked.

"Her mother is deceased," the matchmaker replied. "Her father is a religious advisor," she added with a nod of approval.

Surveying the girl with narrow eyes, my mother plied the matchmaker with more questions, while I made no attempt to look away from the girl.

My mother, seeing my obvious infatuation with her, adamantly opposed the marriage and told the matchmaker outright, in front of the girl and all, that she had never seen anyone more ill-suited for her son. When my mother went home to my father and listed her complaints about the girl—big-boned, no manners, such a stern face, too ugly—he simply held up his hand and silenced her nonsense. She had quite a temper, something that has never changed since her younger days, or so my father told me. She was the daughter of a government official, and though her father was long dead, she still acted as if she owned every road in town. My father rarely berated her or denied her anything, but he was already ill and insisted that I marry before he died. He saw the girl the next day when I fetched her from the matchmaker's place and walked her to our house, and he pronounced her fit for me. We were married two days later in his chambers before his deathbed.

That day, we cleared my father's large room and moved the family altar inside along with the ancestor tablets and Bodhisattva figurine. My uncles and aunts sat on wooden stools beside the bed in the order of their age and rank. My bride and I began the ceremony by kneeling before the altar, but I alone bowed to my ancestors. Her back remained stiff; her head, covered by the red silk cloth of her headpiece, was unmoving. I thought perhaps she had forgotten what to do, but when I tried to signal her by pulling on the sleeves of her dress, she ignored me. It was clear then that she had other intentions. My relatives were aghast and whispered violently behind their hands. I heard my mother, in a high-pitched voice, say, "What is wrong with that stupid girl?" At a loss, I stood up, and Mei-ling did the same. My mother tried to rise out of her seat then, her face pinched with rage, but my father, whom I thought had fallen into a stupor before the ceremony had even begun, kept her at his side with a firm hand on her shoulder.

We did not know that my new wife was one of those Christians then, not until her father arrived the next day and demanded that we submit to a Christian service. He was livid, yelling at my wife for running off without his permission.

My mother behaved no better. She said to me, "I told you we should have waited. Now you see what her family is like!"

Mei-ling and I had already spent our wedding night together, and for me to annul the marriage then would have disgraced her—that is, if I had even considered doing so. My mother knew her defeat soon enough. Her last protest was that my father-in-law could not perform the ceremony inside the house—he would confuse the spirits that the house already harbored. "We cannot take in your gods," my mother told him, indignant. "We already have ours."

Mei-ling's father pointed a shaking finger at her and yelled, "You idol worshipper, if you don't stop that, I'm going to—" He gasped and pounded his chest with his fist, caught by a coughing fit, and my wife ran to him and begged him to sit down.

Since my mother would not let him into the house and my father-in-law would not leave, we held a service outside in the courtyard with the chickens flocking around us. The neighbors poured out of their houses to watch my father-in-law, a stern man in a black suit, reading from a black book things we had never heard before.

The days after the wedding were tense, to say the least. My wife hung up a wooden cross in our chamber. She stood in the center of the room and read her Bible aloud during all hours of the day, and every so often, she would stop her chanting and, with her free hand raised into the air, shout, "In the name of the father, the son, and the holy spirit, I expel evil from this room!" Downstairs, my mother knelt before the family altar day and night and recited the sutras and burned incense until our neighbors came to see if our house was burning down.

Several days after the wedding, my father died. I rode my bike down to city hall to file claims for some properties under my father's name. When I came home that afternoon, my mother greeted me at the door with a smile. It was the first time she smiled at me since I married. It was a proud smile, if not a spiteful one, and I immediately ran up the stairs to my old room.

I could hear my wife sobbing through the door, which was locked from the outside. I had to ask my aunt, my father's unmarried sister who lived with us, for the key, which she warily produced for me. My wife was buried under a pile of blankets. I knew that something had gone wrong, but nothing could have prepared me for the sight of her bloodied face. It had been several hours since the beating, as I later learned, and her face was already swollen. I could not tell if she was bleeding from her mouth or her nose. It was the same with the rest of her body, and I examined her thoroughly, first by prying her shirt away from her tight, sweaty fists and pushing it up to her shoulders. Then before me was her pale torso, her slight rib cage mottled with red welts.

My aunt told me that the minute I rode away from the house, my mother found Mei-ling in the kitchen skinning a chicken for lunch. My mother pulled her away from the sink and slapped her full in the face. Then with the stick my father used on me when I was a boy, she caned my wife.

"She was so angry," my aunt said. "She said that your wife has shamed the family, not worshipping the ancestors, ignoring the monks when they come by to collect alms. There's no one to feed your father's spirit, and it's going to starve and become a hungry ghost." She paused in her fevered speech, her face paling at the thought. And then she frowned again. "And your wife—she's crazier. She yelled at your mother. She said, 'Devil, devil, devil! Elijah's curse on you!' It made your mother so angry to be called a devil."

The next morning, when I went to call my wife down for breakfast, the bed had already been made. The closets had been cleaned out. She sat on the bed with her bags at her feet.

"What is the meaning of this?" I asked, stepping into the room.

"I won't stay here," she said. She retreated to the window and stared down at the courtyard. "Your mother is watching out for you, but she—she hates me."

I didn't know what to say. I sat down on the bed and smoothed the sheets.

"Does it bother you?" She placed a hand over her chest. "What I am?"

It didn't matter to me. And I remembered that it hadn't seemed to matter much to my father either. Perhaps the urgency of his death forced his hand in the matter. Whatever his reasons, I was grateful for his intervention.

"Don't you have anything to say?" she asked. "Are you going to let her beat me again?"

"No," I said, shaking my head. Then I straightened. "Of course not."

"You'll leave with me then?" she asked, and though her voice was sure and steady, she held herself tense, as if waiting for a blow.

I did the only thing I could. I left with my wife.

In our new house, my wife allowed no Buddhist figurines, not even a Bodhisattva. Instead, we have on our wall an ink-sketched painting of a waterfall with biblical verses. At the base of the painting, where the water dissolves into white foam, there is an old man sitting on the grass. I once told my wife that the old man was Confucius. She said no. She said it was a man searching for God.

My wife also did not allow a family altar where I could burn incense for my father, whose ghost is in mourning, punished by his unfilial son. My mother, very old now, tells me this every time I return to my village. So whenever I am there, I sit before my father's altar where my mother has put a framed black-and-white photograph of him, taken the year before he died. I did insist on bringing a picture of my father and nailing it on the wall beside the painting of Confucius; this my wife did not protest. She said it was good of me to think of my father, for he gave me life. I should remember him, she said, not worship him.

Still, when I am alone in the house and it is dark inside, I think my father is watching my every movement. When I sit in my room without the radio or the television playing, I think I hear my father's sandaled footsteps on the floor. Sometimes it is only the sound of birds flapping past the window. Sometimes I go and kneel before my father's picture and seek his forgiveness.

I am driving my wife to the hospital to see Dr. Wu. The second time this week. He will stick a long needle into her side and inject her liver with a chemical that will cut off the blood feeding the abnormality. This is what he told her when he examined her last time.

In the car, my wife tells me that I need not accompany her to these appointments. She says, "It's no big deal, old man. I can take the bus."

"Nonsense," I say. "If I don't take care of you, who will?" But I smile to myself. She is having a good day. My wife hardly has the energy to argue with me these days. Most of the time, she sits quietly beside me and tries to not fall asleep.

Since my wife's been sick, the church folks have been coming to our house more often. They are a group of six or seven women whom my wife has known for years. Now that their children are in college, they have become bored housewives with nothing to do. When these women come over, they bring baskets of food and things like Christmas stockings they darned themselves. When my wife was well, they took tango lessons or knitting classes together.

These days, when I come home in the late afternoons, I often find them in my living room, kneeling on the floor with my wife in the center, their hands extending to touch a part of her body. It is "hands-on praying," my wife tells me, like Jesus touching the sick women in the Bible. I never complain about them because I know my wife needs them, but the women can sense my unease, I am sure, because before I can give them a proper greeting, they crowd the door, say good-bye, and thank my wife for her generous hospitality.

As I steer the car off the street and into the parking lot, she taps the window. "Watch out for the sidewalk!" she yells.

"I see it, I see it." It is no use to reassure her. She makes gasping sounds as the car turns. "See? I saw the sidewalk and I made sure the wheels were far away from the curb and we're both in one piece." I park the car, turn off the ignition, and sigh with exaggerated relief.

My wife shakes her head as she gets out of the car, leaving me to slam her door for her. "There may be nothing wrong with your eyes, old man, but there's something wrong with your head!"

Inside the hospital, I wait in the empty corridor. I sit alone on a bench outside the examination room, where the doctor told me I could not go in. There is a copy of today's newspaper on one of the chairs and I take out the sports section. The Taipei City Little League has won their third game. The team is bound to sweep the series.

I look at my watch. It has only been ten minutes.

My wife likes her new doctor. Dr. Wu. He is tall and slender, too skinny, I think, with large hands and a soft voice. Whenever she sees him, she pats his arm and says things like, "Oh, you're not eating well enough. Your face is pale." She says he is a most handsome young man, and tells him that if she had a daughter, she would give her to him.

My wife likes to talk like that, about children we never had.

A few years after we left the village, when it was clear that my wife could not conceive, she went from one doctor to another. Every one of them diagnosed a different ailment, prescribed a different cure. What made things worse was the family renting the apartment upstairs. The family had two children, and every evening we could hear them come home from school and play. The pounding of their feet on our ceiling as they ran, the bouncing of a ball, or the noise of an electric train shooting down the hallway. Sometimes we could even hear jump roping, the slap of a rope followed by a heavy landing. I would turn on the radio or television to block out the sound of their playing. It was a relief to us when they moved away.

My wife began to buy herbs from Taoist temples too, which her father severely disapproved of. She would bring home a bundle of neatly wrapped packages tied together with strings and set them before her on the desk in the study. She would read the Bible and pray as she always did, but then she would put her hand on the package and say, "Lord, if it pleases you, let me drink this and be well." She cooked the herbs with water in a hefty clay pot over a low fire. Afterward, she forced down the dark brown concoction in three large gulps, and, making a bitter face, she would pat her flat stomach and say, "That should do it."

It went on like this for months, for years. And the only reprieve she could find were the moments she had to herself in the study. There were times when I heard her sobbing through the door, and I could only stand outside and comfort myself with the idea that the storm would soon blow over, that she couldn't possibly carry on like that forever. When she came out, I would busy myself with the newspaper or listen to a game on the radio, pretending not to notice her tear-ravaged face.

After her first unsuccessful tries, I no longer hoped. But things were easier for me. Every morning, I woke up at five-thirty and rode the bus to the dock for work at seven. I was employed by my uncle's shipping company, where I am now a manager; I have worked there since I moved to the city with my wife. I supervised the cargo going on and off the ships, hired or fired workers, and gave men their wages. During our breaks, the men and I would hit rocks with small planks we found along the dock, pretending we were hitting home runs. Those days, baseball was already a popular game. And Jiang or Lou-Lou would tell me about their boys trying out for the Little League, how they were catching the fever as well. At four, I washed myself in the communal shower outside and picked up a fresh trout or two, or, for special occasions, a shark fillet, before I went home.

It was harder on my wife that we never had children. She stayed home all day with an occasional visitor, a neighbor or a friend, as her companion. But mostly she was alone. When I came home and saw bloodshot, swollen eyes, I knew that she was losing the battle that day. But she would not say what bothered her, as if telling me meant the worst kind of betrayal, and my wife would never be disloyal to her God.

Her faith was a frightening thing. She knew no boundaries, and she would have kept on seeking more remedies if I hadn't put a stop to it. It was the first day of the typhoon season, well past dinnertime. On the radio, the news broadcasters said that the streets were beginning to flood and some power lines were taken out by trees that had been felled by the wind. I had been home for hours, waiting anxiously for her, thinking that she had been robbed or molested in the streets or hit by a car. Then she came home, soaked to her bones and shivering uncontrollably as she put away her umbrella. I ran to the front door and demanded where she had been.

"Getting my medicine, of course," she said, blinking at me.

I lost my temper then. I slapped her, just once, but it threw her back several steps. When I raised my hand again, she was too stunned to move away, and the look of utter surprise on her face gave me pause. She was remembering my mother, I thought. I lowered my trembling arm, as dumbstruck as she was. I watched her warily, trying to guess what she would do next, where she would run to. Then she did the oddest thing. She came back to me. When she began to cry, she stumbled toward me and burrowed her face against my chest, like a child seeking comfort. I was so relieved I thought I would fall to my knees, but I touched her wet hair instead and combed my hand through it.

"I don't want a baby," I rasped against her cold forehead. "It doesn't matter to me. Not one bit."

"But your mother," she said, her face still buried in my sweater.

"I'll talk to her," I promised. "I'll make sure she understands that we did everything."

"She's going to tell you that I'm cursed."

"Wife, she already thinks you are cursed."

That night, we lay side by side on the bed, not touching.

"I just don't understand," she murmured.

I shifted to my side to face her. She was staring blankly at the ceiling. "What?" I prodded.

"Why I can't have a baby. I pray day and night. I confess all my sins. I do good things for others. What am I doing wrong?"

Then she turned to me, piercing me with her confusion and disappointment. "Maybe it's me," I told her. "Maybe I am what's wrong." I knew I should stop then, but I couldn't. "Maybe he knows I wouldn't be a good father. Maybe he's punishing me."

"Hmmm," was all she said. Then she reached over and turned off the lights.

The doorbell rings. My wife shuffles to the door in her slippers. It is the new seminary student from church, and my wife has been expecting him since six o'clock. She has dinner laid out on the table. When I picked her up from church last Sunday, she asked me if the boy, Jun-nan, could come to our house. It was usual, she said, for seminary students to pay house visits. It is a part of their training, she said. Then two days ago she told me she also invited him over for dinner.

I was flipping through the newspaper in the living room. She was putting on an apron in the kitchen, having decided that she was feeling well enough to make dinner. "What?" I called out. "You did what?"

"I invited him for dinner, too."

I put the paper down. "Why'd you do that for?"

She stuck her head into the room. "He is living by himself. I can't bear to let him eat at some stand on the street before coming here. The least I can do is feed him."

She smiled very hard at me. I didn't believe a word she said. She has pulled tricks like this before. "Fine," I said, returning to my paper. "Invite the whole church if you want."

This entire day, my wife chattered endlessly about him. Jun-nan this, Jun-nan that. His name means "handsome male," and all the school girls from church flock around him. Now I hear the boy in my living room, saying that something smells very nice.

I look at myself in the mirror above the dresser. My tie is still crooked, so I jerk it off and decide to go without it. I'll see how handsome he is, I say to myself. Then I sit on the bed and wait to be called. I don't want him thinking I am happy about any of this.

"Husband! Husband!" My wife is giddy with delight. "Old man! Jun-nan is here."

"Oh, it's quite all right, Mrs. Liao," the boy says. "I don't mind waiting."

Finally, to save myself the embarrassment of having my wife drag me out by the ear, I stroll into the living room with my hands deep in my pockets. It is all I can do to keep myself from whistling. The boy is standing before my father's picture, studying it very closely. He is tall, and when he turns around, I am surprised to see that he is no boy at all but a young man. Perched on his straight nose is a pair of scholarly black-rimmed glasses. His shoulders are broad, thick, well muscled. An athlete. He is perhaps twenty-seven, no more than thirty. When my wife told me that he was a student, I thought she had meant that he was around the college age.

I nod at him, then turn to my wife. "Let's eat."

Like a nervous hen, she ushers him to the round table where she lifts the lids off of the entrée dishes. When we are seated, she expertly points to each dish with her chopstick. "This is sautéed eggplant, and that's *ma-po* tofu, my own special recipe, and the skewered chicken, also my own—"

"—From Big Wong's Grill down the street," I blurt out.

My wife is aghast. She slaps her chopsticks on the table. "Old man!"

Jun-nan tries to stifle his laughter. When my wife turns to him with a big smile, he pulls himself together.

My wife, thick-skinned as she is, doesn't give up. "Well, if I did make it, it would be exactly like this."

He nods solemnly, his gaze never wavering from hers. "Oh, I'm sure it would, Mrs. Liao."

I reach for the eggplants, but my wife clears her throat. She usually blesses the food by herself before I come to the table, but for the sake of appearances, I know she is going to make me wait. My wife and Jun-nan, the two conspirators, hold hands across the table while Jun-nan says a prayer. I sit there, staring stupidly at the steam rising from the soup, thinking that all this good food is going to be cold before they're done.

As we eat, my wife tries to engage me in a conversation with Jun-nan, but I remain silent, making it clear that I am only here to clean my plate and be on my way. But the young man has a healthy appetite, too. He eats my wife's cooking the way I do: like it's his last meal.

"You are not married, no?" my wife inquires. "No girlfriend?"

He laughs uneasily and chews on another piece of Big Wong's chicken. "My mother wants me to go see a matchmaker. I told her it's a bad idea. I want a Christian girl, someone to serve the church with me."

"I met Mr. Liao through a matchmaker."

He looks back and forth between me and my wife. "Really?"

"I'm not recommending it, mind you. It was a very rash thing for me to do at the time, but we didn't turn out so bad, did we, old man?"

On our way home from the hospital, where Dr. Wu told me that the injections haven't been working and the abnormality is growing— no longer two lima beans but three and a half—my wife says to me that she is very lucky to have found such a good husband. God forgave her, she says, for rebelling against her father when she was young, for not marrying the boy her father had picked out for her and going to a matchmaker instead. "I'm a blessed woman," she says.

I have heard this before, and I know what is coming.

"Church is having an Easter service this Sunday," she says, her finger tapping her purse to no particular tempo. "Easter service is—"

"I know what Easter is," I reply.

"Oh." She plays with her hands, which have become pale and thin. "It'll be nice. We always have a special program for Easter because Jesus was resurrected that day and—"

"Wife!"

She stops talking altogether, but I can see by the frown on her face that she is regrouping for another round.

I give in. "Okay. I'll go and listen to the singing. But that's it."

My compliance takes the wind out of her sails. "Oh." Then she brightens up. "What about the sermon? You know, you haven't gone to one since Pastor Kuo was here, and he's been gone for a year now."

Pastor Kuo. He was the one who pointed at me during his sermon and said, "Sinner! That's what we all are, sinners!" My wife tried to explain that Pastor Kuo didn't know who I was, and I just happened to sit right in front of the altar.

I take my eyes off the road to glance at her. I cannot deny her anything these days. "We'll see."

* * *

The church is packed. The children dress in pastel colors: the girls in pink and yellow dresses, the boys in slacks with baby-blue or purple bow ties. The men are dressed impressively in black suits and silk ties. Some women are wearing the Chinese *qi-pao* and their hair tucked up with butterfly pins, while others, like my wife, wear Western dresses. My wife wanted to wear her high heels, the ones she wore for tango lessons, but I made her take them off before she got into the car.

"I'm not picking you up if you fall in those," I said to her at the door, and, glaring at me, she kicked them off and replaced them with a pair of flats.

But nothing could dampen her spirits today. She clings to my arm as we walk into the church, which is decorated with bows and ribbons like one of those baby parties. She introduces me to everyone she sees, although they all know who I am. "This is my husband. Oh, you've been praying for him? Thank you. God bless you!" I do nothing but stand stiffly beside her and nod and bow to people as they comment on how beautiful my wife is today, how they almost forget that she is sick.

The usher leads us to the front of the room. I try to stagger behind to slip into a seat in the back, but my wife catches my hand and pulls me along with her. "Don't be so childish," she whispers.

I see Jun-nan standing near the podium, casually leaning against the wall. He is wearing a white shirt with a pair of black slacks, and he watches the throng file in through the front door. When he sees me, he waves. I return his greeting with a tight smile.

The orator approaches the podium alone. There will be a short sermon today, he announces, to make time for singing and the children's skit.

The sermon is brief, as promised, no more than ten minutes long. The pastor speaks earnestly about the empty grave, the disbelieving disciples. No one is listening. The women fan themselves with the programs, the men check their watches in agitation. Even my wife is slouched over, struggling to nod off sleep. I am the only one enjoying the story of Doubting Thomas. It is all fairy tale to me.

Then the skits begin. Onstage, the actors are the children I saw in their Sunday outfits earlier, but now they are dressed in ragged clothing and fake beards. Jun-nan hovers around the stage and tries to whisper stage directions to them. The children run about with their costumes falling around them, and a woman, someone's mother perhaps, tries to discreetly toss a mustache to a little boy. I laugh aloud, and my wife elbows me in my stomach. "This is serious!" she whispers vehemently. I shush her in return and look to the stage. I meet Jun-nan's gaze and I hold it. He is laughing too, his arms folded over his abdomen, his thick shoulders shaking with unsuppressed mirth, and for a brief moment, we share our joke in secret.

Right after the service, I take my wife to the car. I know by the way she leans her weight against me that the morning has tired her out. As we maneuver around the people standing in the aisle, I politely decline invitations to stay for cake and tea. By the time we get to the car, I am nearly carrying her. I pin her between my body and the car as I fish for the keys in my pocket, unlock the door, and then guide her into the passenger seat. She leans back and lets her head roll slightly to the side, like the first day when the doctor told me the bad news.

The traffic is light, the city still sleeping on this quiet Sunday morning. The importance of this day goes unnoticed.

"We'll be home in no time," I mumble. "Just hang on."

She says nothing.

"Should we go to the hospital, wife?"

Stirring, she traces the water spots on the window with her fingertips. "No, no, it's just a spell. I'll be fine."

When we get home, I carry her to our bedroom. I have never done that before, not even on our wedding day when she refused to let me carry her into my room. Though I told her I was strong, she was too embarrassed. Nothing has changed except that I am weaker now. The two of us are heavy, my legs threaten to crumble beneath me, and I am running to the bedroom with the fear that I will drop my wife on the floor.

She moans when I lay her down. "I'm so tired." She touches the top of my head. "Tired."

"Just sleep," I say to her, lifting her legs up on the bed, smoothing out the sheets. "Everything will be okay. Don't worry."

I wait for her to fall asleep like that, kneeling beside the bed, my forehead leaning against my fists, my elbows digging deep into the mattress. This must be what my wife feels when she prays on her knees. What does she say to her father, I wonder, and what does he say in reply? What magical spell does she cast to call his attention?

Then I bow my head. Father, if you love my wife as much as I do, you will save her.

I keep my head lowered, my eyes shut, my breathing still. But I hear no answer. Instead, I hear the sound of wooden sandals tapping on the floor. But I will him away. I will him away. Then I hear something else. Running feet, pattering softly across the house.

My wife wakes me in the early evening. She says in my ear, "Old man, it's almost time for dinner." For a minute, I forget that she is ill, and I lie still on my stomach and listen to the pots banging. The water rushing out of the faucet. Her slippers shuffling across the kitchen. The refrigerator opening and closing. Minutes later, the smell of garlic cooking in hot oil drifts into the room. I should get up. I should go help her. But I am content to stay in bed and burrow my face in the scent of her pillow.

Aaron Gwyn

❧

THE OFFERING

An image was before mine eyes, there was silence, and I heard a voice, saying, shall mortal man be more just than God? Shall a man be more pure than his maker? Behold, he put no trust in his servants, and his angels he charged with folly: how much less in them that dwell in houses of clay, whose foundation is in the dust, which are crushed before the moth? They are destroyed from morning to evening: they perish for ever without any regarding it. Doth not their excellency which is in them go away? They die, even without wisdom.

—Job 4:16-21

Her surgeon had explained the procedure would take five hours—one to make the incision and remove the lamina, another to extract the disk, three more to position the bone grafts, fasten the vertebrae with pins and screws. When Kathy began to awaken, struggle against the blur of vision and sound, she saw white brilliance and a ring of figures brightly clothed, supposing, at the age of fifty-one, she'd expired on the operating table and ascended to her reward. Warmth overcame her, and then elation, an assurance, as in those hymns she sang in church, that there was indeed a celestial paradise, and her voice, unparalleled in the congregations of Oklahoma, would attain its chosen place.

It was out of respect for this calling that she'd flatly refused her pastor and his prompting to think toward secular venues. She sang, she informed him, as a type of ministry, and a performance of Wagner or Strauss would jeopardize the one gift she could offer. Her husband and daughter argued against this, but now, as the bright forms encircling her grew clearer, she knew she had acted properly: her compensation would be great and the next face she saw, that of her Savior. Even as the notion suggested itself, a set of

161

kindly features emerged from the radiance and drew close, a voice speaking in calm and measured tones, telling her not to worry, that everything would be okay.

"Mrs. Olaf," it said, "you shouldn't try and talk."

But Kathy tried regardless, the smile that stretched the right half of her face beginning gradually to lower, the nurse providing details of her stroke.

What upon awakening had seemed five hours was, in truth, a month-long coma. During the laminectomy, Kathy's blood pressure had risen, and there was clotting just below her knee. The doctors had not understood what was happening until the anesthesia wore away and their patient lay unresponsive, her face vacant, eyes fixed to the wall. Through the years to follow, she would gather only the vaguest impressions of this time—a stretch in which dream bled to waking, color to speech, one afternoon a figure standing at the foot of the bed grasping her shin, asking could she feel this, and what about *now*?

But when Kathy did awaken, she did so fully, and the doctors were pleased to find that there was no damage to the brain, none to liver or kidney function, very little to the CNS. The left side of her body had been affected, but her recovery in this regard was just short of miraculous. A few days and she was drafting letters; within a week she was walking; after a month she was released from the hospital altogether. The stroke seemed now to involve only her larynx, her tongue and esophagus, and, most notably, her voice.

For the most part, Kathy was able to suppress the terror such an affliction might have caused. The doctors said, given her progress in other areas, she could expect the complete return of vocal ability, and, in the meantime, encouraged her to consult a speech therapist, which she did several times a week. Each morning she would awaken to find something else restored to her, another skill recovered. The left side of her face grew taut; she ceased to drag her foot; her penmanship continued to develop, then attained, almost, the precision of type. She kept pen and legal paper with her at all times, conversing, in this way, with her daughter and husband. Strangely, she found relationships with her family were strengthened, and, viewing it as a temporary state of affairs, Kathy began to experiment. She left mischievous notes on her husband's pillow, scribbled reminders to her daughter, scolding her for a chore left undone, sneaking Post-its into her cereal box or bag of chips. On weekends, she would sit at her desk and write long letters to her mother and sisters, receive replies just as lengthy, speaking of matters they had not been able to discuss. In many ways, the silence that she viewed as a thing to be overcome had fostered a peculiar kind of intimacy. Driving home from the market one day, she realized that the anxiety attacks that had once forced her to carry Valium seemed to have vanished.

And yet, there were nights she went to bed and an apprehension would vibrate in her chest, a flow of acid to her stomach, shortness of breath—the thought she might never again form words, let alone perform. She pushed this away, for the idea held a taint of blasphemy: she was chosen to bring song to the world, and this is what she would do; as long as she was alive, this is what she would offer. How could it even be otherwise?

Time passed. Eight months. Nine. Kathy awoke on a Monday morning with feeling in her tongue and throat. Her doctor removed the tube from her stomach through which she took food, and put her on a liquid diet, then on solids. She was able for the first time to swallow and chew. At the table one evening, just before dessert, the woman suddenly cleared her throat. There were a few moments of absolute silence, daughter and husband staring. They blinked several times, began slowly to clap.

Then came the one-year anniversary of her stroke, and, in a weekly meeting with her therapist, the man informed Kathy her speech might not return, insisted on her acceptance of that. She sat for a while, then nodded, went to her car and drove home. Walking inside, she stood a few minutes in the hallway, scanning the room—dining table and ottoman, recliner and venetian blinds, slats of sunlight dividing the carpet into a checkerwork of shadow. Her husband and daughter were not yet home, and there was, she noticed, a palpable silence, an absence that seemed to vacuum sound into it, to become, in some way, its negative. Blood rushed in her ears. Motes swirled in the afternoon light. When her husband pulled into the drive, Kathy was aware she had begun, after a fashion, to scream—hands clenched, nails cutting into her palms, no sound but the force of air across her teeth, the quiet hum of the refrigerator, the scarcely perceptible ticking of an antique clock.

She began to flood her environment with sound. There were the gospel tapes she played on her morning drive, the headphones in her office at work. She had a radio installed in the shower, a waterproof component that, on most days, was capable of nothing but static. Kathy listened to it regardless, steam beading the shower door, the water turned hot, aimed at her throat.

She became a compulsive watcher of television, she became a lover of malls. Even the Pentecostal church she had attended for the last twenty-seven years seemed far too quiet, the prayer service close to unbearable, and one night, unable to sleep, she saw a program wherein charismatics pranced in the aisles while a preacher stood singing above them, accompanied by an electric band. Kathy observed this with great attention. She fetched the remote from between two cushions, turned up the volume.

One afternoon, her husband—a squat man with thinning hair and glasses that slid incessantly down the bridge of his nose— arrived home late and, with a self-congratulatory smile, sat a cage in front of her, wrapped in silver paper, tied with a bow. Beside it was a smaller, rectangular package, likewise wrapped. Halfheartedly, Kathy reached from where she lay and undid the ribbon. Behind chrome bars, she saw a parrot—green and yellow—shifting from one leg to the other.

Kathy picked up her pen, scratched quickly at the tablet, held it toward Chris.

What the hell is that? it read.

"Parrot," her husband told her. "You can teach it to talk."

Kathy stared at him a moment. She wrote the word *How?*

Chris smiled. Pointed. "Open the other," he said.

She did so and discovered, inside a padded, cardboard box, a device roughly the size and shape of a book, though not nearly as thick. It was dark gray and had a speaker at one end. On its surface was a keypad, a small digital screen. Instinctively, Kathy moved a hand along its side, flipped a switch, and brought the screen to life, bright green letters asking her to enter a name.

"I got it at that store we went to," Chris said. "The one with the wheelchairs?"

Kathy sat staring at the mechanism. She looked up at her husband.

"It's called *a talker*. They make them for people who lose their voice." Chris sank both hands in his pockets, began to rattle change. "I know you're going to get everything back, but for right now, I thought it'd be nice not to have to write all the time."

Kathy forced her mouth into half a smile.

"Wouldn't it?"

She shrugged.

"Well," Chris said, sitting on the couch beside her, "they told me I could take it back if you don't want it. You might at least give it a shot."

Kathy looked back to the apparatus on her lap. She typed her name into the keypad, pressed firmly the button marked *enter*.

Ello, Kathy, the machine welcomed, metallic and harsh, a voice she'd almost come to expect.

Years later, Kathy would find it odd how quickly she came to prefer her machine to the tablet and pen. She had hesitated, at first, to even turn it on, to hear the device pronounce again those words and syllables that ought to have been coming from her. It found a place on the kitchen table beneath a stack of bills and flyers. One morning, she saw her daughter employing it as a coaster. There was a permanent ring on its display from her glass of orange juice.

It was the parrot that occasioned the machine's initial use. Kathy, after taking the week off, was lying on the couch, watching television and, from the corner of her eye, the bird rocking nervously on its perch. When the program went to commercial, Kathy hit the *mute* and turned her full attention to the parrot. She thought it peculiar the way the bird's eyes—glassy and dark—did not permit the expressiveness one associates with the eyes of a dog or cat. There was a vacancy to them, as if someone had taken a drill and bored holes in the creature's face.

Still watching the bird, she got up, walked quickly over, and retrieved the machine out from under the catalogues and Chinese menus. She brought it to the couch, sat down, flipped the switch at its side. When the screen came up, she typed a phrase and pressed *enter*.

The bird stared at her blankly, shifting its feet. It cocked its head to one side and let out a brief croak.

Kathy retyped her message; did so again; was still doing this when Chris entered from the garage, stood next to the piano, and quietly observed the proceedings. He had just opened his mouth to ask what she was doing when the bird, in guttural replication of the machine, uttered one of the words she'd been typing for close to an hour now. Kathy jerked her head toward her husband and smiled. She once again entered the phrase, and this time, the bird repeated it in full.

Over the next week, Kathy would work with the parrot an hour each day. It was the first progress she'd enjoyed in quite some time, and though she pondered the reasons God would bestow such a gift on the bird and not on her, she hoped to make a good showing. Perhaps, she thought, it was a test. Maybe she would be rewarded for her selflessness, for considering God's grandeur and not her own. It was with this in mind that she sat down one afternoon when her husband and daughter were out shopping, pulled the machine onto her lap, and typed *Jesus is Lord*.

The parrot did not hesitate. In a voice that resembled, to an alarming degree, the machine's, the bird spoke loudly back to her the name Jesus.

It was harsher-sounding than she would have liked, but Kathy was pleased with her success. Nodding excitedly to her pupil, she retyped the message.

The bird looked at her, craning its neck. "Jesus," it shrieked.

Kathy continued typing and the bird continued repeating the name. She had been able to accomplish *Pretty bird,* and *Who's that,* and even *Chris and Kathy,* but for some reason, the parrot would not consent to follow *Jesus* with anything but the slight shuffling of its feet.

Kathy tried for a few more hours, but could get nothing else from the bird, and by the time her husband and daughter arrived, she was weary to the point of tears. She stood, walked over to Chris, and put her arms around him.

"Hey," her husband asked, "are you all right?"

"Jesus," the bird interrupted.

Chris turned to look at the cage. The parrot rocked on its perch. "Jesus," it screeched.

"When did you teach it to do that?" said Chris.

Kathy shook her head, made several indecipherable gestures.

Her husband laughed nervously. "Sounds like it's cursing. Like it dropped a hammer on its foot."

Their daughter, a pale-skinned teenager with a shapeless body and eyes that resembled, in many ways, the bird's, went to the cage, stuck a finger in between the bars, and attempted to stroke the creature's head. The bird inched to the far side of its perch, flapped, several times, its wings. "Jesus," it said, and with that, sank its beak into the young woman's hand.

The parrot continued its blasphemous monologue through dinner, and intermittently over the course of the evening, and that night even when they put the sheet over its cage and turned out the lights, its metallic voice would cry out, muffled a bit, but piercing nonetheless. The bird had just seemed to calm itself, and Chris was on the edge of dozing, when his wife broke down and began to cry hysterically. He eased over, took her head upon his shoulder, and held it against his chest, beginning to whisper. But try as he might, the woman did not seem receptive to comfort, and eventually he began to grow upset himself. He scooted slowly back to his side of the bed and lay there, listening to her weep.

"Kathy," he said, after a while, "you need to get ahold of yourself."

But Kathy didn't seem capable of this, and the suggestion only caused her to sob louder. Chris closed his eyes and tried to sleep. The bed began to tremble. Without the use of her voice, the noise sounded as if someone were attempting to strangle her.

"Really, now," he told his wife. "That's not going to help."

"Jesus," said the bird.

She decided, in the days following, she would have to make a stand. No more lying on the sofa cradling the remote, having her husband call work at the last minute, telling them she'd not be able to make it. She had the impression she was beginning to sink, that if she closed her eyes, the recliner would make its way gradually through the floor. It was time, she thought, to stop feeling sorry for herself. It was time to engage with life. She felt like the curator of a forgotten museum, walking corridors and silent halls, occasionally dusting a sculpture, stooping to polish a fingerprint from glass, quiet caretaker scanning obsessively her collection, waiting for the day she would be replaced.

She started by returning to the gym, two hours a day, three on weekends. She did treadmill and weights, swam, and tried step aerobics. Her back had begun to ache once more, but the exercise seemed to help this, and her mood improved greatly as a result of being on fewer pain pills. In the evenings, she and her husband would go to movies—something she'd rarely done since her daughter had been born—or just stay home and discuss the day's proceedings. She had gone back to using the tablet, and it seemed more natural somehow, allowing her to articulate herself with precision. In support, her husband bought a notebook as well, and most of the time they would conduct their exchanges purely in writing. He claimed he felt guilty speaking.

"Besides," he told her, "I enjoy the quiet."

And yet, despite the fact she'd recovered her morale, despite the improvement in her relationships, Kathy was increasingly plagued by the desire to perform. She could avoid the feeling for several days, and then she would hear a song on the way to work, see a singer on TV or at church, and there would be a sudden throbbing at the back of her skull, a sensation she would have to clench her teeth to avoid. It was not, Kathy would admit, that she was no longer able to minister. Neither was it about being praised, a sense of accomplishment. She came to understand that in singing, she made a profoundly human connection: an audience's approval signified validation, an acceptance of her into their community. It was only in that instant of being recognized, in being appreciated and her talent understood, that she could be, in any way, spiritual. It was her primary link to something larger, her only proof of the divine.

At the start of the next week, she met her pastor at his office. In times past, the man had been her biggest supporter, someone who had encouraged her to pursue singing as a career. After they'd exchanged pleasantries, and she had scribbled answers to questions about her health, Kathy slid a note across the desk that expressed her desire to begin, once more, performing.

The pastor—a large man with graying hair and thick unstylish glasses—gave her a kind, confused look.

"Exactly what," he asked, "do you mean?"

She slid another note across, saying she had something in mind.

"What kind of *something*?"

Again, there came another note, telling him it was a surprise.

Kathy would never decide if it was mere pity on his part—or perhaps a vague desire to exploit the situation, to present this woman as someone who, despite her hardships, refused to be silenced, would express her thanksgiving even if she had to do so with sign language—but by the time she left his office, the Reverend Hassler had agreed with reluctance that a week from the following Sunday, he would introduce her just before his sermon, provide whatever accompaniment she required. She told him she would need someone on the piano, that she would be in touch regarding which song. The man told her he would be more than happy to assist.

Over the next two weeks, Kathy devoted several hours a day to practice. Her husband and daughter agreed, during this time, to remain in the living room, to make sure the television's volume was loud enough they could hear nothing of her rehearsal. When, out of utter curiosity, Chris asked what it was she'd planned, Kathy smiled broadly and indicated that the secret nature of the enterprise would cause him to be all the more impressed when the day of her performance came.

He shook his head and told her he was impressed already. After all, it had been weeks since she'd broken into tears, and the parrot, having kept them awake several nights with its outbursts, seemed to have forgotten its new vocabulary altogether.

The first Sunday of April was hot and bright, Oklahoma springtime, already humid. Kathy stood in the mirror, adjusting pearls on her neck, her earrings and collar. Though her face had tightened a good deal since the stroke, she could still detect a slackness. She put a hand to her cheek, pulled the skin to achieve a tautness proper to her age, pulled more, hoping, in this way, to see back through the years. There was forty-two, and, stretching further, there was her thirties—this was how she looked at nineteen. She let go her face and stepped backward. Taking up a large purse, she put an arm through its strap and turned to leave.

Her nerves were such that on the way to service she drummed her fingers in continuous motion on the armrest. At one point, she glanced over and caught her husband smiling. He reached, put a hand to her knee, and gave a gentle squeeze. In the backseat, their daughter asked if she could go to a friend's house for lunch.

By the time they arrived at the First Pentecostal, Kathy had fully installed herself in the mind-set of performance, a curiously numb state wherein she felt her muscles begin to contract, a means she'd

devised of keeping anxiety at bay, failure from drifting into her
thoughts. The family made their way through a barrage of hand-
shakes and hellos, went to the sanctuary's far right, and seated
themselves at the front. Smoothing her dress beneath her, Kathy
caught sight of the pastor sitting upon the platform. The man
glanced over and cast an inquisitive look with slightly raised eyebrows that seemed to ask whether or not he was to go through with
the plan as they'd discussed it, two days before. Kathy stared at him
for a moment, then nodded.

She would never be able to recall the first part of that morning's
service, though she knew the ceremony by rote—the ritual of
hymns and offering, sermon and announcements. It had not been
altered for as long as she'd been a member, and it suddenly
occurred to her that what she and the pastor had planned would
constitute an extraordinary moment in the church's history. When
the man left his seat and approached the podium, Kathy's attention
snapped to, the anxiety once again present. She raised a fist to her
mouth and forced a cough.

"Brothers and sisters," the reverend began, "most all of you
know Kathy Olaf, and you also know the incredible trials she and
her family have endured through the course of this last year. Kathy
has been with us for two decades, and she's performed more solos
than I can remember. When we learned of her stroke—when I
learned of it, at least—I knew we'd lost something special. I think,
for many of us, it was one of those times that I spoke about last
Sunday, one of those times when even those of us with great faith
start to question things. I know I did."

The man paused, let his gaze sweep the congregation. Kathy
watched intently, pleased with where this introduction was headed.
She shifted in her seat, brought her purse onto her lap, and looked
inside.

"But," the man resumed, "we have a real treat for you this morning. Kathy approached me a few weeks ago, expressed how badly
she wished to continue her ministry of song. And when I heard
how she was planning to do this, I can't tell you how I felt. I guess,

at that moment, I realized not only our sister's dedication, but that her willingness to serve God and her refusal to accept defeat would continue to bring blessing to this church, perhaps even more than it did before her sickness. It gives me real pleasure to introduce Kathy Olaf to you, and to announce a new era in her service of the Lord."

Kathy rose from her seat and was met with a roar of applause. It continued as she climbed onto the platform and stepped to the pulpit, as she brought the microphone to a position almost touching the lectern's surface. Even when she stood there motionless, smiling and raising a hand to the audience, it took a full minute to die. She reached into her purse, removed the machine her husband had bought her, and slid it between the podium and microphone. At that moment, understanding her intentions, the congregation began to applaud once more, some to whistle and cry out. When, finally, they had settled, she glanced to the pastor sitting behind the piano, and motioned that she was ready. He began to play the intro, cautiously striking each note as if he were drawing the rhythm behind him on a string. Kathy nodded once or twice, and then started rapidly to type.

She had chosen an older hymn, part of her repertoire from the days when she'd first begun to perform. She pecked out the opening verse, scarcely hearing the sound she made, or even looking to see the crowd's reaction. *I come to the garden,* she typed, *while the dew is still on the roses. And the voice I hear, falling on my ear, the Son of God discloses.* Kathy had practiced many hours just to get to the point where she could make the machine keep tempo, and, since she had no control over its pitch or tone, this was where she devoted her attention. As she worked her way through the lines, that feeling which was now a part of memory began steadily to return; for an instant she was transported, forgetting she had been the victim of a stroke. It was ecstatic—a sense of being controlled by something from outside, of herself being the machine upon which another force was typing. She had never before felt so like an instrument.

When the song turned to the chorus, she took her eyes from the keypad, glanced briefly up. She was smiling, but the expression was soon to fade. All around the sanctuary, people were wincing, sitting with heads lowered, faces plastered with agonized smiles. It was then that Kathy heard the noise she'd been making—*He walks with me and He talks with me and He tells me I am His own*—noticing, for the first time, how the PA amplified the metallic speech, changed its pitch, added a slightly guttural distortion. She'd never found the tone pleasant, but had, after a while, grown used to it. Now she heard it as a sound completely alien, as if her illness had discovered its perfect articulation, an ideal voice.

Kathy began the second verse, trying to focus on the performance, on the idea that her attempt alone was important, that this is what would astound. Her fingers began to feel like they were operating independently of her body, each digit under separate command. She knew she was falling behind, losing rhythm and her place in the song. *The sound of His voice,* she hurriedly typed, *is so sweet the birds hush their singing.* She tried to start the next line, but at this moment her hands seemed to lock, the muscles to freeze. She stopped in midstroke, her fingers balanced over the keys, lifeless almost, as if afflicted with palsy. Drawing them into fists, she blinked several times, and then looked toward Reverend Hassler, abruptly aware that he too had stopped playing. When she glanced back to the audience, she saw her husband and daughter were staring at the floor.

In a matter of seconds, the crowd would begin sympathetically to clap, their applause rising louder as they attempted to drown the note of humiliation that somehow lingered, sustained by the burgundy carpet and curtains, the padded pews and offering plates. Kathy knew that this would come, that soon the disaster would be pardoned, smoothed over, utterly forgotten. She knew that people would extol her courage, congratulate the performance as an obvious success, perhaps even, one day, ask her to repeat it. But now she looked out over the heads of these churchgoers, not only hearing, but, in actuality, *feeling* the silence, noting it as a palpable, even substantial entity, a concrete and sentient force.

It was this, more than her illness or embarrassment, that she found terrifying. That sense of quiet which seemed to turn the congregation sitting before her into an enormous painting, she the lone visitor to some museum where humanity was framed, placed under glass, hung in perpetuity. Or, maybe she was the canvas. Perhaps it was her on the other side of the velvet rope, watching as tourists walked continually past. *Kathy Olaf,* read the small brass plate, people nodding to partners and stroking their beards before moving to the next installation, leaving only the silence, wide and infinite— miles of it, centuries. It wasn't calm or tranquillity, the peace that an irksome voice encouraged her to be mindful of, let grow and develop, even welcome. For Kathy, it was merely silence—a quiet that would remain undisturbed until that day she heard the click of the curator's heels, impeccable suit and tie, flashlight in his grip. He would arrive one afternoon with his assistants, pace the room and then pause, turning his beam squarely on the glass behind which she stood. Without further consideration, he would speak to the helpers, or even lift a hand and point, his voice quiet as a whisper, saying, *That one: take it down.*

Lin Enger

❧

Buffalo Dreams

On the edge of the dry slough below the back pasture, the animal lay half asleep and panting, sweeping his footlong, purplish-pink tongue across the fragment of salt block that had rolled down here in the spring. He was old and blind. He was missing one black horn. Eight years before, on the afternoon the western Sioux obliterated the Seventh Cavalry, he was grazing with his harem beneath the Rosebuds east of the Little Big Horn, felt the screams like a tickle in his ears, heard the popping guns, and urged his cows to move on. Now he lifted his black nose to test the air and got a strong scent—freshwater, from underground. His thirst told him, *Get up,* and the muscles in his haunches tensed and trembled. Then relaxed. He dropped his head. Lodged tightly between fourth and fifth vertebrae was the mushroomed bullet that had failed to knock him down last fall, when the hide hunter perched on top of a Northern Pacific railcar outside of Glendive, Montana, had tried to take him at two hundred yards. From there he'd moved east, away from the hunters who were shooting it up in their last money year. His wound healed, but the bullet was slowly having its way, squeezing off the nerves to his left hind leg. By late February he'd crossed the Missouri south of Mandan. By June he'd entered a country dotted sparsely with shacks and dugouts and sod huts, where great squares of prairie grass were all plowed under.

Now, in fall, he moved a half mile or so a day, no more, stumbling after his great old water-smelling nose, from river to slough to creek to hand-dug well.

His ears pricked up at a sudden sharp striking sound, and he swung his monumental head to the north, where the noise came from, steadily now—but of course he couldn't see over the top of the near rise, beyond which a man in a stained woolen shirt sat on the edge of a kitchen chair in the shade of his sod house, leaning forward and working with hammer and chisel on a small block of oak. Every time the man breathed out, a white burst of steam flowered.

It was seven in the morning. The hens had been robbed of their eggs, the four hogs slopped, the oxen turned out to pasture. This time a week earlier Abel would have been throwing himself at all the work still left to finish before winter: the fall plowing, the new wooden barn waiting to rise from the pile of lumber for which he had paid fifteen dollars. This morning, however, he hadn't so much as glanced toward the additional five-acre piece he'd selected for potatoes next year, hadn't reminded Rough and Ready, his oxen, how lucky they were, getting out from under the sod before he did. Abel was so focused on his work that he didn't notice the old woman who had come up behind him.

As he leaned forward she could see the bare back of his neck, the sun wrinkles there, the unscrubbed dirt. His shoulders were wide, not bent yet from the plowing and lifting and digging and carrying, or from dragging himself through the heat and the devil-inspired cold. The patch on the seat of his pants was attached with a rough stitch that wouldn't hold for long. She cleared her throat. He kept pounding on the chisel, turning his head only slightly to say, "I hope you brought me something from that hot kitchen of yours, Fia."

"You can't smell it? Where's your nose?"

He put the hammer in his lap and turned all the way around to grin up at her. She held a covered plate beneath her large, well-trussed bosom. Her hair she'd pulled as usual into a hard gray bun. Her pure, winter-blue eyes seemed to see more than they had a right to see, and Abel thought, *She can't know.* Instantly he saw not Fia but his mother back home, those same blue eyes wrinkling up as she studied him, her firmly set lips not quite undermining the huge softness inside her, as she gave her head that small shake that told him she wanted to understand, but then twisted away, offering him, finally, her narrow, stooped back. More than a year he'd been gone from home, and it was her face alone Abel could still see, not that of his wife or infant son, his father or his brother. Only his mother—and the oranging pine house with the red-tile roof, the gray-roofed granary and barn, and the hills of pine trees that crept down to the very edge of each small field.

"Will you eat it, then, or should I take it back home?" said Fia.

Abel reached out and lifted the cloth from her plate of flatbrod. There was a little jar of apple butter, too. "You're trying to ruin me." He stood and took the plate from her hands, and set it on the only windowsill of his house.

The old woman aimed her square face toward Abel's stack of barn lumber, then looked down along her large nose at the block of oak Abel had been chiseling. "Important work, I suppose." She accepted the chair Abel offered and, frowning, watched him take the oak block for his seat. "You ought to be starting on the barn. Can't trust this weather to hold."

"I suppose I know what I'm doing," Abel said.

"You're carving on a piece of dead wood, man! Homesick, are you? Making yourself a little troll?"

"No, a hawk on a fence post. For my son."

Fia leaned forward, tipping her head to one side as she peered at Abel's face. She said, "He'll see the real thing soon enough, I should think, as soon as you're able to send for him—and his mother."

Abel only winked and reached out to pat her knotted red hands. "It's sweet relief, Fia, knowing there's somebody close by, worrying over me."

She slapped his hand away, groaned, and stood up from her chair. "Then don't listen to a mother," she said. She aimed a scorching glare at his smile, trying to burn it away, but soon gave up, clucked her tongue, and relented with a half-smile of her own. "Say," she said, "I guess you heard about the buffalo."

Abel hadn't.

"Axel Pedersen saw it moving this way along Hay Creek last night—or so he says. Axel might have been drunk. Said he got too close and it blew smoke and fire at him."

Abel shook his head. "Even west of the Missouri the herds are gone now. I've been looking at the papers. In July the hunters packed up and went home."

Fia shrugged and tilted her head in an easterly direction, toward her son's homestead. "Just so you know . . . Julius said to tell you that he has just the gun for the job." She lowered her voice. "He's always wanted to shoot a buffalo, you understand."

"So have I," said Abel.

Fia gave her hand a little flip, as if tossing away a plum pit. "And every other Norwegian farmer on the prairie. I'll tell my son you've got a gun of your own." She straightened her shoulders as if to leave. "It doesn't take long, does it, to forget where you came from," she said.

Abel laughed. He remembered the speaker some years ago who had come to his parish, a local man who'd gone to America and then returned, working for a shipping line. He'd spoken of high wages, as much sweet milk as you could drink, and land for the taking (no cotters there!)—land occupied only by a few scattered bands of peaceable Indians and black rivers of buffalo thirty miles wide. The subduing of the territory had already begun, the man had pointed out a bit grandly, and if you waited too long, you wouldn't be a part of it.

"Fia," Abel said, rising. She had turned to go, but now turned back and stepped toward Abel, the entire blue world in her eyes—and of course his mother there, too, her lovely weathered face, in spite of the fact that she'd denied him it, turning her narrow back as he left for Kristiania with his trunk on a cart. Did she know that refusing to let him see her face then would cause him to see it everywhere now? In the sooty lamp glass? In the glaze of grease that lined his skillet? Even once, last night, in the amber three-quarter moon?

"Abel? What is it?"

"Fia, you tell Julius I'll give a shout for him, if I see that buffalo."

She frowned and looked over again at the pile of lumber, dampened her pale lips, closed her eyes. She made a little sound in her throat. "You're leaving, aren't you," she said. She looked down at the piece of oak. "And making that thing to take back home."

Abel sat down and breathed in the air, realized the day was going to warm up. Indian summer, they called it here. "Julius has eyes for this piece of mine, anyway, doesn't he?"

"Julius—puh! Julius has eyes for everything. When did you give up, Abel? Your wheat turned out fine. Your animals, they're healthy. I know it must be hard, alone out here, missing your wife, but I thought by now you must be almost ready to send for them."

Abel shrugged. He'd left Petra only months after their wedding, one week after their son was born, and though he'd missed them a great deal at the beginning, and worried about them, the more their images faded, the less he doubted the years of work and love they would have. They had become, almost, objects of his faith, like God. He had saved enough now for an ocean passage and the train, but he'd decided to use the money to pay for his own trip home. He couldn't recall making the decision, only becoming aware in the last week that he'd made it.

A quick shadow passed across Abel's face, a hawk gliding at mid-height above the slough, its head swiveling as it watched something down there. Early to be out hunting, Abel thought.

"Why?" asked Fia. Slowly she sat back down in the chair and clasped her hands in her lap. Abel couldn't look into her face, but put his eyes instead on a point of sky just to her left.

"My mother," Abel said.

Fia patted her lips with her fingers, opened her mouth as if to say, Ah, but said nothing.

"My wife and son, I'll see them either way. They're mine—with land or without land."

"But what life can you give them without it?" asked Fia. She moved her face to the side, trying to catch Abel's eye.

Abel looked at his hands. He said, "If I do not go back, I'll never see my mother again." What he couldn't say was, if he didn't see her again—and he dearly wanted to—he was afraid his mother would never give him any peace.

"Your mother would want you to make a future for her grand-children," Fia said.

"My mother might want to know her grandchildren," said Abel, looking finally into the old woman's face. "As you will know yours."

After Fia had gone home, Abel walked down to the sod-wall barn to get a smaller chisel. Moving past the cow stall on his way to the tack room, which he'd put up as a lean-to on the barn's west side, he glanced out the glassless window in the sod and saw the buffalo. It stood just outside the cow yard and was leaning over the top of the fence to get at the water tank. The weight of its massive black head and neck bowed the uppermost plank. Abel cupped a hand behind his ear and listened to the sound of the animal drinking. He had never seen a buffalo, except in pictures, and what struck him were its hair and beard, the heavy, dark, long, dusty, tangled mess that reminded him of himself last spring, after four months stranded in his hut, burning twists of straw to keep his stove hot.

When the animal finally lifted its head and snorted water, Abel thought of sneaking back to the house for his rifle. Then he remembered what he'd said to Fia. Her son Julius, of course, was rooting himself here. He had resolved to stay. He deserved the buffalo. Its meat would last him the winter, and he could mount the head on a wall, tell the story to his neighbors and children. As Abel watched the animal drop its head back into the tank and slap its tufted tail against its bald, slim rump, he heard a horse gallop into the yard and a man shout, "Abel"—Jacob Hansen, his neighbor to the west, with a letter, no doubt, from town.

Abel crouched low and slipped quickly into the tack room. Hansen could talk the hair off a dog, and often when he brought mail from Ellendale, he stayed for the day. "Post from Norway," Hansen called, and Abel heard him coming toward the barn. From the yard, Hansen wouldn't see the buffalo, although by now it was surely on the run.

"Anybody home?" Abel heard Hansen stop in the barn's low doorway, grunt to himself, then walk off. A minute or two passed, and the horse trotted away. Abel went quickly to the barn window and was surprised to see the animal still there, still drinking from the tank. This time he noticed the gauntness in its hindquarters, the missing horn, the way it stood with one rear leg bent stiffly and lifted from the ground. It was time to go after Julius.

Hansen had stuck the letter between the door and its frame. It was from home—the same brown envelope—but immediately Abel saw that it was addressed in his father's hand. He went inside, sat at the table, and opened it cautiously. He read, "Dear Son," and stopped. His father had never written him before, had always called him by his given name. Abel had to take several deep breaths before he could read on: "I'm sorry to be writing with this news . . ."

He sat for a time without moving, until the square of sunlight passing through the open door had warmed his cold hands. Then he got up and reached under his bed for his rifle, an old Sharps .50 caliber single-shot for which he'd traded a bushel of potatoes. He took two heavy bullets from a coffee tin and went outside. The buffalo had moved a few yards away from the water tank, and Abel, staying downwind, walked to within forty feet of the animal, lifted his gun, and sighted down its barrel, trying to remember if the iron sights required a fine or a full bead.

The old bull stood with his head in the sky, his shovel-like nose questioning the wind, his eyes closed. He was getting the scent of

Fia's apple press a quarter mile away and dimly recalling a flavor he'd known just once, long ago—a green, biting flavor, riotous. His dead eyes saw a flash, and he found himself among his cows again, grazing in the shade of a wild orchard in autumn, apples covering the ground, his cows gorging themselves, crunching and moaning. He walked over to a low-hanging branch, set his teeth around an apple, and ripped it down.

Vu Tran

❧

MONSOON

Father Linh woke that morning from a dream of drowning water buffalo. He sat up in bed, his throat parched, and remembered fragments of the dream: hooves thrashing, a rainy darkness, the hulking forms of countless buffalo tumbling, floundering, in and out of water, and amid the thunder and rain, the bizarre sound of their drowning, like cats screaming. Father Linh tugged at an earlobe, blinked his eyes. It felt like evening in the room, though the wall clock read half past six. He poured himself a glass of water from the nightstand and chuckled at the thought of water buffalo wailing like cats. He passed gas beneath the sheets, smiling again as he imagined an exhalation of evil spirits from the night. Above him, rain galloped on the rooftop. How appropriate, he thought, finally noticing the morning storm at his windowsill.

Unbeknownst to the Father, the first rains of monsoon season had drenched the countryside overnight. Swirling currents overran the roads, engulfed rice paddies, flooded private gardens, seeped into houses beneath the front door. Had Father Linh only looked outside his window, he would have seen the willows and banana trees sagging in the courtyard and, beyond the iron gates, ropes of muddy water snaking their way downhill to the stream that skirted the neighborhood. It had only begun raining last night, and already

183

the stream was overflowing its banks, capable at this point of drowning any number of unlucky animals, water buffalo included.

But Father Linh did not mind the rain. For him, morning showers had the quality of a soothing song, and on this day, in particular, the musical play of water—of life, as it were—inspired him. Next week would mark his ten-year anniversary as pastor of this church, and for days now he had been working on a special homily for Sunday's Mass. Being the lone priest in a mostly Buddhist town, Father Linh felt great pride in the congregation's growth since his arrival. It was crucial, therefore, that his homily be a celebration, a stirring testimony, an affirmation. He had been known to move people to tears with the beauty of his sermons, and the thought now of doing so on Sunday gave him goose bumps. As he mumbled his morning prayers, two decades of the rosary, he wondered if last night's strange dream could offer any possible ideas.

A knock came at his door. Before he could respond, the house boy stuck his bushy head into the room: "Mrs. Phong just called, Father, and says you must come to her house immediately. It's an emergency."

"Someone die?"

"I don't know, but from the sound of her voice, I think it's something much worse."

"What's worse than dying?" said Father Linh with a grin.

When he stepped outside, a thunderous downpour greeted the Father. The church stood on an eminence of land that overlooked much of the surrounding neighborhood, and as he peered down at the houses lining the road, at the clusters of palm and banana trees, at the stretches of farmland in the distance, it seemed everything was sinking and fading under the haze of rain.

He descended the hill toward the Phong house, hunched under his umbrella as a steady stream of water lapped at his heels. This five-minute walk was going to drench him, and the thought of being wet so early in the morning made him sigh dramatically. He loved a rainy day, but preferred loving it indoors and in bed.

Someone was probably ill at the Phong house. Father Linh knew the family well, had baptized the twin girls, confirmed the oldest daughter, and long known how old and fragile the grandparents were, how apt they were to call on him even when nothing was wrong. Mr. and Mrs. Phong were especially fond of him, and as they were the richest rice farmers in town—and one of the few families with a phone—it was difficult for the Father to turn down their frequent invitations to dinner. Their generous contributions to the church were, if anything, an excuse to indulge them. But Father Linh was an uncommonly obliging priest. He had no siblings, and his own parents had passed on years ago, and so even though the townspeople sometimes exhausted him with their personal and domestic problems, he relished their trust and attention.

At the bottom of the hill, a large pool of water had flooded a dip in the road. Father Linh lifted the folds of his cassock and waded across the pool. For a moment, he saw himself as a stylish woman from some French painting, one hand holding an umbrella and the other lifting the hem of her dress. His feet and ankles were numb, but for a moment the chill felt pleasant. Looking back up the hill, at the church's towering steeple and cascading walls, at the small rectory where he lived, Father Linh reminded himself how good it was to have people to help at all.

A few bicycles glided past him on the road, their riders draped in plastic ponchos, and many of the houses still stood quietly with their doors and shutters closed. The Phong house, as he approached it, looked just as quiet, though its four stories and many windows gave it a deserted appearance.

Mrs. Phong met him at the door with a startled expression, her voice muffled by the hand across her mouth: "The boy, Father. It's the boy."

Father Linh stepped inside the dim and silent house, calmly wiped his brow and balding head. "What is it?"

"My only boy," she murmured, and closed the front doors hastily. "I always knew his strange ways would bring about misfortune. All that time he spends locked up in his room, scribbling away, talking to no one but himself—no wonder something like this has happened. Twenty years old and no interest in girls or playing soccer or anything else but those books, books, books. They're the fruit of all . . ." She spoke in intense whispers, as if to herself, and hurried the Father up the winding staircase. She appeared to be the only one awake in the household.

They reached the boy's room, a cove-like place on the topmost floor, and before entering, Mrs. Phong turned to the Father uncertainly. "It is bad enough he was born with a weak heart." She opened the door.

Inside the room, the rainstorm sounded louder, more violent, though it felt to the Father that he had stepped into a cube of silence. The first thing he noticed was the large puddle beneath the open window, then the empty bed, a tangle of sheets. He walked to the window and closed the glass shutters, and it was in turning around that he saw Bao Ninh on the wall.

The boy was awake, but looked unaware of anyone's presence, even his own. His body was fixed upon the far wall, two meters from the ground, at ease as though he were sitting on the edge of an invisible chair, knees out but his feet and back clinging to the bricks, with one arm outstretched like a wing and the other arched over his head as if in the act of scratching it. Frozen in this pose, the boy wore blue and white striped pajamas and the weary expression of a deep-sea diver.

Father Linh shuddered, fell back a few steps. He crossed himself and stuttered at the boy, "Mary, mother of God! What have you done?" He did not expect a response, and indeed Bao Ninh made no sign of having heard him.

Father Linh could feel Mrs. Phong's eyes on him, could feel the rising bubble of a question in her silence. He wanted her to say something so that by sound she might lessen the severity of what they were seeing. Anyone's voice, in fact, would have been welcomed, for his own was presently lost.

The oldest daughter was the first to come. She wandered into the room and muttered sleepily, "I heard something," but when she saw her mother standing wide-eyed, saw her priest backed up against the wall, his palms flat on the bricks, and then saw her brother on the wall, her scream was as loud as the crack of thunder that followed.

One by one, the rest of the family rushed into the room: the father, the grandmother, the grandfather, the impish twin sisters. Flustered by the sudden excitement, their faces demanded answers: *Who screamed?*—*What's wrong?*—*Why is the floor so wet?* But then a gesture toward the wall directed their eyes, and a string of gasps filled the room, a look of terror, a look of grief, a look of shock and disbelief; and once everyone was present and awake enough to see it was no dream, each face turned to the other for something to say.

Finally, Mr. Phong spoke: "Someone come help me find my ax and a pair of scissors." He ran from the room.

"Is he in pain?" said the sister.

"We should go fetch Father Linh," cried the grandmother.

"We should go fetch the Pope," cried the grandfather.

"The Father is here," Mrs. Phong said.

"Who glued Bao Ninh to the wall?" asked one of the twins.

"Did he get up there by himself?" asked the other twin, who then added, "Is he evil now?"

"We need Father Linh, I say," the grandmother cried. "He'll explain all this."

"The Father is right here, Mother."

"Oh, well, good morning, Father. I didn't see you standing there."

Mr. Phong came rushing into the room with an ax and a pair of scissors.

"What are you doing?" demanded his wife. "Let the Father handle this."

"Woman, this isn't Fátima. Why bring God into this when I can just as easily get the boy down myself . . ." With that, he leapt onto a chair and started pulling at his son's feet, which did not budge. He then went for the arms, but they, too, were immovable. When he started cutting into Bao Ninh's pajamas, he quickly discovered that both the boy's shirt and his skin were stuck to the wall. So as the women averted their eyes, he lifted the ax and swung at the bricks. A small crack appeared. He bit his lip and growled, "If I can't pull him off the wall, I'll pull the wall off him." He swung the ax again.

Bao Ninh paid him no attention, hardly even flinched. Though his hair clung to the wall, his head was free, and he now peered down at his body, and for the first time seemed to consider his dilemma. The window had crept open again, and the world outside erupted in a thunderclap as his father knocked down a small chunk of the wall.

Father Linh, as if awakened by the thunder and the chaos of voices in the room, finally roared: "Do you expect to carve him off the wall? Tearing down this house will not help anything!"

Mr. Phong stopped in midswing and looked over his shoulder. It was always rather startling when Father Linh raised his voice, especially since such intensity seemed unbefitting a face so apt to smile, so round and calm—the wide, porcine nose, the thin eyebrows, a pair of eyes as quiet as the voice he almost always used. Mr. Phong's ax fell to his side, and with reluctance, perhaps even some embarrassment, he stepped down from the chair.

The room fell silent again as everyone waited for either the Father or Bao Ninh to speak. The boy coughed awkwardly, then murmured, "Someone please hurry and get me a bucket to piss in."

Father Linh waved everyone out of the room. Mrs. Phong returned with a metal bucket and helped her son relieve himself, and then, with a backward glance at the Father, she closed the door behind her.

Alone at last with the boy, Father Linh felt a chill invade the room. His voice, he hoped, was calm: "What happened here?"

Bao Ninh pondered the question beneath the tangle of hair that draped his brow. The boy had profound cheekbones, which seemed to narrow his already squinty eyes, and together they gave his face a puffy, almost stubborn appearance. Father Linh rarely saw or spoke to the boy, whether at church, around town, or here at the house when he visited, but he had long known the boy to be obsessively studious—"the pouting poet," as he was called by a few neighbors. At his first communion nine years ago, the boy, he remembered, brought along a book and fell asleep during the ceremony.

The Father was about to repeat himself when Bao Ninh spoke up, "Seems I woke up this morning and heard bells, Father. Tiny bells. And then I found myself up here." His voice was barely audible amid the clatter of rain. He was staring blankly at the floor, as though regarding a reflection of himself on the clay tiles, and for a moment Father Linh thought he was under some slumberous trance.

"Are you in pain?" the Father asked.

Bao Ninh shook his head, wiggled his fingers. "It almost feels like I'm lying down and you're the one on a wall."

Father Linh edged closer to the boy and reached for his hand, then thought better of it. He brought his own hands together and said, "Close your eyes, child, and we shall pray together."

But Bao Ninh continued staring, and after a moment finally turned to him, his eyes wide and luminous, as though he had just awakened and recognized who the Father was. His voice was unexpectedly loud: "I have not taken communion these last few Sundays, Father."

"I didn't mean to hear your confession just yet, child."

"I'm not confessing anything. I'm simply telling you that I no longer care."

"About what?"

"As of last night, I've decided to stop praying altogether."

"Stop praying? But why?"

"It's an empty obligation, Father. Merely wishful thinking, I say." The boy stopped and his brow furrowed slightly. He looked wide awake now. "I've memorized these words and repeated them in my head since I was a boy; I could recite them now in a boxing match if I had to. There's no integrity in that, is there? And I'm usually thinking of other things, anyway, like the book I'm reading or what I'll be doing tomorrow. Before bed, I sometimes say my prayers while I go to the toilet, just to get them out of the way."

"And you use the same hand to cross yourself?"

"On many occasions, Father."

"Well, that's just . . . you should be ashamed."

"I've also decided guilt is not a good reason to pray either."

"Now, don't be foolish, that's hardly the attitude. Be wary of where this will lead you." Father Linh heard his own voice quiver. He had a notion of making the boy blink somehow, though his harshest glare at the moment seemed rather ridiculous and futile. Their conversation suddenly felt absurd to him, the boy's indifference as bizarre as his exile on the wall. "Have you no fear?" he asked Bao Ninh.

"Fear of what?"

"Well, don't you realize prayers are for the grace of your *soul*?"

"I don't know what that is, and I'm afraid I've never felt it, or ever will. And you, Father, I doubt you've ever felt it either."

Father Linh considered this accusation and realized he had no personal proof to challenge it. He coughed loudly and reminded himself of the boy's present predicament. "So if not the grace of God," he said, "what *is* important to you now?"

Bao Ninh glanced at the mess of papers that cluttered his desk, at the bookshelves lining the walls of his room. "I have all I need in this room," he said.

"But that's it. Don't you see?" Father Linh looked around the room and crossed himself. "This is a sign. Look what has happened to you—"

"Yes. This." Again, the boy regarded himself. "I must say, this is quite strange. Perhaps it's a mere coincidence, Father. A cosmic blunder." He gave a luxurious sigh. "Or perhaps it is my fate, unexplainable but worth bearing."

Father Linh stared at him. "A vainglorious suggestion, child," he said quietly. The draft was making him shiver, and he went again to close the window. "So why have you told me all this? What do you want me to do?"

"Nothing, Father. Perhaps it *is* my one last confession to you."

The boy lifted his eyes to the ceiling and took a deep breath, as if breathing in the scent of the room, a scent (it appeared to the Father) of some naive and preposterous triumph.

"Father," Bao Ninh said. "Please don't speak of this to my family, especially my mother. I'm certain she wouldn't take this well."

"And what do you suggest I tell her?" the Father replied. He felt like scolding the boy, but then something cold in the boy's demeanor, a coldness in the air, in fact, made him inarticulate, made him want to flee the room. "I'll return tomorrow," he said, "and we shall talk then. Tonight, I *will* pray for you." And he walked out the door.

Downstairs, in the formal room where the windows were still closed and the front doors still locked, the Phong family stood about, arguing quietly.

"I don't want people coming in here and thinking my son's the devil," Mr. Phong said.

"Oh, but this could very well be a miracle," insisted the grandmother.

"Hanging on a wall doesn't sound like a miracle to me. I'm sure it's quite uncomfortable up there."

"Will he be able to sleep on the wall?" asked one of the twins.

The other twin said, "Maybe if we feed him a lot of food, he'll get heavy and slide off."

"Or maybe tomorrow morning we'll find him back in bed," suggested the sister.

"You're all being silly now," Mrs. Phong said. "This is a sign from God, I am sure of it. What it means we don't know. But the boy has his faith and so do we. All we can do is pray and leave it to Father Linh." She turned to the Father and nodded her head. "What did he say, Father? What happened? What should we do now?"

"I don't know," he answered, and avoided her eyes. Everyone in the family looked at him in silence, as if disappointed by his reply. Their quiet sincerity, their solemnity, was something he was unused to on his previous visits to the house. He led them in a quick prayer and promised he would return as soon as he could.

The rain was still raging outside, and on the way home Father Linh gave up on his umbrella and his sandals. Before long, his cassock was soaked and his feet caked with mud. He passed a rice paddy, now a pale green sea where children were swimming and screaming playfully. The Father felt too exhausted to warn them out of the waters. All at once, he was seized with bewilderment and pity, for the family, for the boy, but also an inexplicable outrage. It seemed to him that Bao Ninh had been speaking from the depths of some ludicrous dream, and had the Father not possessed a moral reserve of sympathy and hope, he would have believed the boy deserving of this strange affliction.

At the evening service that night, only half the normal parishioners attended. The Father's homily about familial honor and loyalty was one he had used five years ago, and tonight he recited it indifferently, for the rain, he knew, was drowning out his voice. Later in the night, after the church was emptied, after the cook, the housekeeper, and her two sons had left for their own homes, the Father sat alone in his room and tried to write his special sermon for next Sunday.

Words usually came easily to the Father; he fancied them the sword and scepter in his execution of the Lord's truth. Tonight, however, words eluded him. He managed to write one line—"The might and gift of the Lord lies in the Mystery of our devotion to Him"—but what else to include remained another mystery. For hours, he tried to incorporate anecdotes about his ten years here in town, the weddings he had performed, the funerals he had overseen, the illnesses and recoveries and triumphs he had witnessed. But in light of the events that morning, all these stories seemed insignificant to what now felt like the beginnings of a failure.

Outside, the rain fell about the house as though upon an ocean, and for a moment, perhaps the first time in his life, a tide of loneliness washed over the Father. He murmured his evening prayers, laid his head upon his desk, and, forgetting to pray for Bao Ninh, let the rain lull him to sleep.

When he returned to Bao Ninh's room the next morning, he found Mrs. Phong feeding the boy chicken porridge and his twin sisters

painting his toenails with nail polish. Bao Ninh ate his porridge
quietly and looked satisfied by their company, nodding and shaking
his head when his mother spoke to him. The room was alive with
music and voices. A record player sat on the desk playing old folk
songs, the volume turned high enough to be heard over the ongo-
ing storm. One twin was telling Bao Ninh ghost stories while the
other sang along with the songs on the record player. Spirals of
burning incense hung from the ceiling to keep the mosquitoes
away.

"I'm glad you've come to spend time with us, Father," Mrs.
Phong said. "Your presence, at least, is comforting." She hushed the
twins. "The girls were frightened at first, but now they can't stay
away from this room. We were all uncertain at first, too, but now
the entire family wants to keep Bao company. We've actually seen
more of him today and yesterday than we have all year. I suppose
coming in here makes things feel less terrible."

Father Linh nodded and sat on the bed.

Bao Ninh's sister soon came with needle and thread and sewed
the tear in her brother's pajamas, offering also to sew the small hole
in the chest of Father Linh's cassock, which had been there for
years. He kindly thanked her and said no. As he sat there on the
bed, he watched the women at Bao Ninh's feet, singing instead of
weeping, seeing to his every need like four maids before their king.

When Mrs. Phong and her daughter left, her husband entered
and greeted the Father with a bow. He stood looking at Bao Ninh
for a moment, as if contemplating another strategy, all the while his
right foot tapping in rhythm with the music. He left the room and
soon returned with a cleaver and a plate of mixed cement. Standing
on a chair, he patched the crack in the wall. He looked again at the
Father and said, "His mother is always right."

Before long, the grandmother and the grandfather joined them
in the room. They brought the Father coffee and cigarettes, and
began telling their grandson stories about their life, happy to have
the Father and the twins there to listen in. The grandmother talked
about her days in the convent as a little girl, how horribly mean the

nuns were—"No offense to you, Father"—and how much she missed her family when she was away. The grandfather spoke of his time in the war and, pulling down his pants, showed everyone the scar on his left buttock in the shape of a diamond—"Sat on a dead man's knife, I did." They talked on into the afternoon, invigorated by their own voices, by the strains of music and rain, until Father Linh was overcome by the opulence of his surroundings and the softness of Bao Ninh's bed, and remembered his own chambers back at the church.

The thought of returning home saddened him, struck him as a distance too far to travel, through so much rain, so much mud and silt, all the way home to a church and rectory pervaded by the echoes of prayer, where his housekeeper dusted the pews in silence, where her two sons whispered playfully as they hunted for mice, where the cook prepared his dinner in a kitchen lit by fireflies and a lamp older than she. Father Linh watched Bao Ninh on the wall, watched him staring at the window that had crept open again somehow, and realized at once the envy in his heart. For an instant, he wanted to linger in this house, in this room, and with this family for the rest of his life.

As the day progressed, the Father forgot about his duties at the church, forgot even his plans to call the bishop for assistance, the Pope perhaps if it would come to that. Bao Ninh's family continued frequenting the room, even had lunch and dinner together on the floor. There was no work to be done in this weather, and so it seemed the family brought their lives to the room: the sister her dresses to sew, the twins their toys, the grandparents their photographs from years and years past. Every few hours, the Father was asked to lead everyone in prayer, and it was during these times that he remembered the dilemma at hand, and his voice and will grew more fervent. He noticed that Bao Ninh, who told his mother that he would follow along in his head, had his eyes open during the prayers.

When evening approached and everyone gradually went off to bed, their departure, one by one, left the Father with a sense of impending solitude. When Mrs. Phong finally stood up to go, she beckoned the Father to her and whispered, "I have faith that this will be over soon. You must believe it, too." She smiled and left the room.

The Father was alone again with Bao Ninh, who was staring sadly at his bookshelves. He turned off the record player and stood quietly by the bed.

Finally he said, "I can tell from your eyes that you are not happy up there."

"Only because I must bear the boredom, Father."

"But can you bear the loss of your spirit?"

"My spirits have not yet left me."

"Oh, but the spirit of God—where is *that*?"

"I don't know, Father."

"This is what I fear." Father Linh pointed at the open window. "Take a look outside."

Boa Ninh was looking at Father Linh's finger. The priest dropped his arm. "Can't you see what has happened? Look through the window, and behold the coming flood. Don't you see you are the cause of this?"

"Me?"

"But of course. The Lord works in mysterious ways, and this, all that has happened, is His message to you. Pray with me, and things shall be rectified. Here. Now. We'll pray together."

"I can't do that, Father. Not in good conscience."

"Good conscience? You're stuck on a wall—don't you want to get off?"

"But I would only be pretending, Father. It would mean nothing. Besides, being up here on the wall has allowed me time to think."

"About what?" Father Linh waited.

Bao Ninh nodded at his desk and said, "Look there, Father, at that pile of papers. They are my poems. Hundreds of poems that I've struggled to write for years now, even in my sleep. They mean more to me than anything I know. And yet a week ago I was in despair, ready to throw them away, burn them all, until I realized that part of my struggle has been the presence of God's cold and grieving hand on my shoulder. But now I feel nothing there. Now everything is possible." And again he lifted his eyes to the ceiling. "One day I'll be the greatest poet this country has ever known."

"Not up there, you won't."

"But don't you understand, Father? What motivates life but our own selfish needs: desire, ambition, jealousy? Could it be my choice is the least selfish, the least sinful, of the three?"

"Ah, so that is it. The poet in you will save you as well? You'll break your mother's heart, you know. And your family, who loves you so."

"I believe I love them, too, Father. But in the end, an artist's only responsibility is to his art."

Father Linh grimaced. He remembered how sick the boy was years ago. It was his heart, they said, and at one point the family ordered his coffin and his grandmother prepared his clothes for the grave. Mrs. Phong came to the church every day for three months and prayed for an hour in the morning and for an hour in the evening. Father Linh wanted to remind Bao Ninh of all this, and was about to, but visions of death flickered in his mind. "And what of oblivion?" he declared soberly. "If there is no faith, there is only oblivion. Your art may outlive you, but will it help you bear the anguish of being outlived?"

Bao Ninh leaned his head against the arched arm and looked down at Father Linh. "I'm sorry, Father," he said. "But there is nothing I can do. Please, if you could, turn on the music before you leave."

"But listen, child—"

"The music, Father. Please."

As Father Linh departed, the music from Bao Ninh's room drifted in the air, followed him down the winding staircase, caressing his back and curling over his shoulders, though it seemed also to dull the light from the chandelier, lifting shadows onto the high walls so that when the peals of thunder sounded, the darkness trembled, for the house now felt alive and deep in slumber.

Father Linh found himself descending an endless flight of stairs. He remembered his unwritten sermon at home, and the thought of having to finish it, of having failed here, and now of leaving this house, this family, made him ache inside. It was not fair, he thought, that someone like Bao Ninh possessed what he, a man of boundless faith and devotion, could never have. With a candle in hand, he wandered from room to room and peered at each family member asleep in bed, wrapped in the furious comfort of rain and thunder: the sister under her pink covers, the grandparents side by side, Mrs. Phong, her hand on her husband's chest, and the twins lying on the tile floor, arms draped around each other. Despite the torrential rain, he could hear the sound of their breath rising and falling. Eventually, the Father came upon an empty room with an empty cot in the corner, and without thinking, without even the slightest hesitation, he curled himself under the warm covers and fell asleep.

In the middle of the night, the Father was awakened by the thunder. The darkness and emptiness of the room brought him to his feet, disorienting him momentarily, and he found himself walking blindly back through the corridors of the house, up, up the staircase, and back to Bao Ninh's room, where music still played softly.

He stepped into the room and into a standing pool of water that rose past his ankles. He would never know, later on, if it was a trick of the night, a vision encumbered by sleepfulness, but Father Linh now saw Bao Ninh fixed upon the opposite wall, next to his bookshelves and above the hill of poetry on his desk, still in the same pose like a toy ballerina asleep in her glass globe. Instead of panic, the sight only brought the Father a more intense drowsiness, as though the weight of all he had seen were a swiftly sinking anchor in his chest. He waded, splashing, through the pool of water, toward Bao Ninh's bed, but did not hear the sound of his progress for all the thunder roaring outside. As he lay his head down upon the pillow, he heard a deep voice speaking to him, coming not from the boy asleep on the wall but from the record player, it seemed, but his eyes closed before he could piece any of the words together.

Father Linh woke in the morning with a faint ringing in his ears. He sat up in bed and looked around the dark room, stricken by a feeling that he had been abandoned in the house. The rain had ceased, its sound on the metal roof fading into a hollow kind of silence, sudden and heavy, so that now a forgotten stillness overcame the room. To the Father's left, Bao Ninh had returned to the far wall and was snoring quietly. Perhaps it is no flood, after all, he thought.

The Father felt as though he had been asleep for months, then realized he had forgotten, for the first time in his life, to say his prayers before going to bed. The guilt made him cringe. It seemed the awareness of himself in someone else's bed brought about a weakening of his moral will, so that now he wanted nothing else but to escape from this house and return to the church. And yet, as he stared up at Bao Ninh still on the wall, an intense affection burgeoned in his heart, not for the boy, he realized, but for that sense of himself as a creature reborn, rousing not only from sleep but from a body no longer his own.

Father Linh rose to his feet—the floor, he noticed, was dry—and approached the boy's desk. Bao Ninh's poems lay in a mess of papers, some pristine, some formerly crumpled, his handwriting ornate and frantic across the pages. He lifted them to the light of the window and began reading, one after the other, and soon found himself intoxicated by the power of the boy's poetry. His own unwritten sermon came to mind, and Father Linh could read no more. Bao Ninh's words were more beautiful than anything he had ever written or could ever conceive of in his mind, a beauty so wrought and terrible and truthful that he would have believed God himself had hidden in the ink of the boy's pen. But then this could not be, the Father said to himself. The boy still needed to be saved, had to be saved, and for an instant the deep voice with which he fell asleep last night echoed in his head. He saw the moment had come for drastic action.

Slowly, as quietly as he could, the Father gathered up the papers on the desk and held them to his chest. Cowering from the ceiling, from the closed eyes of the boy on the wall, he hurried out of the room, descended the staircase, and, without once looking back, walked out the front door.

Outside, dawn was approaching. Tree branches leaned over the road, dripping water onto the Father's head as he walked. A cool breeze caressed his face, wafted through the hole in the breast of his cassock. In the far distance, he heard bells, and for a moment, he believed he was the first person to wake in town, in the world, as it were. The countryside had never been this green, this clear, this quiet.

Again he passed the flooded rice paddy, whose waters by now had climbed the roadside as though lying in wait for someone to pass. Father Linh stopped and regarded the paddy with something approaching peace. He felt then that the agony of the world was nothing more than a test, a trial, and if one were to awake from a night of fitful sleep, it was best to say a prayer and go on with things as normal, because at the end of the day the mystery would be all too overwhelming to bear. Two days of rain had now ended, and eventually it would rain again. And so there it was.

With the papers thrust to his chest, he stepped into the paddy and waded into the depths. After some distance, he flung the papers up in the air, watched them flutter and swirl around him, then come to rest on the surface of the water, where they floated.

Father Linh waded in deeper and deeper (not too deep, he thought), until the water reached his waist, his stomach, his chest, the entire time his voice growing louder: "The Lord is my Savior, the Lord is my Savior, the Lord is my Savior . . ."

Charlotte Forbes

THE MARVELOUS YELLOW CAGE

The shopkeeper who sold it to her said this about the cage: that it came from an old hotel in Veracruz where it hung in the lobby and held jungle birds that were so charmed by the genial voices of the guests and the clink of bar glasses that they sang all day and into the night. When the hotel was razed to make way for a new one, the birds refused to budge from the cage, they pecked to bleeding the hands of anyone who tried to remove them, and sang their last song as the cage was heaved onto the ash pile of the past.

She'd thought it such a fine story. And a splendid cage: domed, yellow, with Victorian curlicues about the sides and base, and large. Large enough to contain a human. In the shop she marveled at the cage, imagining it full of troupials of her own, knowing she had to have it. She bought it at full price without bothering to dicker, but when it was delivered to the house it was all wrong, monstrous even, and she had it put in the storeroom under the acacia tree, where it lay forgotten for decades.

That much Ayela Buse remembered right away; it came rushing at her as she opened the door one August afternoon and the yellow form nearly glowed in the dim of the storeroom. At eighty-seven, Ayela Buse was so comfortable with herself and the liberty with which she led her widow's life, free to indulge her midmorning

melancholy, her revulsion for television, her preference for the
Roman practice of drawing the drapes against the heat of the day,
and all the other tics of body and spirit, that not much upset her.
The sight of the cage, the size of it, the look of it, however, sent a
shudder through her, and her usually fine memory drew a blank as
to why she had ever had the urge to purchase such an unreasonable
object.

Xavier Buse poked his head in the storeroom door. *Mother, are
you in there?*

Over here, she waved. *I'm looking for that alabaster statue for you.*

He picked his way through the sea of old armchairs and garden
statuary, still in the suit he had worn for twelve hours on the two
planes and one ramshackle hired car he had taken to drop in unexpectedly on his mother. Xavier Buse frowned. *Look at all this,* he
groaned. *Mother, you've got to start weeding this out.*

Ayela Buse turned toward her firstborn. He had taken nothing of
her, not her caramel skin, her liquid eyes, her instinctive aloofness.
He was all his father: the tall frame, the auburn hair, the fastidious
appearance, a nature similarly inclined toward the dutiful but
devoid of the father's passionate imagination that long ago captured
the fancy and then the heart of Ayela Buse.

At the age of twenty-five Frederick Buse had known that his
first duty was to himself and, breaking free of the stranglehold of
three generations of Buse influence, left the Great Depression and
the sunless city of Boston with only his law degree and an open
heart. He set out overland to South America, but he hadn't even
crossed the Rio Grande when love apprehended him in the form of
Santa Rosalia, a backwater Spanish colonial town possessed of a
certain golden light that flattered its superstitious populace, and lay
close enough to the Mexican border to claim the exotic persuasion
of a foreign land.

Then there was Ayela Garzan, illegitimate daughter of a Mexican
dressmaker and an itinerant judge. What a hard thing she was: will-
ful; haughty; strutting down Dolarosa Street in the flowered dresses
of her mother's creation; her breasts, her chin thrust forward; a

stranger to soft feelings with no use for the sherbet-colored sky of
summer evenings. Her laugh was a sneering, mocking thing, and in
her eyes was a flinty look that both abhorred and craved the inso-
lent stares of the men loitering outside the bars. Ayela Garzan was
eighteen when Frederick Buse first laid eyes on her. He looked
beyond her detached Mayan beauty and saw a spirit that, not unlike
his own, hung by a thread to the things of this world. What she
needs is a life, he said to himself, which gave him courage to
approach her as she sat in the twilight on a bench in the Plaza de
Oro, waiting to throw herself away on the men who perfumed the
night with their cigars and whiskied breath.

They married in the Mission Church, he in a morning suit, she
in a Mexican wedding dress, and took a large stucco house on
Olivea Road, where the jacaranda trees were fuller and the heat
seemed more bearable. After a wedding trip to Corpus Christi,
Frederick Buse set up a law practice in Santa Rosalia, and became a
fixture about the limestone courthouse in his white linen suit and
the ebony-handled cane he carried to offset his youthful appearance. Early in their marriage he filled Ayela Buse with life three
times in measured succession, ensuring that for the next quarter
century she was not without the constant bickering and the frenetic
love and the sudden insurrections that diverted her mind from its
own darker tendencies. When their sons moved away, retreating to
their father's native Boston, she viewed it as betrayal. Frederick dismissed it with a casual, *Whatever we are, they'll be the opposite,* but
immediately devoted himself to assuming their place. He began to
come home for lunch, insisting on elaborate meals prepared with
love, and requiring her presence at the charitable events he headed
in Zaragosa County. They went on this way, eating kingly concoc-
tions, presiding over music festivals, flying over the land in hot-air
balloons to usher in all manner of celebrations until Frederick's
death three years ago.

With a widow's need to invoke the departed, Ayela Buse summoned her husband. He came to her in his immaculate linen suit,
striding across the plaza with blueprints for a new wing on the

Infirmary of the Good Shepherd, and then sitting under the stars, eyes closed as the tremor of violins rose on the evening air in the amphitheater he had mercilessly badgered the politicians of Santa Rosalia to build.

With the vision of her husband came the courage to stand up to the petty concerns of her son, and she turned to Xavier, saying: *I'm too old to have someone telling me what to do with my things.*

At eight o'clock that evening Ayela Buse, in a dress of blue silk that flowed to her ankles, sat at the head of the dining table, with Xavier to her right. Not since the November weekend two years ago when Freddie's family stopped en route to a diving trip on the island of Cozumel had Ayela Buse seen any of her sons. At this point she was not the kind of mother who required her children's presence, preferring to go it alone lest she be robbed of an old age free from the good intentions of her offspring. Surmising that this lay behind Xavier's trip, she postponed the inevitable and leaned a glowing face toward him: *Tell me about the girls.*

With more than a little relief, her son spoke about his own family, the bewildering life of his two teenage daughters and his wife, Hilaire, an accountant like himself, but with a restlessness she appeased by acting in a local theater troupe when a role sufficiently tragic came along. He nearly forgot himself in the balm of his mother's undivided attention and, in a rush of gratitude, stopped short and put his hand over hers.

It's good to see you, Mother.

Before Xavier Buse could say something he might later regret, Chilcha appeared. Dressed in a gray uniform that had grown too big for her, she carried a large platter and the impassive expression of a servant ravenous to learn the situation at the table.

Other evenings, Chilcha and Ayela Buse ate a bowl of cereal together at five-thirty, seven o'clock, nine-fifteen, whenever hunger struck. They sat at the plank table in the kitchen, Ayela reading aloud from the evening paper. But from the first gong of the doorbell and the giddiness that came as her little bird body was twirled around and set gently down by Xavier's sturdy arms, Chilcha threw her entire being at one nearly impossible task: serving his favorite dinner of *ropa vieja*. She bristled at Ayela's invitation to join them in the dining room, saying, *Let us not ruin Mr. Xavier's memories.*

As they ate Ayela Buse spoke of the goings-on in Santa Rosalia. Her son listened, keenly aware of the intelligence in his mother's voice, her dignified beauty, the white hair that was long and wild in a charming way, part of it caught at the back in a tortoiseshell barrette, as she had always worn it. He began to have second thoughts about the business that he, as the eldest son, was obliged to undertake.

But as Chilcha finally cleared the plates, and water ran and pots thunked in the kitchen, Xavier Buse sat up straighter in his chair and cleared his throat.

Mother, we want you to come and live with us in Boston.

Ayela laughed as if a child were making a joke. *But darling, I live here*, she said.

We've talked about this before. It's time now. Softening his words, he hastened to add, *We worry about you down here. If you should need anything . . . we'd be right there to take care of you.*

Ayela Buse fingered the ornate handle of her silver fork. *But there's Chilcha.*

Xavier Buse examined his mother carefully. He spoke gently as if breaking bad news to the next of kin. *Chilcha is . . . old. She's failing. She's probably older than you are, if anyone really knew.* He put his hand over hers. *We have the room. It will be better for everyone.*

Mmmmmmm, Ayela Buse replied. She had taken on her husband's sentiments about the city he disowned, and had no intention of spending her last years in a cold, dreary place where winter lasted for nine months and the inhabitants ate brown beans and cod, and, after church on Sundays, knelt in adoration before portraits of ancestors with huge faces and disapproving eyes.

Mistaking his mother's silence for miraculous assent, Xavier dared to go on. *I've made some inquiries . . . and the realtor has a buyer for the house.*

But I've left the house to Chilcha. It's in my will.

That's ridiculous, Mother. Chilcha would rattle around here all by herself.

It's her home, too. Ayela Buse looked thoughtfully at her son. *And it's what I want.*

The candlelight flattered her, melting away the years until Xavier saw her on those remote nights of his boyhood, lingering at the dinner table, listening to her husband speak of business matters, idly running her finger through the candle flame. He had thought her strange and reckless, knowing even then that if he didn't take a stand against her, he would never find himself.

Xavier Buse put down his napkin and rose from the table. *Boston's not a bad place, Mother. You'll get to like it,* he said, and, brushing his lips over his mother's forehead, went up to bed.

After dinner, Chilcha brought out the coffee and the pralines, and the two women sat on the terrace listening to the soft thud of bugs against the bougainvillea.

Despite the heat, they enjoyed their nightly ritual. The night was kind to them, obscuring their wrinkled faces, making them young again; they were grateful and used the night for sitting and dreaming and divulging the hopes of their past, either sighing with regret or dying of laughter until their will to be awake trailed off. Together, they rose to ready the kitchen for morning with fresh napkins and bone-white coffee cups overturned on their saucers like gleaming mountains, and made their way upstairs.

Without intending to they had slipped into the ways of an old married couple with such ease and mutual delight that it sometimes struck Ayela Buse like a thorn in the heart. When she looked back over the fifty-nine years she had spent with her husband, what bubbled to the surface was not the affectionate regard that was the soul of her life with Chilcha, but such a dark tangle of opposing sentiments, such a snarl of admiration and near-claustrophobic indebtedness, complete trust and bursts of disconsolate rage, that she dared to wonder if it was actually love she had known with Frederick Buse.

You are going to Boston, then? Chilcha asked when she could no longer stand the silence between them.

Ayela laughed. *That's what the boys seem to think.*

Perhaps that is best.

What about you?

I will be all right.

There is no one to care for you.

Señora, there is.

Who?

There is someone. There is always someone. It was a lie and they both knew it, just as they knew what made it a lie had nothing to do with the fact that as a girl Chilcha fled from her home on the ravaged Napo River, shorn of its trees and its caterwauling monkeys into a frightening silence, and landed in the Buse household as a cook, seeing the family through the birth of three sons and the death of the father, and all the raucous joys and sorrows in between, with such single-minded devotion she had forgotten to have a life of her own.

Ayela Buse smiled at the liar, waiflike in the ill-fitting uniform, her short gray hair tucked behind the ears, her ancient face lit by innocence. *Come with me.*

Chilcha shook her head. *No. There is no room.*

There is room. We can live together, like here, Ayela Buse suggested, knowing full well the irreplaceable sanctity of *here.* Here, they rarely went off the property. During the day they played cards, worked in the garden, drank cold chamomile tea, nearly collapsed from scouring the terra-cotta tiles or polishing the heavy English furniture, fell asleep in the coolest spot on the terrace, read to each other the latest anti-aging miracles from the health magazines and the Spanish dime novels from half a century ago, and, when the sun was down, took solace in their own muddied versions of the past. Occasionally they felt the urge to cook the old complicated dishes Frederick had requested, and gave themselves over to grinding pine nuts and roasting quails and coaxing salt from eggplants and baking rings of meringue to the perfection of clouds kissed by the sun, after which a dozen dazzling platters appeared on the dining-room table. Since their shrunken stomachs couldn't digest what they had so laboriously prepared, they hung the colored lights and threw open the doors to the neighbors who christened these sporadic gastronomic affairs The Feast of Two Women.

No, not Boston, Chilcha said. *Think of our life here. Mr. Xavier will understand. He is the one with the heart of an angel.*

Ayela Buse reached for the pralines as though she hadn't heard a word.

You told Mr. Xavier what we want, Chilcha pressed her. *What did he say?*

Without looking up, Ayela rearranged the uneaten candies on her plate. *Mr. Xavier says we're a couple of ridiculous old women.*

For the next three days, on the terrace, over café con leche, in the heat of the afternoon, mother and son debated their future plans in sessions that veered from the quiet and thoughtful to near shouting matches. The endless sessions took their toll on Ayela Buse. For the first time in her life, a fluttering heart, pains in her hip, sudden and disturbing lapses in memory, and other real and imaginary capitulations to old age began to bother her. One insomniac night, she went for a cup of tea and tripped on the stairs in a fall that did no physical harm, but so unnerved her that when Xavier burst from his room and ran to her aid, she let herself be led to an armchair and soothed and scolded, and, feeling as defenseless as the day she was born, surrendered in a whisper: *All right. You win. I'm yours.*

The next afternoon a black truck with ANTIQUES AND ESTATES printed discreetly in red pulled up in the back drive. Ayela Buse was summoned outside and, standing by the gardens she started with a finicky tea rose given to her by her husband for her twenty-second birthday, was introduced by her son to the truck's owner. Mr. Aguilera, a short man with vigorous arms, closed his eyes and bowed, proclaiming it an honor to meet the distinguished lady who had tended to Santa Rosalia as if it were her own child. Having lost the habit of social discourse, Ayela Buse muttered an embarrassed thank-you, while recognizing the man for what he was: a vulture.

Mr. Aguilera knew the Buse family by reputation as one of the old families of Santa Rosalia, discerning in their taste, and he leered at the handsome Spanish colonial house as if it were a woman to whom he would soon have unlimited access. Then his eyes fell on the proud, downhearted face of Ayela Buse, and the desire to console her ambushed him. What came out was the statement, delivered as he examined the cuticles edging their ragged way over his fingernails, but in a tone that made her look up and take notice: *You have raised wonderful roses, Señora.*

She nodded and led him inside and up to the attic, returning to sit in the kitchen, where Chilcha was preparing purple coneflowers for a medicinal tea. Without the vaguest notion of what would become of her, Chilcha waited with the patience of God in her dark Andean eyes, praying to the holy mother to help her lay roses along the burdensome path of Ayela Buse and, in a fierce whisper, vowed to them both: *As long as the lord gives me life I will serve you.*

An hour later Mr. Aguilera appeared in the kitchen still writing in the small blue notebook. Ayela led him outside to the storeroom. From the doorway she watched him defile with his intentions the statue of the one-armed Venus de Milo she sketched while pregnant with Xavier so that he would see beauty in imperfection, the nineteenth-century globe she insisted on so the boys would know the world before it became smaller and less mysterious, and the oil painting of St. Peter's Basilica she bought impulsively in a curio shop in Laredo when the bells of the Angelus floating over the sun-baked streets made her painfully aware of the hollowness of her own being.

Where did that cage come from? He interrupted her thoughts.

I don't remember, she said offhandedly, realizing that it hadn't made her shudder as it had a few days earlier. Its effect on her was so benign that she walked over and ran her fingers along its thick iron spokes nubby with yellow paint, thinking of the birds singing their hearts out inside its cavernous womb. She didn't hear Mr. Aguilera say it wasn't a fine piece, just a curiosity.

Mr. Aguilera raised his voice. *Señora, I'm ready to make an offer.*

Ayela Buse walked out of the storeroom. The impending loss of her possessions made her feel as though she might sit down and cry her eyes out. Mr. Aguilera feared by the sudden wobble to her gait that she was about to have a fainting spell or worse. When asked whether she wanted a glass of water, a light came into her eyes. *I don't wish to sell,* she said.

Mr. Aguilera protested. *But your son. He said to take the things away today.*

The reminder of her son's presumption strengthened her resolve. Ayela Buse repeated her refusal to sell.

As you wish, Señora. He bowed and retreated, thinking Xavier Buse was going to have his hands full.

At six-thirty Xavier Buse stood in front of a pay phone on Dolorosa Street. Having just come from the realtors, where he arranged for the sale of the house with the power of attorney he had insisted be drawn up after his father's death, his heart should have been lighter. But he was plagued by the damnable truth that the brothers' plans for their mother came from selfishness and selflessness, wisdom and foolishness, not in equal parts but in proportions that seemed to shift and refract by the minute, the hour, the day, as impossible to pin down as sunlight falling on water.

His brothers hadn't helped matters. He had telephoned them his news, which was met by a cheer from Freddie and from Jesse a chorus of hallelujah that traveled via fifteen hundred miles of telephone line to strike a sour and impious note with Xavier. He hung up convinced it was a bungled business and that the three of them were about to introduce their mother to the worst years of her life.

Christ, he muttered, resigned to the hopelessness of ever making peace with himself on the matter.

He stood on Dolarosa Street, unsure of where to go next.

Behind the line of stores, his eye fell on the familiar dark three-story facade of the Jesuit school from which he had graduated over forty years ago with high honors and a temporary sense of self-sacrifice. The building was a plain brownstone, the only dark structure in all of Santa Rosalia, and the sight of it produced a sheaf of memories in him, the strongest of which was his fourteen-year-old self late on a Friday afternoon in the empty cobblestone courtyard in a light spring rain. Feeling a strange radiance in being wet and cold and alone, he vowed to forsake the material world and, like his namesake, St. Francis Xavier, walk barefoot amid the pearl fisheries of India with the word of God on his lips. Though he believed the fantasy long since dead and buried, the ingenuousness of it still moved him, and he stood staring into the Dolorosa Street traffic dreaming of himself before the world got hold of him.

Xavier Buse returned to the house in an irritable state and with a bottle of tequila under his arm. He found his mother and Chilcha drinking lemonade on the terrace, not yet ready to take in his presence. Even after he asked what had happened with Mr. Aguilera, his mother had to finish her laughter before she looked at him with a distracted, *I told him to wait. I'm having second thoughts.*

Oh for God's sake. Just sell it! We're lucky to have someone cart this junk away, Xavier Buse shouted with such surprising sharpness that Chilcha fled into the house.

Xavier ran his fingers through his thinning hair and his eyes lit on something that made the blood pound in his veins. Rising from the garden, which was beginning to have a broken-down look of its own, was the yellow cage.

Mother! What are you doing?

I asked the handyman to put it out, Ayela Buse replied, keeping to herself that she was merely obeying the cage's renewed and benevolent pull on her, that after all this time she was ready for it, or it for her. *Lord knows why I ever bought such a thing. Its history, I suppose,* she said, and began to relate the provenance of the cage insofar as she knew it.

Her son cut her off. *I've got to get back to Boston tomorrow, and you've got to pack up the house. We can't have some piece of junk sitting out here!* He began to feel the old suffocation of this place, of the woman who was his mother, her willfulness, her unpredictability, and it made him wish to be anywhere but here.

Ayela Buse sat rigidly in her chair, wishing to God her sons had never given her a thought. Finally she stood up. *Kindly have the decency to allow me to do as I wish in my own house while it is still mine,* she told her son in a steady voice, and, with the air of an injured queen, turned and strode inside.

Xavier heard her moving about within, tidying up, switching off lights. Just as he was about to go and beg her forgiveness for this entire debacle, she pulled the switch on the colored lanterns that lit the terrace, leaving her son in darkness holding his heart like a dashed lover.

He plunked himself down on the chaise lounge. It wasn't the white wicker he remembered, but yellow plastic, which saddened him while making him hotter, as did the thought of the stifling bedroom awaiting him under the eaves at the front of the house. *Damn,* he said out loud. *Damn the heat. Damn her. Who doesn't have air-conditioning in this day and age!*

The words slid like stones into his mother's particular brand of punishing silence. Xavier Buse began to swig on his tequila, recognizing himself, once again, as the victim of grave injustice from day one. He bowed his head, grieving for that small boy who had watched his mother watering with a garden hose and had taken his penis out of his short pants to water the flowers alongside her, and was then sent to his room without dinner, suffering less from her harsh sentence than from knowing in his child's heart that his help had only angered his mother. The longer he sat, the harder it was to resist the ancient feeling deep in his cells that his mother had loved his brother Freddie better, and then the youngest, Jesse, with an all-out devotion, despite what his father had always maintained: that by the time her third-born came along, Ayela Buse had finally gotten the hang of motherhood.

Xavier Buse let loose with a loud tequila belch. *Shit,* he muttered, and cursed himself for his own self-pity, for making this visit in the summer, for making it at all. Alone in the dark terrace in the smothering heat, he thought he might cry.

After the departure of her son, Ayela Buse tried to put the notion of a future in Boston out of her mind. The Buse house was built in the last century. Its large formal rooms with ceiling fans, the black and white marble foyer flanked by two reception areas, a courtyard with a columned arcade where the boys played quoits and Frederick held his chamber-music evenings, and where Chilcha now grew her pots of verbena, prompted Ayela Buse to observe, *The buyer will have second thoughts. People don't live this way anymore.*

She forced herself to float along on this cloud of delusion until a Thursday afternoon three weeks later. Chilcha had fallen asleep on the terrace, and, still dressed in her night clothes, Ayela Buse answered the door.

Hello again. Mr. Aguilera bowed, avoiding her eyes. *Your son asked me to come . . .*

My son has gone back to Boston, Ayela Buse replied, without inviting him inside.

But the house must be completely emptied . . . , he went on.

Yes, she cut him off, fully aware that her reign as mistress of this house ended in sixty days, when the new owners took possession.

Mr. Aguilera bowed his head. The house seemed sadder than he remembered, and leaning toward decrepitude, led by the two stone lions that stood sentinel on the front portico, one of which had lost its back leg, the other its head. When he looked up again it was with apology in his eyes.

Ayela Buse blushed.

There wasn't a grander, more comfortable house than her own, a more desirable place to live out her time. But the truth was that she and Chilcha were collapsing from the weight of it, from the missing flagstones and the sagging tiled roof and the dusty stucco and the ragged emptiness of the formal rooms, and all the other thousands of unanswered groans. The grand old house was losing ground, just like the two of them.

Well then, he said. *Let's begin where we left off. In the storeroom.*

Slowly she unfastened the key from the chain around her neck and handed it to him.

I'll be quick, he said.

There's no hurry. Take all year if you want, she replied, leading him around the back of the house.

He stopped her in front of the garden and spoke to her gently. *And after the storeroom, I'll have to have a look at the house.*

Ayela Buse sighed and averted her gaze toward the sky.

Look wherever you like, she said. *But you'll have to excuse me.* With the sense that something that began a very long time ago was about to come to an end, she left him and retreated upstairs to throw herself down on her bed.

Frederick had ordered the king-size bed when those things first became available, when they hadn't needed it because they still slept with their arms around each other. She'd teased him about it, but over the years it had proven a wise investment as they gradually and without rancor pulled away into themselves until they slept as close to their own edge as possible, up against the night tables piled with books and spectacles and pills.

Chilcha first slept with her in the conjugal bed last fall. *Your cold is trapped inside your head,* Chilcha had told her, nursing her with eucalyptus oil and gentle massages of the frontal and maxillary sinuses, and staying with her to supply the comforting presence of health in the sickbed. They slept in the same bed first out of necessity, then because they couldn't go on any other way.

Dear Chilcha, she murmured, and, lying on her back in the middle of the bed, Ayela Buse thought in a rational way about what time held for the two of them. She could see only a larger flotilla of aids to move their ancient bowels, more of the insomniac nights, the infernal shakes, the fracture of brittle bones, two shrinking women content to remain in their nightclothes for weeks, frantic to know what they had just been told, ransacking the house for the piece of paper they held in their hands.

Desire to have a body would cease. Then would come the unending days of being a burden to themselves and everyone else, left to thieving and disinterested orderlies who would bathe them and change their diapers and put them to bed until they finally submitted to the will of God.

Ayela Buse lay quietly, lost in trying to understand, vaguely aware of the footsteps up and down the stairs, the softening sun, the faraway voices of Mr. Aguilera and Chilcha, then the closing of the heavy front door.

It was nearing dark when she awoke from her thoughts, refreshed as if she'd slept for days. Had the seed not been planted, the revelation may have never seized her by the throat and dragged her down the road of reason. But alone on the bed in which her three sons had been conceived, she had come to understand: *Bless you, Xavier,* she whispered.

She went to Frederick's library to wait for the call she knew was coming. When it came, the bid for the contents of the house was not at all generous; she could have held out, counteroffered, pled unfairness. The bid was not generous, but it was reasonable, and in a short time Ayela Buse had become the most reasonable person on earth.

She said nothing about the offer, but as a lawyer's wife was aware of the business to be done, and the following morning, showered and smelling of sandalwood soap, wearing a simple dress of pale linen, she drove to the office of Mr. Aguilera to sign the papers with the eagerness of a girl on summer holiday.

Two nights later, Chilcha sat with pillows propped up behind her, the tiny black transistor radio on her lap and the earplug in her right ear, when Ayela Buse came into the bedroom with two bowls. *I've made the banana pudding you like,* she announced.

Chilcha's dentures were already soaking in the glass on the night table, and in response she could only grin the gummy smile of a newborn.

The hour was late and they ate without speaking. The only sound was the scraping of spoon against bowl, and when they were done Ayela Buse put the bowls on a white lacquer tray that was waiting on the dresser.

In the immense bed, Ayela Buse reached across the expanse of sheet and took Chilcha's hand in hers. The hand was small, like a child's, though far more knowing and smelling faintly of lemon. Ayela Buse pressed it to her cheek and closed her eyes. *Such hands,* she whispered, and gently let it drop on the bed. She smiled at Chilcha: *Get some rest now.*

Chilcha lay her head back on the pillow and let her eyelids drop. Ayela Buse watched her and did not shift her gaze until Chilcha fell asleep. Then she gently lifted the earplug from her ear and put the radio on the nightstand, watching like an angel of mercy until Chilcha's breath turned imperturbably low and even, and then ceased to be.

Only then did Ayela lie back. Dressed for eternity in the pale blue nightdress she had worn since the early days of her marriage, she gave herself over to the strange torpor that had begun to envelop her at the last taste of the pudding. She opened her mouth as if to say something. But what came out was a single sound, small and joyous, like the song of a bird.

Rattawut Lapcharoensap

❧

SIGHTSEEING

We're on the southbound train, the tracks swift beneath our feet, the windows rattling in their frames. The train crawls slowly down the archipelago, oceans bordering both sides of the tracks. To the east, the Hunan runoff softens the soil, silt spilling into the ocean, turning the Gulf of Thailand brown. Mountains shield the west from the monsoons, leaving the leeward coast barren and dry, the Andaman Sea retaining its crisp, cool blue. We're going through Prachuap Khiri Khan now, where the mountains recede briefly into a flattened plain, the seas pinching the peninsula into a needle. We are going through the slimmest part of the slimmest peninsula in the world, the Indian and the Pacific crashing against both shores. The earth is a tightrope; our train speeds across the flat, thin wire. They say that a century from now this will all be gone, that the oceans will rise above this threadbare patch of earth, creating a strait as narrow as Molucca, as fine as Gibraltar, yoking the oceans, severing this nation in two. I can't quite believe this because I never believe anything I won't be around to see.

We're going to Koh Lukmak, the last in a long chain of Andaman Islands, a tiny fortress of forest and stone. Ma's boss had a picture of Lukmak on the office bulletin board for years and Ma said she wanted to see what all the fuss was about. The fine sand.

The turquoise water. The millions of fishes swimming in the shallows. Her boss had called it paradise, and though I remember Ma telling me as a child that Thailand was only a paradise for fools and farangs, for criminals and foreigners, she's willing to give it a chance now. If paradise is really out there, so close to home, she might as well go and see for herself.

It is not an easy trip—twelve hours by train, eight hours by boat—and Lukmak is so small it rarely appears on most maps. In a few hours, we will step off this train and sleep in Trang. We will leave that small seaboard town at daybreak, hire a boat at Tha Tien. The boat will be small and thin. With the monsoon's approach in a few months' time, our vessel will skip dangerously along the sea's hard current. We will stop to rest and take lunch at Koh Trawen, the first of the Andaman Islands, an abandoned penal colony. We will leave Trawen after lunch, board the same small boat, get to Lukmak by nightfall.

Sightseeing, Ma said when we bought our tickets at the station in Bangkok. We'll be farangs. We'll be just like the tourists.

This is my last summer with Ma. At the end of the summer, I am to leave for a small vocational college up north.

I watch the blue of the Andaman on the right side of the train. Ma is turned the other way, watching the murky brown of the gulf. Her window is open. She presses her face against the warm wind, her long black hair whipping wildly around her, the thin navy blue blouse fluttering against her chest. Our shoulders knock every so often, rocking to the motion of the train. We have barely spoken since we left Bangkok early this morning from Hua Lamphong Station.

I break the silence. I tell her to look straight ahead, toward the front of the car. I ask if she can see both oceans out of the corners of her eyes. She smiles and tells me she can. One eye blue, one eye brown. My mother puts a hand on my knee. Then we are silent again, eyes fixed on the front of the car. We know that soon the mountains will rise and we shall be committed to one side of the peninsula—blue or brown; that the sun shall set and the oceans will soon be dark and inhospitable; that the earth only thins and flattens out long enough for us to see two oceans at a single glance; that only a handful of people ever get to see this in their lifetime. Above all, Ma and I know that if things were different, if our lives were simply following their ordinary course, we would never have taken the time to notice such sights.

The beginnings seem so obvious now, though they did not present themselves so clearly to me then. False steps. Spilled coffee. Porcelain cups ratcheting against the kitchen counter. Cuts and cooking burns, welts white against her dark arm. Bruises on her legs from running into furniture, ebony rosettes blooming on her unblemished skin. Shoulders knocking against door frames. Her penciled eyebrows more arched than usual, uneven sometimes, the naked flesh of a brow peeking from beneath a thin charcoal line.

But I am at first too busy to give these things much thought. I am too absorbed with the life I plan to lead in the north, on my own, away from Ma. I spend nights in my room studying the vocational college's pamphlets, its maps and course guide, brochures of the nearby town. I familiarize myself with the surrounding geography, dream of the mountains that nestle the campus, of a steady provincial peace away from Bangkok's cacophony—its congestion, its heat, its concrete facades. I make copious lists of the belongings I will take with me. I revise this list endlessly. I pack and unpack into the night hours, though my departure is still many months away.

One morning, Ma misjudges the last step coming down the stairs, turns her ankles. She steadies herself with a hand on the banister.

"You all right, Ma?" I laugh. She steadies herself, widens her eyes. She blinks twice. She smooths out her dress with both hands, pulls the strap of her purse back onto her shoulder.

"Oh dear," she says, chuckling. "Don't know what's with me these days. Just a little overworked, I guess. Too many things on my mind."

A few days later, she's not going to work. She's home, reclined on the couch, watching television in her pajamas.

"You sick, Ma?"

"It's just this migraine," she says, holding a hand to the side of her head. A migraine. Migraines never stopped her before. She's a woman who doesn't miss work. Not ever. Not for migraines, not for flus, not for colds. Not for monsoons, not for landslide warnings. Not even for the military's curfew a few years ago, when the Red Cross carried wounded protestors on bloodied stretchers into the lobby of her office building. She's a woman who once went to work with malaria and was asked to go home because her boss found her in the bathroom throwing up. Even then, she insisted on going back to work—until she fainted in the middle of a company meeting. An ambulance had to be called; she went back to work the very next day.

"I'm glad you're taking some time off, Ma. Should I take you to a doctor?"

She smiles at me from the couch, turns back to the television, snuggles up against one of the pillows.

"It's okay. I already took some medicine. Feeling much better already. Go on ahead to school, luk. Don't worry about me."

But two weeks later, there is nothing but worry for both of us. Two weeks later, while I'm downstairs having my breakfast, spooning the last of my rice porridge, I hear a loud crash coming from the upstairs bathroom. I hear the shower trickling, the electric water pump whirring and wheezing in the back of the house, and then there's another loud thudding, the sound of something heavy hitting the ground. I walk to the bottom of the stairs, call up to my mother. I ask if she's okay, but there's just a long unending silence. There's just the slow, steady trickle of the shower.

I'm up the stairs. I'm at the bathroom door.

"You okay, Ma?"

"Sorry. Just dropped something."

There's a weak, sheepish chuckle in her voice and then, as I'm walking back toward the staircase, I hear the sound of skin slipping against porcelain tiles, like a car screeching to a halt. I hear that thudding again, louder this time. It's like the footsteps of giants. Like fists hitting sandbags. Like my mother hitting the bathroom floor.

The door isn't locked. It's as if she knew this would happen, as if she'd left the door unlocked that morning thinking, *Just in case*. I open the bathroom door. I see my mother's silhouette through the shower curtains, a small heap on the floor, thick clouds of steam billowing through the room. I walk toward the shower. I throw the curtains open on my mother's nakedness. I help my mother get up. Her irises roam wildly back and forth across the ceiling. Her small hands reach out for my arms. Her fingernails dig into my flesh. Her mouth opens and closes like a fish out of water, gasping for air.

It is then that the barely noticed details start to fall into place—the clumsiness, the bruises and cuts, the misjudged steps, the misshapen eyebrows, the days off from work. I turn off the shower. I wrap a towel around her small, naked body. I help my mother get up. This is the first time that I have seen my mother naked. I look at the way her breasts sag like upturned bells, nipples bulbous like baby mangosteens. I look at the thick thatch of hair between her legs. I look at that lost look of shame on her face.

My mother is going blind.

The doctors say her eyes have deteriorated beyond repair. Migraine-induced retinal detachment. They tell us that if she had checked in a couple of months earlier, when the migraines started, when the pain behind her eyes began, blindness might have been averted. They tell us it's too late now. We take the three-hour trip to Bangkok Christian—a private hospital that took care of the prime minister when he lost his right eye in a shooting accident—to get one last opinion.

The ophthalmologist at Bangkok Christian mentions experimental surgery. But he informs us that the success rate has been slim thus far. He says Ma would risk going blind altogether from the procedure. It is something called a "vitrectomy": taking my mother's eyes out of their sockets, soldering the fallen retina back to the vitreous, putting them back in again. The ophthalmologist says the procedure will be very expensive. A surgeon would have to be flown in from Singapore. He says this with a smile. His stiff, white lab coat shimmers under the bright fixtures.

"Money's not an issue, Doctor." I say this curtly, though I know it is a lie. My mother and I have never purchased a plane ticket for ourselves, let alone for some stranger from Singapore. Ma tells the ophthalmologist we'll think it over. We leave Bangkok Christian with nothing new. Four doctors now and still the same old story.

Eight to ten weeks before permanent loss of sight. Retinas detached, vitreous shrunken, optic nerves irrevocably damaged. Stay out of the sun. No bright lights. No small print. Do eye exercises. Focus on slowly moving objects. We need to keep the retinas stimulated, on the off chance they might regenerate. On the off chance. In case of a miracle. Get lots of sleep. Don't go to work. You really can't go to work, ma'am. But above all, don't panic. But most important, please relax.

My mother quits her job. Later that week, we look at a map of Thailand together, tracing the hatchet-shaped boundaries, circling places she would like to see. Lop Buri. Chiang Rai. Loie. Samut Songkhram. Mae Hong Son. The doctors tell Ma to get out of the city, take a vacation. We decide to go to the Andaman Islands.

And in my room that week I unpack my belongings once more. I don't repack them this time. I put all of the books back on the shelf, stack the brand-new notebooks under my desk. I move the course guide, the maps, and the brochures from the head of my bed, stow them away in a drawer. Though I still take them out from time to time, flip through the now-familiar pages, I'm finding it difficult to dream of those mountains again. I cannot look at those maps without imagining my mother blind and alone in the house, and I'm starting to wonder, for the first time in my life, about what kind of son I really am.

* * *

The train comes to a stop in Trang. I try to take my mother's arm when we get up.

"I'm not blind yet, luk."

"Sorry, I just thought—"

"You just thought nothing, luk. I'm fine."

The sun is gone, the tree-lined horizon red from the last of its rays. Moths dance against the platform's flickering lamplights. When we step off the train, Ma puts on her sunglasses: horn-rimmed, purple-rhinestoned Armanis we bought at the Chatuchak bazaar. She wears those sunglasses every chance she gets now. Doctor's orders. They suit her well, and if it wasn't for the fact that sunglasses look out of place in the evenings, I'd say my mother might be a Chinese movie star.

We check into our hotel room, have dinner at a noodle vendor in the center of town. We order large bowls of seafood vermicelli, sit at a small table on the sidewalk. We eat by the weak light of the town's streetlamps.

"You okay?" Ma asks, tugging at the noodles with her chopsticks, peering over her sunglasses, thin wreaths of steam unfurling between us.

"I'm fine. Why?"

"You're not being very talkative, that's all. You've been a little morose. A mother notices, you know."

"Is there something you want to talk about?"

"Oh, I don't know. Something. Anything. Everything. For God's sakes, we're on vacation, luk. Smile a little."

"Fine, let's talk."

"Okay, let's talk."

"Okay." She chews off the head of a prawn, smiling, twirling the translucent husk between her fingers. "Why don't you tell me about the school up north, luk. What do you think you'll study? I don't think we've ever talked about that before."

"I haven't given it much thought, actually."

"No?"

"No, Ma."

"But you were so excited a few months ago."

"That was a few months ago, Ma."

"What did you tell me you were going to study? What was it, luk? Libraries? That was it, wasn't it? Oh, I think you'd make a great librarian. You'd be so handsome with all those books."

"Let's talk about something else, Ma."

There's an awkward silence. Ma puts down her chopsticks. She takes off her sunglasses, folds the thick plastic earpieces, lays them neatly on the table. I can see the faint outline of rings already forming around her eyes. I bend to sip my broth.

"Look at me, luk. No. Look at me."

I put the bowl down, lean back in my seat.

"I didn't bring you along so you could brood. I would've come myself, luk, if I knew you were going to act this way. What's wrong with a little conversation with your mother? I'm not asking for much here, luk. I'm just asking you to be courteous. I'm just asking you to be kind."

"Sorry, Ma. I just didn't—"

"Don't 'sorry' me, luk. I don't need your apologies. I just need you to act like you're my son, that's all—not some cranky client I'm taking out to dinner. Be decent, luk. Be nice. Is that too much to ask?"

"Ma—"

"You think it's easy for me to sit here knowing I'm going blind, that there's nothing I can do about it? I could wake up blind tomorrow morning. I might never see you again. And you'll be sorry then, luk. Real sorry. You'll probably be sorrier than you've ever been in your life, knowing that the last time your mother saw you, you were being dreadful."

We finish our meals silently. On our way back to the hotel, there's a blind man playing an accordion on the corner across from the hotel. He sings a southern work song, his contralto lilting across the street. Pedestrians drop change in the tin cup at his feet and he smiles at the sound of each brightly clinking coin. For a moment, as we walk past, I wonder where his children are. Then Ma and I look away. From our room three stories up, we can hear him singing all through the night. We sleep to the sounds of his beggar's elegies.

Every Saturday morning, Ma battles the vendors at Chatuchak. Even the most stubborn of vendors have submitted to her entreaties. It is not only charm she exerts upon them, for charm will get you only so far; Ma slashes their prices through an inimitable combination of wit, commonsense economics, high theatrics, and old-fashioned psychological manipulation. That Saturday at the bazaar, a few days before our trip, Ma was at the height of her powers.

The vendor was a young, homely-looking girl. Throngs of people filed past her booth. I stood at a distance as Ma scanned the hundreds of frames neatly laid out on the table. "What do you think?" she asked, putting on the Armanis.

"They look good, Ma."

"Really?"

"Yeah. You look like Jackie Kennedy."

This pleased her. She raised her hand in a fluttering half-gesture, smiling, bending to look at her reflection in the small mirror. "How much?" she finally asked, taking off the glasses with a swift, dramatic gesture. The vendor said twelve hundred. Ma yelped. "They're real, ma'am," the vendor said. "Real Armanis."

"Real or not, that's an awful lot of money."

The girl laughed—a shrill, sheepish sound. A middle-aged Chinese couple walked into the booth, the husband with a vacant look in his eyes. Ma asked for a discount. "I can't, ma'am. Profit margin's small as it is."

"C'mon. Give an old woman a break."

The girl smiled. She said eleven hundred. Ma yelped again.

"I'm not a farang, na? We're all Thai here. Give me the Thai price." The vendor asked Ma to name one. Not eleven hundred, Ma said. The vendor counteroffered: ten-fifty. Ma put the glasses back on the table. "That's ridiculous," she said, shaking her head, though

I could hear that hint of mischief in her voice. Only now, I knew, would the bargaining begin in earnest. "Let's go," Ma said curtly, feigning disappointment. The Chinese couple glanced at us, smiled, and I tried to return the courtesy. The wife went back to browsing and the husband to looking as if he would rather be elsewhere. "Can you believe that?" Ma asked as we made our way toward the aisle, her voice loud enough for the girl to hear. "Twelve hundred for a pair of fake Armanis."

"Ma—"

"Don't 'Ma' me. You don't think it's a little expensive?"

"Well—"

"It's outrageous."

There is faith in the way Ma bargains, in the way we started to walk away from the girl. Her faith was substantiated that day. The girl called us back.

"Ma'am! Ma'am!" Ma let go of my arm, turned to face the vendor.

"How's a thousand, ma'am?" the girl said, getting up from her seat.

"Oh no." Ma laughed, grabbing my arm again. "Why would I spend that kind of money on a pair of fake Armanis?" Out of the corner of my eye, I saw the Chinese husband snickering softly to himself.

"They're not fake, ma'am."

"Oh?"

"No, ma'am. My boyfriend got them from the factory."

"So they're stolen?"

"Ma'am!"

"Pirated, then. They're pirated. You know I could—"

"Ma'am!"

"I'm just teasing. What's a little teasing?" Ma said. "Don't take an old woman like me so seriously. Here. Let me look at them again."

Ma tried them on once more. The girl told her she looked stunning. "I like them," Ma said, taking off the glasses. "But a thousand? I don't like them *that* much." Again, the girl asked Ma to name a price. Ma took out her wallet, handed me the sunglasses, fished out a few bills. "Tell you what. I'll leave six hundred baht on this table. Then I'll walk away with those sunglasses."

"Oi! I can't do that, ma'am."

"Of course you can."

"No, ma'am, that's impossible." The girl looked at me. I shrugged. "Okay," Ma said. "Let me ask you this, then: How much did you pay for these glasses?"

"I don't know, ma'am. My boyfriend was the one—"

"Oh, just tell me. What's an old woman like me going to do with that kind of information? Your boyfriend's not here now, is he? How else am I supposed to give you a fair offer?"

"I can't do that. I'd lose money if I gave it to you for six hundred, though."

"So six hundred it is, then," Ma said emphatically, laying the money down. The Chinese husband let out a bellowing laugh this time and the girl shot him a look that suggested, suddenly, that she was much older than I had originally assumed. "I can't let you do that." The vendor's voice was strong and curt now, a new pallor on her face.

"Now you're talking," Ma teased, smiling. "No need to 'ma'am' me all the time. Now we can talk like adults. How much did you pay for these?" The girl shook her head. Six-fifty, Ma offered. The girl shook her head again. Ma took another hundred-baht note from her wallet. Seven-fifty.

"No."

Ma held the note in her hand, and for a moment they just stood there—the vendor and my mother—locked in a mute battle. I'd seen this type of standoff many times before. I pitied the girl.

"How old are you?" Ma asked suddenly.

"Excuse me?"

"How old are you?"

"I'm twenty-six, ma'am."

"It's a good age to be, twenty-six," Ma said. "You might not think it from the way I look, but it wasn't so long ago when I was your age. It wasn't so long ago at all—though you're far more beautiful than I ever was then."

The girl just blinked at my mother's flattery. The Chinese wife, for the first time, looked our way.

"Here's the situation." Ma put the hundred-baht note on the table with the other bills, patting the pile of money like a bettor blessing her ante. "I'll tell you my problem and then you can decide whether or not to give me those glasses for seven-fifty today. Thing is, those glasses aren't an accessory for me. They're not an optional luxury. You see, I'm going blind. By this time tomorrow, I might not be able to see a thing. Do you understand what I'm saying? You're looking at a woman who's going *blind*. The doctors say those glasses might mean a few more days of sight for me—ask my son if you don't believe me. Now, you don't strike me as the type of girl who'd let a woman go blind over a few hundred bahts. But maybe you are. Maybe you're that type of girl . . ."

"Oh come now, child, have a heart."

It was the Chinese woman, her voice raspy like sandpaper.

Later that day, snaking our way through the aisles of the bazaar, Ma took the bag from my hands, put on the Armanis, and laughed a wild laugh of triumph, turning heads in the hot market.

I wake to the sounds of birds. The beggar has left his corner. Ma is already up, smoking a cigarette on the patio, warm wind rushing through the screen door, her small silhouette dark against the sky's red and yellow hues. She's wearing her sunglasses. When I approach, she flicks the cigarette over the railing.

She's taken to smoking lately, something she's never done before, a pack of Benson & Hedges a day. It's one of many things that make my mother seem a stranger to me now. The sunglasses. The smoking. Ma and I, for the first time, taking a vacation together. The case of Tsingtao beer we've lugged down here with us from Bangkok. My mother drinking beer at all. She wears jeans and blouses and baggy T-shirts instead of neatly tailored business suits. She's stopped wearing makeup as well, and—without the rouged cheeks, the crimson lips, the penciled eyebrows—I sometimes feel like I am seeing my mother's face for the very first time. And I have woken up many times now to Ma sitting at a distance, watching me sleep.

"How long have you been up?" I ask groggily, sinking into the chair next to hers.

"A while. Just wanted to see the sunrise."

"Feeling okay?"

"Fine," she says. "It's better this morning. No black dot yet."

A few days ago, she told me that when her vision faltered, it was like looking through a kaleidoscope. A cold white flash flooded her eyes, and when her eyes refocused, it was like the world was breaking into a million tiny pieces. She had to shut her eyes for a while before the shattered world rearranged itself—before pieces of brown became a chair, pieces of red became a shirt, pieces of cream became her own reflection in the bathroom mirror. Sometimes, when she opened her eyes, the world would still be murky, blurred, like opening her eyes underwater, and it often took a while before things came back into focus again. These spells were getting longer and longer now, but she said she didn't really mind them so long as they went away. What she did mind, however, was what she calls "the black dot": a small black pinprick that begins in the center of her vision and expands in an ever-widening circle, like a dark flower whose blooming slowly smothers her sight. It grows larger and larger every day, and when this happens, Ma has to blink hard to keep the dot at bay.

We watch the sunrise together, the fiery orange slowly peeking over the sea, the first of the Andaman Islands a ghostly shadow on the horizon. Ma gets up from her chair. "I'm going to miss this," she says.

The sea is a sheet of blue. We arrive at the port in Trang, buy our tickets to Koh Lukmak, sit down for a bowl of fish soup. We have a long journey ahead of us—eight hours at sea. The stench of fish is in the air and, in the distance, ships bob on the horizon in a line, as if strung together by some invisible thread. Gulls swoop down upon docked junkers, pecking at fish guts left to waste on the ply-wood decks, squawking in their loud, discordant tones.

When we board, Ma promptly falls asleep, lying down across the narrow bench, a life jacket as a pillow beneath her head, the sun a soft blue glow through the tarpaulin. The boat is long and thin, a sixteen-seater manned by a boy my age. He sits at the stern with the rod of the motor in hand, the blades behind him gurgling beneath the sea's surface, the wind blowing through his reddish, sun-soaked hair. The sun climbs the sky. Waves gently slap against the boat's wooden hull. A couple of farangs sit at the bow, outside of the tarpaulin shade, two white men in gaudy batik shirts passing a thin flask of Mekong whiskey between them. Koh Trawen—the island where we will drop off the farangs and stop for lunch before going on to Lukmak—is a faint hazy specter in the distance.

Before she fell asleep, Ma told me that during the 1930s and 1940s, Trawen was a penal colony, a place where the government sent con men, Royalists, dissident writers, and communists. After the war, the prisoners rebelled, murdering all of the authorities on the island. As retribution, the government cut off their rations and left the prisoners there to die, with no means of transport back to the mainland, surrounding the island with a naval patrol so the chao-lay—the sea gypsies—could not come to their rescue. The government claimed they all died there after a few years, starved to death on the edge of the maritime border, but there are fishermen who swear that they still see fires in the hills at night, tiny orange flames flickering out across the open sea, the rebels—or perhaps their children, or perhaps their ghosts—waiting to return to the mainland, preparing for their next assault against the military government.

I watch Trawen's faint outline on the horizon. One of the farangs lies down against the bow, his feet resting on the first bench, a cap pulled over his eyes. His friend stashes the whiskey flask into a backpack and smiles at me. I nod. Then he joins his friend on the bow, face up to the sky, draping a towel across his face. The tarpaulin beats overhead like a light sail. Soon, I am the only person awake except for the boy at the stern directing our small boat out into the Indian Ocean. I watch Ma sleeping for a while, watch the rise and fall of her chest. Every time she sleeps, I wonder if she will wake up blind, and I wonder what I'll do then, what we'll say to each other when the time comes. But soon I, too, start to feel drowsy, the small boat rocking like a cradle on the open sea.

When I wake up, Ma is hunched over, her head in her hands.

"Are you okay?" I ask, trying not to panic, though I'm thinking, *It's happened, it's happened. She's blind now.*

"I think I'm seasick, luk. I'm not used to being on boats." I reach under my seat, hand her a bottle of water. "Here," I say. "Drink up. Breathe deep. Don't look at the floor. I hear it helps if you keep your eyes on the horizon."

Ma sits up straight, takes a couple of deep breaths. She sips from the water bottle. Her face is flushed, beads of sweat clinging to her brow. Trawen is larger now—I can almost make out the shape of trees—and I realize that what I had perceived, from a distance, to be one large island is actually a series of them, four or five smaller islands rising around a larger mound. They seem a thousand shades of green now, the colors multiplying with the closing distance.

"Do you need to vomit, Ma?"

Ma shakes her head from side to side, a hand over her mouth. "We're almost there," I say.

Ma lets out a groan. "How many more hours from Trawen to Lukmak?" she asks.

"Five, Ma."

"Maybe we should stay at Trawen for the night, then, luk. I don't think I can get on this boat again today."

Then Ma is on her knees, her head hanging over the side of the boat, retching and heaving and vomiting. Long streams of light liquid splash into the blue-green surf. I sit on the bench beside her, pull her hair from her forehead, stroke her back. I feel her body tense and relax, tense and relax beneath my hand. She vomits until she cannot vomit any longer, as the farangs look over occasionally before quickly looking away.

"It's best to get it out, madam," the boy says from behind us, his voice carrying over the sputtering engine. From the tone of his voice—easy, matter-of-fact—I can tell that he has tended to many a seasick middle-aged lady. "Just hang on, madam. Trawen won't be long now."

Ma's body relaxes. She reaches down into the surf, scoops up a few mouthfuls of water, spits it back into the ocean. She wipes her mouth with one arm, rests on her elbows against the side of the boat. "You okay, Ma?" She nods quickly, not looking at me, trying to catch her breath. And then Ma widens her eyes, blinks twice. Widens her eyes, blinks twice. Widens her eyes, blinks twice again. She blinks twice, she blinks three times. She reaches out with one hand and grips my thigh tightly, her fingers pinching the skin. I stifle the impulse to yell. I rest a light hand on hers. I urge her on. Widens her eyes, blinks twice. Widens her eyes, blinks twice. Finally, she relaxes her grip and I can feel the blood rushing back to the skin of my thigh. She puts both of her hands in her lap, takes a few deep breaths, and gets up to sit on the seat beside me. "Look at me, luk," she says, her voice weak and frail. "Oh, just look at the state I'm in."

Her hands pat the breast pocket of her blouse, move wildly over her heart. Her eyes dart across the boat's watery bottom.

"What is it, Ma?"

Ma's lips are quivering. Ma's teeth are biting down on the trembling, whitening flesh.

"My—My—Where are—My sunglasses, luk—"

And I imagine the sunglasses slowly falling, the horn-rims and purple rhinestones and the word ARMANI in tiny gold letters spiraling down the blue-green abyss, searching for a resting place on the soft and sandy seafloor.

We decide on a bungalow on the west side of Trawen, a small crescent beach far away from the farangs. With the approaching monsoon, only two of the six bungalows on the beach are occupied. One of the smaller islands around Trawen is but a few hundred meters away, directly facing our bungalow, a modest mound no larger than a city block rising out of the ocean. Earlier, when I asked the boy on the boat if the island had a name, he told me it didn't, it was too small to warrant one. Ma rented one of the bungalows for the boy so he could take us out to Lukmak in the morning and he tied the small boat to one of the pier's barnacle-crusted posts.

Ma falls asleep again after we unpack our bags on the wicker floor, her body splayed across the mattress. I change into my trunks and decide to go for a swim, gently closing the screen door behind me.

The water is as warm as the evening air. I walk out a short distance, my knees slicing through the calm surface. Though we are not at Lukmak yet, it is as Ma hoped it would be: the water like a clear skin stretched over the earth; the sand fine and white and soft as a pillow; the schools of tiny rainbow fishes moving in quick unison. Wind crabs scuttle across the floor, burrowing themselves, leaving fresh divots in the sand.

When the water is up to my waist, I plunge beneath the surface, doing quick breaststrokes away from the beach. My chest skims across the soft, sandy bottom. I come back up for air, take a deep breath, plunge down again. I do it once more, the bottom deeper this time. I can feel the soft incline dip a little more, sense the surface slowly rising above me with every stroke I make along the bottom of the sea. I push up off the bottom with my hands, come up for air, plunge back down again.

I open my eyes this time as I rush to the bottom, kicking hard against the surface. I see soft shafts of sunlight slicing through a thick, bleary haze. Clusters of blue, clusters of yellow, clusters of green disperse all around me, moving as if suspended midair, little pellets of color swimming through a depthless tapestry of light. I hear my feet kicking, my heart beating, the warm water rushing around me. An indistinct seafloor rises up to meet me. I crash into the sand. Perhaps, I think, this is what Ma must feel in the grips of her oncoming blindness. These indistinct visions. These fragmented hues. This weightlessness.

I come back up for air. When I break the surface, I look back onto shore, eyes stinging, lips parched and dry. The bungalow looks small with the island rising up behind it, the sun a golden crown around its peak, the beach a thin white slit in the distance.

I see a door opening, a woman sitting down on the bungalow stairs. She's a red and black dot resting back on her elbows, her feet in the sand. I raise my hand up out of the water to wave to my mother. I'm hoping my mother can see me. I want to believe that she's waving back, that the red and black flutter is the sign of a mother waving to her son. It's me, Ma. Me. I'm swimming back to shore.

The island's electricity generator cuts off with a loud crash at eight. Ma goes inside to fetch the oil lantern, comes back out to sit with me on the beach. The tide has peaked and is beginning to recede.

"Feeling better, Ma?"

"I'm a different person, luk. Sorry about this afternoon."

"Don't be silly, Ma," I say, stretching my legs out in the warm sand. "I'm sorry about the sunglasses."

"Oh," she says, chuckling, lighting a cigarette, fingering the neck of her Tsingtao beer, "they were just silly little things anyway. Probably retribution for taking advantage of that poor girl at Chatuchak."

We sit there silently for a while, listening to the breeze rustling the coconut trees, the waves lapping against the beach, watching the fast shadows of wind crabs racing sideways across the sand.

"Can I ask you a question, luk?"

"Sure."

"Are you going up north at the end of the summer?"

"Well," I say. "Honestly, Ma?"

"Of course."

"I don't know, Ma."

"I was afraid you'd say that."

She takes a drag off her cigarette, the ember casting a soft red glow on her face. She stares out into the darkening ocean. She stubs the cigarette against the beer bottle, sparks flying off the glass.

"Listen to me, luk. Listen to me very carefully." She reaches over and cups my cheeks with her hands. Her palms are cool from the beer. Her touch startles me. "You're going up north at the end of the summer. I don't care what you think—you're going to college. It's what I want for you. You have to go. I don't want you taking care of me, hanging around. I don't expect you to, if that's what you've been worried about all this time. Don't worry. I can take care of myself."

"But Ma—"

"Just listen to me. It's enough that I'm going blind, luk. I don't want you to suffer too. Besides." She takes her hands away, tilts the beer against her lips. "I'm not dying here, luk. I'm just going blind. Just remember that. There's a big difference—a whole world of difference—even if both of those things happen to good people every day."

I wake up to the dark, to the sound of the screen door swinging on its hinges. Ma's sheets are neatly folded on the mattress beside me. I get up, put on a shirt, walk outside, down the bungalow steps. It's quiet save for the wind whistling through the trees, dark except for a flickering flame, bright and orange, throbbing in the distance, moving across the surface of the sea.

I think of the spirit of dead prisoners, of fishermen's tales, but realize quickly that it's only Ma with the oil lantern, that the tide has receded considerably since I went to sleep, the edge of the beach where the water meets the sand some distance away.

The flame of the oil lantern gets smaller and smaller and soon it is merely a pinprick against the dark night. *It's my mother walking on water,* I think. It moves sideways now, moves along the bottom of the dark shadow across the bay, comes to a resting place. *It's my mother on an island with no name.*

I walk toward the water, toward the flickering light. The flame is like an orange eye winking at me from across the divide. The sand is damp, soft as a slab of fresh clay, my feet sinking into its warmth as I walk.

When I come upon the water's edge, I realize there is still considerable distance between where I am standing and the light of Ma's lantern on the island across the bay. Perhaps the water is shallow enough to walk across, but I remember from swimming here yesterday that the bottom quickly falls away and that my mother is not a very strong swimmer.

And then I see it. I see a thin luminous line out of the corner of my eye. I see a thread running faintly across the bay. An opaque sandbar stretched between the islands like an exposed vein.

I walk toward the sandbar, across the beach, my eyes fixed on the flame. I see that the path is no more than a meter wide, a white trail running across the surface of the water. The black sky turns a deep indigo, night slowly relenting to day, and I can make out Ma's small shape sitting beside the flickering lantern. I'm walking onto the sandbar, warm waves licking up across my bare feet, out to watch the sunrise with Ma, and then to bring her back before the tide heaves, before the ocean rises, before this sand becomes the seafloor again.

Thomas O'Malley

NIGHT SLIDES FALLING TO LIGHT

The Greelishes sat at their evening supper and watched as the first snow began to fall over the hills and valleys of Loch Garman. It was a cold, wet December evening in 1954, a week before Christmas. Clouds the color of slate rolled in early and even the animals became silent. The light beyond the hills turned silver, and snow fell with the soft twinkling glow of tapers at midnight mass, and one imagined the soft-hushed, short-breathed prayers of penitent schoolchildren bent in genuflection. Young Matt, who'd been busy doing his chores since he came in from school, helped his mother hang chestnuts and mistletoe and curving lintels of dark green ivy still smelling of black earth and deep rocky raths. Something about the scene beyond their window suggested silence and peace, and the Greelishes were reluctant to break that spell.

John Greelish laughed suddenly, thinking about some local such and such come into the shop that day, and Jenny Greelish smiled as she set the fine china on the table as she always did for the supper, as he proceeded to tell his tale, nodding every once in a while, or shaking her head at the nonsense her husband brought to the dinner table, but it was the sound of his voice she loved—he could have been saying anything and she would have loved it—and all in a language like music she couldn't understand but could feel.

He was a kind-spirited man who never had a bad word for any-one, who would rather smile than frown if he could in the least will himself to do it, as he had all through the previous two winters when he'd gone without work and had traveled to England and to the job sites of Manchester and farther north, Newcastle. Even then, she marveled, the man had found something—anything—to smile about.

How she had waited on his letters, and when they came they never spoke of his hardships over there, although she knew there were plenty; instead he wrote of how much he missed her, and how was young Matt doing at the Good Council, and had the potatoes and turnips he'd sowed come up all right, and the six acres beyond were probably in need of cutting about now, and if she was to talk with Walsh he'd promised him that he'd give him a good price on the topping, and with each letter he'd enclose his paycheck. And though the distance kept them apart and she feared at times—outrageous times in the middle of windy rain-swept nights in which she could get no warmth from either the pillow or the hot-water bottle, and after, she'd chide herself for being so skittish and silly—that he might never return. Still, she'd managed to skimp and save and work the fields frugally, so that by the time he did return late one night, unannounced, having ridden in Pat Burke's pig lorry the thirty miles from Rosslare Harbor, jigging and rolling over the broken macadam of the back roads, they'd embraced and held each other close while young Matt looked on wondering at the serious air of the spectacle— how much weight and significance seemed pressed upon this moment, a weight and gravity he could not quite comprehend. John held her face in his hands, and after they'd kissed she told him proudly, *One thousand pound, John, we've one thousand pound in the bank.* That meant they could buy the house they'd leased from Grennan the past ten years, and John smiled and kissed her again and again, and then nuzzled into her neck until she squealed and pushed him away. Matt smiled and John called to him, and then he held his son and his wife together against him, holding them as if he were holding them for the first time, and as if he might never hold them again.

A sliver of an ashen dusk peaked the far high fields of snow, and Jenny began lighting the paraffin lamps. John Greelish complimented the decorations, the fine, interwoven garlands of ivy, the wildberries and mistletoe, the warm, rich smell of chestnuts that Jenny had baked so that Matt could string them, and he talked of Christmas. Matt sat at the far end of the table listening to his father, enjoying the heavy laughter that spilled from his mouth, the way it jostled and rumbled and shuddered and faded only slowly in his jowls, and in the bristly hair of his wide sideburns. The fire was blazing and smoke from the slag coal intermittently sent a black shiver up the flue, and Jenny dimmed the lamps so that the shadow and spill of light-filled snow danced upon the windows and threw shadows about the room like the images cast by the light of an illuminated picture carousel.

After the dinner they would listen to Radio Luxembourg as they always did with the second draft of tea, and they'd sit before the fire and listen to the news from Britain and Europe and beyond. Matt would stretch out before the fire with the dogs and halfheartedly work on his Irish and on his sums. Most often he'd fall asleep, and Jenny would rouse him for bed, hand him the hot-water bottle she'd already filled with boiling water. That night they heard the gate swing open and footsteps crunching the fresh snow, so slow their progress through the thickening that it seemed forever for them to arrive at the door at all. John rose, wiping his mouth on his napkin, a welcome smile already on his lips, and said, *Put the kettle on for they're sure to be frozen to death, Jenny.* When the knock came he opened the door without hesitation, throwing the latch and the bolt. Then the gunshot rang out. A spike of bone and blood splintered the back of his skull, and he pitched backward to the floor, eyes wide, a charred bullet hole steaming his left temple.

The man at the door stepped over the threshold and into the room as if he had just stepped from a painting, some foreign winterscape projected from the frame of the doorway, its white tableau at his back. A long black overcoat billowed about him, a peaked hat pulled tightly to his brow, a dark scarf drawn across nose and mouth. His boots, thick with crusted snow, sparkled in the light as his coat whipped his calves. And for a moment as he stood there they stared at the startling sight of him with something akin to wonder and horror. Then he fired three more rounds into John Greelish's body, each one shuddering through him and ringing out on the stone floor beneath.

Parabolas of light-filled snow swung and arced across the walls and ceiling. The paraffin lamp flickered, scorched and blackened the glass it bent its flame against. The fire rushed and whined and roared in the flue. *Informer,* the man said, and again, *Informer,* and then walked back out into the night.

Sobbing, huddled together at the base of the table, Jenny held Matt to her, then crawled across the floor on her belly to John. She laid herself over him as if she could protect him, wrap him up and bundle him from the snow that swept in and covered his legs before the open door. She looked out on fields, darkening, and yet so bright and luminescent that she had to blink to see, and the gate swung wide and opened into a white expanse so great and vast and unfamiliar she could not comprehend it.

At a corner of a field in the shelter of an old stone shiel the man pulled the black scarf from his mouth and nostril, pursed his lips and spit. A plume of breath frosted the air before him. He had thin yet well-shaped lips pressed firmly together like the stamp of a seal, high, robust cheekbones razed an hour earlier with the blade, scrubbed raw so that his skin gleamed and the clenched bone of his cheeks seemed as polished as stone. Lifting his hat, he ran a hand through thick, curly hair glistening with Brylcreem. His eyes were glints of blue like sapphire glittering from dark rock, and bluer now against the white.

He rested his long legs upon a fallen capstone, pulled tobacco from his pocket, and slowly, meticulously rolled a cigarette.

Lighting it, he dragged deeply as he watched the snow falling about him, as casually as if it were a smoke after his supper and he'd just consumed a satisfying meal. He smoked the cigarette to the nub, and when he was done he threw the cigarette into the ditch with a sigh. *Greelish is innocent,* he thought, and then dismissed the thought just as quickly—it was no business of his.

He stamped his feet to shake the cold from them, and the ground felt solid and good beneath his feet. He smelled his fingers, the odor of cordite and burnt metal, and he lingered on that smell, turned a gold wedding band slowly and methodically around his finger. He ran a hand through his curls, adjusted his hat, then straightened the crease of his pant leg; he could have been coming from mass.

He pulled up his scarf, climbed easily over a fallen wall, and trudged in a straight, unerring line across the fields toward the car he stole in Enniscorthy that morning and parked a mile distant. Within a matter of minutes his footprints would be gone. There was no one on the roads, and the farms and cottages were all still: an occasional bare light burning dimly from a window, the meager tendril of black smoke bending from a chimney, and snow falling without cessation.

He did not confuse duty with religion or love or with any higher ideal.

This man.

My grandfather.

Years later, Moira—my mother—hears him calling for her—wheezing like a tire puncture from down the hall, past whitewashed walls and crumbling plaster and the fish-gut smell of the river, the stone beneath her feet echoing and clattering and resounding like the footfalls of a penitent walking the halls toward her cell in a cloister, to the small door, dark and fragile as shell with rot. From beyond here she can smell his sickly-sweet sweat, urine-soiled sheets, his brimming chamber pot. A candle burns in a small wall sconce beneath a picture font of the Blessed Virgin, and from this she draws holy water and blesses herself before proceeding through the door.

She lifts the iron latch, dipping her head to avoid the low stone lintel, steps down into the dark cell, and still he is calling for her, urgent now, as if he senses she is there, calling for *Moira* and for the last rites, calling for *Moira* and for God, *An Dia, Toig me on bian seo,* calling, *For the love of God, Moira, come and comfort me, come and take me from this pain.* He always calls Moira because her mother, thankfully, has been dead and in the ground the past two years and beyond his touch; but still it was this way when her mother was alive; it has always been this way since she was old enough to remember, and more so since his illness. This hard, unyielding, implacable man, with his lantern jaw and his face like an inscrutable lock set against the world and all outsiders—all except Moira—is dying.

She sits on the edge of his bed, its weight dipping beneath her, occupying the space that his body can no longer fill. *Daddy,* she whispers, *I'm here, I'm not leaving you. Daddy.*

She leans over his chest, the odor of him and of his chamber pot filling her nostrils, and as her fingers tenderly graze his lips, his mouth, his ragged breathing whispers warm upon her skin with the suggestion of prayer. Her hands enclose his face, and she leans farther over him and pushes against him, and he struggles and fights, and she pushes and pushes, her hands like a fan spread across his nose and mouth, mucus and spittle breaking upon her palms as he sputters for life. She pushes and pushes until his eyes bulge and the veins burst and blood seeps through them, bright blue eyes becoming bluer still, and pink blossoms of blood spilling like ink drops through the white. His Adam's apple stretches hard and round through puckered skin, the freshly shaven patch of gorse she had sheared herself that morning, lathering him from a cracked porcelain bowl of soapy froth, drawing the blade back and forth across his neck, bedeviled and loose and wrinkly and haggard as a scrotum, distended now and reflecting candlelight as bone might. Her father's chest rises and falls like a steam shovel so that she wonders how he can have so much fight and struggle left in him after all these years. His pupils contract and cloud, and a long, lurching hiss of air escapes from between her fingers—one final exhale with chest and body rising, pushing up from the bed—his bladder and bowels emptying in the struggle and the sudden acrid odor filling the room—and still she is forcing her hands down upon him, mashing his lips and nose, his teeth gnashing at the callused bottoms of her hands until they draw blood, and then—he is still.

In the silence she hears wind sighing and snow tapping against the small windows of the darkening room, and her sobs muffled against her father's soiled undershirt, the hard protruding bones of his shrunken chest against hers, and beneath, the vacuum of his absent heartbeat and the silent, swirling sense that in killing her father she has utterly and completely damned herself to his side forever.

A stillness falls over the house and we, the children, blink as if waking from a deep sleep. I hear the snow falling in great clumps from the roof and the wind moaning in the eaves, a crow cawing from the fields, pigs and cows chuffing and snorting from the shed backed up against the wall. And in that moment I know that grandfather is dead.

My mother emerges from his room, shaking her head madly, hands clutched as fists to her mouth. She walks the hall to the main room, footsteps clattering and loud in the silence, and with dusk coming on, everything seems to be lightening around her. An opaque sliver of snow covers the far sedge, and twilight turns it the color of char. Through the small center room with its blazing hearth are the small moon-faces of her children, the Os of our mouths, the sheaf of wheat her mother wove into a St. Bridget's cross, now black and dry and dusty with age, grandfather's fishing tackle, husks of torn line and rotted eel creels, his oversized Wellingtons turned aslant the fire, his shiny, rosin rosary beads—his oiled shotgun above the mantel gleaming dully. She opens the door to the outside world and steps through.

Snow hurls against her face and into her eyes. It gathers in her hair. It is colder than she expected, and the going is difficult, out into white fields, an expanse that seems to grow and grow until nothing else remains. There is nowhere to turn to or to look back to, nothing to break the unerring point of sky and field and horizon, and when she closes her eyes to it, the whiteness wipes clean the slate of her mind, everything that she has known and ever will know again, until there is nothing left at all—just the fields spreading before her.

Dear God, she says to the air—to the sky—to no one at all—*Dear God,* and she cries, but cannot say what it is exactly—this feeling—this weight—this expanse growing within her. She opens her eyes, and there is the wide orbit of the sky and the weight of the land pressed to a horizon curving away like a moon, and the sky seems to occupy everything and hold her there within its impossible arc. From somewhere comes the sound of a sheep bleating, and then nothing. Her feet are numb, her thighs heavy from moving through deep snow. Her heartbeat slows in her chest as she stares at the expanse before her—all color and sound are gone—all thought and emotion. She hesitates for a moment, listening for some sound, a voice, a chorus of trilling souls perhaps, and then she is stepping forward into that other, and the wind catches her back and lifts her up and brings her to it, her wide blue eyes bled of color and turned to white.

Daniel Villasenor

❧

TO A STRANGER

Winter in the east is good for thought, the student was thinking as he left the musty alcove of his apartment stairwell and crossed Fourth Street to the neighborhood park. Each morning he followed the frozen, rutted paths through the park to the subway station on the opposite side. The brief walk enabled him to assemble his thoughts for the day. He knew exactly how much time it took for him to walk at a leisurely pace to the station, and he never missed his train. The Divinity School was in the center of the city, and often he did not return home until eight or nine o'clock in the evening. That morning he was thinking about the gray endlessness that characterizes eastern winters, a kind of protracted sobriety that holds within it a paradox: the sharp, cold knife of each breath and at the same time a diffuse watercolor softness in the low, even clouds and in the dun-colored air, in the grainy dissipations of buildings and in the quiet remove of trees. An impressionistic softness, not nourishing but its opposite, so that the frozen face of winter is really like a human face, like the unyielding and yet fathomless face of someone you have not seen in years, who has experienced more of life's pain and inconsolable joy than you have, who sits across from you and looks discompassionately at your mediocrity, and yet with a kind of surfeit pity for your inexperience—and thereby withholds. So winter in the east is good for thought, the student was thinking.

Not more than three weeks ago he had seen fall from the trees the last perhaps half dozen leaves heretofore clinging to the top-most wind-raked branches of the last be-leafed tree, watching them loose on his way and feeling that incongruous lift of the spirit that the falling of leaves brings, as if death and gravity were pregnant withal with a bizarre levity. He remembered that although the park had not been peopled as it was in warmer months, he had seen a few sparse couples walking together on the Saturday, holding to each other in that intimate way that lovers do as if the ample, inter-twined fabric of their coat sleeves were an electric charge upon their marriage. Upon marriage, he had then thought, if marriage was that endless lean of two souls in weather, two coat sleeves lost and yet supporting each other through the dark contracting months of the year, making the mouths whisper to each other where the bodies leaned, so that wish and dream and shame might thus be absorbed in the amplitude of wool and goose down, scarves and collars and hats. If, he had thought, that padded indivisibility was what mar-riage was.

The student, whose name was Peter, had hardly spoken a word to his wife in recent weeks. In truth it had been many months since he had come home in the evening from his courses and they had eaten supper without an almost unbroken silence, whereas once they talked quietly at table and by the light of the one shapely glass-ensconced candle that had often burnt down and pooled in the pewter before they had done with the elaborate meal. In the first year of their marriage they had sometimes made love in the evenings, before they were too tired, and in bed they were attentive and familiar with each other. The sex was uneventful, tender, and quick. Now he could not remember the last time he had made love to her, and the thought of that would enter him as a train approaches a tunnel and enters and rushes forth, blotting out the light of day, and with its insufferable clamor, all sound and sense and recognition, even the fact of the very train. So that it wasn't a thought at all, but a non-thought ushered upon the roaring back of a thought. He stood as the thought, in all its violent and remorseless inarticulation, entered and passed through him, rocked back on his heels by the wake of it. But then it would just as suddenly be quiet. Looking up, the day appeared blue and lit, just as in the depths of some all-but-entombed railway station light pricks the darkness again upon the passing of a train. And then there was somewhere to go, and something to do. Then the thought, the train, was like a forgotten bad dream that makes one feel all the day a gnawing physical weariness that is just barely untraceable to the stress and impasse and bitter confusion of the nightmare. He never said to himself, You have not made love to your wife. He merely watched the thought approach like an implacable apparition from the distance, even longed for it—longed to feel it smash its brute and inarticulate volume against the wall of his consciousness and the faintly effervescent numbness through his body after—almost a tenderness of absence. He longed for it as a depressed man longs for sleep.

That morning crossing the somber park he recalled again the Saturday just three weeks before when he had seen a few skateboarders trying to outdo each other with their tricks, and a theatrical young black boy wheeling his wonky bicycle in grand curves, speaking to himself without a care to the world's eyes, and earnestly debating something upon himself. There had been the gardeners cajoling each other, raking back the last pulverized leaves into the sallow grass. There had been children of all races about the swings, dressed and clumsy in their vibrant colors, alive in their voices. And walking then through the park he had been able to see the world moving in its turns, and thus turn himself back upon his world: his work, his studies, which were coming along fine. He felt that he was quietly impressive to all his teachers; that he was making headway; that in no long time he would command a similar quiet respect in the university, in the community, perhaps from within the pulpit. He felt confident of his destiny.

But over the course of the previous three weeks, as winter came
on with a terrible finality, especially in the last fortnight, which was
as cold as anyone could remember, so that people began to lose
even that animation which accompanies the advent of terrible
weather, so that their faces began to withdraw in their hoods as dust
into the corner of a room, and they failed to meet each other's eyes,
he had been plagued by a relentless sense of doom and purposeless-
ness. Not just of his own life, for he was not habitually a self-
absorbed man, but an unremitting sense of the folly and pointless-
ness of all human behavior, of all endeavor. That morning, looking
at all the faces in the subway, he could see that there was not a
spark of originality or intelligence on any face, that not a one had
what could be called an internal life, a respectful conversation with
oneself; that they stared blankly in stupefied un-wonder at their feet
or each other or their own alienated jostling images in the darkly
teeming glass; or that they traced with their thumbs spastic patterns
along a briefcase handle or upon a thigh that itself jumped and
twitched under the stress of some facile, visionless ambition; or
they folded and refolded the day's newspaper not so much to learn
of the terrible and innocuous repetitions of the news but simply in
order to refrain from having a thought themselves to which they
would be held accountable by some higher authority within.
Because there was no authority. They had thrown away the authority with the rest of the refuse in which they waded. Or perhaps,
Peter thought, it had never been there, the authority. And here he
shuddered, because the line between an authority within and God
without was a fine one. The disappearance of one meant, did it not,
the disappearance of the other? He had never conceived of the
divinity as an essence apart from human potentiality, and his sudden (or was it sudden?) misanthropy plagued his soul. And he wondered if his ostensible love of mankind was perhaps a fiction he had
created about himself that he might have a path, a course of study
and a position, lacking as he was in other gifts. Looking at the faces
in the subway, he could see no innocence, nor complex awareness,
nor honest grappling, nor that which was called suffering, if suffer-

ing was a clarity of grief. He could see only listless unconsciousness, so that people resembled nothing so much as cattle, and he even began to see or imagine (in his dreary state of mind it was nearly impossible to tell the difference) drool coming from out the corners of people's mouths. He considered what his own face might look like under the strain of such images and he shuddered again. Distraction, he thought, ceaseless distraction and lethargy and the shortsighted mercenary pursuits that feed the pathetic and nearly homogeneous egos of modern people—this is what we call human life. He looked down at the floor of the subway, at the Styrofoam cups, cigarette packs, sections of old newspaper, pamphlets advertising pornography, plastic shopping bags, the wrappers of fast food, and he thought, These people who must ride this same subway every day, who throw down their trash only to look upon it the next day and the next; this heedless discard swelling about my feet is the measure of human life. We care no more than a cow does for his place at the slop.

He had gone through the day with an unshakable torpor. He had even opted to miss his early-evening class, thinking that a swim in the lap pool, and a long steam after, would lift his spirits. The community recreation center was just six blocks from the Divinity School, and passing another park, this one even more humble than the one near his home, he could not help but remark to himself upon the terrible still life of the little brown corner of earth. The hopeless attempt at an idea, an intimation of wilderness eked out within an urban zone the concrete of which stretched as far as a small sea. That too was some figure for the desperation of modern life, he thought, shrugging his shoulders so that his coat collar might cover the pale lobes of his ears (that morning he had forgotten his hat). He looked up at the trees against the monotone press of the sky and he could not help but see the branch tips as inkless writing implements dithering emptily upon the air. Just as in the subway car, the whole dead scene of the park seemed fraught with a terrible animism. Unwittingly he saw, in the large leaning trunk of a tree, in the knots and torqued runnels of the bark, the reclining figure of St. Peter as he is laid on the wooden cross in the crucifixion by Caravaggio, the complete incredulity of abandonment, the stake somehow blood-less through the left hand, the body rising up off the wood even as the men are carrying him inverted, the world-dead eyes of the man as if there has been some mistake, and there has, he thought. There has been a mistake.

In the pool he swam thirty-six lengths of crawl stroke, which was his routine. He dried off and did fifty sit-ups on the mat on the deck, and for a time lay flat on his back and listened to the electric hum of the lights high above like great fluorescent beehives in the vaulted space. He showered and returned to his locker and sat naked on the bench and absently mopped at his neck with the towel, feeling the quiescence of the body after exercise, thinking, If I could just sit here. If only I didn't have to move.

There had been only one other man swimming in the pool and presently he entered the small locker room. By chance, or by fate, of all the lockers in the room his was the one directly next to Peter's. He stood near for a moment, his hip at the level of Peter's bent head, until Peter, who was lost in thought, who was in fact thinking about Jesus, moved a few feet down the bench. He was thinking about the parable where the people are asking Jesus about access to the Kingdom. *Whoever is shut out is shut out, Jesus said. And one of them was heard to say, O Lord, is this thing definite? And Jesus said, Listen: Insight, Knowledge, Obedience, Endurance, Mercy. These have slept in those who have believed and acknowledged me. And since those who slept did not fulfill my commandment, they will be outside the kingdom and the fold of the shepherd; and whoever remains outside the fold will the wolf eat. And although he hears he will be judged and will die, and much suffering and distress and endurance will come upon him; and although he is badly pained and although he is cut into pieces and lacerated with long and painful punishment, yet he will not be able to die quickly.* How, Peter thought, could the bearer of magnanimity speak in the rhetoric of such punitive ultima-tums? How, with an ordinary stone, could the Son of the Father of the universe draw in the sand such a sure line between right and wrong?

Could you help me with this? the man said.

His voice, though it came out of a silence punctuated only by the somnolent drip of a showerhead, did not startle or even surprise. Even as it broke his meditation it seemed to Peter inevitable, faithful as a line delivered upon the stage. In fact directly upon the sound of it Peter suddenly had an omniscient sense about the scene; that he was in a play, or that he and the man were thus composed in a painting of nudes and the one was standing quarter-turned while the other sat ruminating on a bench: Could you help me with this? And the voice! So calm, so light and quiet and sure; unobsequious and yet blithely courteous. Immediately it made him feel lonely. No—it was not a sentiment. Something in the voice made even the possibility of its absence unbearable.

The man, turned thus, looked down at Peter, a silver bracelet dangling from his hand. Could you clasp this for me?

Again the voice! Even as Peter began to take in the man's features—the articulate shoulders, the long muscular limbs, the helix and the faint arch beginning in the low back and tapering to the neck so that his torso looked like a wet paintbrush, and finally the quaint Renaissance face with the graze of a dimple in the chin, eyes the color of molasses in sunlight, the wet light brown hair already beginning to lift up into waves of curls—even as he began to look at the man it was still the voice that disarmed him. Neither low nor high, it had within it at once some improbable conjunction of meditative introspection and mirth. And intelligence, wry but not ironic. And confidence—he had not even said so much as Pardon me. And humility, as if he knew too well that part of human folly that asks of others what should not be asked, and yet here he was standing naked, asking this simple thing. Courtliness, Peter thought, out of nowhere. And then he met his eyes.

The man laughed, pleasantly, and turned from his locker to face Peter. This bracelet, I can't—

Sure, Peter said, standing. Yes, yes, of course.

He took the bracelet and the man held out his arm, underside exposed. Peter brought the chain around the wrist and began to try and open the clasp and fasten it to the diminutive ring. But he couldn't do it. He tried several times but his manual dexterity had never been good, and his hands were damp from the wet towel and his thumb kept sliding off the catch just at the moment when it looked as if he had it. The man stood completely relaxed, his hand neither flaccid nor tense, as if in his open palm he held some invisible seed for invisible birds. Peter redoubled his effort, but the more he concentrated the harder the task seemed until his eyes were burning (he had lately misplaced his swimming goggles) and he could not properly see. The chain slipped off the man's wrist and fell to the bench, and from the bench it slid to the floor. They looked at it together as if it were some saurian presence somehow slipped onto the cold tile of human affairs. Peter rubbed his eyes with the back of his hand. He could hear his own breath, three breaths for every one of the man's. For a moment neither of the men moved to retrieve the chain. Then Peter bent down and gathered it in his hand. Do not look, he said to himself, Do not. But against all willpower, as he stood his eyes grazed for an instant the tight balls and the clean, tapered shaft, flaccid and circumcised, the one vein traversing a diagonal and voluted path along the relaxed curving beauty of it. Velvet, he thought, banishing the word from all future discourse even as he thought it. The man leaned closer to avail himself more earnestly to the task, and as he did so a current of what we call power—the quality of quality restrained—came off of his body or his breath, Peter could not say. Only it seemed he could not get enough air. He brought the chain once more around the wrist, but he could not even manage to pull back the tiny spring. I can't get it, he said.

He looked briefly into the man's eyes. He knew that those eyes had watched his body as it bent down. Even before he had begun to bend he had acquiesced to that, known that the eyes would follow him quietly and shamelessly, that he would for that time be blind to their gaze, helpless before it. He had bent to the floor as one bends back into a dream upon briefly waking, knowing that the conclusion might terrify and betray him, but unable to resist the sensation of the plummet. The man for his part looked at Peter evenly. His look was not prurient per se, but alive, abundant, and if there was the suggestion of sex in the flare at the heart of the pupils, it was more the suggestion that sex might be where the intelligence places it, and that this might be such a moment, and it might not be. The eyes were simply interested. At which point Peter saw himself in his situation. He began to panic. The locker-room door swung open and a man entered and heaved his bag onto the end of the bench and looked at the two men standing there like some statuary of delicate communion, Peter's fingers actually grazing the other man's wrist veins as if he were poised to press some strings to the frets of an instrument. The man picked up his bag and went to the next row of lockers and coughed. I can't do it, Peter said again, whispering it fiercely as if it were some desperate secret between them. I'm sorry.

Just try one more time, the man said quietly. I think you've almost got it.

And so he did. With tremendous concentration Peter bent to the bracelet, his eyes leaking from chlorine, tiny sweat beads breaking out now upon his upper lip. He could barely see; he felt as if he were trying to thread a needle underwater. And when the chain did finally clasp it was something of a small miracle. He breathed, straightening, pressing his eyes again with the backs of his hands. He looked at the man and smiled broadly, and the man smiled at him. Suddenly they broke out laughing together and clasped each other by the arms as if they had accomplished something perilous and of consequence. Thank you, the man said.

You're welcome, Peter said.

The man turned around and lifted his shirt from its hook and held it open in front of himself. He stood examining the shirt a long time, holding it thumb and forefinger each to the seam of a shoulder, like a mirror in whose draping folds he seemed to be noting the current of life in his own body. Peter watched him. Then they dressed in silence. Peter hurried. He could feel his clothes absorbing the dampness he had neglected and he cursed himself. It's the coldest day of the year, he said.

I was just thinking that I didn't want to go outside.

The voice! Again that resonant calmness! The paradox of it! The anchored levity of it! How did one live into such a voice? He was desperate to hear it again but he could think of nothing trivial enough, or important enough, to say to him. And he was equally as desperate to get away. He finished dressing and ducked his head under his satchel strap, but as he made for the door the man said, Wait, just a second.

Peter turned. The man was fully dressed now but his shirt was still open, and he held one sock in his hand. He stood looking at Peter a moment, and then suddenly he put the sock in his mouth— a gesture that should have seemed ridiculously childish, but with the man it was simply spirited, gamy—and bent, rifling through his duffel bag. He pulled out a worn paperback book and sifted through the pages until he found the one he was looking for, and then he carefully ripped the page from the welt. He walked toward Peter, folding the paper once before he placed it in his hand.

It hardly matters if you feel the same, he said, or even understand. It's just very rare, and Whitman says it best. And I happen to have him with me. It would trouble me always if I didn't tell you.

He spoke in the same easy, direct, and unaffected regal timbre. A voice that could incur no debt, Peter thought. Thank you, Peter said, not looking at the piece of paper. He turned and pushed open the door and walked, echoing down the hall.

When he reached the far end and opened the door to the street he could not believe how cold it had become. And now there was wind. Debris flew down the avenue in fits and starts, and in the harsher gusts the street signs buckled. Outside, he pulled the door shut with difficulty and stood leaning against it, breathing as if he had been walking uphill. In the light from the sign above the lintel he examined the paper. It was a poem of Walt Whitman's entitled "To a Stranger":

Passing stranger! You do not know how longingly I look
    upon you,
You must be he I was seeking, or she I was seeking
    (it comes to me as of a dream),
I have somewhere surely lived a life of joy with you,
All is recall'd as we flit by each other, fluid, affectionate,
    chaste, matured,
You grew up with me, were a boy with me or a girl with me,
I ate with you and slept with you, your body has become
    not yours only nor left my body mine only,
You give me the pleasure of your eyes, face, flesh, as we
    pass,
You take of my beard, breast, hands, in return,
I am not to speak to you, I am to think of you when
    I sit alone or wake at night alone,
I am to wait, I do not doubt I am to meet you again,
I am to see to it that I do not lose you.

He read it twice, then he folded it and stuffed it in the pocket of his wool duster. He walked half a block and then he stopped: It would trouble me always if I didn't tell you. He repeated this last sentence of the man's over and over again, and then he laughed suddenly, a short, hard burst of submerged air. I have never in my life uttered a single true sentence, he said out loud.

He began walking again, his hands jammed into his pockets so hard the inverse pressure seemed to pump his feet lightly up out of the ground. The clarity of the man! And to preserve his dignity by telling a truth to a stranger, and yet to ask nothing of him! In word or tone or demeanor—to ask nothing of him. Where did such reserve come from? Peter silently screamed the question to himself. And he answered himself: He has no shame. And how much shame must one openly eat, he thought, until shame disappears?

He was walking rapidly with his head down. When he looked up he saw that he had passed his subway stop. Retracing his steps, he thought, If he has no shame, then his conscience must not thwart him. And if he spoke that way to me, to a stranger, naked and in a locker room, then he must carry himself always without fear, and he must believe what he thinks and think what he believes, and he must be at once undivided and variable, and the world must be full of endless possibility and mystery for him. And he felt, for a moment, what an adventure life must be for such a man. He was suddenly struck with a blow of nausea, and he wanted to go home. He stood in the walk and breathed and looked about the city, at the lights along the converging streets in their endless processions, and upward at the buildings and the sporadic yellow squares of light—so many fulgent paper cutouts upon the sky. And he thought that behind each window someone must be mulling over sentences, words in the mind that he or she was trying to shave closer and closer to truth, so that they might thereby untrouble themselves; that people everywhere, this very minute, were answering the terrible summons of their souls, together or privately, performing small acts of bravery that would release them from the prison of their fears. And he had a tremendous desire to go home, to open the door of the apartment, and to blaze upon his lovely wife these thoughts and words.

He got off the 6 train at Fifty-ninth Street and walked up the station stairs into the freezing night, then crossed the street and descended the south-side steps and entered the F to Brooklyn, and sat, all the while talking to his wife. But by the time the train entered the Seventh Avenue station he was growing numb. Words, revelations, and entreaties, which so immediately prior had been prompt and eloquent on his tongue, slipped from him now, down through his body like schools of dead fish sinking through a chemical sea. There was an acidic taste in his mouth. And by the time he was walking through the familiar paths of the park, abruptly he had nothing to say. The words were gone; he could not have found them to spare his life. And the warm woman he had pictured taking him prodigally in her arms, this anima-wife, this sibling figure of endless compassion, had become again the cold companion of his house. Even their friendship was dead. They could not please each other if they tried. He stood stock-still in the middle of the park, as silent and as cold as one of the trees.

When he finally climbed the steps to his landing it was late, and he knew he had missed dinner. He stood freezing outside the door, wishing he were wet with snow, wishing he could shake out some dampness in two or three snaps of his elbow, that the drama of the action might help him enter his house. Jennifer, he said, as he stepped into the hall and shut the door.

His wife did not say anything. He heard her rise from the couch in the living room and pad into the kitchen. He heard the refrigerator door open and close. She is laying out the cold brisket and the boiled string beans on a plate, he thought. She is lifting, as if it were the grossest impertinence to have to do so, a dead dollop of mashed potatoes and slopping it cold on a plate, and she is not even going to ask me if I want it heated up. She's put her hair up tight and her face is pulled back as if by wire, and her eyes are the color of gunmetal, and she is looking at the food right now wondering if she should heat it up, and she's not going to.

Baby, his wife called from the kitchen, I'm heating up your dinner. Do you want a roll?

He turned and leaned his forehead against the wall. Yes, thank you.

He walked down the dark hall to the kitchen and stood in the door looking at her back. She wore a faded midnight-blue silk nightgown and her old sheepskin slippers with the clumped wool lining. Her hair was not tied back but swung loose and pendular, dark blond, past her shoulders. He could see the remnants of auburn tint in her hair where she bent under the overhead light of the stove. I met a man today, he said.

Hmm, she said.

In recent weeks, nay, months, they had grown used to speaking to each other in short blurts of meaningless data, miserable non-attempts at conversation, such as, I met a man today who reminded me of someone, or, So-and-so's wife has an old Volvo, or, There are some students from the department meeting next week at that Cuban restaurant we read about last year. And these phrases lately went unanswered, as if they were fragments of some background broadcast of radio or television that interrupted the silence when the distant signal came in. She turned from the stove and set his plate on the table and turned back to the sink and started placing the not-yet-dry dishes in the cupboard, loudly. In recent months she had become noisy, whereas once she seemed to attend even inanimate objects as if they had a vulnerable sentience. This was one of the qualities about her that he had loved. Now she seemed to try to sound every object she handled and test its strength to the breaking point against another. In fact she had broken several dishes inadvertently lately. And her back, her body on the whole, as he sat now looking at her, moved in hard, jutting motions; her shoulders were high in a perpetual shrug. I met a man today, he said, not lifting his utensils.

She paused and moved her hair from about her face, but did not say anything or turn around. When she finished storing the dishes she stood looking down into the empty sink. She stood on her toes a moment and then she arched her back slightly, rising further on her toes, and as if her whole body was inflated with a single breath, she exhaled, slumping at the sink in sudden and profound diminishment, her body vibrating minutely as she braced herself to keep from falling to the floor. I can't go on like this, she said, her mouth hardly moving, as if she were cold. She stood and turned. I can't, Peter. I can't go on like this anymore.

She leveled at him terribly now, and she looked, Peter thought, gutted, like a house after a savage storm. That is despair, he thought—if you can just get up and touch her you will be her husband.

He rose and walked to her and put his arms around her. He wanted to tell her that he understood, that they shared a like despair, and that if they could just realize it together all would be fine. But he could not find those words. I met a man today, he said instead. At the pool, a swimmer.

Peter, are you listening to me, she whispered fiercely into his shoulder. I can't take another step like this. I'm dying.

Yes, he said. I understand. I am too. I'm trying to tell you something.

What are you trying to tell me?

I met a man.

For a moment they were in a complete unbridgeable privacy. He felt her falling a great distance, speeding through his arms. There was a muffled horn from the street, and laughter, a greeting, a door slamming somewhere in the apartment complex. She caught her breath. She leaned back and looked up at his face a long time. Her eyes were swollen and her mouth was a deeper bordeaux, and blowzy, and there was an almond glow about her skin. He realized that even before he had come home she had been crying. Are you saying—

Yes.

What are you saying?

Yes. I don't know.

When?

Today. I said so. Maybe all my life.

She looked into his eyes, one and then the other, as if she were measuring the yield of one truth against the other. Perhaps five minutes passed. She looked at him without reprieve. Peter, she whispered finally. She had never been so still, and yet it seemed to Peter that all the faces of her life, the oeuvre of her mien, her selves, those he'd heard of and seen in pictures, and the tidy array of faces he'd married, it seemed they passed across her face until they passed, or rather bypassed, the two of them as there they stood, and then she was unrecognizable. And he saw, from far in the reaches of her strange eyes, from the inscrutable underside of the world, he thought, a flicker, a flare begin to dawn as slow and circumspect as the day's dawn itself, until she seemed to shed and gain her innocence in a single stare, like a child who, with its finger along a blade or in a flame, experiences the first numb awareness of the ecstasy of pain. She was almost smiling; one corner of her mouth began to quiver and lift with that wry ascent to paradox that so quickly becomes a kind of irrepressible glory, and profoundly female. She began to walk him back to his chair, shaking her head back and forth slowly, her eyes wet and confounded and full of tragic resolution. When his calves pressed the edge of the seat he sat. Tell me about him, she said, and directly she had said it she clapped her hand over her mouth. With her other hand she began to loose the tie of her gown.

Are you laughing at me? he said.

Tell me about him, she said, sliding off her slippers.

I want to laugh, Peter said.

Her gown swung open. She squatted and unzipped his trousers and pulled down his boxer shorts and took his sex in her hand. Laugh, she said, looking up at him, her mouth trembling, expressions of indignation, seduction, and the spur to tears fleeing about her face like leaf-shadow. And rising now, laughing herself with a sound more like gasping for astonishment, or pleasure, she swung one leg over his thigh, and then the other, and then lowered herself upon his lap, her gown spread around her, his sex still in her hand. And he did fairly harden. And she placed him inside herself and began slowly to move. Tell me about him, she said.

Jennifer, he said.

Him, she said.

He was beautiful.

My God, she said, lifting up and angling herself the better to have him.

Not God, Peter said, moving into her now.

I don't care, she said.

Don't you? Peter said harshly. Don't you? Don't you?

God, she said. Just take me.

He thrust vigorously then, bracing himself with his hands and rising up off the chair.

Tell me, she whispered fiercely in his ear.

I'm going to come, he said.

And she stopped instantly, leaning back and looking into his eyes with some shifting admixture of compassion, arrogance, lust, pity, wonder, and terrible need. Let me watch you, she said. You never let me watch you. I've always wanted to watch you.

And she began to move again even as he started to come. He looked at her as long as he could and then he flung his hands over her face.

No, she said, knocking his arms away. She threw her arms about his neck, sobbing as his convulsions died into her.

He held her in stillness a long time after, listening to the house. At some point he shucked off his shoes and underwear and his trousers and stood and carried her into their bedroom and laid her down on the bed. He took off his shirt and moved naked alongside her, his body against her back, feeling her breathe. In the low light of the bedside lamp he studied her face. He looked at her skin, at the pores of her skin. He saw the faint sickle-shaped marks outlining her mouth, lines he had never seen before in repose, only when she smiled or frowned. Her mouth was dry; small flame-shaped flakes of skin rose upward on her lower lip like the peaks of spume upon ocean waves. He bent into her nape and inhaled her. It seemed to him that in a single breath he could imbibe her whole life, her childhood, her brief, rare, irrepressible moments of happiness, and her shattered dreams. It seemed to him that a multitude of lungs dilated throughout his body, that his body was a lung, that there was in him an infinite invitation to air. Her eyelids flickered, and he remembered the first time he had watched her dream. He leaned back and traced with his eyes the line of her neck from where it extended from the soft hair on the back of her head to her small, sharp shoulder. He looked at the wing of her scapula, rising and falling, or rather opening and closing in a breaking rhythm in time with her breath. Her skin—all human skin—seemed so frail, so thin, to house such subtle convergences. She seemed to him a delicate bird that had flown headlong into his care, given him her life. And it occurred to him with a resolute clarity that he had deceived her as he had deceived himself. It had so little to do with the swimmer, beautiful as he was. If they failed at marriage it would be because, undisguised, they did not help each other live. My God, he thought, marriage . . . marriage was not, as he had surmised just weeks before, some soft contract of mutual absorption, but something far stranger, and more harrowing. Perhaps it reached its shining significance only in the moment of its dissolution, like a god; perhaps it went on expanding, like a galaxy. His hand was poised over his wife's hair, not wanting to touch her lest he keep her from sleeping, and wanting all the same to stroke her into sleep. We can care for no one, he thought, beyond our ability to hurt them. And it was as if she heard his mind, for she turned and looked up at him and said, Peter, I'm so scared.

I know, he whispered. I am too. But I don't want to lie anymore.

Are you lying?

No, but inside.

Inside? Are you lying inside?

I don't know. I'm so glad it's winter. I need time.

Time for what?

Time to begin to think without lying.

I'm afraid, she said, that if I sleep when I wake up it will be like it was before.

It won't be, he said.

And he lay there with his arms around her, and she did finally sleep, and he felt that they were traveling, that if they looked out the window they would see earth and trees and cities moving by them, landscapes of places and peoples they had never heard of, or read about in the books of such things.

Charles Baxter

REINCARNATION

We had reached that part of the dinner when all the guests, smoothed out with wine and the meal, the first and second helpings, sit back and speak their minds. "Hearts," I would once have said, "sit back and speak their *hearts.*" I used to think that this was the basis of civilization, such conversations. Late spring, and the last of the light flowed through the west windows over the radiators, and over the boards on the radiators, and the houseplants on the boards. We were sitting in Ryan and Alicia's house, and we had eaten the dinner they had served. We were there, my wife and I, and Gray and Brant, who had been together for six years and might as well have been married.

In houses like this one where all the furniture is worn, the fabric frayed by use or scratched and shredded by the cats and children, the music stand knocked over, the flute on the mantel, and the sheet music for flute jammed in underneath the scattered books on the coffee table, you feel an atmosphere of *Sure, why not, go ahead, let it happen,* a kind of relaxed tattered permission. You wouldn't have that permission if you hadn't been invited in the first place, but the hint of squalor really lets you go. Alicia had taken her shoes off. She was sitting next to me, and she was wearing a white cotton dress, and her legs were crossed and glowing in the last of the spring light. She is a pretty woman with rust-colored hair and warm, intelligent brown eyes that go sleepy when she's amused, and she's a close listener who watches you as you talk and remembers your gestures and gives them back to you, though not exactly in a mocking way. Of course I was in love with her a little, but it was friendly and comfortable and didn't have an emergency feeling to it. She was an anthropologist and a semiprofessional musician who had given up anthropology for a year or two of motherhood.

The talk had turned to reincarnation. Was this bourgeois, this topic? Yes. Okay, fine. If that needs to be acknowledged.

"In my previous life," I said, "I was a hedgehog." I nodded, agreeing with myself. "A hedgehog, nosing around under the hedges, eating grubs."

"What kind of grubs?" Brant asked. "It makes a difference."

"No," I said, "it doesn't make any difference. But since you ask, the grubs I ate, as a hedgehog, were larvae, beetle larvae. That's a fact."

"Is it?" my wife asked. "Is it a fact?" We had recently quarreled.

"Yes," I said, "it is." We're still friendly, though, my wife and I. "What were *you,*" I asked her, "in your previous life?"

"Why don't you ask Ryan over there?" she said. "I don't know what I was. He might know."

"Okay, Ryan," I said. "What's your opinion?"

Ryan is an incredibly—actually, preposterously—handsome accountant who works for the city. When you're walking with him, women and men turn helplessly to gaze in his direction. He's baffled by his own good looks and doesn't know what to do with them. It's like a freak accident. He's a bit dull, though, as handsome people often are. As the genial host, he was sitting back and smiling at us, his arms crossed, leaning back in his chair. "In my previous life," Ryan said, "I was a swan."

"Ryan," my wife said, "you *are* a swan."

"No," he said, "I was a swan, I'm not a swan now. I'm an ex-swan."

"So," my wife said. "I've always been curious about this: what *do* swans eat?"

Ryan, quite nonplussed by my wife's question, raised his arms up and touched his brow, as if he were thinking. The light was disappearing from the living room and the dining room, as if leached out by the window facing the street. Alicia and Ryan's children were making a racket downstairs.

"What were *you?*" Alicia asked, turning toward Gray and Brant, but directing the question to Brant, who's funnier and more talkative than Gray usually is. Gray doesn't always make eye contact, even when he's speaking to someone. This particular evening he was playing with his water glass. "I was a priest," Brant said.

"Where?"

"In a little rural parish," Brant said, smoothing out his ponytail, running his fingers through it. "In Saskatchewan. I heard confessions. All my previous adult life I heard the confessions of the rural farmers. Run-of-the-mill sins. I waited for the big sins, but I never got any. It drove me to drink. Run-of-the-mill sins drove me to a run-of-the-mill addiction. I kept hoping for something hugely awful, but it never came my way. In disappointment, I died after a fall down the parish stairs."

"You would have made it to the hospital," Gray said, looking up from his water glass toward Brant, "if that swan hadn't been crossing the road in front of the ambulance."

"I never did that," Ryan said, shaking his head. "I never crossed the road in front of an ambulance. I would never do that. It's not swanlike."

My wife had taken her sandals off now, down there under the table somewhere, half in imitation of Alicia, half not.

Gray said, "What's all this about animals? I thought people in their previous lives were exalted. You know, like Napoleon and Judy Garland." He had a pleasingly melancholic delivery, a great FM voice, and, in fact, worked at the local NPR station. Today his nose was sharper; he was a bit too thin, I thought. It was worrisome.

"I was never Judy Garland," Brant said, raising his face to imaginary footlights. "I was never anybody famous. I wasn't even as famous as Ruth Roman. I was a parish priest, that's all. I listened to confessions, verbal leftovers of desperate fun."

"Well, I was," Alicia said. "I was famous."

"*You* were famous?" Ryan asked, reached down to touch her in a husbandly way on the ankle. I would have envied him at that moment for having married Alicia if I had been an envious man. "You?"

"Yes, I was."

"Well, who were you?" Brant asked her. "What name did they give you?"

"That would be telling," Alicia said. "But I was beautiful. There was this thing that I did, this endearing little turning-of-the-head, kind of a shy pout thing. It broke hearts."

"Alicia, dear," Brant said, grinning, "you do that *now.*"

"You were Marie Antoinette," Ryan near-whispered to her. "You told the rest of us to eat cake."

My wife drank the rest of her wine and raised her arms in an exasperated stretch. She's class-conscious and generally doesn't like whimsy in any of its forms, especially this kind. "Marie Antoinette! Why do middle-class people, people like us, talk so much about incarnation and reincarnation? We should be talking about our lives right now. I just don't understand it, or maybe I do understand it. It just seems vain to me. Actually, no, it doesn't seem vain so much as habitual." She stretched again, and her beauty, her earnest small-town integrity and physical grace, flared up in that one movement. I could tell she was going to start something. "I'm sure about one thing," she said. "When I'm dead, I'll be dust. No more of me anywhere. I'll be among the happy dead. I don't want to go around this routine one more time. No thanks. Once is enough, is my opinion. You know what I saw today?"

"Katherine," I said.

"This is what I saw," my wife said. Alicia was nodding in her direction and pouring more wine. "What I saw was couples, or I mean *a* couple, in Ridgeway Park down by the reservoir. I was hurrying home. Speeding to pick up the kids. So there was this couple.

And, of course, they were beautiful. She was beautiful and he was beautiful and they were being beautiful together. They had a blanket and a picnic basket and, of course, it was a warm day. She was wearing a dress a lot like yours, Alicia. Ah, no," Katherine said, correcting herself, "she wasn't. I just remembered. She was wearing blue jeans. So was he. His hair was longer than hers, and more blond. They were sort of nestled together like one of those French paintings, picnics on the lawn, one of those *popular* paintings.

"They were happy, naturally. I could tell that, even though I was speeding by and was behind the wheel. So I gave them a wave. I don't know if the girl saw me. They had leaned forward to kiss, and it was pretty slow, the way youngsters take their time when they're kissing, exploratory. I might have been speeding by, but I could tell that, at least. And it set me to thinking. Why do people, when they're as happy as that, insist on being happy in the most public place? I'm not guiltless. I used to do that. I used to put on public displays. Sometimes lovers find bushes or trees to hide behind, but more often these days they're right out there. And you know what I felt like doing?"

"Yes," Gray said. "You felt like standing up in the movie theater and shouting, 'Don't do it! It's not too late to change your minds, both of you.' "

Alicia interrupted at that point. She was rather good at interrupting in such a way that you would never notice that she was interrupting. "Brant," she said, "I can't get it out of my head what you said a minute or two ago." She stopped and inserted a little interim of silence into the evening so that we could all get our breath. "Those run-of-the-mill sins that you listened to, when you were a parish priest. What sort of sins were they? You never said."

"I couldn't tell you."

"Why not!" Alicia was gently imitating Brant's head motions.

"I couldn't tell you," Brant said, "because it would violate the sanctity and the privacy of the confessional box."

"But it's over," I said, recovering myself somewhat. "You're dead, and the Saskatchewan farmers are dead, so you can tell us now."

"I try not to remember the bad things in my previous lives," Brant said huffily. "I try only to remember the good things."

"Oh now, *that's* an exaggeration," Gray said, touching Brant on the arm.

"Well, I can tell you that they masturbate a lot," Brant said.

Ryan was pouring the wine, making his handsome and pleasingly dull presence known. "Oh, I doubt it," he said. "I don't think farmers masturbate all that often." Then he stopped as if he had thought of something. "I don't think they need to."

"I wasn't talking about the men," Brant said. "I meant the women."

"What do the men do?" I asked.

"Oh, them? Well, they get into land auctions, and fights, and bankruptcy hearings, and they farm and farm and farm. How should I know? All I heard about was their sins, and then I died. Oh, listen: I just remembered." He drank what was left of his wine, and instantly Ryan poured more. "Here's a story I remember. This isn't run-of-the-mill. This is a story you'll all like.

"We had this neighbor when I was a kid, I mean when I was a parish priest—no, forget that—a really nice guy to the neighborhood kids, very kind and all that. He was the father of two daughters, and they were about age ten or something. He was so nice, and everyone *said* he was so nice, that, after a while, he became the sort of guy who can't discover himself doing anything wrong. It's like Elizabeth Taylor coming to believe that she's Elizabeth Taylor. And what this man did was, he fell terribly in love with the woman who lived down the block and across the street. Whose name, if you can believe it, was Claire Carlson. The guy's name was Jimmy Palantier. Anyway, this guy, Jimmy, fell in love with Claire Carlson, the neighbor, and she must have been touched by him because they had an affair. That's not the interesting part of the story. No one would care about the story if that was all there was to it.

"No, the interesting part of the story has to do with Jimmy. And the fact that he thought he was a nice guy and could not discover, I guess you'd say, a flaw in himself. Here he was, in love, and married to someone else. He couldn't feel guilty. He knew he was supposed to, but he couldn't. And what he did—this is where the story begins—was to become friends, or better friends, with Claire Carlson's husband, whom everybody called J.T. I can't remember what the initials stood for. He wanted to be friends with the husband of the woman he was sleeping with. Maybe he thought that he would get closer to her that way. Or that he'd keep everything on this positive social level. I don't know what he thought.

"So Jimmy would call up this big, burly guy, J.T., or somehow arrange to borrow a shovel or a power tool, and they would chat. The thin guy and the burly guy would talk. They were both ex-navy men. They had that in common. The important feature of this story is that J.T. would chat *back*. Like the family man he was. Like the family men they were. Straight men are quite a puzzle. Anyway, they started doing householder whatnot together. They'd give each other help on repair projects, chopping and sawing down dead trees in the yard, that sort of thing. Sometimes they needed a tool, a gizmo, and they'd go off together, and you can imagine Claire's surprise when she saw her lover and her husband hunkering down inside her husband's truck, dusting up the driveway, doing various errands. It terrified her, seeing this.

"Meanwhile, she and Jimmy were sleeping with each other whenever it could be arranged. She probably asked him to stop being friendly with her husband and he probably refused."

"How do you know this," I interrupted, "if you were a child at the time?"

Brant took off his glasses, pulled out his shirt from his trousers, and polished the lenses on the shirt flap. I noticed a food stain on the fabric. "Don't ask me how I know," he said. "I just know, that's all. Where was I in my story?" Brant sighed. "Oh, yes. Jimmy and J.T. out in the truck, passing a bait-and-tackle shop. They discovered that they both liked to fish. They stopped and bought some new line and lures. Guy equipment. It turned out that Jimmy had a boat with an outboard motor. They bought fishing licenses. One day, one summer day, let's say in mid-July, they went fishing. They left Claire behind. I don't know what Jimmy's wife was doing. She's not part of this story.

"So the lover and the husband stepped into the boat with their fishing poles and lines and out they went into the bay of Henryson Lake, about fifteen miles west of here. It's a good lake for fishing, particularly on the west side, I'm told. Pike and bass, so they say. How would I know? You won't catch me catching fish. So they're out on the boat. Whenever I think about this, I think of the air, the *largeness* of the sun and the air and the sky, and the wind, you know, causing the water to lap against the boat. I think about these things. I even think of the strength of the fishing line they were using, and if it broke. I think of those two guys in the boat, fishing."

"You weren't there," Katherine said.

"No, I wasn't there."

"So, you're making this up. So, this is all academic."

Brant put his glasses back on. "No, it is not academic. Not at all. I keep thinking about the water and the wind, and sometimes I wonder if there was a smell of inland lakewater vegetation, you know, one of those heavy green smells."

"So, they're out on the boat," my wife said.

"Yeah," Ryan said, leaning back, so that a bit of light from the west window rushed across his face, streaking it. "Which guy killed the other guy?"

"I keep forgetting that I'm in America," Brant said. "That's surprising, because I'm an American and I've never been out of this country. I keep forgetting about the necessities of violence in the U.S.A. Well, if you were expecting violence, you'll be disappointed. Something else happened."

"Brant, don't be coy," Gray said. "Just tell the story."

"All right," Brant said. He leaned forward, instead of back, and he put his elbows on the dinner table, and he grinned suddenly and unexpectedly. "J.T. caught something; the line pulled and the reel sang, and he yanked and pulled in a tremendous fish, and together they brought it in. Jimmy scooped the fishnet down into the water and pulled the monster into the boat and then they put it on the what-do-you-call-it, the . . ."

"The fish pail," I said.

"No, not the fish pail. The stringer. They looped its gills and put it back into the water to keep it fresh and alive, and they laughed over their luck with the fish, and in the laughter that followed this catch, this triumph, with J.T. smiling and Jimmy smiling, in that moment of camaraderie and fellowship occasioned by the catching of the enormous fish, J.T. turned to Jimmy, and he said, quietly and suddenly clear as day, clear as a shiny knife, '*I know what you're doing.'* "

Brant sat back in his chair, crossed his arms, and looked at all of us with satisfaction.

"That's what he said?" I asked. " 'I know what you're doing'?"

"That's it."

Alicia, who was still sitting next to me, moved her chair back away from the table and she tapped the wood floor with her bare foot impatiently. "I don't get it. That's your story? That's what it leads up to?"

"Yes." Brant was apparently pleased that his story's success had been wasted on us. "Two people in a boat. One man has a secret, he thinks, and is cheating the other man. But the other man knows. The other man says, 'I know what you're doing.' And that's the end of the story. That's all the story has to tell. Because it's enough to know that one of them recognizes what the other one is up to."

"Men don't act that way," Alicia said.

"How do they act? Tell me about men."

"I don't know. They just don't act *that* way. More wine, anybody?" She held up the bottle.

"They go into rages," Gray said. He hadn't said much until now, and I had been thinking, and not for the first time, how well his name suited him. "They fight. Or they're silent. They don't settle for *knowing.* That's an untrue story. That's always been an untrue story. You heard that story from your mother, and she got the facts wrong or she remanufactured them. That story doesn't come third-hand. It comes fifth-hand." He was picking at something on his face as he said this.

Brant raised his hand slyly and then pretended to toss away an invisible ball the hand had held. "Doesn't matter where the story comes from, or who got it. It doesn't even matter if it's true. The topic of conversation was run-of-the-mill sins."

"No," l said, "we were talking about reincarnation."

"Well, it's about that, too."

"It does matter if it's true," Ryan said, standing up, motioning us away from the dinner table. "It matters if it happened. If those guys were in the boat."

Brant looked at him, one of those slightly unpleasant looks when there's too much intensity in the gaze. "No, it doesn't matter if they were in the boat. It only matters if you think it could have happened. I think it could have. Maybe you don't think so. Do you think it could have happened? Come on, Ryan. Give us your view."

Ryan was walking into the kitchen. I don't know what he had in mind to get there. Without turning around, he said, "All right. Yes. It could have happened."

Alicia leaned toward me. She said, "It's not enough to know something. You have to tell somebody that you know. Your knowledge has to be known."

"What happens then?" I asked.

"Then the wind dies and you're out in the boat together," she said.

An hour later, we had all stepped into the backyard in the semidark with one small floodlight aimed toward the trees. The floodlight was on a bad switch and would go off from time to time. What Ryan and Alicia had built out there was something of a wooden platform without railings where you could squat or stand or sit while you contemplated the stars or the darkness of the woods beyond the floodlight. There were chairs, a few. Like the rest of the house, it wasn't quite enough of anything to be festive. The boards were sagging inwardly, and the deck gave the impression of being in

remission from an attack of the natural, organic sort. Ryan and
Alicia were looking after the drinks, and Brant and Gray were gazing up at a treehouse that Ryan's son from his first marriage had
built. The talk had slowed down and evolved into mutters and one-
liners and half-lit noddings in the dark.

"Incarnation," I said, my words aimed straight up into the
largely empty sky. "I happen to know one thing about it. I saw it
once. It happened in New Jersey."

From behind me, I heard Gray saying, "No one ever got reincarnated in New Jersey. Can't happen."

"I didn't say 'reincarnated.' I said 'incarnated.' Do you want to
hear this story or not?" I asked, irritable in my most sociable manner. "This story actually happened because I saw it. I had been in
Philadelphia and had gone over to Camden, New Jersey. Not a
lively place, except crimewise. I was about a block away from the
Campbell Soup factory, which smelled that particular day, as I
remember it, of chili beef soup, and I was on my way to Walt
Whitman's house on Mickle Street. I just wanted to visit the place. I
was in town anyway, and it was a spring day, and I knew it was
there in Camden, New Jersey, and I found it right there on Mickle
Street because I knew the address. It was fortunate that I knew the
address because the historical-marker plate had been unscrewed
from the front of the house, and stolen."

"And probably," Brant said, "reattached to somebody's summer
house in Duluth."

"Probably so," I said. "I went to the house and rang the bell. A
very beautiful woman answered the door. I said that I was an
admirer of Walt Whitman's poetry and wished to see the house. She
was quite obliging. That was her job, I suppose. She was an
African-American lady, and she spoke about Walt Whitman as if he
were, or had been, a close relative. Just as if he were her crackpot,
but lovable, uncle. She would tell stories and jokes about him and
then start laughing. She took me to the deathbed. She showed me
his rocking chair and the highboy. Several handwritten letters were
stashed in display cases. I saw his hairbrush and his comb. She took

me all around. I signed my name in the register. I was the first visitor in three days, and the last visitors had been from Japan."

"So what was reincarnated?" Alicia asked. "You didn't see his ghost, did you?"

"No," I said. "Of course not." I was telling this story, but I was looking off toward the woods beyond the yard, and I thought I saw a raccoon there, getting curious about the potato chips we had left behind when we'd been out there having drinks before dinner. "I think there's an animal over there," I said. "Just a curious little raccoon.

"Anyway," I said, "after the tour, the bed and the hairbrushes and the highboy and the rocking chair, I thanked the lady and stepped out the door onto Mickle Street. And as I watched, an alley cat crossed the street, and as my eye followed this cat, I saw what was across the street. I hadn't noticed before. Right there, right across from Walt Whitman's house, was a brand-new prison. Yellow brick with slit windows. This one was as ugly as men can make them. Barbed wire around it? I don't remember. It was so ugly they didn't need barbed wire.

"I looked up at the slit windows and I saw a boy there, looking back out. We exchanged glances, but I sure wasn't the person this kid was waiting for. And I figured that this place must be one of those holding prisons, one of those places where they hold kids and adults until their trials come up. So there's this kid standing there at the window and he's got a sign that he's put in the window and the sign is in capital letters and it says HI DAD. So, I figured his dad was coming along, and, sure enough, while I was standing there, literally at the stoop of Walt Whitman's house, along comes one of those airport limousines. It's not a limousine, it's a van. A van for taking people to the Philly airport. And it stops and parks and this big guy gets out, this big Italian-looking guy.

"And this guy runs out into the middle of the street, into the middle of traffic, though there isn't too much in Mickle Street because it was a residential street until they built the prison there. I guess this guy, this father, doesn't have time to visit his son, or it's not visiting hours, or something. Anyway, he stands there in the middle of the street and he waves at his son, and his son waves back at him.

"And then the kid sort of jiggles or shakes the HI DAD sign, and the father, this big guy, acknowledges it by nodding and smiling, and then he starts holding up his hands, all ten fingers, and then one hand, four fingers, and the kid seems to understand because he moves the HI DAD sign up and down. I figured it meant that the kid had fourteen days until trial. Anyhow, the kid nodded, too. I couldn't tell if he was a nice-looking kid or a mean one or anything—you can't tell about things like that from a distance.

"And, at last, the father looks up at his son and he presses both of his hands with the palms inward to his lips, and then he throws his son a kiss with both hands. Standing in the middle of the street, he throws a kiss to his son. He's standing there in the middle of Mickle Street with his hands flung out in the air, and then he turns around and gets back into the airport van, and he starts it and drives away. The kid removes the HI DAD sign from the window, and that's the last I ever saw of him."

I sat back, momentarily tired out by my own story.

"That's a good one," Katherine, my wife, said. "You never told me that one." She scratched at her scalp. "But you said it was about reincarnation. I don't get that part."

I almost didn't hear her question, because I could see the raccoon more clearly now. They're shy animals but courageous at night, and no one can deny the intelligence visible in their eyes.

"See that raccoon?" I asked, pointing. Gray and Brant said that they saw it, but no one else apparently did. "Oh," I said, "the reincarnation part is about Whitman. Whitman's poetry is about love you don't have to earn. It's about love that you just have or that you just get or you give but not the kind that you did something to earn. It's not Protestant love. It's love for being itself. If you're a father, you love your kid, no matter what. In jail or out. That's what I meant."

"That kid had earned his father's love," Ryan said. "He earned it by being his father's son."

"That's not *earning*," I said. "He didn't have to do anything right or wrong. There wasn't any test his father had given him that he'd failed or passed. He just was. He just *was* that kid. That's what Whitman talks about."

"No, that's not Whitman, that's being a parent," Katherine said, "about which many people know nothing. You love your kids because they're your kids. You don't love other people that way. You don't love Arab terrorists that way. You don't love Afghan tribespeople that way. You wouldn't want to."

"I need a drink," Brant said. "I could use a digestif. Just a spot of brandy for the road. Ryan, I don't mean to bully you in your host duties or anything, but you got any brandy? I could use some."

Somehow, my Mickle Street story had created the wrong tone or put some element into the air that the other guests were forced to ponder. A silence without depth or extension drifted down over us like an invisible black fabric. You would have thought that I had committed a terrible social blunder, courageous in its rudeness. The night sky was dimly visible overhead, and I had had too much to drink, so that when I looked up at it, the stars appeared to be swirling, or blindly racing some sickening stellar soapbox derby, right to left, right to left.

"There's no such thing as unearned love," Katherine said, out of the dark. Then she took my hand. "You should know that. You earned mine. You have it. I'll never give it up." Then, appearing to remember that we were in some sense in public, she said, "I love this guy. I love the sight of him."

Ryan was back with the bottle of brandy and the tray, and the brandy glasses he'd once bought at the discount store. The signs, as opposed to the essence, of civilization in the Midwest can be a pretty hasty and contingent affair. He had already poured it out, and we took glasses and drank in silence together. He had turned the floodlight on in order not to stumble and now turned it off again.

"I love *him,* too," Alicia said, "that guy." She angled her head in Ryan's direction. "And not because he looks the way he does. If he looked like a bowling ball with hair he wouldn't have caught my attention in the first place, but he doesn't look a bit like that. You know what I love about him? He cleans up. He does the dishes. I make these messes, and he cleans them all up. How can you not love that?"

Gray and Brant were listening to all this but not saying anything.

"Right," Ryan said. "I know about cleaning up the messes. I do that. But sometimes, sometimes in the middle of love you just want all of it, all those attachments, just to go away. You think it would be a fine idea if the whole thing just flapped its tired old way into flames. A great burning shell of flames. And took itself up to . . . I don't know what I'm saying."

"Yes, you do," Katherine said.

"Well, all right, maybe I do. What if . . . what if we could all get beyond attraction somehow. Being drawn by people to people. Don't you ever get tired of affection, every damn form of affection, and of being aroused, and beauty, and all that stuff? Don't you?"

"Not as long as you're young, you don't," I said. "Alicia, where's your flute?"

"Living room somewhere," she said. "I'll get it."

With the floodlights still off, Alicia came out with her flute and played for us. She was first chair in a local semiprofessional orchestra. Even in the dark, I could see the eyes of the raccoon watching us. Alicia played Debussy's "Syrinx"—she told us what it was—and then she played it a second time. It takes two and a half minutes to play.

The nymph Syrinx was pursued by Pan and disappeared into a reed bed, where she was transformed into a reed. Once, upon waking from a terrible dream, I felt as if I had been turned into a piece of wood, like Pinocchio, and for ten or fifteen seconds I could not remember how to move my limbs. Years ago, during the summer between my junior and senior years in high school, I worked in a geriatrics ward, where one old woman who always wore pink bedroom slippers told me that she was a prizewinning horse, and one old man with a bright gray mustache believed that he might be—he whispered this to me—a box turtle. He said that he was actually a turtle because he moved so slowly and there was a weight on his back, either his shell or death. I asked him how it was, being a turtle, and he said it was okay once you got used to it.

A breeze from the south moved through the plant life in Alicia and Ryan's backyard. Of all of us, Alicia and Gray had known each other the longest. Before we had sat down to dinner, Gray, who had brought over a little wooden train for Janey, Alicia and Ryan's older daughter, had been upstairs chatting with her. You could hear them laughing and giggling from downstairs.

At that moment, sitting there with the breeze going through the apple trees, and Alicia playing her flute, and, in the dark, Katherine taking my hand in an emotion like happiness, but not identical to it, a *hopeful* feeling or sensation, I felt as if I would be transformed beautifully or frighteningly, I wasn't sure which. I would explode or levitate or turn slowly into another thing. I felt *as if* that, but not exactly that. I waited on Alicia and Ryan's half-completed back deck to see what would happen next.

The raccoon turned around and lumbered away.

"Mom?" It was Janey, calling down from her upstairs bedroom window. "Mom? I can't sleep when you're playing!" I looked up. Her silhouette stood there studying the lot of us.

Alicia's notes stopped in mid-phrase. I could hear her putting down her flute.

"All right," she called. "Go back to bed."

"I will," Janey said. Then her voice faded as she said, "Just don't play any more."

"Now, there's a motto," Gray said.

It was so dark that I couldn't tell where anyone was except by voice. The stars were still unpleasantly racing from right to left. "Gray," I said, "you've been pretty quiet all evening. What's new?"

"When we expire," Gray said, after a moment, "where do you suppose we go?"

The wind continued to flow through those same trees. Its sound filled up the quiet and apparently empty moments. "Oh," Ryan said, "I'll bet we float."

"Float?"

"Yeah, float. Float between worlds, maybe."

"You think it's painful?" Gray asked.

"No," Katherine said. "I don't think it would be."

"Why not?"

"Because you've done all that by then," my wife said. "You've done pain. You don't need to do it, after you've done it."

"Nice to think so," Gray said. "Nice to think you could get past it."

"Yes, isn't it?" my wife said. "It could even be true."

"Yes. It could be. I went to the doctor this week. Those people certainly think about pain a lot. Though, have you noticed, they never mention it."

"They mention it sometimes," I said. "Not very often."

"Not as often as they should," Gray said. Where was Brant? He hadn't said anything, not a word, during all this. "Not as often as they will."

"What does that mean?" Alicia asked.

"I know what you're doing," Gray said. "You're all holding hands. You're all dancing on the lawn. Slow two-steps. You're all going home. You're all fine."

"And I know what you're doing," Ryan said, out of the dark. "You're—"

"—No, you don't know what I'm doing," Gray told him, more loudly now. I could hear a few crickets and that same persistent wind. "You don't know what I'm doing. You know that I'm sitting here, but what you don't know is that Brant's hand is on my face, and his thumb is caressing my cheek, back and forth, just a caress, that's all. And you don't know that his hand is wet. And the water isn't from his body. It's from mine." He waited. "It came out of my eyes."

A few minutes later the floodlight went back on, and when it did, Brant's hand was still there, where Gray had said it was, and still wet. I know because I looked.

Mary Yukari Waters

~

SINCE MY HOUSE
BURNED DOWN

They are burning leaves at Toh-Daiji Temple. The monks do it constantly this time of year, in late afternoon when there is the least amount of wind. From upstairs, above the pantiled slate roofs of neighborhood houses, I watch the smoke unravel above branches of red maple. Even from four alleys away it reaches me through the closed glass window: pungent, like incense; reminiscent of some lost memory. Impending recognition rushes through my head like the feeling right before a sneeze, then is gone.

They say that snakes are sensitive to smell. Some species can sense their prey from a distance of several kilometers. This seems significant because when I was born, eighty-six years ago, it was in the year of the snake. Though I've lost much of my hearing, as well as a steadiness of hand and jaw, my connection to smell has deepened with age. It's not that I'm able to smell better, but that I have stronger physical reactions to it: sometimes a tightening of the throat, a bittersweet stab in the breast, a queer sinking in my belly. My convictions have always been instinctive rather than logical. "Snake-year people," my mother used to say, "lie close to the ground. They feel the earth's forces right up against their stomachs."

Stomachs. Yuli, my daughter-in-law, must be cooking dinner

downstairs. For just a split second, I thought I detected the metallic whiff of American tomato sauce, which always makes me feel vaguely threatened. I sniff again but it's gone.

I never knew about tomato sauces until a restaurant in the Shin-Omiya district first introduced the western omelette on its lunch menu. That was a long time ago, years before the war. I remember my daughter Momoko, fourteen at the time, begging permission to go with her friends.

"But Momo-chan," I said to her, "I make you omelettes every morning."

My daughter gave me a pained look. "Mother, western eggs are *completely* different!" They use no sugar, Momoko said; no fish base to mellow the flavor, no soy sauce for dipping. Her classmate's father had described them as salty. They were spiced with grated black peppercorns and spread with a thick, acidic paste made from tinned tomatoes.

"Ara maa! How revolting," I said. "But go if you must." The problem of not knowing how to use silverware did not cross our minds till later. That was where Yuli came in. My daughter-in-law, Yuli, who at this moment is downstairs cooking something that I pray is Japanese cuisine. I haven't caught any other smells yet, so what struck me as tomato sauce may have been a fluke.

Back then Yuli had been a new bride in our home for only a few months. She was raised in Kobe, a cosmopolitan port city well known for its foreign restaurants and boutiques. Yuli's family was very modish, and very rich; her trousseau included, among the traditional silk kimonos, a twelve-piece set of blue and white English china and several knee-length dresses from France. One dress was sleeveless and black; all along its hem hung long tassel-like fringes. Yuli said it was a tango dancing dress.

Naturally I had reservations about this bride. I hope, I said with polite concern, that this city has enough culture to appreciate your taste in foreign clothes. I doubt if Yuli caught the sarcasm. Our city of Kyoto: Japan's capital for centuries, inspiration for *The Tale of Genji*, focal point of the ancient arts. We are far inland, strategically cloistered by lush green hills on three sides, the Kamo River along the fourth. I offered this last fact on a more genial note, saying it provided a year-round cocoon of moisture, which gave Kyoto women the finest skin in the country.

But my reservations went deeper. Yuli being born in a horse year had bothered me even before the marriage. It wasn't just me. Our extended family took a double take when they learned that my son, a rabbit year, was considering marriage to a horse. No doubt neighbors gossiped in the privacy of their homes; the dynamics of such a union were only too obvious. How could a timid rabbit (a male rabbit—the shame of it) control a headstrong steed? In the end, however, we all decided in favor of it because Yuli came from such a decent—and wealthy—family.

When I was a child, a horse scroll hung in the tokonoma alcove of our guest room. It was ancient, originally painted in the Chinese royal court, and presented to my family by a city dignitary on the day of my great-grandfather's birth. If females born in horse years were to be pitied, then males born in those years were cause for celebration and gifts. The stallion was painted on white parchment using no more than ten or twelve brushstrokes. The strokes throbbed with contained energy: the haunch a heavy, swollen curve of black ink; the tail a drag of half-dried, fraying bristles that created the effect of individual hairs swishing in space. The stallion's neck, lumpy with muscle, was caught in midturn. One large black nostril flared above bared teeth. What I remember sensing about this horse, captured by the artist in the split second before it bolted, was its imperviousness to anything other than its own alarm. That black eyeball, rolling back, would not see a small child like me underfoot. Its hard hooves would not feel what they crushed. That thick neck would not respond to reins.

I thought of that horse as I watched Yuli teach my Momoko how to use silverware. She looked very unlike my daughter, who had our classic Minamoto features: long, oval face, eyes slanting up like brushstrokes. Yuli had a wide, square face; bold, direct eyes rather than dreamy ones; short, intense laughs like yelps. She was all smiles, eager to please. But some indefinable tension in her vitality reminded me of that horse. Something about her neck, too, though it wasn't thick or muscular. (But then, any neck would look slender under that enormous face!) Yes, there was inflexibility in that neck, noticeable when she inclined her head sideways in thanks or in acknowledgment, that robbed the gesture of a certain soft elegance.

Momoko was thrilled that Yuli's Kobe upbringing had included western-style restaurants. "Aaa, Yuli-san, you've saved me from becoming a *laughingstock!*" she breathed in that exaggerated way of teenagers. "I would have made some horrible mistake, not knowing any better, and shamed my whole *family.*" At that moment, I wanted to slap my daughter. And Yuli, too. Momoko's innocent words could not have cut me any deeper. We Minamotos were one of the five oldest samurai families in the Kansai region; Yuli's family crest came nowhere near ours in distinction. Since girlhood Momoko had been trained, as I once had, in every conceivable form of etiquette befitting her heritage: classical dance, stringed koto, tea ceremony, flower arranging, different degrees of bowing for each social situation. She had nothing to be ashamed of. As if eating with outlandish foreign utensils even counted as manners!

Yuli had cooked up a traditional Japanese egg loaf for Momoko that night, since I kept no peppercorns or acidic tomato sauces in *my* kitchen, and served it at the low dining-room table. Forks and knives glittered among her English china with the malevolence of surgical instruments. I sat quietly behind them on a floor cushion in the corner, sewing and watching this woman teach my child social behaviors I knew nothing about. Momoko's clumsy attempts made the metal utensils clang alarmingly against the plate.

"Place your forefinger here, like this," said Yuli, standing behind her and leaning over her shoulder to demonstrate. "Or else that fork'll slip right out of your hands." Momoko giggled and made a little bow of apology over her plate.

What a barbaric way to eat, I thought. Wielding iron spears and knives right at the table, stabbing and slicing—chores that should be done in the privacy of a kitchen, leavings diners' energies free for thoughts of a higher order. At that moment a strange foreboding rose up through my belly, a sense that my world, indeed my entire understanding of it, was on the threshold of great change. I felt my fingers tremble over the sewing.

"Momoko," I called out from my corner. "Momoko. Sit up straight."

I have carried with me to this day the image of Momoko begging permission to go to the restaurant: a slender girl in a fall kimono the exact shade of those maple leaves down by the temple. She stands beside a tree with its bark sodden black from the heavy rain. Moss creeps up its trunk, and her fine white Minamoto complexion is a luminous contrast to those bitter autumn hues of black and green and rust. The poignancy of the picture strikes me now as it did not then: that fine play of color, worthy of a Hiroshige etching; youth blooming in a season of endings. Momoko was to contract pneumonia that winter, and die months later.

My instincts were right.

There was the war, for one thing, the magnitude of which none of us could have predicted. Its hardships need not be discussed. We tacitly understand this, those of us who have survived: our long-time neighbors; my rabbit-year son; even Yuli, who, as I always suspected, is 100-percent horse. "Remember that crazy old Uehara-san?" I occasionally say, laughing, to our old neighbor Mrs. Nakano in the alley. "How he missed his sushi so much, he used raw chicken instead of fish?"

"It didn't taste bad, ne . . . ," she always says, and we both chuckle, as if looking back on happy times. We go no further. We never discuss the bombings.

Mr. Uehara was lucky; at least he owned chickens, living out in the country. He was our contact for black-market rice. Back then, wartime currency was useless. I hate to think what that rice cost our family: bolts of fine watered silk, priceless porcelain vases handed down for generations since the Yamamoto Period.

We neighborhood women took the train into the countryside,

since our men were either fighting abroad or, like my own husband, reported dead. Our train bumped leisurely through the crowded east-side weaving district on its way out to flat farm fields, past narrow doorways of slatted wood and somber, shrinelike roofs. In prosperous times one could have leaned out the train window and heard the deafening clatter of looms—*gat-tan-gat-tan*—coming from each house. Now, silence, except for the occasional screech of ragged boys playing swords with long bamboo poles.

For the physical task of carrying, we wore navy-blue mompe of the peasant class (I'm reminded of them when I see today's popular pajamas). On the way there, we lugged our family treasures concealed in large furoshiki wraps; coming back, half a sack of rice each and no more. We all knew about the cases of women who had developed hernias from too much heavy lifting. At the farm, old Mr. Uehara treated us to his startling lunch menu of raw chicken sushi. On one occasion, he served grasshoppers crisped over a fire and crumbled into brown flakes—these looked identical to the shaved cod flakes we had eaten with our rice before the war; the texture, too, was identical, and with soy sauce the difference in taste was barely discernible. "Plenty of nutrients," Mr. Uehara told us with a sparkle in his eye. "In times of trouble, we must use our heads." It was hard to say whether that sparkle came from his own good health or from the anticipation of receiving yet another installment of our family fortunes.

The loneliest time was afterward on the platform, sitting on our sacks of rice and waiting for the whistle of the train. We had no energy left for small talk, and each of us sank down into her own private gloom. By now, no doubt, Japan Railways has replaced that wooden platform with a concrete one, complete with an automatic ticket-vending machine, but back then it was rickety, its planks weathered gray by the seasons. Orioles' nests swung from the exposed rafters on the roof. The roof rose high above the surrounding fields, throwing down long shadows. A breeze swept over long sasaki grasses, and the black shadows quavered over them like reflections on a rippling sea. I had a sense of being marooned while the sun set on the end of the world.

I tried not to think of my husband, lying in some unmarked grave in Iwo Jima. I tried not to think of Momoko, dead these five years. But in such weak moments misery gathered in my breast so thick and clotted that it blocked my breathing. The sound of crows cawing on their lonely flight home was unbearable.

At one point during those trips I heard the music of the fields. It wasn't so significant at the time. But some random memories, like my image of Momoko, are like that. Over time, they acquire a patina the way pearls gather luster. The sound I heard, a hushed soughing, brought to mind countless blades of grass rustling together and the millions of tiny lives—insects and birds and rodents—feeding and sleeping and growing beneath their cover. The breeze, filtering through the grasses, dislodged the sounds so that they rose up and, wafting on currents of air, hummed and whispered all around. A Masahide poem I learned in childhood floated to mind:

Since my house burned down
I now own
a better view
of the rising moon.

Peacetime ushered in what I refer to as Yuli's era. Children became versed in silverware usage, as the Americans instituted hot-lunch programs in the decimated schools. Knee-length cotton dresses, too, became common. Yuli dragged out her French trousseau dresses—practical-minded Mr. Uehara hadn't wanted those—and paraded through the open-air market among rows of chives and lotus roots, glamorous in silk. It was so embarrassing.

Yet for the first time I desired her friendship. We had gone through a terrible war together—known so much loss—and like it or not, she was now part of my life: someone who remembered our old quality of living, our family's stature. I was a bit frightened, too, by this harsh postwar energy sweeping the city: children marching through our alleys wearing western school uniforms of navy and white, garish billboards with English words (which Yuli had learned to read back in Kobe, and was now teaching my son). But as I said, this was now Yuli's era. She had no interest in friendship; the horse was already running with the bit between its teeth.

"Mother-san, I'll finish up here," she often said brightly as we were cooking together in the kitchen. This, before I had barely even finished washing the rice! I had to fight back now just to stay standing.

"A, a, that's not necessary," I would reply. "I'm happy to do it. You just go relax, put on some cosmetics for when your husband comes home." Do *something*, so I can have grandchildren.

"I'm already wearing cosmetics." That short laugh of hers, like a yelp.

Our struggle progressed over the years until Yuli stopped playing fair. Her final big victory, driving me out of my own kitchen, arrived just last week. To my credit, it was decades in coming. It was Toshihide, my own son, who delivered the blow to me in the garden, stepping cautiously across the moss to where I was bending over to feed the turtle in the stone vat. "Yuli has noticed," he said slowly and loudly into my ear, "that more than once . . . left on . . . gas on the stove. More than . . . refrigerator . . . closed all the way. Perhaps . . . old age . . . Would you mind . . . ?" From the corner of my eye I saw Toshihide's Adam's apple shifting about like the nose of a rabbit. Aaa, I should have had another son! Momoko should have lived.

My whole life has been a process of losing security. Or identity. Perhaps they are the same thing. I may not be a true snake. For each skin I have shed, there has been no new replacement.

I sit upstairs now, relieved of all my household duties, and look down at the smoke rising from Toh-Daiji Temple. I wonder if the monks there contemplate life's cycle as they tend the fire, or if their mundane task is simply a welcome break from more serious duties.

Leaves and twigs and straw, all leaving behind their inherent forms and evaporating into space. Next spring their ashes will reemerge without a trace of their former characteristics: as moss, as an earthworm, as a cherry tree whose fruit will be eaten by children in summer, then converted to human matter. A pitiless world, this: refusing you the slightest sense of self to cling to.

Two weeks later I go for a stroll down to Kamo River, which is three blocks from home in the opposite direction of the temple. I shuffle through the dappled shade of maple trees and hear cicadas shrilling *meeeeee* overhead, which is impossible in November; a combination, no doubt, of ingrained memory and the hearing aid I wear on my walks in case I meet someone I know.

I head toward a sunny bench overlooking the water. These days walking exhausts me. The river flows past, sunlight glinting on its surface like bright bees swarming over a hive. I fancy I can hear the bees buzzing, so I take out my hearing aid and put it in my handbag. I sun myself like this for a long time, eyes half shut. I conjure up from memory the surface sounds of the river, its tiny slurps and licks as countless currents tumble over one another. I remember, too, the soft roar of the undercurrent in flood time as it drags silt and pebbles out to sea.

The music comforts me. I imagine dissolving into the water, being borne along on its current. Something slowly unclenches within my chest. I am pared down, I think suddenly, to Masahide's poem. And I sense with a slow-burning joy how wide this river is, and how very deep, with its waters rolling out toward an even vaster sea; and the quiet surge of my happiness fills my chest to bursting.

Bilal Dardai

❧

THE EMPTY BOWL

Wrapped in green cotton and the dependable glare of the test pattern, Fred Lester has a dream about Cheerios. Light and crisp and bumpy, the first spoonful of the cereal goes in his mouth without him even realizing it, his jaw so eagerly clamping down that he tastes the cold steel of the teaspoon along with the milk and toasted oats. He has barely swallowed when a second spoonful has been deposited onto his tongue. The sound of his chewing reminds him of an army regiment marching through snow.

The kitchen is his own, but in a shade of blue neither he nor his wife, Ellen, would ever have considered kitchenish. Fred does not recognize the table or the chair he sits in, nor the backyard he can see through the screen door. *My kitchen has been moved,* he thinks, but somehow this does not seem unusual. *Or, I am not in my kitchen, but in one very similar.* Fred considers for a moment that he may be eating somebody else's Cheerios. The box, a familiar kindergarten yellow, faces him from the opposite end of the table. The bowl of cereal on the front of the box is a twin to the one in front of him, making the cereal box into a goldenrod mirror for which he does not exist. Fred is stretching across the table to grab the box, perhaps to casually browse the nutrition information, when he awakens.

Fred sees his left hand hovering above him, colored with cathode rays and set against a shadowy background. He wills his fingers to close and then brings the fist to his chest, grunting softly. Fred tries to mentally restructure the test pattern in front of his feet into the last thing he saw before drifting off to sleep, his brow furrowing with the effort. There was a police officer of some sort. There was a doctor of some sort. A woman screaming, and there was a commercial break of some sort.

The empty space next to him should be occupied by his wife, but she is not there. 4:07 AM. An empty space in the shape of a woman. Fred sighs and mumbles words to himself that not even he can decipher, finds the remote nestled in the sheets, and banishes the glow from the room. He stares into the fading colors of the ceiling, trying to see around the pulsing violet blobs left behind by the television set. At this moment, he becomes unsettled by the notion that perhaps nobody closes their eyes, that the best all of humanity ever manages is to spend long periods of time staring at the backs of their eyelids. Perhaps eyesight is never turned off, and perhaps his dreams, be they of sharp-toothed monsters or of breakfast cereals, these dreams are nothing more than another television set directly in front of his eyeballs. This thought haunts him for several minutes. He accuses his eyeblinks of fraud.

The empty space next to him. Ellen should *be* there. *This is a dream bedroom,* he considers. *I am traveling from one imagined room to another.* Fred rotates and plants his bare feet on the carpet, propels himself from his bed to the door, opens it, steps into the hallway. He recognizes this hallway. This must be his hallway, the bathroom door closed at one end, his daughter's room next to it, slightly ajar, allowing only slivers of small light. Fred finds himself conflicted about checking on his sleeping little girl; Lucy being in her bed should be a given. Even in this house, where the dark room behind him was clearly not true, where his wife, Ellen, should have been but wasn't. *Lucy is asleep,* he reassures himself. *She is dreaming of a house where her mother must be, since her mother is not in this one.*

The stairs protest. They scold Fred Lester for his physical girth, the carelessness with which he drops his weight onto each step as he descends into the front foyer. Fred hears and notes these complaints. He makes silent, empty apologies and promises. This foyer is not his own. He can see the cedar coat rack standing tall and silent before him, suffering its burden with practiced stoicism. His long brown coat, Ellen's long maroon coat, Lucy's blue windbreaker, everything is there, and yet this feels wrong, somehow. This foyer is not his own, but it maintains appearances regardless, almost as if making a calculated effort to trick him. *Ha,* thinks Fred, *you do not fool me. You are not my foyer. My foyer is different.* The illusion so vanquished, Fred walks through the false foyer and enters his kitchen.

Fred Lester is a sensible man. Fred Lester is an educated man with a family and a home of his own. The reality that he inhabits is also time-shared by millions of people in the world, and in this reality, his wife, Ellen, is asleep in his bed, his true foyer has usurped the impostor, and there are no Cheerios on his kitchen table. The Cheerios were a dream; a nutritious and tasty dream, but nonetheless a dream. When Fred Lester turns on the light to his kitchen, it is the proper shade of yellow that Ellen had picked out herself, that Fred had agreed upon. This is his kitchen. There is no question.

And yet, there is the box of Cheerios on his table.

He blinks when he sees it. He blinks several times in rapid succession, ignoring the impulse to yelp. *Cheerios do not follow men from dreams into their waking lives,* Fred deduces, *so these must have always been here.* With further contemplation, he decides that these must be Ellen's Cheerios, or perhaps Lucy's, although Lucy favors raisin bran or oatmeal, doesn't she? Fred stalks around the kitchen table, blindly opening drawers and cabinets behind him and seeking out a spoon and bowl, worried about taking his eyes off the cereal box, lest it vanish into another room, or into another dream that he will have later. There is whole milk in the refrigerator, and Fred procures that as well. He sits at the table—at *his* table—and pours himself a bowl. The Cheerios clatter as they hit the ceramic, piling on top of one another, and Fred resolves now that he will eat every one, that he will eat every tiny circle in his bowl, every one in this box. *Are the dreams of Cheerios memories of Cheerios long since eaten, or of Cheerios waiting to be born?* This seems a mad question, and as such he lets it go.

He asks himself instead what it is that his wife likes about this cereal, as he takes his first bite. It is hardly as satisfying as the bowl he was having moments ago. This is what she eats every morning? He can see Ellen now, dressed in her white lab coat and tennis shoes, sitting down and eating breakfast, idly chatting about something her coworker or supervisor said to her. The Cheerios crunch between his molars. Ellen is reminding Fred that she is working a double shift today, reminding him that he and Lucy are on their own for dinner tonight. Lucy has soccer practice today, she adds. Make sure you call the landscaper, she adds. I love you, she adds. Ellen Lester deposits an emptied bowl in the sink and leaves the house.

The kitchen seems to shift around him as Fred Lester slowly awakens. No. This is not his kitchen. He can feel cold realization rushing through every pore of his body, saturating him. Not his kitchen, not his house. A dream. Fred sees himself in the memory of his house, answering a phone call, his daughter watching a rented movie in the living room, the walls of the living room flashing blue and white. A spy of some sort. A meeting of some sort. An explosion of some sort, and the voice on the other end of the phone tells Fred Lester that there has been an accident. There has been an accident, please come quickly.

Fred stands outside his memory of himself, seeing the man with unblinking bloodshot eyes carry his daughter to bed. Fred shuffles down the hallway to his bedroom. He falls asleep and dreams of Cheerios, and when he awakens, his house has been replaced in parts. His bed should have Ellen in it. His kitchen should have Ellen in it. His foyer should have Ellen in it. Fred continues eating his cereal, barely conscious that he is weeping again. The kitchen blurs through the saline, the colors and shapes of the cereal box melting and distorting like a ruined oil painting. The blank gold mirror of the box struggles to communicate to Fred from a small red icon on its face. *Good for your heart,* Fred reads, chewing tersely. Good for your heart.

Fred Lester sits in a home not his own, and he eats.

Louise Erdrich

❧

RESURRECTION

During the days Marie spent cleaning her house, she slept less and less. There was so much to do. Now that Nector was gone Marie shut her mind on loss by keeping busy. She went through her husband's belongings, repacked clothes to keep or give away, sorted his books into piles of the same size and shape. Lastly, one night, she came to a long and brittle skin bag. One end was quilled with rawhide strips of pale, washed-to-sand colors, dyed with butternut, wild grapes, ocher, fading sere. A horned man radiating wavering lines of power was beaded onto the other end. Marie drew out the pipe. She held the cool red bowl in her scarred palm, rattled it a bit, but before he'd stored it Nector had cleaned it well. The stem of the pipe was wooden, carved in a spiral, crosshatched and fitted with a tiny cross of myrtle and a string of the oldest white-heart trading beads. The feather of a golden eagle, grown ragged at the tip, dangled as she lifted the stem. She brushed the feather to her cheek, and then returned the pieces of the pipe to their case as they were, for to fit them together, Nector once said, was to connect earth and heaven. She put the pipe away for their niece.

Marie went to bed early. She had peaches and tomatoes to can, chokecherries to boil down, venison to pound. Old Man LaGrisaille had left her two bushels of ripe corn. She woke in the dark, real anxious to seal it fresh in jars. In the iron-black air before dawn, she rose, poured water into the speckled blue enamel coffeepot, put it on the range to boil, and sharpened her knife. When the water was hot, she put in two fistfuls of coffee.

While it was heating up again, she peeled back the stiff husks and pulled away the strands of silk from pale, white-gold kernels. She drank her coffee and then, sitting at the scored wood table, pushed the short razor-thin blade down each cob. The meat of the corn fell away in milky rows. She filled half a dishpan by the time the air was lighter. The window went gray to blue-gray, night blue to the blue of day. The grass was trembling, the sun pushing over the spines and arms of trees in their gold and rust, when Gordie walked into the yard.

Marie had reached the age where her skin was soft again, smooth as rainwater in a drum. She kept herself moving, though, and she was strong. She hefted the pan onto the stove now and used a plastic measuring cup to scoop corn. There was a large red jug of water near the stove and she began to pour from it, drawing for the great round steamer she used to sterilize her jars. When she had put her water in the right place, she turned to the window. He was still standing there. She didn't need to look twice. He had no jacket and his shirt hung open, trailing, the tails stained flaps. The pants that had fit him when he began drinking weeks ago were falling off, barely held up by a piece of clothesline. He had shaved, or someone else had shaved him, once, twice. The soles of his shoes seemed to take root. He swayed, arms close to his sides, a doll with weighted feet. The circle of his motion grew rounder and wider until in one movement he uprooted himself and sprawled headlong, diving forward to the margin of spent grass that Marie cultivated with the leavings of her kitchen water. It was as if he saw that bit of grass, focused on the bitter green as some minor salvation, or perhaps he just wanted sleep.

He lay curled, one arm crooked beneath his car, then legs hunched. He slept like a sick child, a thin dog, like he was dead. Marie went out to cover him because the day was so cool. Windblown leaves scattered around his face, folded heavily against the ground. She unfolded a quilt cut and stitched from the woolen clothing too tattered to repair. Each square was tacked down with a knotted piece of yarn. The quilt was brown, mustard yellow, all shades of green. Looking down at it, Marie recognized the first coat she had bought Gordie, a faint, tough gray patch, and the blanket he had brought home from the army. There was the plaid of her husband's jacket. A thick skirt. A baby blanket half turned to lace by summer moths. Two old blue pants legs.

Gordie stirred and turned, his face twisted, but he wasn't sick. Marie bent, shoved him the rest of the way over so that he was sleeping on his stomach. She straightened slowly, went into the house, and then turned off the gas beneath the boiling water, though she didn't like to lose the heat. Her bed was already made, so she lay down across the covers and pulled a crocheted afghan over her knees.

An hour must have passed, two maybe. She didn't sleep at first. Then she dreamed that the barn was still standing, needing to be tamped and locked against the growing cold. The cows stamped, udders swelling, aching for her bands. Potatoes touched cold eye-sprouts in the cellar. There were two or three babies, always diapers in the tub, and on slaughter day a basin of bloody shirts and pants the men had come home wearing. Milk to skim, cream to keep. Bread still rising underneath a clean rag. Sweetgrass. Long tails of it to pick, braid, and store in the dark for Rushes Bear. Mice. Mice in everything. She would have to catch them with that tiny rind of bacon that she used over and over in the trap. There was a horse, white and gray. One day it fell over and just lay there. Someone needed to bury it. Someone had to dig a hole, but the men were gone again. She thought of the Skinners, a desperate people who lived a mile along the trail. Marie always peeled her potatoes with thick skins, dumped the peels across the fence. By morning, the peels were gone. She would tell the Skinners about the horse, know that the horse would vanish too. So much to do, too much. She couldn't stop planning her time. She now awakened, having slept hard.

The first thing she thought about was Gordie, and sure enough, he was awake in the kitchen. She heard his footsteps as he shuffled from the refrigerator to the table, back and forth, dragging out the stew, the chili, the uncut pie she had been saving to take to the nuns, bringing out the bread, the butter, pouring himself a cup of Kool-Aid, pouring more running from shelf to shelf down the refrigerator, putting everything that was there into himself. She didn't get out of bed until she heard him rummaging through the cupboards, poking a butter knife down through the jars of sugar and the bags of flour where she kept her little envelopes of money. Where she used to keep them. Now she had another place.

"Ahnee, n'kawnis." She stood in the doorway. Since she had lived among other old people at the Senior Citizens, Marie had started speaking the old language, falling back through time to the words that Lazarres had used among themselves, shucking off the Kashpaw pride, yet holding to the old strengths Rushes Bear had taught her, having seen the new, the Catholic, the Bureau, fail her children, having known how comfortless words of English sounded in her ears.

"Hey Mom." He sat down quickly at the fall of her steps. He started blowing across the surface of a cup of cold coffee.

His face had gathered in the poisons and he looked pinched and soft. His mouth hung slack like an old sock and he dropped food on his plate from his shaking fork. The long black hair he had from his father, hair that made him so proud when he was a teenager, fell in thick ropes every which way. She wanted to take a brush to it, to slick it back. The shirt he wore was ripped across the neck and stained across the arm with old blood. He smelled like the bad life—shit, wine, vomit.

"Take that one off," she said, shuffling to the corner behind the door where she kept the extra clothing in the house. She chose a shirt that Gordie's father used to wear to work, a green twill from Sears.

"Beeskun K'papigewyaun," she told her son.

"I don't want to wear that." Gordie eyed the shirt from underneath the ripped crown of his hair. "It was June's."

Marie carefully folded the shirt and went back to the corner. There was a sweatshirt at the bottom of the pile, something that June herself had once left. The sleeves were cut off and curled around the edges, and the front of it said BISON. She had washed it carefully and now she unfolded it and put it on the table across from where her son sat. He nodded when he looked at it, and then his body seemed to jump as if he had been given an electric shock. He was sick, sick again, blindly sick, knocking into shelves and pulling down the flour bin, throwing himself toward the door, hitting wall, hitting stove. He didn't burn himself and he missed the knife, landed with his head in the wood box. He pulled himself out, reeled toward the window, backed toward the door, lost his pants, tangled his feet in the crotch, pulled them back up and lunged at the refrigerator, slipped down its side, fell upon the floor, and did not move.

Marie came out from behind the door. From the little utility room that Gordie himself had tacked on during his last good six months, she took her cleaning rags and a bucket. She poured two careful measures of ammonia into the water, stirred it around, took the rag, and began to wash. While he was lying there, she cleaned up everything and put all that he had disturbed back where it belonged. She turned on the heat underneath the big kettle and she began to boil her jars and her lids. She started cooking her corn, too, stepping over Gordie's legs when she needed to get something from the refrigerator or the cupboard just behind him. She was absorbed in the task of putting on the lids and wiping the tops clean when she felt a slow stirring behind her and gradually, as she moved aside, glancing at him over her shoulder, she watched him crawl forward across the linoleum. He rested under the table.

"Hey Mom." His voice was thin, rough, ground pellets shaking in a can.

Marie didn't answer.

"Hey Mom," said Gordie again, his voice lower, tentative. "I could use a drink now."

"I don't keep nothing here."

Gordie's arm appeared first, wrapped around the back of a chair. Slowly, he dragged the rest of himself upward, rung by rung, until he was leaning on the slats of the backrest. He turned himself around and with bewildered simplicity sat down directly at the table.

"Don't you, didn't you, I mean I thought you used to take your whiskey in a little milk. Or was that the nun I heard about?"

Gordie started to laugh, to wheeze. His lips went red and he used his face, talked with animated fervor, his arms propped underneath his chest. "I guess it was this Mother Superior I remember, the one that wouldn't take the doctor's medicine, the whiskey, so her sisters, they mix it up with milk and she drinks it and drinks it and when she's all well her nuns say, 'Now that you're better, do you have any advice for us?' And the Mother Superior says, 'Whatever you do, don't sell that cow!' "

The laughter seemed to churn him up, he rumbled with it, shook, and after a few moments he put his head down on his crooked arms.

"My little mother," he said. "I hate to be a pest. But would you give your old son a good blast?"

"What did you do last night?" Marie sat down across from him.

"Last night?" Gordie raised his head and looked at her, swimming in the air. His face assumed an altar-boy slyness. "I stayed awake all night praying."

Marie nodded. "So you're down to wine now."

Gordie gathered himself, sat momentarily tall.

"N'gushi, I'm sorry. I feel I must apologize to you. Allow me to say that I am sorry."

Marie's expression did not change.

"Give me that shot." His demand was sharp, sudden, sober. He rose toward her, bigger, expanding his chest, pushing out his neck cords.

Marie did not move, but when his hand came near she raised her paring knife and slashed him lightly where his palm would have connected.

Gordie drew his wounded hand back to himself with slow indifference. Marie got up, pushed a dishcloth across the table. Gordie took the cloth and wrapped it loose around his bleeding cut.

"We match now!" Suddenly he blurted words out, laughing, thinking of the raised scar in the center of his mother's hand, thinking of how he'd always felt it when she smoothed her hand over his face. He closed his eyes as he sat there and Marie, without turning her back, worked on her canning.

"My socks are too tight," he said after a while.

"You don't have on any socks," Marie said, looking down. "You need some."

"I feel like I do." Gordie's voice was fascinated with himself. "I feel like my socks are too tight."

For a long while the two stayed in the kitchen. Marie went about her business and Gordie slumped. He was somewhere else. Motionless, eyes open, he watched as a dark line connected and reconnected over different markers in his life. The pointer stopped over the year he married June.

They were lying in the dark of the hottest night of that fierce blue summer, panting in the sodden air, when June leaned across the bed and put her fingers on Gordie's mouth.

"Now," she whispered.

He rolled carefully away, rose as quiet as an animal. They left, out the room, out the screen door creaking shut, out the yard and down the dirt road, out of town and off the reservation. They walked east, hitched south, walked east again, and woke as the sun rose, dry and sucking, along the tilted black outline of the World's Largest Prairie Chicken. The town's pride, made of fiberglass, it drummed for a mate near Rothsay. They sat down beside it and took their money out to count. Together they had fifty dollars. Maybe it would be enough for a few nights at a lake cottage. By noon, hitching, walking fueled by ninety-nine-cent breakfast specials, they reached the first lake of Minnesota's ten thousand, a small and reedy oval.

"But anyway, it's water," June said. There were lots of little wooden signs along the road—jigsaw-cut arrows with painted names, TROLLMERE, THE LOON'S HAVEN, JOHNSON'S RESORT. The sign to Johnson's had actually fallen off its post and stuck point-down in the grass, which is why they thought they could afford to stay there. It had once directed people down a rutted dirt track, so they took the winding seam through a field with a few thirsty-looking horses in it, then some woods and undergrowth, until they arrived at a group of buildings, some large, some small, all peeling the same dull red paint.

There was a man of about sixty years sitting on the back porch, reading through a pile of newspapers. He wore a pair of loose cutoff jeans and no shirt. His chest was smooth and thin, though his arms looked strong. His face was wrinkled, darker than his chest, and bearded with a pale, whitish mat.

"Johnson?"

"Sorry, we're all closed up."

The man waited, looking at June and Gordie with no expression. He was like a teacher, used to having his intentions read. June didn't know the rules, though, of being a student, and for that matter she didn't act much like she knew she was an Indian, either. She approached Johnson as though they were two regular people, as though there were nothing but the usual between them. Two strangers meeting. She introduced herself and introduced Gordie as her new husband.

"Are your cottages closed up or are they just 'closed up'?" June asked, getting down to business.

"Well"—Johnson sat back a little—"we aren't part of the resort owner's association anymore."

June considered that. She looked over at the four tiny board cabins, shaded by trees. "Do you mean they might be lacking . . ."

". . . some of the amenities." Johnson nodded.

"And what," asked June, "would those be?"

Johnson shrugged. "Running water, for one. Bathrooms. Beds."

Gordie's ears sharpened. "Maybe," he suggested, "you could give us a reduced rate?"

Johnson's eyes took on a figuring gleam, and he spoke reluctantly. "I don't know," he considered. "They are kind of unique places in that they don't have your basic conveniences."

"Look," said June. "Gordie and me here, we just got married and we're looking for a vacation. All we have is thirty dollars. It's a take-it-or-leave-it deal."

"Since you put it that way." Johnson rose, holding out his hand.

Gordie shook with him, then June did.

"Come on." Johnson picked his way on tender feet down a path studded with roots and twigs. "Down to the end we have our honeymooners' suite. I had to take out the furnishings a while ago. Skunk got in. Two winters should have aired it out, though."

The little cabin had a back entry. The door seemed locked but Johnson kicked the baseboard and it creaked open. The inside smelled of old wood with the sun on it. Whether the floor had been swept long ago, or scoured since by wind and mice, it was clean enough. There was a big glassed window in the room, with just one pane taped, and shining outside of that, the green lake, much bigger and longer than it had looked at first. There was a dock, a gray boat tied to the pilings.

Johnson sighed.

"Let's go up to the house and haul down a mattress. I got an extra."

They did, and brought an old brown bedspread for a blanket. Johnson gave Gordie a fishing pole to use, line and hooks. "You buy yourself ten dollars' worth of bread and apples and butter at the Lucky Six, catch your own fish, you can eat good all week."

"All week?"

"Twenty dollars, that's my rate."

June took their money out and paid. Johnson put the money in his pocket, walked back to his porch, and sat on the steps again.

June closed the cabin door, wedged a stick of wood beneath the knob, and propped the windows wide. The mattress was on the floor. The two lay down on it and fell asleep almost immediately. When they woke up it was early evening and the light was low and green-blue. They walked outside and went down to the water. They took off their shoes, then looked around. The whole lake was still. Lights shone far off on the opposite shore and there was no sound but the nicker of a horse beyond Johnson's house.

"I'm going in," June said. She stripped off and rolled together her T-shirt, jeans, and underwear, and then she pushed off and floated through the reeds with just her head showing, like a turtle. Gordie watched her from the water's edge.

The air was still heavy with the day's heat, oppressive. He tried to breathe deeply and calmly but it was hard to pump the air in and out of his chest. He looked all around, sharply noting each light, closely listening. There was nothing to disturb the peace. No one to watch. Slowly, he eased his jeans down his hips and then waded in over his knees. The water was warm but the sandy bottom almost cool. June had gone under, then all of a sudden she rose before Gordie, reeds drooping off her shoulders, the water streaming down her face and the snaky ends of her hair, running down the smooth well between her breasts and flying off her arms when she smoothed back her hair. She blotted out the last of the sun. She laughed at Gordie, so uncomfortable in his baggy shirt, his hair caught on one side from sleep, his arms awkward.

June pushed Gordie over in the shallows and he started laughing too. They swam past the reeds together, out to where the water was colder. Across the lake, the lights of boats spun back and forth. June swam without effort, rolled, dived up and down like a fish, took Gordie farther and farther, away from the shore, toward the middle of the lake.

It was deep, fresh, cold beneath the surface, and so dark that he could barely see his wife.

"Bother me," she said.

"Out here?"

"It's easy. The water's so calm. There's hardly any waves."

They were treading water, facing each other.

She put her arms on Gordie's shoulders and floated her legs out to either side of him. He tipped himself back and balanced in the water, finning his hands.

"Try to stay still."

He aimed for her but he missed. He tried to draw her close to him, holding her hips, but as soon as he put his arms down, his entire body sank. They both went under, clasping in the dark, their bodies cold and slippery.

June came up choking, laughing, drank a mouthful, broke away from Gordie.

"That water's damn cold," Gordie said.

"Oh so what. Let's go back." June stroked along behind Gordie, gliding through the water.

Suddenly she grabbed him. He gulped the air convulsively, then sank in her arms. They went down, Gordie fumbling, awkward in surprise. When his air ran out he panicked, twisted from June, and kicked to the surface. He leveled off and made for shore. Pulling deep with his arms, he heard the regular and resounding thump of his kicks boom in his ears.

Heavier once he stood, touching sand, dazed, he gathered his clothes and waited for June on the thin, foamy shore.

June slogged out of the shallows and followed Gordie up the path to the cabin. They went inside, silent. Gordie sat down on the mattress and immediately she pushed him over and lay down on top of him. The air in the cabin quickly grew too steamy, and mosquitoes droned. Making love felt like work. It wasn't any fun, but they couldn't stop. They sweat. Gordie felt tears burning up behind his eyes. Not that he would quit. They went on and on until they gave up and fell asleep right in the middle of it, mouths open, hot, unhappy, bitten by insects, on a mattress with little buttons that left round sore marks all over them so that the next morning they looked awful and felt worse, and all that day, as they swam and dozed and fished off the dock, as they woke up and gutted their fish and went to the store, swam again, and slept, then woke, fried the fish in a little cornmeal and butter, as they ate their Bunny bread, sweet apples, drank iron-brown water, they were each hoping that the other would not suggest sex again.

That night they sat on the dock, holding hands. The moon rose. They watched until finally it seemed clear they were much too at peace and tired to do anything but sleep. June shrugged. Side by side they walked the little path to the cabin, went in, and lay down without speaking. They kissed each other's hands and then folded them together and lay that way, like two people carved on stone caskets, staring up at the starless ceiling.

Outside, the afternoon drew quickly along to its peak, the light of early fall short and radiant until the shadows poked blue from the tiny spruce Marie Kashpaw had planted. Darkness spread from the tough little oaks and split box elder that never had been cut, from the hollyhocks, all rattling in seed. There were a few squash vines left, soft brown, the leaves brittle, the squash left to cure, to gather a little sweetness, covered up by burlap sacks. The shells were dark green, tough as turtles. There were almost twenty that Marie had grown this year, all for the cellar. She stood on the porch steps and watched the light blaze out behind the trees, listened to the oak leaves, leathery and ticking.

She stood out there for too long and didn't keep her head turned for her best ear to pick up her son's whereabouts. Then the chemical smell hit her and the light suddenly faded fast once it sank beyond the trees. She turned to go back into the house and heard him jump. Everything was out of the closet in the added room she used for storage, and on the floor the Lysol with its bottom punched, the can opener next to it, and the remains of the loaf of white bread. He was down on the floor, jumping, his entire body sprung by heels and head. His torso arched and up he went, fast, faster, so fast she couldn't catch him. He was a grasshopper, leaping up and down around the room, hair flying, arms slapping at the furniture and knocking the stove and dangerous and cooling jars.

She tried to follow him, to keep things he could knock over from him, blocks of wood, ax, more jars of canned corn on the table, harder, faster, springing through the soft blue dusk. The floors and walls thumped as he drummed along, and then he suddenly spun through the door into the bedroom. When she followed she saw he'd landed on the bed and for a long time after, as the light went entirely and as the wind came up a little, rattling the twigs and leaves outside the window, she heard the bed singing and complaining in a rhythmical creak that slowed and softened as the stuff let go of his body, gradually, until, when she lit the kerosene lamp she liked to have at night, he had gone still. She stepped next to him, bent over with the lamp, and smelled the harsh rapture of the Lysol on his breath.

And then, fearing almost that she could ignite his lungs if she put the burning flame too close, she stepped away and out of the room.

She set the lamp down on the kitchen table, picked up the chairs and put them right, except one, which she placed against the closed front door. Nothing that had fallen was broken badly, and she restored all that was out of place. The bedroom had one window, only large enough for a ten-year-old boy to crawl through. He would have to come out this way, past her, when he did. She filled another lamp and left it by the first, wick trimmed, ready. She put some matches in her pocket, then sat in the chair with its back to the locked door. She bent over, loosened the laces on her shoes, picked up the ax that was lying beside the chair, and placed it carefully across her lap. Her head fell back. She quickly went to sleep, she was so tired.

In the deep of the first watch of the night, around midnight or one, the lamp sputtered and she felt it as an absence at the heart of her dream, a mess of scenes that contained no one, and ran black and long as time. She woke startled, and her hands tightened on the ax handle. Weakness of age had loosened her muscles and she had to make an effort to raise her arms. They hurt, already sore, and all through her hands the nerves pinched, tight as fence wire. He was moving in the bedroom. She could hear him stumble from the bed, hit the wall with a hand, a leg. Then he appeared in the doorway, outside the dim circle of the lamp.

His face was naked and drawn sharp. His eyes shone, green-white, empty in their deep sockets, glowing as if they gave back the reflection of a car's headlights. His hands ran up and down his shirt, the fingers long and spidery and ceaseless. She stood up, the ax dangling. She put it down carefully across a chair, watching him for any movement, and as soon as she turned the flame higher in the lamp, she picked up the ax again. The light leapt upward, smoking, and consumed the wick. But by the time it guttered out, Marie had her other lamp going. Gordie vanished soundlessly, as if the light wounded or upset him. There was something horrid and gentle about his movements. He had lost the clumsy weight of humanness. He retreated with the tiny shudder of a sigh into the darkness.

She thought of letting him out, of simply opening the door and standing to one side. But then, too many passed out cold and slept in the woods. There was the danger of being run over on the roads. There was no question in her mind that if she let him go he would get himself killed. She would almost rather have killed him herself. She was wide awake, more alert than she had ever been. Her brain was humming in the dark, her head was full of nails. Gordie was her firstborn. He had lain in her body in the tender fifteenth summer of her life. Now she could sense him gliding back and forth, faster, faster, a fox chasing its own death down a hole. Forward, back, diving. She knew when he caught the rat. She felt the walls open. He connected, went right through with a blast like heat. Still, she sat firm in her chair and did not let go of the ax handle.

Thomas E. Kennedy

୧୨

DONNA AUBE

In the kitchen, by the light of the open refrigerator door, Binzer popped three cubes into a rock glass, bowing to the ritual. The vodka sizzled agreeably and steamed, crackling the ice. In the back window of the apartment across the way he noticed an illuminated statue of the Virgin Mary, blue and white, facing across the courtyard toward him. He speared two olives on a little plastic sword and dropped it in the drink, decided against the peanuts in favor of one of the Wilde Havanas remaining in the box.

At the living-room window he lit up, puffing as he stared out at the vacant lot across the street from his building, a broad expanse of weed and rubble, broken bottle glass glittering in the light of a streetlamp beneath the windy, darkening sky. Someone had placed a dilapidated plastic table and chairs amidst the weeds.

The cigar was marvelous. So was the vodka, a Russian distilled Smirnoff. And the music, Rautavaara, a modern Finnish composition of quiet passion. It was good to be alone in the dark.

Something drifted to consciousness. A question: *The Virgin Mary?*

Back in the kitchen he looked again at the window across the way. No illuminated statue of the Virgin Mary stood there, only a blue and white lamp. Then he saw how the angle of the shade resembled the arms of the Virgin draped in a robe, palms open to welcome and offer solace. Not the Mary of clasped hands; this was the Mary who looked down, not up. The image stoked nostalgia for his childhood, and he stood there transfixed by the lamp for several moments, the angle of the shade, a classic form. He marveled over the chance beauty of it, lifted the cigar to his lips and sucked. It was cold.

Pausing in the hallway, he studied a framed photo of himself with his arms to either side around his children beneath the Bridge of Sighs in Venice. His children were very young, and he wore sunglasses and a short-sleeved shirt. It was taken the summer he had completed his doctoral thesis, and the person missing from the photo was his ex-wife, who had taken it. The shadow of her arm could be seen on the wall behind them. How happy his children looked, leaning into him, beneath his crooked elbows, a seven-year-old girl, a nine-year-old boy.

The phone rang. He listened to his own voice answer on the machine, the beep, the voice of a woman he knew saying she had only called to say hello. Her voice conveyed desire. He pictured her body, remembered the silken feel of his palm gliding down the delicate skin of her back, sipped his vodka, and wanted her. Then it occurred to him he was tired of wanting her, tired of the rituals of easy passion, the ever-ready love of the lover within. If he lifted the phone now he knew the evening would end in her bed or his, the little death, inevitable sadness, nothing.

Back in the living room, he stared again at the empty lot. The music had ended. A tall, angular man stood on the corner, silhouetted in the silver light of the streetlamp, doing some slow, meticulous ritual of movement. Binzer felt a trembling in his pulse, for he knew the figure was without meaning, merely a man performing a series of exercises. It frightened him vaguely to have glimpsed himself perceiving significance in this chance coinciding of a moment in his life with a moment in the life of an unknown person on a street corner, as though the slow, angular movements of his limbs and shoulders were a metaphor for something, challenging him to comprehend.

I see you there, he thought, and that is all, and felt sad that the woman who had called was lonely, had chosen him to fill her lonely night, and he had nothing in him to offer just now but the blankness of standing alone in the quiet dark of his living room, a cold cigar between his fingers, holding a glass of vodka diluted with melted ice.

He knew that if she were here now, at just this moment, their eyes would meet and perceive an undeniable ending following the extended passion of their last meeting, the perception of an emptying completed.

The chill warmth of spirit comforted his tongue. He saw a large bird glide above the lamppost across the top of a tall tree, wings hung in the pale dark sky of his fifty-second autumn.

He wondered what things meant, whether anything meant anything, wondered what he meant by wondering that, and for just an instant feared suddenly, unexpectedly, inexplicably, for his sanity.

He turned his mind to the lecture he would deliver next day, some quotes from Plato's *Apology,* which he had been inspired to reread visiting Syracuse two summers before, when there was still money for that sort of thing. He could not think of Syracuse without considering the two ancient theaters there—the one where Greeks had watched Oedipus live through his ruthless fight to see, and two hundred yards and two centuries away, the one where Romans watched men and beasts tear out each other's throats. The Romans, he thought, were more like us, centralists, well organized and bloodthirsty. And what was God's position in all this? The immortal hand that forged the tooth.

At some point during the night, he sat up in bed, groggy, slid from beneath the sheet, and stepped across to his desk to write some words on a piece of paper. Then, so he would not forget, he folded the paper and tucked it into the pocket of the shirt he had hung out for the next day, and returned to his bed, sinking gratefully back into sleep.

* * *

There was no room for moodiness in his professional life, and the air of the brisk October morning braced him for the lecture he was due to deliver. It was a talk he'd given many times before about the distinction between reality and realism in fiction and, by extension, in the fiction we create of our own lives. As he spoke, his words were sufficiently familiar to him that he was able to stand back behind himself as behind a prop, and watch through his eyeholes the students in the class.

"Let us not forget," he said, "the origin of the word 'persona,' from the Latin, *per sonare,* to sound through. The narrative persona in a fiction is a mask through which the author sounds the words of the fiction, just as the actor in the Greek theater held a mask before his face to indicate the character he portrayed."

As he spoke, he looked from face to face in the classroom, making eye contact to secure their engagement. Autumn sunlight slanted in through the tall windows, across the pale wood of the desks, the hands of the students writing in their notebooks. He looked at Marissa, the young dark-eyed girl whose last story was about a man who would not put his hands beneath her narrator's shirt; he watched her face go tense in his gaze, then shifted to the face of the heavy, jocular woman who wrote breezy tales of deep longing. To the tall young man with the damaged eyes, whose last manuscript was a sympathetic portrait of a child abuser.

"Time for questions," he said then. "Anyone? Anything?"

The young dark-eyed Marissa had a question so powerful her voice quavered to deliver it. "I keep wondering," she whispered. "Asking myself. What . . . *is* a story?"

She reddened at the snickers, and Binzer hastened to say, "Good question. I'm glad you asked that." Then removed his eyes from her to take in the entire class.

"A story is just an account of something that happened, or might have happened, given the shape of art, even if that shape reflects nothing so much as the shapelessness of life. That's all."

"Sounds easy," said the jocular woman who wrote breezy stories of deep longing, and whose name he never could remember.

"Even less," Binzer said. "In point of fact, a story is nothing but words flung into a pattern on a page . . ."

"My question," interrupted the quiet, thin, black girl who had not yet spoken this term, "is how much do you have to, like, understand?"

"Don't worry about understanding a thing. Just drench the parched page with words. Wander in the woods and let your unthinking eye describe a pattern in the leaves. Remember Stevens: To discover, not impose. Williams: Not adjectives, but verbs. Sometimes the truth depends on a walk around a lake. Often the best fiction is a puzzle the reader has to forge a key for, to unlock a fragment of contemplation that brings us *that* much closer to a vision of ourselves."

"Wow!" said the black girl in search of understanding, and Binzer sneezed. He dug out his handkerchief and mopped his nose.

"Remember your Plato," he said. "Your Socrates: *Not by wisdom do poets write poetry, but by a sort of genius and inspiration—they say many fine things, but do not understand the meaning of them.* Or what Beckett said when someone asked him to explain the characters in Godot: *I know no more than what they say, what they do, and what happens to them. If I did manage to get slightly acquainted with them, it was only by keeping very far away from the need to understand.*"

This silenced them for a moment, and in the gap, he remembered a dream fragment—his lips gliding down her spine, remembered Gass: *I dreamed my lips slid down your back like a skiff upon a river*—remembered, for some reason, Ovid: *Don't let the light in your bedroom be too bright.*

"Okay," said the plump, jovial woman, with a truculent dip of her rounded shoulders, "but what about—"

The bell rang, and he stopped her with an eyebrow. Playfully, he finished with Plato: "*The hour of departure has arrived, and we go our ways. You to live. I to die. Which is better, God only knows.*"

During lunch he discovered a folded piece of paper in his shirt pocket on which was written the words *Donna della Aube*. Then he remembered the dream from which he had awoken during the night. A seated woman with no face had shown him a piece of paper on which these words were written. He had risen, copied them down. He smoothed the paper out beside his plate, studying it as he munched his cafeteria pizza, and sipped a club soda.

While he ate and gazed at the paper, the woman who had phoned him the night before came past with her tray of soiled dishes. Her back, his palm; her spine, his lips. She did not stop or look at him. Just as he turned his head to call her name, he noticed that the cafeteria sound system was playing an old Rolling Stones number. "Time Is on My Side." Mick Jagger sang about having the real love, the kind that she needs, and he wondered what the old singer was implying.

Binzer wondered whose side time was on.

That evening he attended a family gathering at the home of his ex-wife's uncle, a retired professor of history. The occasion was the forty-ninth wedding anniversary of the uncle and his wife. The uncle greeted Binzer warmly at the door.

"You are always welcome here," he said, clasping Binzer's hand in both of his. Binzer's gaze fell across the little heap of their hands and fingers, his own still strong, though worn red, framed by the uncle's—pale, thin-boned, corded thickly with blue veins. "I consider you an agreeable chapter in our family history. I always liked you." He paused, shifted gears. "Why not throw a party for our forty-ninth, ey? Should we wait for our fiftieth? One of us might be dead. Both of us." Without pause, he added, "Your wife couldn't make it. Your ex-wife. Some sort of flu."

He followed Binzer into the rooms throughout which the party ranged, clutching his elbow. "How are you managing? I hear you've taken rooms downtown. My own girls are spread all over the place now. It's a puzzle in an enigma. Can you figure? Rose and I together for forty-nine years, and every single one of our five girls divorced at least once. I gave them away one by one. They took the names of other men. Put their own names in a bottle and threw it in the sea. I strike you on the head with the shoe of your father. My daughter, my ducats. Fuck it. This world is no longer mine."

"Your world was a better one," Binzer said to the old man. "Your life was blessed. My two probably won't even marry. Then who's gonna pay our pensions?"

The uncle shrugged elaborately. "Come have some wine."

Binzer could not help but envy the sprawling North Shore house, vast rooms with windows over the sound, the white walls, plank floors, the antique luxury of space. B & O speakers filled the house with jazz improvisations on "Autumn Leaves." He recognized Miles Davis's trumpet, Cannonball Adderley. He knew this piece had to be at least forty years old, yet somehow new still, and the flattish tones of Davis's horn filled him with sweet melancholy.

He carried his wine with him as he greeted people. The aunt, whose once vividly pretty face now resembled melting wax, kissed his neck and whispered, "Go back to her."

"It's hopeless," he said, and went to embrace his newly bearded son, who stood chatting to a tall, thin couple with drawling voices and superior expressions on their long faces.

"Pops," his son said, and Binzer thought he saw an ironic pull to the boy's lips in the moment before the embrace. Am I a joke now?

"Another beard?" Binzer said.

"Same one. I sculpted it."

"Ready to defend your thesis yet?"

"Not quite. In the spring, I think."

"You think?"

"I might do something else first."

"Why not do something else afterward?"

Now the ironic lips were unconcealed. "How's the new rooms, Pops?"

Binzer hid his wound, swallowed the injustice, but reminded himself that his current circumstances were a result of the generous settlement in his wife's favor, the trust accounts for his children's education. You fool, he thought, you self-pitying, half-fat, half-bald, half-old fool.

"They're fine for a writer," he said. "Plenty of light." He noticed his son was not wearing the wristwatch he had given him, which had been his own father's, a St. Gaudin's double-eagle piece, half a century old. Last time they met over dinner they had argued about time. His son insisted it was an arbitrary invention, that clocks were instruments of tyranny, time a postulate of Swiss jewelers. Binzer had let himself get into it, and he wanted none of that this time.

With reluctance he continued on his round of greetings, after first squeezing his son's strong bicep to reassure himself the boy would manage, reminding himself how long it had taken him to realize he was no better than his own father.

His daughter intercepted him on his way into the next room.

"Daddo!" She hugged him tight and kissed his cheek. He studied her face, wondering if it really was as beautiful as it seemed to him, or whether that beauty was pure subjectivity on his part. He felt somehow that her heart was farther from him than his son's, but that she understood him better and knew how to make him feel unconcerned about her. Yet he saw this as a sign of untroubled devotion for which he was grateful. She was younger, yet less at odds with life, with her lot. Perhaps men are more alone than women, he thought. Thanks to all the necessities they subscribe to. Biological maybe. Or the remnant of a community of the subjugated. Of course, she had a partner, and as far as he knew his son did not.

"How is your mother?" Binzer asked.

"Fine."

"I thought she was sick."

"Not too bad," she said, indicating with her eyes that it was nothing at all. She just didn't want to come.

"Give her my love. How about you? School going okay?"

"Fine."

"And your, uh, Bernie?"

"Fine. He's studying for an exam."

Binzer had met the young man a couple of times; seemed okay, although he had been startled to see black Celtic bracelets tattooed around either bicep. He also knew from his ex that the girl had recently acquired a tattoo on the back of her shoulder, a scorpion, her birth sign.

"How's the spider?" he asked, and wished he hadn't, but she laughed, a little nervously—a tribute he was grateful for. "I was just going to tell you . . ." He held his tongue. Perhaps he would get a tattoo himself if he could find some smooth part of his body to put it on. Why not? Perhaps he would fling himself into dissolution, a ruinous dispersal, disordering of his senses. To hell with productive concentration. Why not? Then it occurred to him that what he might have said to his daughter, how sad a fading tattoo looks on fading skin, was even worse in opposite: how ridiculous a *new* tattoo would look on fading skin.

"I love you, honey," he said. "Please take good care of yourself. You're my treasure." My daughter, my ducats.

It warmed him that she seemed to receive the statement with warmth, kissed his cheek again, and he squeezed her tight before she was taken by a favorite cousin to dance to music he could not imagine how to move to. He watched for a few moments how subtly they moved together, the young man's eyes turned down to her face, his smile private as hers. He was a tall, slender boy, with a slender face and long nose, wore a black shirt and silver tie, his blond hair tied in a ponytail, and suddenly Binzer could not bear to watch any longer.

He retreated to the library, where an attractive young woman sat alone watching television. Binzer recognized the film as *The Maltese Falcon*. Humphrey Bogart moved toward Peter Lorre, who backed away like an Apache dancer. Bogart smiled cruelly, a cigarette taut between his lips, and Lorre's eyes turned up fearfully to his face as Bogart smacked him, knocking him unconscious.

Binzer glanced at the young woman. "Talk about your homophobic glee," he said.

She smiled sidewise up at him and said nothing. Her blouse was scooped low. Conscious desire to dress that way, he thought. "The quest," he said. "Ey? The jewel-encrusted bird of tribute. The cobalt-blue eyes." Then, because he was attracted, he turned away, busied himself studying the spines of books on a shelf, tilted back his head and held his glasses at an angle for a look at a sculpture on a pedestal. Some goddess who wore an array of many orblike shapes around her neck.

"Artemis," the young woman said. "Those are bull testicles."

"Indeed," he said, trying to remember.

"A thousand years before Christ," she said.

"You know your gods and goddesses, all right." He could not remember. Artemis. Diana. "Some cult, was it?"

"In Turkey. The bull testicles did for her what the Angel did for Mary."

"Ah!" He still could not remember and was miserable to find himself wondering if this young woman . . . No. "Are you a teacher?" he asked, glancing into the crease between her breasts, wondering why he could never break the relentless program that drew his eyes to the luscious forms of women.

She smiled. "I work in a doughnut shop," she said, and lifted a glass of sparkling water from the table beside her. A movement in the corner of the room startled him. A dog rose to its feet and yawned, a black Labrador.

He laughed. "Startled me!" he exclaimed. She made a movement with the water glass—as though she meant to splash it at him—and he ducked back, offended, confused. On the TV screen Sidney Greenstreet was saying to Humphrey Bogart, "By gad, sir, you are a remarkable fellow. Extraordinary!"

Binzer drained his wineglass as an excuse to get away.

Already tipsy, he poured a vodka in his kitchen, glanced across the courtyard at the blue and white lamp. It was not even blue and white, it was green and beige. He snorted, stood swaying at the sink, infinitely grateful that he had said nothing suggestive to the young woman in the library. Yet the mere chance that he might have troubled him. Why? She might have wanted me. And? He thought of his dark-eyed student Marissa, of the woman who had phoned him the night before whom he perhaps would never see again, of his ex-wife's once-beautiful aunt with the melting-wax face, and reached up to the box of Wilde Havanas. There were still two in the box.

He decided abruptly to allow himself to smoke them both. And then what?

"And then nothing," he said aloud. "And then nothing. Not a goddamned fucking thing."

In the hallway he looked at the photo of his children flanking him beneath the Bridge of Sighs in Venice the summer he had defended his thesis. *Realism & Other Illusions.*

The thick, bitter cigar smoke was a comfort in his mouth, the Russian vodka, and he stood looking out the front window at the vacant lot across the way. Someone sat at the plastic table among the weeds, and Binzer had the impulse to go down to him, bring the vodka bottle, ice, offer the final cigar. "By gad, sir, join me for a touch of the creature!"

"Alone," he murmured. *"Alone, alone, all all alone, alone on a wide wide sea,"* he snickered, and sipped vodka, and recognized happily how tipsy he was.

I don't ever want this night to end, he thought, sat on his sofa, and leaned back against the cushions, and soon was one with a kind of paradise of mindlessness.

Two Anacins and a glass of tomato juice constituted his breakfast. He sat staring at the smoothed-out piece of paper on which were written the words *Donna della Aube.* In truth it was so simple. He knew a little French, but he did not remember knowing that *aube* meant dawn. Yet something led him to a French-English dictionary on his shelves that solved that riddle. He had been thinking about anagrams, but it was much simpler than that. *Donna* was no puzzle, nor was *della—de la.*

What a blessing! A veritable revelation.

Yet another hour passed, and he had come no further. The words, defined, left him blank. He scanned his books. Jung, of

course, but so what? Anima, animus, women are monogamous.
Oh? There was so much knowledge, so much wisdom, in all the
wonderful books on his shelves, but this was a message from a
woman with no face who had visited him in a dream. Jung would
be intrigued. Coleridge would approve. Aristotle would say in
dreams we sleep with our mothers. He ran his index finger across
the spines of one shelf, pulled out a little brochure that he had been
given by a blind man on the subway train one summer day, opened
the cover, and read, *What is your life? It is even a vapour that
appeareth for a little time and then is gone*. He closed it again, slid it
back into its place.

What to do with this?

Many spaced-out moments passed, his eyes filled with the
vacant lot, the weeds, the now abandoned table, the glittering bits
of broken bottle glass.

He had a class in four hours. Time enough for a good long walk.

He crossed the park, strolled along the lake where the necks of
swans floated past like questions, paused to admire the magnificent
symmetry of a chestnut tree, yellow-brown, red with the fall. The
aroma thrilled him as it had all his life, the death of summer. Rilke:
*He who has no house now, never will. He who is alone, alone will stay,
will sit, read, write lengthy letters through long evenings, will wander the
boulevards restlessly, up and down, while the dead leaves scratch past his
feet.*

He came out of the park onto the boulevard, crossed the street
to the Church of Our Lady and climbed the steps, pulled open the
heavy door.

Blessing himself from the holy-water font, he sat in the last pew,
remembered how his father had knelt each night to pray at the side
of his bed before he slept. Binzer wondered now what the man
prayed for, what he had believed.

For a moment then it was as though his parents stood on either
side of him, a hand on each of his shoulders. The simmering quiet
anger of so many years it had taken him to forgive them for God

knew what, first the one, then the other, and now at last he felt that they, too, had forgiven *him* for God knew what.

He could have sat forever in this modest church, gazing across the dim expanse of light, filtered through stained glass, to the altar stone, the statues. He stood, crossed to the right of the altar where a statue of Mary rose above a tray of flickering red vigil lights, arms extended, palms open. The quietness of her face, stone eyes gazing down, the calm, the stillness of the space around them. He might have been a boy again, up at dawn for summer morning mass.

He lit a candle, knelt.

"Oh, mother," he whispered.

Andrew Roe

❧

ROUGH

Anna told Aaron that she liked it kind of rough. They were walking back to his apartment, mildly drunk, shuddering against the streaming fog and cold. He wasn't sure what that meant exactly, "kind of rough"—but he didn't want to disrupt the flow of the potentially epic evening (so far so good) with stupid questions that would reveal his staggeringly sedate suburban roots and quasi-conservative leanings (shit, he'd voted for Bush, both of them, actually), which he still felt vaguely embarrassed about even after having lived in the famously liberal city—The City—for close to seven years now. That's what they called it here, The City, capital T, capital C, as in "I've been living in The City for close to seven years now," as if there were only one city and where else would you live?

As it turned out, though, whether or not Aaron was sexually qualified in the rough department didn't really matter. After a poorly executed elevator kiss (his initial overture drew ear and hair instead of lips), and after opening a bottle of blueberry Schnapps (the only alcoholic beverage he could forage in the kitchen; it was either that or NyQuil), and engaging in some subsequent sofa groping and minimalist dialogue right before (Should I? . . . There . . . How's that? . . . Maybe if . . . Okay, good . . .), he came in like five seconds and then it was over.

"So much for rough," he said, going for levity, because at that point what else could he do? And then because she didn't say anything back right away he added, "It's been a while."

"Me, too," she said.

Aaron's brother gave the toast at the wedding. He was in AA so he didn't raise a glass of champagne. He raised a glass of water instead. The speech incorporated all the standard themes and conventions of the rather limited wedding-speech genre—the use of humor and embarrassment mixed, ultimately, when it came time for the 150 or so guests to uniformly hoist their glasses upward and wish the happy couple the best, with sincerity; covering Aaron's nontraumatic childhood, his bumbling yet endearing adolescence and teenage years, his partying college days (and here Aaron's brother inserted a cautionary note about the perils of excessive drinking, offering himself as an example), and his eventual relocation to The City—except Aaron's brother, being a lifelong Midwesterner, made the faux pas of saying the actual name—and then bringing in Anna, what a great girl she was, and how she made such a great addition to the whole curmudgeonly Cahill clan, and of course ending with the final thought of how now there was one family instead of two, et cetera.

Everyone agreed that the wedding was a major success (although, granted, the goateed deejay ignored Aaron and Anna's emphatic request *not* to play "Y.M.C.A."). Guests mingled easily, naturally; trays carrying wine and hors d'oeuvres kept appearing just when more food and drink was needed, as if on cue; time slowed to a tranquil, celebratory hum; and the outside world temporarily receded away like a spent wave returning to the ocean. There was one point during the reception when Anna looked across the room to see Aaron talking to a pregnant cousin of his, and then he turned, and their eyes met at just the right time, and it was one of those totally clichéd yet very real cinematic moments (complete with orchestral sound track swelling in the background, or so it seemed to their mutual internal stereo system), where everything falls into place and you know you're doing the right thing and that people are meant for each other and, no, we're not all essentially alone, and, yes, a life can in fact be shared, truly, wholly, deeply.

Why do we say what we say, do what we do? Can reason and motive and certainty ever be completely confirmed? How does love begin? How does it end? Does it end at all? What, if anything, lasts? This was the babbling brook of thoughts and questions that flowed through her on the cab ride home, still dark, the city still asleep, but the night just about ready to expire, to become something else, the sky slowly lightening.

She didn't know why she said she liked it rough, which wasn't true, which was just a dumbshit line that came to her, an utterance penned by someone else and that slipped out by mistake. It was something to say when you're tipsy from too many cosmopolitans and your body is alive with the electric blood-buzz of discovering a new person (a very *promising* new person), and you're walking past elaborate mansions that no doubt house elaborate lives, and in the distance there's the bay's steadfast foghorn lament and the occasional cable car clank, and you're periodically looking at him and thinking a million different things and then only one thing.

Afterward he was sweet, offering her tea and control of the remote. But she didn't stay, and she could tell the decision made it worse for him. Immediately she regretted it—"I think I should go," which became the harshest sentence she'd ever spoken—but it was too late. And plus she really did want to go. She suddenly had the postcoital—if you could even call it that—desire to be alone.

It wasn't like this hadn't ever happened before. She had a boyfriend in college who'd been that way, chronically, who'd even read up on the subject to try to increase his stamina. One tactic he tried was to masturbate while watching himself in the mirror and then stop right before he came. Which didn't work. Neither did thinking of sports or Bea Arthur or the ghastly shrunken old woman who replenished the salad bar in the school cafeteria.

She remembered, too, a film appreciation class she'd taken in college, and one of the films they appreciated was *The French Lieutenant's Woman*. According to her professor, the sex scene in the movie represented the most realistic sex scene ever put on film. Why? Because after Jeremy Irons has endured all this unbearable pent-up passion and stinging desire for Meryl Streep, he finally gets his chance to fuck her and he comes in like five seconds and then it's over. He didn't say anything about it having been a while, although that was probably the case, it being Victorian England and all.

Seconds, minutes, an hour—what did it matter, really? It was all transitory, over before you knew it, she thought. There were other things to consider.

He never saw himself as the type to videotape the birth of his children, but he'd done it for all three. In fact, he became something of a delivery-room auteur, jockeying around nurses and orderlies and anesthesiologists to get the best angles, making use of natural lighting, trying to create a Scorsese-inspired gritty realism and edginess. When reviewing the tapes he could see a definite progression in his work, from the first birth to the final one—and it was the final one. There'd be no more kids, they'd decided, no more home movies of blood and birth and beauty. Three was enough.

By then they no longer lived in The City, but in a house in a city (a suburb, that is) where it was okay to say the name. They had neighbors who always waved, gym memberships that did not go unused, financial portfolios with mutual funds that were considered "moderate aggressive." He felt lucky. He was lucky. Sometimes he'd sit in the backyard and soak in the multicolored sunset and pleasantly marvel at the simplicity, the fundamental ordinariness of his life. He'd playfully pat his ebbing stomach and not worry too much about its slow yet determined expansion. He'd see Anna inside the house, knowing that she'd eventually come outside to join him. He loved the waiting, the anticipation of that, knowing that soon he would reach out to touch her and she would touch back. His wife. They'd come a long way since that bar in the marina. Every year they went there and had a drink to celebrate the anniversary of their first date.

It did not look good. It did not look good at all. He stayed up until it got light, unsuccessfully trying to console himself in the numbing whirl of late-night/early-morning cable until his eyes stung too much and he could no longer watch.

In the afternoon he made coffee. While it was brewing, he walked to the café around the corner to get one of those big-ass poppyseed muffins he liked so much. It was all part of his Sunday ritual. He went back to his apartment and read the paper. Twice. Even the travel section. He listened to early R.E.M. and thought about a screenplay that he knew he'd never write. Which was also part of the ritual.

He would see Anna the next day. They worked together, after all. Well, not really together, but at the same company, along with about a thousand other people. They had little work-related inter-action, a fact that now made him grateful. They'd struck up a con-versation at the office Christmas party a week before. Hence the date. Hence the fuck that was over before it began.

People started dying. Parents, uncles, aunts, coworkers. Even neighbors. Mr. Tillman, for instance, who only a year ago was run-ning in 10Ks and doing tai chi at the nearby park (he once showed Aaron a few of the moves, the names of which still stuck with him: Cloud Hands, Grasp Swallow's Tail, Parting Horse's Mane, Sleeves Dancing Like Plum Blossoms). Cancer, of course. You could see how utterly devastated Mrs. Tillman was. Then she died too. And plus there were the more random, middle-aged, you-can't-fucking-believe-it deaths: Terry Finkel, car accident; Jenny Blackstock, also cancer, breast; Dave Gingrass, some kind of ski-lift accident in Austria. And even kids, teenagers, which was the worst. Through it all, they held each other closer, tighter. They didn't sleep as well as they used to (had they ever slept well?), especially when they knew their two daughters and one son, all full-fledged teenagers now, one about to leave for college and seriously considering becoming a vegetarian, were out, away, doing things they didn't want to know about—but of course they did want to know, and that was part of it too, the wanting to know and the not wanting to know. It could happen no matter how good you were, no matter how you lived your life. No big revelation here, they admitted, but still, it made you think. How terminally fragile life was, is. It was true: Being a parent changes everything. Your children—they become everything. You make them but then they remake you. And then they leave.

That afternoon she canceled her plans to catch a movie with a friend. Instead she stayed in, writing letters, doing laundry, enjoying the lonely hum of Sunday. The weather was shitty anyway, and what else was new, the fog pouring in as if propelled from a hidden machine. She saw it from her apartment window, pulsing with what seemed to be a secret purpose, the wind bowing back the trees and swirling garbage and dust. (Anna lived three blocks from the ocean, in the Sunset District, where the sun could disappear for weeks on end. Fogville, she called it, which, sure, eventually got to you psychologically, but she'd been desperate to find a place and had unfortunately signed a yearlong lease.) Repeatedly, she tortured herself by playing the night back in her mind. Fuck. She shouldn't have left. Why did she leave? She should have stayed. Everything would have been better if she had stayed. Now there would be this awkwardness, because of that, and because of Aaron's, well, brevity. Fuck. Would it have killed her to stay, to lie in his arms and wake up together and then maybe even go out to breakfast and talk about how they've both always wanted a house with a porch and isn't Cormac McCarthy amazing?

The last few men she'd dated were fond of wearing black (and nothing but black) and hanging postcards of obscure Latin American poets on their bedroom walls. So that's why Aaron seemed like such a breath of fresh air. She was just beginning to think she only attracted a certain kind of guy: angst-ridden, distant,

unable to accept their anonymity in the world. They usually played
in bands or were trying to start bands. Aaron did not play an instrument and he did not quote Rilke. He was from Ohio.

One of her coworkers, Cheryl from Product Development, had
pointed him out to her. "Hottie alert," Cheryl had said as Aaron
approached, and then passed them on his way to the kitchen.

Anna usually didn't pay much attention to what Cheryl said. She
was one of those women who Anna had decided to tune out—the
kind who were always criticizing other women as too fat, too thin,
too slutty, too librarian. But she was right about Aaron. He made
her tingle in all the right places.

When she saw him at the Christmas party she hesitated about
going over to talk to him. She felt that high-school dorkiness that
had never left her completely, especially when it came to situations
such as this. *Just do it. After all, this could be your husband,* was the
weird random thought that whispered its way into her head, one of
those out-of-the-blue aberrations that you think of every now and
then because at some point in your life it's going to be true, it will
be your husband. *Think of something dazzling to say so you'll have a
good story to tell your kids.* Then she laughed to herself. But she
didn't have to do anything: he was the one who came over to her.
She told herself to remember what song was playing as he made his
way toward her, but she got so involved in the conversation, and so
taken by his smile (genuine, sexy, a little shy), that she forgot.

There are mysteries, though. He had to admit that. No matter how
close you think you are, no matter how truly double-helixed your
lives seem to be, you can't know everything. Secrets exist, uncer-
tainties linger. Inevitably there are those things that get lost along
the years, that happen and somehow are never picked up again.
Like what she said the night of their first date: how she liked it
rough. What was that all about? They'd never discussed it, not once
in all these years and decades together (there were grandchildren
now, the mortgage paid off, a second home in Lake Tahoe, etc.). It
had passed. It had simply passed. Although somehow it had

haunted them, too. At least it had haunted him. He wondered periodically over the years, whenever there was an especially long silence or when they felt out of sync and foreign to each other, if she was thinking of that, how they'd never talked about it, how she'd liked it rough and she'd never had it rough all these years.

She hadn't wanted to die in a hospital. So they brought her home. They gathered around the bed—their bed—and took turns gently pressing ice cubes to her mouth, to moisten the perpetual dryness. "Dad," his children said. "Don't stay up too late. Get some rest, 'kay?" Then he was alone with her. Somehow, he knew. He sat and smelled her smell and remembered as much as he could and watched the last breath of air escape from her lips. Then he kissed them one last time.

All right: he told himself not to dwell on it on the bus ride to work, but of course he did. His only distraction was the woman standing next to him. She was stunning. Occasionally the sway of the crowded bus caused their shoulders to haphazardly rub, and every time it happened a pinching little ache bloomed in Aaron's chest. Was she thinking the same thing he was, which was this: What if they started talking? What if he made some comment about the book she was reading (a thick fucking doorstop of a novel, something called *Underworld*), and then that spurred a conversation and it went so well that they exchanged e-mail addresses (safer, better than phone numbers), and that led to a date and another date, and isn't it funny how love can strike where you least expect it, like for example a rush-hour bus that reeked of old bread and had no empty seats, and because of this, the lack of seating, they happened to be standing next to each other on a certain day at a certain time . . . But he didn't say anything, and neither did she. And his would-be wife/lover/soul mate/mother of his children got off at the exit before his and he watched her disappear into the downtown crowd, lost forever, his life completely altering in a space of five seconds, and then returning back to the way it was. He often had these inwardly dramatic commutes. And

Mondays were particularly fertile for such imaginings and long-ings.

First thing at work, he got settled in for the week, checking his e-mail, returning phone calls, planning out his calendar. He wasn't ready to do any real work yet. He was easing into the day, pacing himself. And all the while Anna hovered in the back of his mind like a bad movie he'd seen a few days ago but couldn't stop thinking of. How would he approach her? What would he say? How would she react? Where was the best place to talk to her?

She worked on the other side of the floor. Her cube had an actual view. You could make out part of the Bay Bridge, the stream of cars and invisible commuters constant, never ending. People driving no matter what. He still wasn't clear on her job and what she did exactly. Some kind of market research, he thought uncer-tainly. When time for lunch rolled around he hadn't walked over. He decided to let it go a little while longer, to see how the afternoon developed.

But not long after making that decision (or rather nondecision), he was proofreading a report on the ability of young children to rec-ognize company mascots and logos and then there she was, stand-ing at his cube.

"Hey," she said.

"Hey," he said.

"Have you had lunch yet?"

"No, I was just starting to think about it, though."

There was something in her eyes, her entire face, even—a look. A definite look that said yes, maybe something could happen here, it wasn't too late. He told himself not to stare, to continue to use language and stand up and grab his jacket and ask where she wanted to go, what she felt like eating. But the look paralyzed him. He just sat there, happy. At least now there seemed to be, if nothing else, the possibility of the possible. It gave him hope.

Quinn Dalton

❦

MIDNIGHT BOWLING

I t was Mr. Ontero from across the street who found my father stretched out in the front yard next to his IV tree as if he'd gotten tired of waiting for someone to let him in. Lettie and Harold Bell and fat Ms. Parsons and the triplets, and other people whose names I don't remember anymore, stood on the lawn watching Mr. Ontero trying to save him while my mother was at work and Donny Florida and I were at school. It was a cloudy day and still pretty brisk out, typical Ohio spring; I imagine the red and blue flashes splashing the treetops on our street like the disco lights dotting the Star Lanes. Mr. Ontero checked my father's pulse and puffed into his lungs because no one else would do it. In between breaths he told the neighbors he was an old man and had seen the Spanish flu, and everyone had said the world was ending then, which it hadn't, so he wasn't scared of any so-called plagues.

After the funeral Mr. Ontero offered to sell back our lawn mower at the price my father had sold it to him. "Fair is fair," he said to my mother on our doorstep, tulips from his garden quivering in his outstretched hand. "No profit-mongering here."

My mother slammed the door in his face. A couple of weeks later, when I started back to school, I'd see Mr. Ontero as I walked to the bus stop, bent like a question mark in his front yard, picking leaves and twigs from his silky, trimmed lawn and stuffing them into his pockets. Whenever I stopped to say hello he told me stories about making lard soap in the Depression and earning a dollar a week on the oil rigs in Missouri City; he spoke like a typewriter, in a kind of emergency Morse code, never pausing to allow me to say "that's nice" or "good-bye" until I had to walk away or miss my bus. I'd hear his voice trail off like a plane passing overhead and feel too embarrassed to look back.

Then Donny started giving me rides to school and work whenever his car was working, and I hardly saw Mr. Ontero at all until he died last week. I rode my bike to the funeral in my pink Eatery waitress uniform, having just been fired, to say good-bye to him in his casket.

Now Donny's driving me to orientation, and I'm thinking about Mr. Ontero as a little boy, cutting the tip of his nose off with his toy plane propeller and having to sit still with no anesthetic while they sewed it back on with thread, real thread; and my father swimming in dark Lake Erie to impress my mother; and Mr. Ontero's squinty black eyes, the last to see my father alive. His reedy-thin voice hums in my ears on and off during the two-hour drive, while my mother thinks I'm at work, saving money for our big move. The voice is saying, "You've got moxie," which he said every time I won the Junior Tournament Bowlers Association of Ohio—Rookie of the Year when I was thirteen, Bowler of the Year at fourteen, and Highest Average the next two years. My father put the trophies in the front window to signal each win. He was Joe Wycheski, the Buckeye Champion of the Ohio Bowlers League eight years running. Donny's uncle Leo, who owns the Star Lanes, puts your picture on the Hall of Fame wall if you get the Buckeye three times. My father's picture has a permanent space in a gold-speckled plastic frame.

Donny pulls into the visitor lot, singing at the top of his lungs to Led Zeppelin. A girl pulls in next to us in a red convertible and hops out; Donny doesn't notice her crinkling her nose as if she smells exhaust from Donny's brown T-Bird with the racing stripes he painted himself—she's walking fast, bangles clinking. A gold chain gleams on her ankle.

"I'll meet you here," Donny says, and for a moment I forget why I thought this was such a good idea, going to college, where he won't be.

The first session is Campus Culture. The tour leader, a blond woman with a pointy chin that turns white at the tip when she talks, says State has a strong gay/lesbian association, and the girl with the bangles says fags shouldn't be allowed because it runs against the Bible, which is why they're being punished with AIDS. Nobody says anything to this. Of course now people are saying you can get AIDS from mosquitoes, or saliva, and that we're all being punished.

Then there's the Student Services and Learn the Library tours, and a packed lunch, and at the end I'm in the parking lot waiting for a half hour with my slick gold and black folder, looking at this wide green campus filled with people I don't know, wondering if there's any good lanes around. I watch the girl with the bangles get in her car and drive away without looking at me, even though she smacked gum in my ear for five hours. Donny strolls from behind some buildings like he's at the park, in no particular hurry. He stomps out a cigarette, unlocks my door first.

"Where were you?" I ask.

He shrugs, doesn't answer. We get on the highway again. "You know what I heard," he says, not asks. "If you can't go to college, go to State."

I roll my window all the way down and hot air blankets us, wisping hair out of Donny's thin, rubber-banded ponytail. Donny hates driving with the windows down, but I like it, because it feels like flying, like the roller coasters at the park.

"Oh really?" I say. The road melts air at the top of the next hill; radio announcer's drilling the record temperature and humidity. At night, planes crisscross our town, spraying the mosquitoes breeding over ponds. I turn the air-conditioning on, to compromise.

"They don't care about you," Donny says.

"You just don't want me to go."

"Whatever." Donny shoves another tape in the deck, Rush this time, singing, *Exit the warrior / Today's Tom Sawyer*. Head swinging forward on the guitar and drums.

What I know is, Donny applied to State, too; didn't even type out the forms. Sent it out like it was no big deal. And didn't get accepted. We haven't talked about what he plans to do this fall, unless he goes full-time at the lanes like his uncle Leo wants. Me, I just got fired from waiting tables at the Eatery because I forgot to bring ketchup to some guy. A bottle of ketchup. I didn't know what I was going to do until Mr. Todd told me about his wife's brother who works at the College of Arts and Sciences at the university, which is weird to think about, a college inside a university. He said his wife's brother would nominate me for a scholarship, even though I've already missed all the deadlines. He called yesterday and told me to go to orientation, said he had something for me. He said there's no need to talk about it to anyone, because these scholarships are for special cases. But I did tell Donny, because I want him to know everything.

"I'm taking a nap, okay?" I say.

No response. I lean back and close my eyes, AC mixed with hot outside air rolling over me in waves, music vibrating my ribs. Donny's driving because my mother finally sold my father's car, which I was using, because she says we need money for our future more than we need things. Our future, according to my mother, is at the Savior Missionary in Marietta. The Savior, as she refers to it, is where I can get real-life experience. "Millions are waiting for the Lord's word right here in Ohio," my mother informed me yesterday. For two thousand dollars, I can get into the missionary program and travel all over the country handing out flyers and visiting foster homes. She thinks I'm going to save that much from waiting tables. So I've been going to work with Donny; I wear my Eatery uniform and change in the bathroom at the lanes. Leo's paying me under the table to balance the books, says he can't see the numbers anymore.

My mother often can't see details that don't fit her "vision," or

"God's plan for us," such as the fact that I've slept with Donny, which she decided not to conclude upon discovering a package of condoms in my dresser drawer while looking for my boat-neck sailor top. Or that she's wearing her seventeen-year-old daughter's clothes and dyeing her hair a lot. Or that she's exchanging love letters with a forty-year-old married man named Jake.

Yesterday I wanted to tell her there was no way I was going to Marietta, but then she said we could sell the house and get away from here together and start a new life, and her eyes were shining and her face was flushed, and I couldn't bring myself to do it. Because I want to get away, too.

My mother went to the Savior a couple of months ago for a conference, Faith in the Eighties, and met Jake, who actually just lives across town, except now he is a reformed Episcopalian and went to the Savior to rescue his soul. He's apparently perfect for her, except he's married, so my mother and he write each other letters and talk about Jesus' will. They actually mail them to each other, like the apostles, they say. I know because I've read them, locked in the bathroom pretending to take a shower, which is what I do when I need privacy. My mother believes in privacy, meaning not being naked in front of anyone unless you're married, or unless you're an innocent child, which neither of us is anymore.

I steal Jake's letters from Time-Life books stacked along the wall underneath the couch. They are stacked there because she gave away our coffee table, along with most of our furniture and all of my father's things. My mother gives things away because the Bible says to. "We won't need any of this where we're going," she said the day the church van came to pick up our kitchen table and chairs. That was two weeks ago. Now we eat our meals standing at the kitchen counter.

I guess my mother thinks I don't look at those books anymore, at the 1920s discoveries of Egyptian tombs and artists' renditions of the solar system. But I found the letters right away, because I still like to imagine the dry desert heat, the pyramid shadows sliding over sand, ancient priests worshipping glowing planets. I've only seen one of my mother's letters, since she mails them while I'm pretending to be at work. The one I found in a stack of bills and long-distance Bible-study offers wasn't what I expected. While Jake talks philosophy, she talked plans—what do houses cost in Marietta? she wanted to know.

After I read the letters, I take off my clothes and stand on the toilet with the water running, inspecting myself in the mirror until it's too steamy to see. I don't know what I'm looking for. Sometimes I try to imagine what Donny sees when we're doing it, how I look from above, or bending over him, or from behind, when I can get him to do it that way.

My mother says I am one of the cleanest people she knows. She says it like she knows something is up. She has started threatening to make me pay the water bill. After I read the letters I put them back between the exact pages of the exact books where I found them.

Donny rolls up the automatic windows, and I turn my head and sigh, still pretending to be asleep, and for a second it feels like we're in space, every sound wrapped in silence, and then I really do fall asleep. Then we're slowing down, sunlight sliding orange on my eyelids. Donny puts the car in park and I hear the seat squeak as he leans across to kiss me. I want to turn away, because I am annoyed with him for reasons I can't explain. But I know it will hurt him, especially after he took me all the way to State and back, so I let him think he's waking me with a kiss. Snow White. I watch him through the blur of my eyelashes. He always closes his eyes, which also annoys me. I open my eyes and stick my tongue all the way into his mouth, and then I start laughing. He pulls back, surprised, then comes at me, head down, trying to lick my face. He slides his hand up my T-shirt and pinches a nipple. I sit up and grab his hands and then I see my mother's car in the driveway, a surprise. Also there's Jake's minivan with the matching car seats in back. I thought they were volunteering at the Terrace Spirit senior citizens' picnic all day.

"I gotta go in," I say, grabbing his hand. He manages to lick my nose and lets me go. I wipe my face with my T-shirt, leave my orientation folder on the seat.

These days our house smells of bleach. My mother carries a spray bottle of cleanser around and washes her hands whenever she thinks of it, which is often. I find her in the living room, flipping through the *Greater Marietta City Guide*. Jake's on the deck, drinking a can of pop and smoking. He keeps cases of pop in the minivan, now that he's sober. He wears khakis and knit golf shirts with athletic shoes all the time. He doesn't know I'm here or he'd be coming in to give me one of his tight hugs and ask me what I've been praying for.

Deliverance, I'd like to tell him.

On the walls are plastic-framed religious paintings, the kind you can buy mail order in three easy payments. They don't quite cover the pale rectangles where my father's pastels used to hang—a historical study of duck and candle pins, lightning over a lake, a pregnant woman in a sheer nightgown standing at a window—all given away. The woman was my mother, but her face is turned away, so no one would know. But my mother didn't think it was "appropriate" anymore. She has told me she won't give away any of my stuff because that's up to me: I have to find my own place in God's plan. Still, I worry. There are things I don't want to lose, like my AMF Angle bowling ball and my father's shirts, which are Buckeye beige with "Wycheski" sewn in maroon cursive on the sleeve and shirt pocket.

I lean over her shoulder, moving slow so as not to catch Jake's attention, which isn't easy since a lot of things I do seem to get his attention, like when I sunbathe or wear miniskirts, but he drags on the cigarette, squints into the backyard, oblivious. My mother's hair is pink in the sunlight; she doesn't look up. She's wearing one of my halter tops and my favorite chino shorts. Now, when I find her looking through my closet, she explains it's because she's given away too much and has nothing to wear. She studies a page in the *Greater Marietta City Guide,* glossed lips pursed, penciled eyebrows a frowned line. There is a photograph of gleaming white Victorian houses on the river. Advertisements for complexes like Eagle's Crest and Indian Falls. There's sparkling pools and workout rooms, happy blond families strolling from their concrete patios to their minivans. My mother drives an old Buick. The spy car, as my father used to call it. Neither of us is blond, at least not right now.

"Aren't these places built on Indian burial grounds or something?" I ask her, and immediately regret it. Jake hears me; he bear-slaps the sliding glass door open and lumbers in, grinning at me, neck muscles straining the collar of his Polo. "Tess! The Lord be with you!"

"Hi, Jake."

Jake moves in for the hug. He's blunt and square, an ex–football player, impossible to get around. I think of squeezing behind the couch but I know this is not an option, so I just hold my breath and let him wrap one meaty arm around my shoulders and the other around my waist so my hips jam forward and my nose presses into the hairy V of his collarbone. Behind me, I hear my mother snap another page. She misses a lot.

"How's business?" I ask when he lets me go. Jake sells disaster insurance, which is odd since he believes the world is ending, and how do you insure for that? In the meantime, he talks about God like He's some cosmic weatherman or the neighborhood fortune-teller, always ready with free advice.

"Glorious!" Jake says, smiling as if he might break into song. "Your mother and I were thinking you should have your own policy."

I look at my mother and she looks at me, smiling distractedly. I sit down next to her, angling for a better view of the *Greater Marietta City Guide*. "I'm not kidding about the Indians, Mom. Isn't it bad luck to build on consecrated ground?" I point out. Also, the river gave people malaria. I learned this in Mr. Todd's American history class. I also took journalism with him, which was my college-prep elective last year, and he says I could be a good reporter because I call it like I see it.

"There's no such thing as luck," my mother says, ruffling her fingers, mixing my words into the air. "How was the Eatery?" she wants to know, glancing at the absence of my uniform and then turning back to the Dogwood Estates.

I bend to inspect the mosquito bites on my ankles. "The bugs are terrible," I say, scratching. My mother makes a face and stands up. She brings back a bottle of peroxide and a paper towel from the kitchen.

"Listen, honey," Jake says, landing next to me. The cushions sag in his direction, pulling me to him like the black holes in the Time-Life books. I concentrate on not crossing my arms. "About the insurance."

"What, are you going to knock me off, Jake?" I smile at him and touch my upper lip with the tip of my tongue, enjoying how his eyes focus on it. He is gathering himself for a response; I can see a thought working up his brain stem, but my mother beats him to it.

"Where were you all day?" she asks, pushing the paper towels and peroxide into my hands. The latest letter from Jake advises her not to get angry at me if I'm FLIPPANT, to act NONCHALANT because it stumps REBELLIOUS TEENAGERS. Jake writes in all block letters, under-lining for effect. Mr. Todd says never to underline. He says it's a sign of immaturity.

"I was with Donny, Mom," I say. I dab peroxide on my bites, which my mom heard on the evening news will kill the AIDS virus in the event it is carried by mosquitoes. I watch it fizz on my red-dened skin and wonder if my mother has slept with Jake.

My mother looks out the window, where everything is still and washed out, like an overexposed photograph. "I'm talking to a real-tor tomorrow," she says, folding her arms and turning to me, pink-polished nails pressing half-circles into her skin. She seems to be bracing herself. Jake watches her bend to hunt through her pile of church bulletins. She hands me a shiny white folder with a red and purple seal and "Savior Missionary" scripted in gold.

"Here you go," she says, smiling as if she just gave me a prize. From the corner of my eye I can see Jake nodding at her. He's obviously coached her on the delivery. I take it from her and open it. Inside are several complicated-looking forms, including an injury release and a pledge sheet with a long list of things I will agree to do and not do, such as renouncing homosexuality, or using the word "Zen." There is a signature line next to a pair of floating hands pressed together in prayer. The application is titled "Foreign Missions Adventure Form."

"This is a chance for you to do something truly great," my mother says, echoing a sentence in the brochure I have just opened. My eyes fall on the words as she says them.

"Praise God," Jake says.

My mother sits on her heels on the floor in front of us, and both of them watch me read. The AC comes on and she shivers. "God has plans for us, Tessie, I really believe that. But we have to win His love. Most people can't do it."

Like your father, she means. I know this because her habit of going to church three times a week and attending conferences and seminars and subscribing to every religious booklist and newsletter she finds only started when my dad got sick a year and a half ago, first with a flu he couldn't shake, then pneumonia, then so many illnesses they couldn't be distinguished from each other anymore. He accused her of trying to make up for him, and trying to make me crazy, but she didn't care what he said at that point. By then you could hardly understand him.

The memory makes my stomach feel tight and bruised. I concentrate on deep breaths, press my fingers into the ultrasuede cushion.

Jake stands up with a grunt. "Tess, why don't you come see me tomorrow at my office," he says, closing in for another hug.

I sidestep, dropping some papers from the application. "I'm working tomorrow," I say.

Jake picks up the papers and holds them out to me, just far enough away so I have to step forward to take them. He winks when I do. "That's fine. This weekend, then," he says with his song smile. He turns to hug my mother, who doesn't seem to mind his chest hairs going up her nose. "Bless you," he says to her, as if she just sneezed.

"Bless you," she says. She walks Jake to the door, leaving me with the Savior folder and a bottle of peroxide, all the safety there is. There is some soft talking. There is perhaps a kiss. The front door shuts and locks and my mother returns. "I'll need those forms by tomorrow," she says.

"I don't think this missionary idea is the best thing for me."

My mother motions me to the couch. I don't want to, but I sit.

"What is the best thing for you? A waitress job?" She looks at her glossy nails and then at me. "Bowling?" She presses her lips together and waits.

I let this pass. I want to tell her about the scholarship I think I'm going to get, but I decide to wait. I saw the signature line on those forms: parents can sign for kids under eighteen.

My silence seems to satisfy her; she stands, smooths my chino shorts against her thighs. Perhaps she thinks she's convinced me. Stairs squeak as she heads for her room, where, aside from the bed and a few clothes in the closet, she keeps Beta tapes with titles like "Loving God in Pain" and "Self-Denial for Self-Fulfillment." I notice she doesn't count the TV in our required sacrifice.

I hang my feet off the end of the couch. The AC hums; ice drops in the freezer. It's been a year since the overdose, which is how my dad actually died, not from the AIDS. That's how my mom refers to it in private, which she rarely does. As if the overdose was an event all its own, not happening to anyone in particular. Days after they sent him home, my father took all of his painkillers, dragged his IV outside, and collapsed in the front yard, where Mr. Ontero found him while my mother was at work and I was in school. The coroner called it narcotic-induced cardiac arrest. Outside the family, my mother calls it a heart attack.

At the funeral, my aunt Belinda and uncle Percy, my mother's sister and brother, who live together and take tea bags with them whenever they travel, told me that because my father was a drug addict, I would have to be more careful, I could get addicted to anything. Me standing by the hole with the velvet skirt around it and the coffin looking like it was hovering, about to blast off. Nobody said anything about the AIDS. It was easier to think about the drugs.

My dad's connection was a guy at the molding plant, where they cast the chairs for plane interiors. The police discovered this after the connection left town, and I guess he could be anywhere now, poking holes in people's skin and shooting in just the tiniest amount of his own blood, too.

Weekends my father and I went bowling. He taught me the roll was all in the release. He was wiry, with a little pot belly I made fun of, and thinning reddish-brown hair that showed the pale skin and light blue veins of his scalp. He wore button-down flannel shirts tucked into jeans in the winter, button-down cotton shirts tucked into jeans in the summer. After years of making plane chairs, he said he would never fly because of what he knew.

When I was twelve, he gave me the AMF Angle, the first-ever urethane make: custom teal with gold sparkles, teal being my favorite color at the time, with my name in gold. We watched each other in tournaments, holding our breath while the other one glided across the floor. When we rolled for fun, he made me discuss current events and my form, and what I could do to improve it. Mostly, though, he talked about how good I was, and how I could do anything I wanted with an arm like mine.

These days, when I release is when I most feel my father in me, or actually, that I am my father. I feel the ball weight in my shoulder, not the elbow joint, which is where most people tend to hold it, and I know I look like him, and that I'm feeling the things he felt, the light strain at the collarbone, the tightening of the muscles in the back of the arm, the turn of the bones in their sockets as the arm drops, swings back, then forward. I imagine my muscles are his muscles, and this is how I keep him alive.

The last time we rolled was at Rock and Bowl, which is on Fridays from 10:00 PM to 2:00 AM. Donny had just gotten the disco ball and the colored lights—he hadn't talked Leo into the laser and the smoke machine yet. My father had had the flu for weeks by then, but he hadn't been to the doctor. The meetings with teams of doctors and the weeks in the hospital were ahead of us.

His hook was way off that night. "You're pulling the ball," I said. I was annoyed. Once he pulled it five boards or more—amateur mistakes.

He ignored me. "Go," he said, as we watched six pins wobble and stay up.

I rolled and got a strike. When you're on, you hardly feel the weight; it's just a part of you that you let go.

My father powdered his hand. "What's a perfect strike?"

I rolled my eyes. "The ball knocks down the one, three, and five pins," I said. I paused, wondering if he was going to make me recite the whole thing. He was waiting. "The five pin takes out the nine pin, the three pin takes out the six, and the six takes out the ten pin," I said. "The head pin knocks down the two, which knocks down the four, and the four knocks down the seven."

"Close. The five hits the eight pin and the ball hits the nine. You remember that," my father said without looking at me, surveying the lane. He rolled, shuffling forward slowly. Three pins down. Miserable.

I won with the next roll, 168 to 132. Not a good night. "You could've done better," he said.

"So could you," I shot back.

"I'm just saying you shouldn't let your game go. You could get a scholarship, you know?"

I was going to tell him he wasn't my coach and I didn't want to hear his plans for me, but then this happened: he sat down hard in the booth as if someone had knocked his feet out from under him. I stared at him and he gazed back at me, as if this were just a movie he was watching.

He handed me his wallet. "Go pay," he said softly. His fingers were damp and cold.

"Dad?" I said.

He made a sound in his throat and held on to the table. I paid

Leo at the bar, forcing myself not to look back at my father, not wanting Leo to see and ask me what was wrong. As I walked back to the booth I felt strangely calm, the sounds of toppling pins muffled and distant.

My father held his arms out to me. "Help me up," he said. I leaned down to him and he held on to my neck as I pulled him to his feet. Somehow I hadn't noticed before that I was almost his height, and that he was thin, very thin. He smelled sour, like overripe fruit.

"Thanks," he said. I pulled away from him as soon as I felt him balance, and he knew it, and I could sense his eyes on me as I put on my coat. "Let's go to Harry's," he said. He patted my arm, smiling at me, waiting until I looked at him. He was breathing shallow and fast.

"I don't think so," I said. But somehow we ended up there. I remember waving to Donny in the DJ box as we left the lanes— Donny wasn't my boyfriend yet; that would be in the summer, after my father was gone and my mother had let the lawn grow to torment Mr. Ontero—and I remember I could see the sweat on my father's face, but I smiled at Donny anyway and waved to Leo, too, like there was nothing wrong.

I drove to Harry's and my father bought me a beer, which I don't even like, and Harry, who runs a tight ship, didn't say a word about it, even though he knew how old I was. My father drank while I scanned a *People* magazine, at the movie stars and cowboys and sick children starting foundations, and I didn't care for any of it, except for being with him in that place.

Two days later he went to the doctor. Then he went into the hospital—full quarantine. My mother and I had to get tests. A nurse quit rather than take care of him. They couldn't handle him at Carter so they moved him to Cleveland, where at least some of the doctors had seen AIDS before. Then they sent him home to die, and then he killed himself.

So I understand why my mother wants to move. She wants to get away from the house my father grew sick in, from Mr. Ontero's pinched eyes that watched him die in the front yard, from the town that knows our story like it's a TV special.

The voice on the Beta floats through the vents. I'm on my knees, sliding *The Solar System* from under the couch, checking for mail. My heart squeezes tighter, like it does when a roll really counts, and I am measuring the space between me and the strike.

There's a new letter. No postmark—Jake probably hand-delivered this one right before I got home. I slip it into my shorts. "I'm gonna get ready for work," I call upstairs.

No answer as I head down the hallway to the master bedroom, where my father stayed after he came back from the hospital, and where I now sleep. Sometimes I still think I can smell his cologne in the master bedroom, even though it's been over a year. Fifteen months to be exact. Donny says he can't smell it, but I think he just doesn't like the idea of breathing Joe Wycheski's cologne after sneaking into bed with his daughter.

I fell in love with Donny's skin first and moved in from there. The day he came to the front door he was brown with a flush underneath. He had gotten taller and full in the shoulders, his voice deeper in his chest. I hadn't seen him since school let out because I hadn't been able to go to the lanes—I wasn't ready for my father's picture on the wall with his hair slicked back and the smile he gave to people he didn't know.

It had been three months since my father had died, and Donny came to the door acting as if he'd just happened to notice the Wycheski lawn, even though it had been a wet spring and summer and his chinos were soaked to the knee. "On the side," he explained to me when he asked if he could help out with the mowing. He meant on the side from his jobs at the lanes and selling water softener and concentrated soap products to county people who have wells and brown teeth.

He came in for a glass of Vernon's and didn't look worried about breathing the air or sitting on our furniture like other people had, the few who visited after it came out why my father was sick. He borrowed his uncle Leo's tractor the first time, but after that he rolled his own push mower the three blocks and one street over to our house, and I watched him through the window or sat outside and pretended to read while he leaned on the mower, muscles moving under his skin. When he left the air smelled like wet soil and the grass tips gleamed like a million little lights.

Then fall came, and Donny asked me to go to the Cinema Six, and later we decided that if we still loved each other by graduation we would get married. Donny didn't mind my mother's tapes, and he said nothing when my mother started replacing my father's pastels with airbrushed pictures of Jesus walking in a crowd of children, preaching on the mount, crying on the cross.

I lock the master bathroom door, turn on the water, pull a single sheet out of the neatly slit envelope. Jake's letters are getting shorter. The first ones were three or four pages on both sides.

This one gets right to the point:

PAULA,

I DREAMED I SAW JESUS FLOATING OVER THE GARAGE AND I THINK IT MEANS WE SHOULD SKIP TOWN. MOVE ON LIKE JESUS, YOU KNOW? LIKE A ROLLING STONE. YOU'RE MY SPIRITUAL SOUNDING BOARD, HONEY, HOW YOU KEEP SAYING, BUT THERE'S MORE TO IT THAN THAT. NOBODY UNDERSTANDS ME BETTER THAN THAT. NOBODY UNDERSTANDS ME BETTER THAN YOU DO. ANYWAY, I NEED TO SEE YOU ALONE.

LILLY'S TAKING THE TWINS TO THE LAKE THIS WEEK. LET'S GO AWAY THIS WEEKEND AND FIGURE IT OUT. I'LL TELL HER I'M VISITNG MY MOTHER.

DON'T WORRY ABOUT TESS. THE MISSION WILL TAKE CARE OF EVERYTHING. I'LL MAKE SURE. I'LL CALL TOMORROW.

BLESSED BE THE LORD,
JAKE

I can see Jake scrawling in the toilet while his wife piles orange floatie wings and beach towels in the back of the minivan, the twins rolling around in the soft front lawn in matching outfits. Then I see us all together in Marietta, on top of the burial mound the Indians made, which is in the middle of town, me with a twin hanging on each hand, Jake with my mother on one side and his wife on the other. Trinities.

I slip the sheet back into the envelope. I stand in the shower, and what I want to know is, what exactly does Jake mean about the mission taking care of me?

I pull on my Eatery uniform over my still damp skin, pink skort sticking to my thighs, and shove shorts and a halter top into my pocketbook. Through the vent a soothing male voice says, "Think of Christ as your friend who walks with you when you push your cart down the grocery-store aisles, when you get the paper, when you go to work." Music swells on the tape. Then I hear the squeak of Donny's brakes outside. "I'm going!" I call up the stairs.

No answer. I slam the door shut behind me. In the car, Donny leans across the seat to kiss me. He's redone his ponytail, name tag already attached to his turquoise-blue Star Lanes shirt.

"Do you have to do that?" I ask, pointing to it.

"I'll forget it if I don't." He puts his arm across the top of my seat as he backs down the driveway. I look at the veins running in blue ropes from his wrist to the inside of his elbow, where the skin is soft and white. It looks like a man's arm, like my father's arm, and it makes me ache.

Donny's smiling. "I sold three purification systems this week," he says.

I roll my eyes. "You know they don't do anything except add salt," I say. The company has this big color brochure on how it saves plumbing from mineral buildup, but it really doesn't.

"You just can't stand it that people like this stuff."

"They like it but they don't need it. You tell them they need it."

"You're worse than Leo," Donny says, looking at me, trees blurring behind him. I try to stare back but I can't. I hate it when he gets mad at me. "Well, who got Leo to buy the new sound system and the laser and disco ball? Now you have to wait an hour for a lane on Friday."

"He just didn't want to go into debt."

"He's an old man, what does he know? He's still saving all his rubber bands off the paper in case there's another Depression. I guess we'll sell rubber bands then. Now, *that's* thinking."

"At least he's not a bullshitter!" I'm yelling now, my ears ringing.

"Oh, and I guess you got the corner on honesty. What about you and that scholarship deal, huh?" He slaps the wheel, shouts out a laugh. "Sitting there in your little uniform pretending to have a job."

"Asshole," I hiss.

"That's right," Donny says, voice low now, eyes steady on the road, jaw clenched. "I'm an asshole for trying to make my own way." Smoke slides out of his nostrils.

There's nothing I can say to this, except that I want college the way I wanted Donny last fall, when the nights got cooler and he didn't need to come over as often to mow, and he crawled in the window of the room my parents used to sleep in, and we undressed under the blankets, and our skin was so warm and slick against each other that we could have been underwater.

Neither of us speaks until we get to the lanes. "I'm sorry," I finally say as he pulls into the gravel parking lot, even though I'm not sorry; I'm just tired, and I don't want to be angry. In front of us is the turquoise fan roof of the Star Lanes with the two round windows like eyes over the door. It's early yet, and there are only a few cars in front.

Donny opens the car door and stares ahead, one hand on the door handle and the other hanging down his thigh right at his crotch, the way guys do. Then he swings his legs out and slams the door behind him, walking away as if he had no one to wait for.

I lean across the seat and pop the trunk so I can get my ball. I can hear the hollow sound of the pins on the buttery wooden floor even before I open the glass doors. Then I pull the handle and the smell of leather and beer and sweat flows out on the cool air, although bowling doesn't make you sweat unless you're nervous. It's just the smell of men who come here every Friday and never air out their shoes. It's a good smell. And a good feeling to look across the lanes, the balls coursing down the boards, through the tunnel, out of the machine, and into the hands, circulating like air, like blood.

I change into my shorts and halter top in the bathroom and take a stool at the bar. Two guys I recognize from high school are drinking draft between rolls on the end lane, my father's favorite lane. Their girlfriends, or wives maybe, both pregnant, sit in the plastic booth, smoking, flicking ashes on the floor, permed hair teased up over pale foreheads, dark circles under their eyes. Staring at the balls going back and forth.

Leo comes over when he sees me, smiling. He's wearing his favorite Beers of the World shirt with all the labels in different languages and eating a bag of potato chips, even though he's supposed to be on a diet. He hands me a catalog, points to a picture of a smoothie machine.

"Tessie," he says, clapping my shoulder. "You think I should order this?"

"I don't know," I mumble.

"I think it's going to be the wave of the future. You can chop up candy bars in it." Leo smacks the magazine against his thigh. "Hey, sweets, what's the problem?"

I decide not to mention the fight with Donny. "My mother wants to move to Marietta."

Leo shakes his head, strokes his mustache. He looks across the lanes, to the lounge area, where the local branch of the Mafia used to entertain themselves after whacking members of the Polish contingency in Cleveland—this my father told me. Leo has never been one to ask for details. "Maybe she could go somewhere nice, like Atlantic City?" he says.

"I don't know what she's thinking, Leo," I tell him, and this is the truth.

"Could you check my math in a minute here?" Leo asks me.

"Sure thing."

"Maybe Florida?" Leo suggests as he heads to the back office.

My parents took me to Disney World on my eleventh birthday, the only time I've been out of Ohio. My dad chain-smoked and bought me foam Mickey Mouse ears and called me Minnie all day, even after I lost the ears on the Witch Mountain roller coaster and cried, while my mother sat down every few feet, putting her head between her knees to keep from passing out in the heat. I used to keep a list of the best days of my life, and this was at the top. I didn't want to leave, even though I was old enough to know that there were people inside the costumes and the park closed at night. "Just leave me here," I remember saying to my father. I can still see his face tilted down to mine, almost close enough to kiss me. But now I think his expression looked something like defeat.

The sun dips behind the buildings across the street and the white stones in the parking lot turn pale purple under the sky. More people are showing up, a couple of teams practicing for the next league event, some regulars who don't play for any team but come all the time. A shark or two scanning the talent. I find Donny at the control board in the DJ box. "Hey, can I come up?"

Donny pushes open the door without looking at me and turns back to the control panel. He's acting serious as an astronaut, when we both know he's only got one button and a joystick.

"Donny," I say. "Don't be mad at me."

"For what?" he asks, looking distracted. He doesn't lose his temper often, and I can tell he's embarrassed. He pulls his chair closer to the board, surveys the stands below.

I want to say, For leaving you. For putting you down even though I believe I'm right. For feeling like I see more than you can. Instead, I kneel behind him where no one can see me and press my face against the back of his neck until he turns enough to put an arm around me. We stay like that until Donny has to start the show.

It's after two when I'm helping Leo cash out in the office room— I'm doing change and he's doing bills. Donny's setting up for the next day. When we're done Leo pats a box of napkins beside him. I sit and wait until he's finished bundling the take. His face is deep red, hairlike veins fan from his nose. He smells like cigarettes and potato chips. He takes a deep breath, slaps his thick hands on his lap. "You know, Donny's like a son to me. His parents are ghosts," he says.

I keep my eyes on the coins. Leo's never talked this way to me before, like Donny's the child and we're the adults. In the whole time since I've known Donny, I've only seen his father once and his mother maybe a handful of times. They're both old; Donny has a brother and a sister that moved out ten years ago.

"You got a good head, Tess," Leo says, smoothing his gray mustache. "So I got an offer for you." I can feel his eyes on me, adding me up.

"Thank you," I say, feeling foolish.

"Year-round work, good pay, full benefits."

"Doing what?"

"What you been doing. Helping me keep the numbers straight. You got a good head, Tess. You think about it." Leo waves me away and I get up to leave. I open my mouth to say something, but Leo lifts a hairy hand to stop me. "I'm glad Donny's got a girl like you. That's it."

When I wake up the next morning the house is hot and bright, and I'm alone. Upstairs, I peek in the doorway of my mother's room, and I can see the open closet, nearly empty except for her Sunday dresses and a neat line of shoes, and the TV in the corner on what used to be her bed stand, tapes stacked on the floor. I push open her door the rest of the way. Sitting in the center of her bed is a lavender duffel bag, open and waiting.

I check the coffee-table books for mail, but there's none. I shower and ride my bike to the high school, which is across the street from the cemetery, where my father is buried. In the hospital, when he knew before we were ready to admit it that he was going to die, he said he wanted to be cremated and scattered in Lake Erie; I remember the air in his voice, his hand on my arm, but my mother picked out the coffin and headstone as if he'd never asked for anything different. I wouldn't go there after the burial, even though I could see the marker from the school-bus window every day. Now Mr. Ontero is buried there, too, his tombstone bone white.

Mr. Todd's summer-school government class is just letting out. After my father died, Mr. Todd came by every few days with homework and lecture notes, so I kept up, and after a while I could have conversations again, and then I came back to school.

Mr. Todd sees me coming down the hallway and waves. He's younger than my parents, with a son in eighth-grade special ed and a fat wife with perfect creamy skin and red curly hair who always chaperones proms and wears the same cobalt-blue satin sheath dress with a black rose on one shoulder to every dance. Mr. Todd wears thick glasses and was probably a nerd in high school, but now he's a man, with sloping shoulders and beard shadow all of the time.

"Tess," he says, motioning me in. The last of the students file past us, all of them with bad cases of lecture face. He pulls a brown envelope from his desk and hands it to me. "Open it."

The letter starts with "Congratulations." I see the words "full tuition" and "special funds." There are several forms. Also a check made out to me for five hundred dollars. I bring the check, printed with an ocean scene, close to my face, studying Mr. Todd's leaning handwriting that I know so well from the margins of my papers, where he wrote, "Defend your pt. here" or "Don't leave me hanging." Ian and Leisel Todd, it says in the upper left-hand corner, above the beach scene. I look at Mr. Todd and he smiles down at me as if I were his daughter, the way I believe my father would have smiled at me. I thank him, and he hugs me, and I hear his heart beating low in his chest, and what I feel is fear, and then relief.

"Let's go to lunch," he says.

He puts my bike in the back of his station wagon. The breeze bends the envelope forward in my hand, as if pushing me along. The rectangular brick building, the gravel teacher's parking lot, the line of pines edging the practice field all look familiar, but changed, flattened by my absence.

It's after three and the restaurants in town are closed until dinner. That's the kind of town this is. Mr. Todd brought in a writer from the *New York Times* to speak to our journalism class last year, a college buddy of his, and I remember him asking where a guy could get a late-night cup of coffee around here, and we all stared back at him as if he'd asked where he could get laid.

We end up at Harry's. It's the first time I've been there since my father died. I wouldn't have gone in there if it weren't for the fact that I know I'm leaving now. I wanted to preserve his presence there, waiting for me. Mr. Todd orders, and I choose a booth in the corner, where my father and I almost never sat because you couldn't see the TV.

Mr. Todd buys a beer for himself and soda for me and two cold salami sandwiches. He sets my soda down and clinks the lip of his bottle against my can as he sits across from me.

"Thanks," I say. The backs of my thighs are sticking to the bench. I peel them up, settle them. We bite into our sandwiches. Mr. Todd drinks most of his beer in two long gulps.

"So. How do you feel?"

"Good. Nervous." The salami makes my eyes water and Mr. Todd notices, misreads it.

"Are you okay?" he asks.

I nod. He puts his hand heavily on mine and keeps it there. "How about your mom?"

I understand he's asking whether I've told my mother or not. He knows about our empty house and about Marietta, and about how my mom's job at the church day care doesn't pay the bills, and she was taking my tip money, which is how he came up with the scholarship in the first place. He knows enough about both of us to be my father. "She's having an affair with a married man," I answer, watching for his reaction.

He pulls his hand away, rubs his eyes. "Oh."

"She's going away with him this weekend."

"She told you?"

"No. But I know." I watch Mr. Todd pick at his beer-bottle label and I can tell he's trying to decide whether to ask about my sources.

I debate whether I'll tell him about the letters and the duffel bag, about how Jake underlines for emphasis. But Mr. Todd doesn't ask. My legs are sticking to the seat again, and I squirm to adjust.

"The forms," he finally says, tapping the envelope. "Get those turned in right away."

I nod, and we finish eating in silence. Mr. Todd swallows the last of his beer. "Tess."

I look up from the crumbs on my napkin, waiting.

"Your dad and mom." He pauses, opening his hands as if to catch the right words. "They're two extremes. You just shoot down the middle and you'll be fine."

Outside, Mr. Todd offers to take me back to the high school, but I tell him I'd rather ride. He pulls my bike out of his car. "Don't forget about me, now," he says, sounding something like my father and Donny combined.

When I get home I hear the shower running in the master bedroom, the metallic bird-call sound in the pipes. On the radio, the announcer's talking about a cold front; there'll be record lows. The AC is dry and cold on my skin; sweat rolls down my spine. I check the coffee-table books in the linen closet for mail, put the scholarship envelope in my backpack at the back of my closet, and lie down on my parents' bed, listening to the water hit the floor of the bathtub.

When my mother opens the door, a cloud of steam behind her, she's startled to see me. She's got a pink towel around her middle and a white one around her head. Her face is shiny and flushed. "I was trying to figure out what you think is so great about this shower," she says.

"And?"

She shrugs. "Good water pressure. Better than upstairs. I'd forgotten." She unwinds the towel from her head and sits slowly on the edge of the bed, as if trying not to sink in too far. As the towel flops around her neck I see she's gotten a haircut and another dye job, so all the frizzy pinkish copper is gone, and the dark shiny hair drips in soft, water-slicked waves around her face. "What do you think?" she says, turning her head so I can see the back.

I sit up. "Are you going anywhere?"

My mother's eyes meet mine. She studies my face. "Where would I go?" she says. Her eyes narrow, searching. Maybe she thinks she isn't really hiding anything because her plans aren't firm, the bag is not yet packed. I don't answer, and she stands, looking down at me. "How about you?" she wants to know. "Where are you going?"

"I'm going to State," I tell her. My heart is pounding. My mother opens her mouth to speak, and then the phone rings. I am nearer to it but she reaches past me and picks up.

"Hello?" she says, turning her back to me, and I know she thinks it's Jake, hopes it's Jake. But then she turns and hands the phone to me.

"Donny," she says.

"Not the rolling stone?" I ask her, and I feel like I've jumped off a high dive, my stomach in my throat, my heart in my ears. I've shown my hand now; she knows what I know. My mother looks at me, sucks in air like she's been hit in the stomach, and I know she's putting it together, all the letters unfolded and refolded, all those words reread. I swing my legs off the other side of the bed and stand up, so the bed's between us. My mother isn't moving. I put the phone to my ear. Donny's saying, "Hello? Hello?"

"Yeah."

Donny can hear something's up from the tone of my voice. "Everything okay?"

"Great," I say with exaggerated cheer. "Are you picking me up?"

"I'll be there."

I listen for the click of the phone line, put the phone against my chest. My mother is watching me as if I'm someone entirely new to her. Her eyes are wide, almost amused. She turns and walks out of the room. Then I hear her running up the stairs.

I pull from the closet my backpack and my favorite jeans. I also pull all four of my father's bowling shirts, which I saved before my mother cleaned out his closet. I take some T-shirts, some underwear, a notebook I didn't use up all the way from the spring. And the pictures, one of my father and me at the Buckeye tournament, one at my graduation from junior high school, one of him holding me when I was a baby, his nose to my forehead. I slip them into the scholarship envelope so they won't bend. I change into my work clothes and I put the bag back in the closet, in the corner where it can't be seen even if the folding doors are open all the way.

I hear my mother going downstairs again and then to the kitchen. My hands feel shaky, weak, as I pick up my purse and bowling ball and carry them down the hall. My mother's chopping carrots for a salad. She seems perfectly composed, her hair gleaming under the fluorescent light. She doesn't look up when I come in. She slides the carrots into the bowl and puts the mushrooms under the faucet.

"I'm going to be late tonight," I announce.

My mother slices a tomato in two. "The house goes up for sale tomorrow," she says.

I wait for her to say more, to tell me the next step. I think of hot Marietta, where the Indians buried their dead, where white apartment buildings stand like grave markers. "Why now?" I ask. I hear Donny's car rolling up the drive.

"Saturdays are the best days to start," she says calmly, misunderstanding me on purpose. "There's going to be an open house on Sunday from two to five. I'll need your help."

"Would you like me to dust the couch?" I ask.

My mother glares at me. Donny honks the horn, and I bend to pick up my things. I look at my mother, her hand small on the knife, her hair dripping and quivering as she starts in on lettuce, pulling the good leaves away from the bad. I decide not to say good-bye.

In the car I tell Donny about the house and then the scholarship. "Are you excited?" he asks me, even though he knows the answer.

"I'll have three roommates," I say. I reach for his hand. "Are you going to visit me?"

Donny rolls his eyes. "It's only two hours away."

This is true, but it feels farther. Donny drives with one hand and holds my hand until our palms are sticky and we can't feel the pressure on our skin anymore. I want him to say he'll go with me, find a job, save money for school. I want to cut his hair, buy him a suit, or even a nice button-down shirt. I want to tell him everyone will understand.

Donny pulls into the Star parking lot and cuts the engine, and we sit still as the car heats.

"Nothing's going to change," Donny says, and I believe him.

That night, Donny does a great show. You'd think it would be the same every night, but it's not. Sometimes the smoke rolls out evenly over the lanes like a piece of cloth, and the laser seems to become different things—a spaceship, a man swimming, someone dancing. Tonight the music's from *Close Encounters of the Third Kind*, and people lean back on the booths, their faces open in the blue light. Donny makes the laser disappear and then reappear in a sweep that washes over us all. He makes it a knife, cutting light into the sky, then a layer of water that lifts above the lanes and spreads itself so thin it's nearly invisible.

I close my eyes and lean my head back and wonder what we look like from the air, from space. I see my father leaning out the window of his car to wave at me, gliding forward to roll. I just want to shoot down the middle, I tell him. The music gets louder until it pounds in my rib cage, and the laser breaks apart over the lanes, coming back together into a single glowing point, and then goes dark. Everyone yells and claps.

Afterward, I help Leo serve up last beers and popcorns. In the control booth, Donny is shutting things down, the board lighting his face like a ghost. He sees me and waves, and I wave back, and then he turns off the desk light, and I can't see him anymore.

Then it's cash-out time. I hurry to the back room so I can get to Leo before Donny does. He's smoking a cigarette, which he quickly puts out, because it's against fire regulations to smoke around all the paper plates and napkins. "Tess!" he says, waving at the smoke as if he's just noticed it.

"Leo, I've got to ask you something."

"Ask."

"I got into school."

"I know."

This surprises me and then I realize Donny must have told him. "I want to know if I can come back. In case things don't work out."

"Oh, sure you can, Tess," Leo says. "But you won't." He pats my head with his paw hand, and I feel as if something has broken loose in my ribs, and then I'm crying into the brown polyester warmth of his shoulder until he helps me sit down.

"Breathe, sweetheart," he says. "Just breathe."

Then I feel Donny's hands on my arms, warm. "Let's roll some," he says.

I let him lead me into the dark lanes. We take my favorite one on the end, where I can concentrate. Donny puts change in the jukebox and goes back up to his light board. He puts on the disco ball, white lights circling slow, like stars in a planetarium. I sit down, switch my shoes, pull my AMF out, and turn it in my hands. It's a little sparkling planet, all lakes and waves. I move to the head of the lane, shoes slick like a pillow of air. I pull in a deep breath, inhaling the place, which smells like wood and oil and beer and my father. I balance the ball and let its weight take my arm back, my body moving forward, my hand behind the ball, pushing it through the air. My thumb comes free and my hand turns into an almost handshake, fingers flicking the skin of the ball as it leaves them, all this in a split second, like air leaving the lungs, like a kiss.

I shut my eyes and bring my father's face close to mine, skin around his gray eyes crinkling. I'm leaving, I tell him, as the ball topples the pins. I know from the sound it's a strike.

By the time we get to my house it's very late. I make Donny stop several houses down the street from mine and turn off his lights. We sit there in the hollow car silence.

"What are we doing?" Donny asks.

"Shh." I get out quietly, shiver in the cool air. "Just wait for me here, okay?"

Donny nods and sits back. On my way down the street I glance at Mr. Ontero's dark house, the windows small and black. Every room is lit at my house, porch lights glowing over the FOR SALE sign leaning against the steps. My mother passes through the empty living room. She's wearing my pink sundress.

I wait until she walks upstairs and I let myself in the front door. There is the lavender duffel bag on the floor, full and zipped, the keys on the counter.

I head down the hallway and grab my backpack, checking for the envelope, my father's shirts, making sure it's all still there, ready. In the kitchen I hear my mother humming upstairs. I lift her keys slowly from the counter and pull the front door closed behind me.

I take the brick path around the side of the house to the edge of the woods and set down my backpack. The keys are cool in my hand. I hold them up to chin level, setting. My arm is trembling, tired but warm. I let it drop, fall back, my feet sliding with long, low strides, my arm swinging forward now, fingers relaxing on the upswing, then releasing the keys, which fly upward for quite a ways, because they are lighter than what I'm used to. They land somewhere in the dark trees with a muffled clink of metal. I listen to the quiet air for a moment and then walk back to the car, where Donny is waiting to take me to school.

Monica Wood

❧

THAT ONE AUTUMN

That one autumn, when Marie got to the cabin, something looked wrong. She took in the familiar view: the clapboard bungalow she and Ernie had inherited from his father, the bushes and trees that had grown up over the years, the dock pulled in for the season. She sat in the idling car, reminded of those "find the mistake" puzzles John used to pore over as a child, intent on locating mittens on the water skier, milk bottles in the parlor. Bent in a corner somewhere over the softening page, her blue-eyed boy would search for hours, convinced that after every wrong thing had been identified, more wrong things remained.

Sunlight pooled in the dooryard. The day gleamed, the clean Maine air casting a sober whiteness over everything. The gravel turnaround seemed vaguely disarranged. Scanning the line of spruce that shielded the steep slope to the lake's edge, Marie looked for movement. Behind the thick mesh screen of the front porch she could make out the wicker tops of the chairs. She turned off the ignition, trying to remember whether she'd taken time to straighten up the porch when she was last here, in early August, the weekend of Ernie's birthday. He and John had had one of their fights, and it was possible that in the ensuing clamor and silence she had forgotten to straighten up the porch. It was possible.

She got out of the car and checked around. Everything looked different after just a few weeks: the lake blacker through the part in the trees, the brown-eyed Susans gone weedy, the chairs on the porch definitely, definitely moved. Ernie had pushed a chair in frustration, she remembered. And John had responded in kind, upending the green one on his way out the door and down to the lake. They'd begun that weekend, like so many others, with such good intentions, only to discover anew how mismatched they were, parents to son. So, she had straightened the chairs—she had definitely straightened them—while outside Ernie's angry footsteps crackled over the gravel and, farther away, John's body hit the water in a furious smack.

She minced up the steps and pushed open the screen door, which was unlocked. "Hello?" she called out fearfully. The inside door was slightly ajar. *Take the dog,* Ernie had told her, *she'll be good company.* She wished now she had, though the dog, a Yorkie named Honey Girl, was a meek little thing and no good in a crisis. *I don't want company, Ernie. It's a week, it's forty miles, I'm not leaving you.* Marie was sentimental, richly so, which is why her wish to be alone after seeing John off to college had astonished them both. *But you're still weak,* Ernie argued. *Look how pale you are.* She packed a box of watercolors and a how-to book in her trunk as Ernie stood by, bewildered. *I haven't been alone in years,* she told him. *I want to find out what it feels like.* John had missed Vietnam by six merciful months, then he'd chosen Berkeley, as far from his parents as he could get, and now Marie wanted to be alone. Ernie gripped her around the waist and she took a big breath of him: man, dog, house, yard, mill. She had known him most of her life, and from time to time, when she could bear to think about it, she wondered whether their uncommon closeness was what had made their son a stranger.

You be careful, he called after her as she drove off. The words came back to her now as she peered through the partly open door at a wedge of kitchen she barely recognized. She saw jam jars open on the counter, balled-up dish towels, a box of oatmeal upended and spilling a bit of oatmeal dust, a snaggled hairbrush, a red lipstick ground to a nub. Through the adjacent window she caught part of a rumpled sleeping bag in front of the fireplace, plus an empty glass and a couple of books.

Marie felt a little breathless, but not afraid, recognizing the disorder as strictly female. She barreled in, searching the small rooms like an angry, old-fashioned mother with a hickory switch. She found the toilet filled with urine, the back hall cluttered with camping gear, and the two bedrooms largely untouched except for a grease-stained knapsack thrown across Marie and Ernie's bed. By the time she got back out to the porch to scan the premises again, Marie had the knapsack in hand and sent it skidding across the gravel. The effort doubled her over, for Ernie was right: her body had not recovered from the thing it had suffered. As she held her stomach, the throbbing served only to stoke her fury.

Then she heard it: the sound of a person struggling up the steep, rocky path from the lake. Swishing grass. A scatter of pebbles. The subtle pulse of forward motion.

It was a girl. She came out of the trees into the sunlight, naked except for a towel bundled under one arm. Seeing the car, she stopped, then looked toward the cabin, where Marie uncoiled herself slowly, saying, "Who the hell are you?"

The girl stood there, apparently immune to shame. A delicate ladder of ribs showed through her paper-white skin. Her damp hair was fair and thin, her pubic hair equally thin and light. "Shit," she said. "Busted." Then she cocked her head, her face filled with a defiance Marie had seen so often in her own son that it barely registered.

"Cover yourself, for God's sake," Marie said.

The girl did, in her own good time, arranging the towel over her shoulders and covering her small breasts. Her walk was infuriatingly casual as she moved through the dooryard, picked up the knapsack, and sauntered up the steps, past Marie, and into the cabin. Marie followed her in. She smelled like the lake.

"Get out before I call the police," Marie said.

"Your phone doesn't work," the girl said peevishly. "And I can't say much for your toilet, either."

Of course nothing worked. They'd turned everything off, buttoned the place up after their last visit, John and Ernie at each other's throats as they hauled the dock up the slope, Ernie too slow on his end, John too fast on his, both of them arguing about whether or not Richard Nixon was a crook and should have resigned in disgrace.

"I said get out. This is my house."

The girl pawed through the knapsack. She hauled out a pair of panties and slipped them on. Then a pair of frayed jeans, and a mildewy shirt that Marie could smell across the room. As she toweled her hair it became lighter, nearly white. She leveled Marie with a look as blank and stolid as a pillar.

"I said get out," Marie snapped, jangling her car keys.

"I heard you."

"Then do it."

The girl dropped the towel on the floor, reached into the knapsack once more, extracted a comb, combed her flimsy, apparitional hair, and returned the comb. Then she pulled out a switchblade. It opened with a crisp, perfunctory snap.

"Here's the deal," she said. "I get to be in charge, and you get to shut up."

Marie shot out of the cabin and sprinted into the dooryard, where a bolt of pain brought her up short and windless. The girl was too quick in any case, catching Marie by the wrist before she could reclaim her breath. "Don't try anything," the girl said, her voice low and cold. "I'm unpredictable." She glanced around. "You expecting anybody?"

"No," Marie said, shocked into telling the truth.

"Then it's just us girls," she said, smiling a weird, thin smile that impelled Marie to reach behind her, holding the car for support. The girl presented her water-wrinkled palm and Marie forked over the car keys.

"Did you bring food?"

"In the trunk."

The girl held up the knife. "Stay right there."

Marie watched, terrified, as the girl opened the trunk and tore into a box of groceries, shoving a tomato into her mouth as she reached for some bread. A bloody trail of tomato juice sluiced down her neck.

Studying the girl—her quick, panicky movements—Marie felt her fear begin to settle into a morbid curiosity. This skinny girl seemed an unlikely killer; her tiny wrists looked breakable, and her stunning whiteness gave her the look of a child ghost. In a matter of seconds, a thin, reluctant vine of maternal compassion twined through Marie and burst into violent bloom.

"When did you eat last?" Marie asked her.

"None of your business," the girl said, cramming her mouth full of bread.

"How old are you?"

The girl finished chewing, then answered: "Nineteen. What's it to you?"

"I have a son about your age."

"Thrilled to know it," the girl said, handing a grocery sack to Marie. She herself hefted the box and followed Marie into the cabin, her bare feet making little animal sounds on the gravel. Once inside, she ripped into a box of Cheerios.

"Do you want milk with that?" Marie asked her.

All at once the girl welled up, and she nodded, wiping her eyes with the heel of one hand, turning her head hard right, hard left, exposing her small, translucent ears. "This isn't me," she sniffled. She lifted the knife, but did not give it over. "It's not even mine."

"Whose is it?" Marie said steadily, pouring milk into a bowl.

"My boyfriend's." The girl said nothing more for a few minutes, until the cereal was gone, another bowl poured, and that, too, devoured. She wandered over to the couch, a convertible covered with anchors that Ernie had bought to please John, who naturally never said a word about it.

"Where is he, your boyfriend?" Marie asked finally.

"Out getting supplies." The girl looked up quickly, a snap of the eyes revealing something Marie thought she understood.

"How long's he been gone?"

The girl waited. "Day and a half."

Marie nodded. "Maybe his car broke down."

"That's what I wondered." The girl flung a spindly arm in the general direction of the kitchen. "I'm sorry about the mess. My boyfriend's hardly even paper-trained."

"Then maybe you should think about getting another boyfriend."

"I told him, no sleeping on the beds. We didn't sleep on your beds."

"Thank you," Marie said.

"It wasn't my idea to break in here."

"I'm sure it wasn't."

"He's kind of hiding out, and I'm kind of with him."

"I see," Marie said, scanning the room for weapons: fireplace poker, dictionary, curtain rod. She couldn't imagine using any of these things on the girl, whose body appeared held together with thread.

"He knocked over a gas station. Two, actually, in Portland."

"That sounds serious."

She smiled a little. "He's a serious guy."

"You could do better, don't you think?" Marie asked. "Pretty girl like you."

The girl's big eyes narrowed. "How old are *you*?"

"Thirty-eight."

"You look younger."

"Well, I'm not," Marie said. "My name is Marie, by the way."

"I'm Tracey."

"Tell me, Tracey," Marie said. "Am I your prisoner?"

"Only until he gets back. We'll clear out after that."

"Where are you going?"

"Canada. Which is where he should've gone about six years ago."

"A vet?"

Tracey nodded. "War sucks."

"Well, now, that's extremely profound."

"Don't push your luck, Marie," Tracey said. "It's been a really long week."

They spent the next hours sitting on the porch, Marie thinking furiously in a chair, Tracey on the steps, the knife glinting in her fist. At one point Tracey stepped down into the gravel, dropped her jeans, and squatted over the spent irises, keeping Marie in her sights the whole time. Marie, who had grown up in a different era entirely, found this fiercely embarrassing. A wind came up on the lake; a pair of late loons called across the water. The only comfort Marie could manage was that the boyfriend, whom she did not wish to meet, not at all, clearly had run out for good. Tracey seemed to know this, too, chewing on her lower lip, facing the dooryard as if the hot desire of her stare could make him materialize.

"What's his name?" Marie asked.

"None of your business. We met in a chemistry class." She smirked at Marie's surprise. "Premed."

"Are you going back to school?"

Tracey threw back her head and cackled, showing two straight rows of excellent teeth. "Yeah, right. He's out there right now paying our preregistration."

Marie composed herself, took some silent breaths. "It's just that I find it hard to believe—"

"People like you always do," Tracey said. She slid Marie a look. "You're never willing to believe the worst of someone."

Marie closed her eyes, wanting Ernie. She imagined him leaving work about now, coming through the mill gates with his lunch bucket and cap, shoulders bowed at the prospect of the empty house. She longed to be waiting there, to sit on the porch with him over a pitcher of lemonade, comparing days, which hadn't changed much over the years, really, but always held some ordinary pleasures. Today they would have wondered about John, thought about calling him, decided against it.

"You married?" Tracey asked, as if reading her mind.

"Twenty years. We met in seventh grade."

"Then what are you doing up here alone?"

"I don't know," Marie said. But suddenly she did, she knew exactly, looking at this girl who had parents somewhere waiting.

"I know what you're thinking," the girl said.

"You couldn't possibly."

"You're wondering how a nice girl like me ended up like this." When Marie didn't answer, she added, "Why do you keep doing that?"

"What?"

"That." The girl pointed to Marie's hand, which was making absent semicircles over her stomach. "You pregnant?"

"No," Marie said, withdrawing her hand. But she had been, shockingly, for most of the summer; during John's final weeks at home, she had been pregnant. Back then her hand had gone automatically to the womb, that strange, unpredictable vessel, as she and Ernie nuzzled in bed, dazzled by their change in fortune. For nights on end they made their murmured plans, lost in a form of drunkenness, waiting for John to skulk through the back door long past curfew, when they would rise from their nestled sheets to face him—their first child now, not their only—his splendid blue eyes glassy with what she hoped were the normal complications of adolescence, equal parts need and contempt.

They did not tell him about the pregnancy, and by the first of September it was over prematurely, Marie balled into a heap on their bed for three days, barely able to open her swollen eyes. "Maybe it's for the best," Ernie whispered to her, petting her curled back. They could hear John ramming around in the kitchen downstairs, stocking the cupboards with miso and bean curd and other things they'd never heard of, counting off his last days in the house by changing everything in it. As Ernie kissed her sweaty head, Marie rested her hand on the freshly scoured womb that had held their second chance. "It might not have been worth it," Ernie whispered, words that staggered her so thoroughly that she bolted up, mouth agape, asking, "What did you say, Ernie? Did you just say something?" Their raising of John had, after all, been filled with fine wishes for the boy; it was not their habit to acknowledge disappointment, or regret, or sorrow. As the door downstairs clicked shut on them and John faded into another night with his mysterious friends, Marie turned to her husband, whom she loved, God help her, more than she loved her son. *Take it back,* she wanted to tell him, but he mistook her pleading look entirely. "She might've broken our hearts," he murmured. "I can think of a hundred ways." He was holding her at the time, speaking softly, almost to himself, and his hands on her felt like the meaty intrusion of some stranger who'd just broken into her bedroom. "Ernie, stop there," she told him, and he did.

It was only now, imprisoned on her own property by a skinny girl who belonged back in chemistry class, that Marie understood that she had come here alone to find a way to forgive him. What did he mean, not worth it? Worth what? Was he speaking of John?

Marie looked down over the trees into the lake. She and Ernie had been twenty years old when John was born. You think you're in love now, her sister warned, but wait till you meet your baby—implying that married love would look bleached and pale by contrast. But John was a sober, suspicious baby, vaguely intimidating; and their fascination for him became one more thing they had in common. As their child became more and more himself, a cryptogram they couldn't decipher, Ernie and Marie's bungled affections and wayward exertions revealed less of him and more of themselves.

Ernie and Marie, smitten since seventh grade: it was a story they thought their baby son would grow up to tell their grandchildren. At twenty they had thought this. She wanted John to remember his childhood the way she liked to: a soft-focus, greeting-card recollection in which Ernie and Marie strolled hand in hand in a park somewhere with the fruit of their desire frolicking a few feet ahead. But now she doubted her own memory. John must have frolicked on occasion. Certainly he must have frolicked. But at the present moment she could conjure only a lumbering resignation, as if he had already tired of their story before he broke free of the womb.

They would have been more ready for him now, she realized. She was in a position now to love Ernie less, if that's what a child required.

The shadow of the spruces arched long across the dooryard. Dusk fell.

Tracey got up. "I'm hungry again. You want anything?"

"No, thanks."

Tracey waited. "You have to come in with me."

Marie stepped through the door first, then watched as Tracey made herself a sandwich. "I don't suppose it's crossed your mind that your boyfriend might not come back," Marie said.

Tracey took a big bite. "No, it hasn't."

"If I were on the run I'd run alone, wouldn't you? Don't you think that makes sense?"

Chewing daintily, Tracey flattened Marie with a luminous, eerily knowing look. "Are you on the run, Marie?"

"What I'm saying is that he'll get a lot farther a lot faster without another person to worry about."

Tracey swallowed hard. "Well, what I'm saying is you don't know shit about him. Or me, for that matter. So you can just shut up."

"I could give you a ride home."

"Not without your keys, you couldn't." She opened the fridge and gulped some milk from the bottle. "If I wanted to go home I would've gone home a long time ago."

It had gotten dark in the cabin. Marie flicked on the kitchen light. She and Ernie left the electricity on year-round because it was more trouble not to, and occasionally they came here in winter to snowshoe through the long, wooded alleys. It was on their son's behalf that they had come to such pastimes, on their son's behalf that the cabin had filled over the years with well-thumbed guidebooks to butterflies and insects and fish and birds. But John preferred his puzzles by the fire, his long, furtive vigils on the dock, leaving it to his parents to discover the world. They turned up pine cones, strips of birch bark for monogramming, once a speckled feather from a pheasant. John inspected these things indifferently, listened to parental homilies on the world's breathtaking design, all the while maintaining the demeanor of a good-hearted home owner suffering the encyclopedia salesman's pitch.

"Why don't you want to go home?" Marie asked. "Really, I'd like to know." She was remembering the parting scene at the airport, John uncharacteristically warm, allowing her to hug him as long as she wanted, thanking her for an all-purpose "everything" that she could fill in as she pleased for years to come. Ernie, his massive arms folded in front of him, welled up, nodding madly. But as John disappeared behind the gate Ernie clutched her hand, and she knew what he knew: that their only son, their first and only child, was not coming back. He would finish school, find a job in California, call them twice a year.

"My father's a self-righteous blowhard, if you're dying to know," Tracey said. "And my mother's a doormat."

"Maybe they did the best they could."

"Maybe they didn't."

"Maybe they tried in ways you can't know about."

Tracey looked Marie over. "My mother's forty-two," she said. "She would've crawled under a chair the second she saw the knife."

Marie covered the mustard jar and returned it to the fridge. "It's possible, Tracey, that your parents never found the key to you."

Tracey seemed to like this interpretation of her terrible choices. Her shoulders softened some. "So where's this son of yours, anyway?"

"We just sent him off to Berkeley."

Tracey smirked a little. "Uh-oh."

"What's that supposed to mean?" Marie asked. "What do you mean?"

"Berkeley's a pretty swinging place. You don't send sweet little boys there."

"I never said he was a sweet little boy," Marie said, surprising herself. But it was true: her child had never been a sweet little boy.

"You'll be lucky if he comes back with his brain still working."

"I'll be lucky if he comes back at all."

Tracey frowned. "You're messing with my head, right? Poor, tor-

tured mother? You probably don't even have kids." She folded her
arms. "But if you do have a kid, and he's at Berkeley, prepare yourself."

"Look, Tracey," Marie said irritably, "why don't you just take my
car? If you're so devoted to this boyfriend of yours, why not go after
him?"

"Because I'd have no idea where to look, and you'd run to the
nearest police station." Tracey finished the sandwich and rinsed the
plate, leading Marie to suspect that someone had at least taught her
to clean up after herself. The worst parent in the world can at least
do that. John had lovely manners, and she suddenly got a comforting vision of him placing his scraped plate in a cafeteria sink.

"The nearest police station is twenty miles from here," Marie
said.

"Well, that's good news, Marie, because look who's back."

Creeping into the driveway, one headlight out, was a low-slung,
mud-colored Valiant with a cracked windshield. The driver skulked
behind the wheel, blurry as an inkblot. When Tracey raced out to
greet him, the driver opened the door and emerged as a jittery
shadow. The shadow flung itself toward the cabin as Marie fled for
the back door and banged on the lock with her fists.

In moments he was upon her, a wiry man with a powerful odor
and viselike hands. He half carried her back to the kitchen as she
fell limp with panic. Then, like a ham actor in a silent movie, he
lashed her to a kitchen chair with cords of filthy rawhide.

"You wanna tell me how the fuck we get rid of her?" he snarled
at Tracey, whose apparent fright gave full flower to Marie's budding
terror. That he was handsome—dark-eyed, square-jawed, with full,
shapely lips—made him all the more terrifying.

"What was I supposed to do?" Tracey quavered. "Listen, I kept
her here for a whole day with no—"

"Where's your keys?" he roared at Marie.

"Here, they're here," Tracey said, fumbling them out of her
pocket. "Let's go, Mike, please, let's just go."

"You got money?" he asked, leaning over Marie, one cool strand of his long hair raking across her bare arm. She could hardly breathe, looking into his alarming, moist eyes.

"My purse," she gasped. "In the car."

He stalked out, his dirty jeans sagging at the seat, into which someone had sewn a facsimile of the American flag. He looked near starving, his upper arms shaped like bedposts, thin and tapering and hard. She heard the car door open and the contents of her purse spilling over the gravel.

"The premed was a lie," Tracey said. "I met him at a concert." She darted a look outside, her lip quivering. "You know how much power I have over my own life, Marie?" She lifted her hand and squeezed her thumb and index finger together. "This much."

He was in again, tearing into the fridge, cramming food into his mouth. The food seemed to calm him some. He looked around. He could have been twenty-five or forty-five, a man weighted by bad luck and a mean spirit that encased his true age like barnacles on a boat. "Pick up our stuff," he said to Tracey. "We're out of this dump."

Tracey did as he said, gathering the sleeping bag and stuffing it into a sack. He watched her body damply as she moved; Marie felt an engulfing nausea but could not move herself, not even to cover her mouth at the approaching bile. Her legs were lashed to the chair legs, her arms tied behind her, giving her a deeply discomfiting sensation of being bound to empty space. She felt desperate to close her legs, cross her arms over her breasts, unwilling to die with her most womanly parts exposed. "I'm going to be sick," she gulped, but it was too late, a thin trail of spit and bile lolloping down her shirt front.

Mike lifted his forearm, dirty with tattoos, and chopped it down across Marie's jaw. She thumped backward to the floor, chair and all, tasting blood, seeing stars, letting out a squawk of despair. Then she fell silent, looking at the upended room, stunned. She heard the flick of a switchblade and felt the heat of his shadow. She tried to snap her eyes shut, to wait for what came next, but they opened again, fixed on his; in the still, shiny irises she searched for a sign of latent goodness, or regret, some long-ago time that defined him. In the sepulchral silence she locked eyes with him, sorrow to sorrow. He dropped the knife. "Fuck this, you do it," he said to Tracey, then swaggered out. She heard her car revving in the dooryard, the radio blaring on. Now her eyes closed. A small rustle materialized near her left ear; it was Tracey, crouching next to her, holding the opened blade.

"Shh," Tracey said. "He's a coward, and he doesn't like blood, but he's not above beating the hell out of me." She patted Marie's cheek. "So let's just pretend I've killed you."

Marie began to weep, silently, a sheen of moisture beading beneath her eyes. She made a prayer to the Virgin Mary, something she had not done since she was a child. She summoned an image of Ernie sitting on the porch, missing her. Of John scraping that plate in the college cafeteria. With shocking tenderness, Tracey made a small cut near Marie's temple just above the hairline. It hurt very little, but the blood began to course into her hair in warm, oozy tracks. Tracey lifted the knife, now a rich, dripping red. "You'll be okay," she said. "But head wounds bleed like crazy." The horn from Marie's car sounded in two long, insistent blasts.

"You chose a hell of a life for yourself, Tracey," Marie whispered.

"Yeah," Tracey said, closing her palm lightly over the knife. She got up. "But at least I chose."

"You don't know anything about me."

"Ditto. Take care."

For much of the long evening Marie kept still, blinking into the approaching dark. She had to pee desperately but determined to hold it even if it killed her, which she genuinely thought it might. She was facing the ceiling, still tied, the blood on her face and hair drying uncomfortably. She recalled John's childhood habit of hanging slothlike from banisters or chair backs, loving the upside-down world. Perhaps his parents were easier to understand this way. She saw now what had so compelled him: the ceiling would make a marvelous floor, a creamy expanse you could navigate however you wished; you could fling yourself from corner to corner, unencumbered except for an occasional light fixture. Even the walls looked inviting: the windows appeared to open from the top down, the tops of doors made odd, amusing steps into the next room, framed pictures floated knee-high, their reversed images full of whimsy, hard to decode. In time she got used to the overturned room, even preferred it. It calmed her. She no longer felt sick. She understood that Ernie was on his way here, of course he was, he would be here before the moon rose, missing her, full of apology for disturbing her peace, but he needed her, the house was empty and their son was gone and he needed her as he steered down the dirt road, veering left past the big boulder, entering the dooryard to find a strange, battered car and a terrifying silence.

"Oh, Ernie," she said when he did indeed panic through the door. "Ernie. Sweetheart. Untie me." In he came, just as she knew he would.

And then? They no longer looked back on this season as the autumn when they lost their second child. This season—with its gentle temperatures and propensity for inspiring flight—they recalled instead as that one autumn when those awful people, that terrible pair, broke into the cabin. They exchanged one memory for the other, remembering Ernie's raging, man-sized sobs as he worked at the stiff rawhide, remembering him rocking her under a shaft of moonlight that sliced through the door he'd left open, remembering, half laughing, that the first thing Marie wanted to do, after being rescued by her prince, was pee. This moment became the turning point—this moment and no other—when two long-married people decided to stay married, to succumb to the shape of the rest of their life, to live with things they would not speak of. They shouldered each other into the coming years because there was no other face each could bear to look at in this moment of turning, no other arms they could bear but each other's, and they made themselves right again, they did, just the two of them.

Erika Krouse

✑

ALL OF ME

About four months after my heart transplant, I came to the door with my towel wrapped around my waist, still wet from an aborted shower. Someone was pounding steadily, like a metronome. Nobody I knew visited me anymore. I was like an old man—suspicious, uncertain. The noise broke off as I swung the door open. A short girl with pink hair and a torn leather jacket stared at my chest with big eyes. I covered the scar as best I could with one hand. The girl pushed past me into my apartment, brushing my hip so that I had to grab the towel before it fell down. Her face had splotchy freckles and a corn-fed look underneath all the piercings. Her age was indecipherable.

"Hi," I said.

She nodded at me.

"Um," I said, "who are you?"

The girl walked over to my couch and sat quickly, crossing her legs. She wore red and white striped stockings. The street made noise behind me. There was still water on my chest, and I was getting cold in my towel.

"Can I help you?" I asked, finally shutting the door.

The girl clasped her hands together. A pretty old-fashioned gesture for someone with a bull's-eye tattooed on her neck. I glanced at the pizza boxes in the corner and the underwear on the floor. I hadn't had a woman in my apartment since I broke up with my ex-girlfriend a year ago. This girl followed my gaze and didn't say anything. I picked up the underwear and held it behind my back. "Do you speak English?" I asked.

"Yes," she said. She took off her shoes.

I looked at her empty shoes and said, "Wait right here." I hustled into my bedroom to change into a T-shirt and jeans, skipping boxers in my hurry. When I skidded back into the living room, the girl was spread all over the couch, like a growth. She didn't move when I slapped my hands together and said, "So . . . your name?"

"Lucy." Lucy balled up her jacket under one shoulder. I noticed a scar on her cheek, and a brownish one on her forearm. She wiped her nose on the scar and sniffled, suddenly. Was she crying? Girls like her didn't cry. She looked like if you punctured her, she'd bleed motor oil. But she was crying.

Her nose stuffing up, she launched a story about her boyfriend, a man named Chucky Thor ("his real name," she insisted until I nodded) who rode a motorcycle. He was my age, thirty-five, a Scorpio. Chucky Thor was a gentle man, she said, but he had a little bit of a cocaine "thing" and a drinking "issue." He also had a master's degree in Chinese studies and a yellow car, long like a banana, filled with flyers for the cat he had lost the year before. Chucky Thor had insomnia. Chucky Thor had sulfa allergies.

Lucy met him a few years ago at a karaoke bar infested with bikers. He was pissing drunk, standing with a bunch of other wasted Harley dudes. When their eyes met, he had his thin arm around a fat, hairy biker, singing roughly, "I've got a brand-new pair of roller skates, you've got a brand-new key." She and Chucky Thor fell instantly in love. "Destiny," she told me.

I tried several times to interrupt, but Lucy raised her voice over mine. In December, Chucky Thor crashed on his motorcycle with Lucy riding in back. He landed on his head, exclusively on his head. The rest of his body was pretty sound, but his brains were mashed potatoes. The doctors in the hospital put him on a respirator. Lucy was also banged up, but she had been wearing leathers and a helmet. His helmet.

Lucy waited by Chucky Thor's bedside for a week, barely sleeping. At first she talked to him, reading aloud or whispering endearments. Then she fell silent near the third day. On the sixth day, she took a safety pin and jabbed him hard in the hand. Then in his leg, his feet, even his neck. His eyelids didn't even twitch.

Lucy spent another week trying to locate his meager family, and then gave up. The doctor told her that Chucky Thor would never speak again, would never walk, think, feed himself, or control his bowels. She said, "Pull the plug," and then passed out.

By now I was just staring at Lucy, who had become animated during this story. I could tell that this was, in some ways, the story of her life. Her cheeks were pink, and she was breathing fast. I said, "I'm very sorry, Lucy."

Lucy said, "Thanks."

"What a terrible thing," I said. "Awful. I can't imagine."

Lucy looked down at her lap.

"Jeez," I said.

She nodded.

"So, um, what does this have to do with me?" I asked.

Lucy's head was in her hands. I listened to her breathing as she rubbed her eyes for a while. Then she looked up. She put her hand on my knee. Her eyes were red, but her expression, when I looked through all the crap covering it—chains, makeup, jewelry—was kind.

"Well," she said. "You have his heart."

This new heart doesn't respond like my old one. With Lucy there on the couch, it still kept a regular beat, while my mind struggled to compensate. I pushed her hand off my knee and covered my chest with my hand, instinctively.

Lucy still wanted to talk. She fumbled with a cigarette, her hands shaking. "At first there was just numbness, you know? Numbness, with sobbing. Now I can't stop thinking about him.

And how you have the last piece of him." Even with a cigarette in her mouth, she had very good diction. Polite. I wanted to tell her not to smoke in my apartment.

"Listen, Lucy? You want coffee or something?"

Lucy shook her head, pink hair flying everywhere.

"This is a little . . . odd," I stumbled. "I don't know what to say. I mean, how do I know you're telling the truth? I don't know you. No offense, but maybe this is just some weird scam for my . . . ah . . ."

Lucy stubbed out a cigarette on my sandwich plate. She glanced at my plywood coffee table, my dreadlocked carpet.

It was true. I had nothing to offer.

Four months before, I had collapsed outside a convenience store. I was unconscious when they wheeled me in, and I stayed that way until after the surgery three days later. I was still fuzzy when they explained the condition to me, postsurgery. After all the talking and diagrams, all I understood was that mine had been a weak piece of machinery, a Darwinian mistake. I had a rotten heart. They helicoptered a new one across town and sutured it into me. Replacement flesh. That's all I knew about it.

Now I told Lucy, "I still don't understand why you're here."

"I wanted to meet you." She lit another cigarette and exhaled smoke. "You're interesting to me."

"What about the other people? Why don't you go find his kidneys or something?"

"I went through a lot of trouble to find you. Besides, I don't care about his kidneys."

"A heart is just a muscle," I said.

"He loved me."

"You don't love with the actual heart, Lucy."

"What do you love with, then?" she asked sharply. "Yeah, Steve, tell me all about love." She looked exhausted.

I opened my mouth and shut it. "Anyway, I . . . feel for you and all, but it's over. This is my heart now."

"No," she said quietly. "It's not."

"Do you want it back?" I snapped. Lucy slitted her eyes at me. I felt threatened, as if she could reach inside and rip my chest open. We glared at each other for a little while.

"He looked kind of like you," she finally said. "But I think he would have been a little disappointed in your attitude."

I shook my head to clear it. "Listen. Lucy." I softened my voice a little. "I am really, truly sorry." I went to the fridge and took out two beers, holding one out to Lucy.

Lucy accepted a beer.

I did feel bad for her, of course, but after doing nothing but recover for months, I was having trouble concentrating on anything but myself. I mean, that guy, this girl—they were nothing to me. I glanced at Lucy's solid, silent body. She was looking out the window at the brick wall next to my building. Every now and then she would breathe in and out, quickly.

I finally said, "I'm going to watch the game now, okay?"

Nothing from Lucy.

I switched on the television.

Lucy didn't drink her beer. I felt her turn her head to watch me. I watched the screen.

I drank my beer.

After about five minutes of this, I couldn't stand it anymore and switched off the television. I leaned forward and pressed my hands together. "Okay. What exactly do you want, Lucy? Money? Because I don't have any."

She didn't move except to push her lip out. She said, "You have Chucky Thor's heart, and I'm going to make sure you take care of it."

I laughed a little, shaking my head. "Yeah?"

"Yeah."

"Yeah?"

"I'm moving in," Lucy said.

Of course I told her no, but Lucy picked the lock the next day while I was at the doctor's office. When I came home, Lucy looked up from the television with a bright "Hi!" Boxes were stacked in a corner of the living room and a turkey roasted in the oven. I tried to imagine kicking her out, closing the door in her face as she stood there, cradling a half-cooked turkey. Or should I keep the turkey? How long do you let those things cook, anyway? I didn't have it in me. So I said, "I shower at 8 AM. Stay out of my way."

Lucy took some getting used to. Her habits. I had never lived with a woman before, besides my mother. Lucy not only smoked constantly, she would do things like ash her cigarette into the cuffs of her pants. Her orange pants. Her purple pants, the green cuffs of her shiny shirts. Sometimes it hurt to look at her.

Then there was the cocaine. Lucy snorted it about once a week. There it was on Saturday afternoons, coating the mirror Lucy had taken down from the wall and ripped out of its frame. Her little silver straw poking out of her button nose. I wondered where she got the money for all that cocaine, but she said, "I do trades." I didn't want to know.

Her constant colds. That girl had the constitution of a bowl of soup. She kept infecting me, since my antirejection meds reduced my immune system. She sneezed in alarm, opening her eyes right after to check on me. Sometimes I would clutch my chest and fall over, just to screw with her.

Lucy's diet consisted of sugar and caffeine. I've never seen a human being put so much sugar into a cup of coffee. I've never seen a human being eat so many cookies on a weekly basis. But she baked, you know? There was something about seeing an apron on over all that junk she called clothes. I had forgotten that ovens were used for anything other than storage space. I had kept ski boots in there, files, old canned goods. The first time Lucy preheated the oven, my tax returns caught fire.

Sometimes she decided to change all her piercings. She'd attack her left eyebrow, her navel, her lip, and her nose with a pair of pliers. When she was finished, she looked the same, but a little pinker and worse for wear and tear.

Lucy ate salted Crisco sandwiches.

Lucy drank caffeinated water.

Lucy had an irrational fear of small coins and buttons. "I'm like the Amish," she said. "Except I like zippers."

"Just like the Amish," I said.

Lucy slept on the hide-a-bed couch in the living room. From inside my bedroom, I listened for noises out there, feeling guilty, rationalizing with myself. After all, she didn't even pay rent. She did buy groceries sometimes, and she cleaned the toilet bowl before it even turned orange, which was great.

Lucy worked three days a week at a homeless shelter, making all the Christmas donations stretch the year around. She said it was like putting together a puzzle. She had to figure out how to feed forty people with three boxes of matzo, two cans of peas, and twelve pounds of coleslaw. "What do you do with one can of creamed pumpkin? One? What do you do with wasabi powder? I make a lot of soup. It doesn't taste good, but I think it's got to be healthy, with all the junk that's inside it," she said. Lucy had twelve cookbooks. She read them in the evenings, staring off into space occasionally, adding up ingredients. She rode her bicycle to work with garlic bulging out of her pockets. Garlic made all the difference, she said. They had forty-eight frozen turkeys in their freezers.

I didn't invite Lucy out on the rare occasions I went to a party or bar. I wasn't ready to have a girlfriend. Especially one I had never even kissed. Sometimes I felt a little frisky, and I'd look at Lucy sitting next to me on the couch, watching a movie with her fingers crammed in her mouth. Then I changed my mind.

But she was so small-town, kind of homey. She made butter-and-honey crackers and ate them, honey dripping all over her chin. She never swore. She said, "Shucks." She knitted me a hat out of yarn, although it was early spring. Bright red. I was getting used to her ways.

A heart can live four to six hours outside a body. During that time, what does it experience? Does it know it's been dispossessed? Does it suffer the feeling of abandonment? Does it have any memory at all?

Ever since the operation, I've had strange cravings. For example, chicken fingers. I can't get enough of them. I always hated them, insisting that chickens don't have fingers. And I drink light beer now. Ever since the arrival of microbrews, I had forgotten that there was such a thing as light beer, "lite" beer. But I find myself ordering it in bars.

Another thing—women. I threw away the picture of my ex-girlfriend I had been carrying around in my wallet. Kathy. She must have wondered why I stopped calling her, after dialing her number and letting her hang up on me for so long. I even saw her on the street with her new boyfriend. I felt nothing. I asked her, "How about them Broncos?" and shook the guy's hand.

Kathy said, "You seem . . . ," and then stopped.

I said, "Oh, I had some health problems. Lost some weight. Gained it back. Back to normal."

"No, something else."

"You look great, Kathy, really, super. Just great. Happy."

Kathy frowned.

As they walked away, I heard the boyfriend say, "He doesn't seem like *such* a bad guy."

Even though I wasn't such a bad guy, I wasn't feeling too good.

Organ recipients usually live less than nine years, postoperation. It's not because the heart dies. A heart is a simple thing. It pumps. It's the meds, the antirejection drugs. They kill you. They also make you hairy, with warts on your feet and hands. I trembled. My kidneys hurt. I took twelve pills every morning, and ten each night. Sometimes I'd vomit from all the pills, and then I'd have to guess how much my body had absorbed and how much I threw up, and take extra.

This heart has a couple of dents, but it's a good heart, a fine heart. It could last forever. But I did notice a difference after the operation, even after I healed. My chest felt heavier. It took some time to settle. Kind of the way your bite changes after you get a filling. There was much anxiety over this heart, since it was my only shot. You don't get a freshly killed heart every day. There are lists.

The thing is, someone has to be in your spot—dying—except just right before you.

It never escaped me that I'm alive because that guy isn't.

I say it's fate, it's for the best. But just as history is always written by the victor, the words "for the best" are always spoken by the survivor. Still, I repeat those words often, every time I do some little good in the world. When I pick up litter, or when a baby gives me a smile, or when someone says, "Steve, you just made my day." Then I whisper it to myself. *It was for the best.*

But it doesn't make me feel less strange, like this life is a loaner. I tend not to wish for better things. I have a heart I'm still making payments on.

About a month after Lucy moved in, I got a job with my friend Henry. He was surprised to hear from me after so long, saying, "I can use you right away. A fifty-yard footbridge and a big deck for a rich lady on a ranch outside town. Eight AM tomorrow." He gave me the address. Henry's a big black guy who has a pierced cheek because he'd always wanted dimples. He's fattish, strongish. We've been friends for three years. A year ago Henry fired me because I couldn't drive a nail into a board in one blow. He probably felt sorry about all that now.

The next day, I showed up fifteen minutes early with a Styrofoam cup of tea, face raw from a new shave with an old razor. I felt cold and a little wobbly, but okay. It was an enormous place, with a cabin-style mansion, stables, a pristine barn, and acres of high pasture, snow crusting random edges. Nothing looked like it had ever been used for practical purposes. The stables held no animals in them. The fields were fallow. Rich people.

They wanted the bridge to cross a little human-made babbling brook (they had installed a water pump so it would babble), and one shallow corner of a duck pond. They had bought ducks with brilliant jewel-green heads and clipped their wings. I asked Henry if that was legal and Henry said, "Anything's legal if you've got money."

The architect had made a mess. The plans were interesting,

mostly because the bridge as designed would never actually hold weight. Henry argued with the lady. "I *like* the design," she pouted. She was wearing an embroidered denim jacket and white cowboy boots, flecked with thin tongues of mud.

Henry said, "Then I hope you like swimming." While they argued, I reviewed and stacked the materials. After not working for so long, the wood felt good through my gloves. Familiar, comforting. When you don't work for a long period of time, the thought of it becomes intimidating. But doing it just felt nice, simple. All the pressure-treated lumber was stacked on a blue tarp, the nasty chemical-green clashing with the pine needles. I organized it, then I scoped out the area. The ground sank under my boots, dead grass rotting under patchy snow. Then Henry called me over and asked my opinion and we discussed the design together, which made me feel good because I'm not a real carpenter like him. The air was raw and damp until the sunshine cleared it out. We revised the plans, arguing fine points, measuring the land.

Driving home that night, I felt normal for the first time in a while. I was tired. I had worked all day long. I was coming home from my job. My job. And there, inside my apartment, was a girl. Technically. Waiting for, well, for me.

I owe the hospital one hundred ninety-seven thousand dollars. With all the drugs and checkups, my medical bills just get worse each month. I send the hospital all my extra money. It's not enough. They send back an invoice, with some of the right-hand numbers crawling ever upward. I worry about it a lot.

Henry says, "Man, let it go. What are they going to do? Repossess?"

Chucky Thor was the only child of dead parents. Lucy said that he was quiet and shy. He loved drugs, but mostly he loved the ritual of drugs—the carving of cocaine into lines, the rolling of the joint. He sometimes crossed himself—forehead, chest, left, right—for no good reason. Lucy said that he had almost gone to law school and was a great believer in justice. He would talk about it the way some people talked about freedom or love.

In my old life, I used to pick up Kathy's hamster Poopsy and throw him across the room. Not at a wall or anything, and pretty low along the ground. But still. Poopsy would roll and roll and then roll onto his feet, and run fast, and maybe lose himself, or maybe just lie there, stunned. His fat ass wiggling under him. I laughed at this. Kathy cried when I did it, when I made her choose between us.

I had gotten fired from every job I ever had. I got fired from a job where all I had to do was chase a broom around. Unreliable, they said.

Once I punched a bartender in the nose because my drink was weak.

Lucy said that Chucky Thor believed that a person only gets so many heartbeats in his life. A fixed number. So Chucky Thor never got angry or exercised. He didn't want to use up his heartbeats.

"But he snorted cocaine," I said. "But he rode motorcycles."

"Yeah," Lucy said. "They're worth it."

Which was weird, because for the first time in my life, I wanted a motorcycle. And I wanted to sleep with Lucy. I didn't know why. I thought about her all the time. She was like a loose tooth to me.

One day Henry noticed my lunch box lying on the ground. Lucy had bought it for me. It was black, and if I held it a certain way I could hide the King Kong sticker on the front. Lucy fixed it each morning, packing me a peanut-butter sandwich wrapped in wax paper, an apple, a little bag of Cheetos, and a thermos full of decaf. Each thing had its own compartment. Carrying it every day, I felt like a little kid, but in a good, if ashamed, way.

When Henry saw the King Kong sticker, I was worried he would make fun of me, but he just said, "It's cool."

Abruptly, I told him everything. The girl, the confusion, all that. He just listened and nodded his head. I kept talking as Henry poured concrete mix and water onto a tarp. We each took an end and pulled it back and forth, mixing the concrete, then pouring it into the footings. Then we placed the posts in the concrete. We leaned against them, our hands smooth against the rough materials.

We got out our lunches, sat down, and ate. The whole time, me talking, Henry nodding.

When I finally wound down, Henry said, mouth full, "It sounds like love, son."

"No!" I said. "No."

He swallowed. "A new heart. Wild. How does that feel? Having a piece of somebody else inside you?"

"A little awkward. I'm always kind of wondering what it'll do."

Henry was quiet for a second. Then he said, "I wonder if that's the way women feel during sex."

We both thought about that.

"Anyway," Henry said, "you also got a girlfriend out of it."

"No, Henry. Not her." She was nothing like Kathy. Kathy had floral stationery and wore silk blouses. Lucy dressed like a cartoon character. She bit her toenails. But Lucy's was the face in my head.

"What exactly is wrong with her, man? She seems to like you. Packs you *lunch*." Henry looked at his cold slice of leftover pizza, the cheese hardened into clots. He dropped it into his lunch sack.

I shook my head. "You've got to see this girl. I mean, she's a piece of work."

"That's right," Henry said, packing up his leftovers. "You never did like work."

I stared at him. "I do now," I said. "I do fucking now."

"Okay," he said, a little sheepish, and threw me my tools. "Prove it."

Anyway, I liked this bridge. It was going to be a long bridge, winding around the property, pretty useless. The lady kept changing the plans. I think she liked having us around. The lake bed was mostly dry in the drainage area, and the ducks swam right up to the barrier as if they were checking on our progress.

I wish I could explain the beauty of it—a hand on wood, fitting two pieces together that have been crafted to match. Finding that some rules do, in fact, apply. That some mistakes can be fixed.

In my old life, I had told Kathy that she should lose weight. I asked her to put on more makeup when we went out with my friends. Sometimes I did this thing where I treated her extra special nice, then the next day I was very polite, so *polite,* it made her cry. I did it to see how much she loved me, and then I dumped her.

These things seemed so stupid now. That night, Lucy fell on her bicycle and needed three stitches. I took her to the hospital and held her squeaky hand while her forehead beaded up with sweat. The mushy skin of her knee wiggled around under the doctor's finger, the needle looping in and out of it.

I wondered what it would be like to be a father.

I wrote Kathy a letter and paid her back the three hundred dollars I owed her. I didn't mention that I owed her money, did I? I thanked her and added an extra fifty bucks as interest. I apologized for everything I had done, listing out everything I could think of. Every single mistake. Then I put a stamp on it and dropped it in a blue mailbox on a blue day. Watched it slip from my hand into the slot, irretrievable. Headed for the world. It didn't feel too bad. No. It felt good.

One Saturday night, I watched Lucy with her new cocaine purchase spread over the mirror, her razor blade carving it slowly.

I asked her, "Why do you snort cocaine?"

"I don't know." She looked up. "It's just something I do. I need ritual in my life."

"You could go to church," I said, and we both smiled.

"It's only once a week, anyway," Lucy said.

"Don't you worry about getting addicted?"

"You can't be completely independent. We're all addicted to food, water." She looked at me quickly and then said, "You're dependent on your meds."

"They keep me alive," I said.

"They're also killing you," she said.

"Yeah." I looked at the cocaine quietly. Then I said, "Hey, forget that stuff. Let's go out on a date." There, it was said and done, yes or no.

Lucy looked up. She had a big pimple on her cheek. "What?"

"Out on the town. Put on your party dress." I was kind of nervous, smacking my fist into my palm a couple of times. "It'll be fun," I said.

"A date," Lucy said. Her fingers loosened on the razor blade. "Okay," she said, setting down the mirror. "Um . . . you sure?"

"Sure I'm sure," I said, unsure. Lucy shrugged. I went into my bedroom to give her a chance to change her clothes.

I'd like to say that it was like one of those movies where the freaked-out girl transforms herself into something all sweet and sexy, like *The Breakfast Club* or something. But she didn't. When I came out of my bedroom, Lucy was still Lucy. "That's a cool dress," I said. It was yellow, with green tile-like patterns all over it.

"I think I look like a kitchen," she said, looking down.

"Really? Then why did you put it on?"

"I like kitchens," she said.

We went to a movie, then dinner. A date in reverse. Lucy was quiet, acting strange until she said, right after we ordered our dinners, "I guess I've never been on a date before. A real one, I mean."

I stared. Lucy was twenty-nine.

"They just kind of kiss me or something, first. Or we have sex. Or they fall in love with me. It's never like this."

"Is this bad?"

"No," she said.

Lucy told me that she grew up on a sheep farm in eastern Colorado in a rural town named Nunn. Apparently there was this big water tower with absolutely nothing around it besides pasture and the occasional cow. A stray chicken or two. Stenciled all over the water tower was the town slogan: Watch Nunn Grow. As a teenager, Lucy would drive out there and spend hours sitting in the field and looking at it. In order to leave town, she had to pass a billboard that said, "Jesus. Every knee will bend, including yours."

When she told me these things, pink hair made sense. I told Lucy about my childhood in the South, where I had simultaneously decided, at age eight, to become both a vegetarian and a veterinar-

ian. It was rough. Down there they had this thing called "Meat &
Three" in most of the restaurants. You get your choice of one type of
meat and three different vegetables, which they also made out of
meat. Potatoes and bacon, corn and ham, like that.

"How did you manage?" Lucy asked.

"I scraped stuff off until I gave up at age twelve."

"Sounds hard," Lucy said.

"It was okay."

"That takes a lot of discipline," she said.

"I had good intentions. Originally," I said.

I didn't touch her except for when I was opening her car door
and our shoulders brushed. When we got home, Lucy went to the
bathroom and changed into her pajamas right away. They had pictures of Wonder Woman all over them. She pulled out the hide-a-
bed. I wasn't sure what to do. Lucy didn't look at me. She got under
the covers while I clutched a beer bottle in the kitchen. I decided to
err on the side of fear, so I washed a dish, took my pills, and then
headed for my bedroom. As I swung through the doorway, I heard
Lucy say something. "What?" I asked, doubling back.

"Thanks," she said. "Mumblemumble lovely time."

Then I figured what the hell, and I walked over to the hide-a-
bed, the side Lucy was on. I leaned over her. She looked up at me,
horrified. I swooped down and kissed her wrinkled-up little forehead. Then I retreated, hands up in surrender position, and went to
bed.

The cocaine stayed on the mirror in two little white lines the
whole next day, and the next. And the next. Then it was gone.

Every autumn, sap flows out of the knots in the ceiling wood beams
of my apartment. It pools on the floor in gummy blobs, or drips on
my head. The building is fourteen years old, but the wood still
pushes its blood around because, even dead, all it knows is the
logic of seasons.

I had begun taking Lucy out more regularly. Weekend nights,
and Wednesdays. After the first night, I never touched her at all.

We went to a play, dinner, lunch, an indoor skating rink. Lucy could skate like a hockey pro. I was getting used to having her around. I was getting used to people staring at us—me in my short hair and button-down shirts, Lucy in her costumes. I was proud of her outfits, actually. They were nothing I could have invented myself.

Henry joined us one evening. I was a little nervous about them meeting, but it was fine, fun. Henry ate Lucy's limp French fries. Lucy told a really stupid joke, and Henry laughed anyway, his big belly jiggling, *haaaa ha ha ha*.

On these nights Lucy was patient with me when I had to leave early, or when I got sick in the bathroom. I tried to excuse myself discreetly. But she always knew, and she was anxious. The truth was, I was getting worse. One night I woke up and my kidneys felt like hot rocks, poking everything inside. I snuck past Lucy's hide-a-bed and drove to the hospital. The night doctor pursed her lips and said, "Well, your heart's fine. It's the meds; you knew this would happen. They will ruin several of your organs over the next ten years. Kidneys, liver, digestive system."

"What can I do?"

"Drink a lot of water. There's not much you can do. Without the meds, your body would most likely reject the heart, since the donor wasn't a relative. Just take care of yourself. It's just a matter of time, after all," she said.

I teared up involuntarily, as if she had punched me. "But that's true for us all," the doctor said hurriedly, rubbing my shoulder.

One night, Lucy and I were in the kitchen doing dishes, me washing and Lucy drying. She twirled the dishtowel like a burlesque singer, waiting for me to finish scrubbing. She said that in high school she was the lead singer in a Patsy Cline cover band with a bunch of firemen. I begged her to sing something, so she sang "Walking After Midnight." She sounded warbly, like a singer from the 1920s.

I turned to Lucy with wet hands.

"What?" she asked. "What?"

"Your voice."

"*What* about my voice?" She put her fists on her hips. Something jangled there.

"It's funny. Cute."

She snorted. "It was good enough for Nunn." She stopped. "What? *What?*"

"I can't decide if you remind me of Charlie Brown's Lucy or of Ricky Ricardo's Lucy."

"I can't decide if you remind me of . . . um . . ." She stopped. "How come I can't think of a single Steve besides you?"

"Because you like me," I said. I took a step forward, toward her, watching myself do it. I said, "You have a thing for me."

"I do not."

"Come here."

"No. Steve Martin," she said. "Steve Jobs. Steve McQueen." But she didn't move away.

"Come here."

"Yikes."

"*Come here,* Lucy."

"You're not the boss of me," she said.

I grabbed her roughly, wetly. I kissed her, my mouth prying hers open. She clutched my head. She was surprisingly strong under my hands. Like a steel wire, my Lucy. I left wet patches all over her shirt. I felt like I was starving. I didn't let her up for air.

Then Lucy's face mushed up and she turned away, gripping the counter with one scarred hand. "Lucy?" I put my hand on her shoulder and bent down to catch her eyes.

Lucy looked up with wet eyes and blotchy lips. She reached for me. She was so small. I felt like I had to be very careful, touching her lightly so she wouldn't shatter. She was doing the same thing to me, laying the side of her face gently against my chest, like she was listening, waiting.

One night we were lying in bed. It was perfectly dark, the way Lucy likes it at night. The meds were giving me the shakes and I couldn't sleep. I let my voice float out, disembodied and temporary in a place where there was no light to track events.

"I love you," I said.

Silence from Lucy. She didn't touch me.

"I can't help it," I said.

More silence. I couldn't see her.

"I'm sorry," I said.

Lucy didn't move.

"I haven't always been a good person," I said.

Lucy was asleep.

"I'm better now," I said into the dark. My body shook on its own accord.

Can you undo the past with the present? I am not a religious man. Even remorse doesn't cut it—there is always devastation somewhere. Sometimes all you can do is an even exchange.

I started shaking harder and harder. Lucy woke up. My body shook so hard, the headboard rammed against the wall over and over. It was loud. Lucy held me down with her arms. She said, "Stop it, stop it. Please. Steve." She started crying, but I couldn't. I couldn't stop.

I had my operation almost one year ago. Funny that I have no memory of the one event that changed everything. Last Saturday, Lucy asked me about it while we lay on a blanket in the park, her head on my stomach. I traced the road scars on the back of her hand. We tried to piece the events together, the timing of everything, her tragedy and mine. But then we just gave up and watched the clouds push the world around so gently, we couldn't even feel it.

It has been twelve days since I stopped taking the antirejection medication. I flushed the pills down the toilet, emptying bottle after bottle. I feel great. I've stopped trembling. I have laughed hard. I went running yesterday after work with Henry, and left him bent over, panting, his fat hands on his knees while I ran next to the creek, beating that, too. I rub the heart through my shirt. It thumps back at me. When I touch Lucy, I feel my pulse in the tips of my fingers, pressing against my skin.

Lucy hasn't done cocaine in months. We've hung the mirror back on the wall. She says she doesn't miss it, any of it. I know she might mess up, but that she'll keep trying. She's a human being and she loves me, all of me, in all my components. That's no small thing. She wakes me up in the night and asks me to hold her hand. She puts my hand on her head and goes back to sleep, and I wake up in the morning with my fingers still knotted in her scratchy hair. I say, "I love Lucy," and she hits me.

Yesterday at work, I stood still and closed my eyes, holding some stray piece of wood. I just stood there over dry land on the footbridge I'm still building. Across the barrier, the ducks swam next to me and I heard them plunge their heads under the surface, just to get wet, just to see what life is like down there. Henry didn't tell me to get back to work or anything. He just watched. I thought about how you take a tree. And that tree has a shape, and you cut it down, and you slice it into parts. Then you combine those parts with the parts of other trees to make this completely new shape. And you hope it holds up.

This is my life. I build things out of fragments. I love a strange girl.

Sometimes I look in the mirror and suddenly beat my own chest with my fists. I'm a better man. There's a miracle happening right now inside me, in the blood pushing through my veins. This heart beats faster than my last one. I'm still alive. Every second is a mystery.

The Writers

Charles Baxter graduated from Macalester College in St. Paul, Minnesota, and earned his PhD at the State University of New York at Buffalo. *Saul and Patsy* (Pantheon, 2003) is the most recent of his novels, which also include *The Feast of Love, Shadow Play,* and *First Light*. His first collection of stories, *Harmony of the World,* won the Associated Writing Programs Award for short fiction; it was followed by the collections *Through the Safety Net, A Relative Stranger,* and *Believers*. He has also published a book of essays about fiction, *Burning Down the House*. He teaches at the University of Minnesota.

Christopher Bundy returned to the United States after five years of living in and traveling through Asia, where he first began to write. His work has appeared in the *Sunday Reader, Beacon Street Review* (now *Redivider*), *Creative Loafing,* and *Japanophile*. His novel, *Plum Rains,* was a 2002 finalist in the AWP Thomas Dunne Novel competition. He is currently working toward a PhD in English in Atlanta, Georgia, where he lives with his wife, Jennie, and his daughter, Harper Lily.

Robert Olen Butler has published ten novels, most recently *Fair Warning* (2002) and *Mr. Spaceman* (2000), and three volumes of short fiction, one of which, *A Good Scent from a Strange Mountain,* won the 1993 Pulitzer Prize for Fiction. The most recent collection is *Had a Good Time: Stories from American Postcards* (2004). He has received the National Magazine Award for Fiction, the Lotos Club Award of Merit, and fellowships from the National Endowment for the Arts and the Guggenheim Foundation.

Ron Carlson is the author of eight books of fiction, including the story collections *At the Jim Bridger* (Picador USA) and *The Hotel Eden* (Penguin Paperback). His most recent books are the novel *The Speed of Light* (HarperCollins) and *A Kind of Flying: Selected Stories* (W. W. Norton & Co.), both published in 2003. He teaches at Arizona State University.

Yunny Chen was born in Taipei, Taiwan. She moved to the States in 1989 with her family and lived in Denver, Colorado. In 2002, she graduated from Amherst College and went on to attend the MFA program at the University of Michigan, Ann Arbor, and now lives in Sacramento, California, with her husband.

Quinn Dalton's first novel, *High Strung,* was released by Simon & Schuster's Atria Books in July 2003, followed by a collection of short stories, *Bulletproof Girl,* from Washington Square Press in April 2005. Her stories have appeared or are forthcoming in literary magazines such as *ACM (Another Chicago Magazine), Baltimore Review, Cottonwood, Emrys Journal, Kenyon Review, Indiana Review, Ink, Mangrove,* and *StoryQuarterly,* and in anthologies such as *Sex and Sensibility* and *American Girls About Town.* She is the winner of the Pearl 2002 Fiction Prize for her short story "Back on Earth" and a recipient of a North Carolina Arts Council 2002–2003 artist fellowship.

Bilal Dardai lives and works in Chicago, where he is an ensemble member with the Neo-Futurists Theater Company. He is an accomplished and award-winning playwright who has seen his work performed in several venues throughout the United States and Europe. Although he doesn't steadily write prose fiction, he has great respect for the medium and hopes to write more short stories in the future.

Andre Dubus III is the author of a collection of short fiction, *The Cage Keeper and Other Stories,* and the novels *Bluesman* and *House of Sand and Fog.* His work has been included in *The Best American Essays 1994, The Best Spiritual Writing 1999,* and *The Best of Hope Magazine.* He has been awarded a Guggenheim Fellowship, the National Magazine Award for fiction, the Pushcart Prize, and was a finalist for the Prix de Rome Fellowship from the Academy of Arts and Letters. Made into a motion picture and published in twenty-nine countries, his novel *House of Sand and Fog* was a fiction finalist for the National Book Award, the *Los Angeles Times* Book Prize, the L. L. Winship/PEN New England Award, and Booksense Book of the Year, and was an Oprah Book Club Selection and number one *New York Times* bestseller. A member of PEN American Center and the executive board of PEN New England, Andre Dubus III has served as a panelist for the National Endowment for the Arts and has taught writing at Harvard University, Tufts University, and is currently teaching at the University of Massachusetts at Lowell. He is married to performer Fontaine Dollas Dubus. They live in Massachusetts with their three children.

Lin Enger has an MFA from the University of Iowa, has published fiction in a number of journals, including *Ascent* and *American Fiction,* and has received James Michener and Minnesota State Arts Board fellowships. In collaboration with his brother Leif Enger, he has published five suspense novels with Simon & Schuster. He lives in Minnesota, where he teaches in the English department and MFA program at Minnesota State University Moorhead.

Louise Erdrich was born in 1954 and grew up mostly in Wahpeton, North Dakota, where her parents taught at the Bureau of Indian Affairs schools. Her fiction reflects aspects of her mixed heritage: German through her father, and French and Ojibwa through her mother. She is the author of many novels, the most recent being *The Painted Drum* (HarperCollins, 2005). She lives in Minnesota with her children, who help her run a small independent bookstore called Birchbark Books.

Nomi Eve has an MFA in fiction writing from Brown University and has worked as a freelance book reviewer for the *Village Voice* and *Newsday*. *The Family Orchard,* her first novel, was based on her own family's history. Her stories have appeared in the *Village Voice Literary Supplement* and the *International Quarterly*. She now lives outside of Philadelphia.

Charlotte Forbes's work has appeared in *Prize Stories 1999: The O'Henry Awards*. "The Marvelous Yellow Cage" is the penultimate in a series of linked stories about the town of Santa Rosalia, which is located entirely in the mind of the writer.

Aaron Gwyn grew up on a farm in central Oklahoma. He received his PhD from the University of Denver and now teaches at the University of North Carolina–Charlotte. *Dog on the Cross,* his story collection, was published in 2004 by Algonquin Books of Chapel Hill. His novel, *Ink,* is forthcoming from Algonquin as well. Aaron's fiction has appeared in *New Stories from the South, Indiana Review, Texas Review, Black Warrior Review,* and others.

Thomas E. Kennedy's credits include nine works of fiction, a collection of essays on the craft of fiction (*Realism & Other Illusions*), four volumes of literary criticism (including studies of the short fiction of Andre Dubus and of Robert Coover), and several anthologies. His work appears regularly in the United States and Europe and has won Pushcart, O. Henry, and various other prizes. He lives in Copenhagen, where he serves as international editor of *StoryQuarterly* and advisory editor of *The Literary Review,* and is a core faculty member of the Fairleigh Dickinson University MFA program. His most recent novels are *Kerrigan's Copenhagen, A*

Love Story, Bluett's Blue Hours, and *Greene's Summer,* all set in Copenhagen. Two further Copenhagen novels, *Breathwaite's Fall* and *Copenhagen Xmas,* are scheduled for publication in 2005 and 2006.

Erika Krouse's fiction has been published in *The New Yorker, The Atlantic Monthly, Ploughshares,* and *Story.* Her collection of stories, *Come Up and See Me Sometime* (Scribner, 2001), was a *New York Times* Notable Book of the year and winner of the Paterson Fiction Prize. She is currently living in Boulder, Colorado, and working on a novel.

Rattawut Lapcharoensap was born in Chicago and raised in Bangkok. He studied at Cornell University and received his MFA in creative writing from the University of Michigan, where he won the Meijer Fellowship in Creative Writing and an Avery Jules Hopwood Award. "Sightseeing" is the title story of his first collection, published by Grove Press in 2005. His stories have appeared in *Granta, Zoetrope,* and Harcourt's *Best New American Voices* series.

Thomas O'Malley was raised in Ireland and England. His work has appeared in numerous journals, including *Ploughshares, Shenandoah,* and *Crab Orchard Review.* He is a graduate of the Iowa Writers' Workshop and has been a Returning Writing Fellow and recipient of the Grace Paley Endowed Fellowship at the Fine Arts Work Center in Provincetown, Massachusetts. His novel, *In the Province of Saints,* was published in 2005.

Karen E. Outen's short fiction has appeared in *Essence* magazine, *conditions* literary magazine, and *North American Review.* Her story "Family Portraits" was included in the anthology *Meridian Bound,* published by Philadelphia's Meridian Writers Coop; and "What's Left Behind" appeared in *Glimmer Train's* first anthology, *Mother Knows.* She received her BA from Drew University and her MFA from the University of Michigan. She has received a Pew Fellowship in the Arts and the Pennsylvania Council on the Arts Fellowship. She taught writing at the University of Michigan. Presently, she lives in suburban Washington, D.C., where she is completing her first novel.

Paul Rawlins works as an editor and writer in Salt Lake City, Utah. His fiction has appeared in *Tampa Review, Southwest Review, Paris Transcontinental, Western Humanities Review,* and other journals, and has received numerous awards, including the Flannery O'Connor Award for his first short-story collection, *No Lie Like Love* (University of Georgia Press).

Andrew Roe's fiction has been published in *Tin House* and *One Story,* and his book reviews and articles have appeared in the *San Francisco Chronicle,* on Salon.com, and in other publications. He was recently nominated for a Pushcart Prize. He lives in Oceanside, California.

Born in Saigon, Vietnam, **Vu Tran** grew up in Oklahoma. He has recently finished a collection of short stories, seven of which have been published or are forthcoming in *Fence, Harvard Review, Southern Review, Michigan Quarterly, Antioch Review,* and *Nimrod.* He recently received his MFA from the Iowa Writers' Workshop and now lives in Las Vegas.

Daniel Villasenor received an MFA in poetry from the University of Arizona and attended Stanford University as a Stegner Fellow in poetry. His novel, *The Lake,* was published by Viking/Penguin in 2000.

Mary Yukari Waters's fiction has appeared in various anthologies: the 2002, 2003, and 2004 *Best American Short Stories; The O. Henry Prize Stories; The Pushcart Prize 2000 XXIV* anthology; *The Pushcart Prize Book of Short Stories: The Best Short Stories from a Quarter-Century of the Pushcart Prize;* and *Zoetrope All-Story Anthology 2.* She is the recipient of a grant from the National Endowment for the Arts, and her fiction has aired on NPR's *Selected Shorts*. Her debut collection, *The Laws of Evening* (Scribner, 2003), was a Barnes & Noble Discover selection, a Kiriyama Prize Notable Book, and a selection for Book Sense 76. It was named by the *San Francisco Chronicle* and *Newsday* as one of the Best Books of 2003.

Monica Wood is the author of four works of fiction: *Ernie's Ark, My Only Story, Secret Language,* and *Any Bitter Thing*. Her short stories have been widely published and anthologized, read on Public Radio International, awarded a Pushcart Prize, and included twice in *The Best American Mystery Stories*. She has also written two books for writers: *Description,* a guide to technique; and *The Pocket Muse: Ideas and Inspirations for Writing*. She lives in Portland, Maine.